AN ETERNITY IN A MOMENT

K. CAROTHERS

LUMINARE PRESS
WWW.LUMINAREPRESS.COM

An Eternity in a Moment
© 2018 K. Carothers

All rights reserved. This book or any portion thereof may not be reproduced or used in any manner whatsoever without the express written permission of the publisher, except for the use of brief quotations in a book review.

Printed in the United States of America

Cover Design: Claire Flint Last
Luminare Press
438 Charnelton St., Suite 101
Eugene, OR 97401
www.luminarepress.com

LCCN: 2018960091
ISBN: 978-1-64388-002-0

This book is dedicated to all those who have ever bravely fought through tragedy, and to those who have helped them.

Love seeketh not itself to please,

Nor for itself hath any care,

But for another gives its ease,

And builds a Heaven in Hell's despair.

—William Blake

CHAPTER

1

"We just lost her pulse!" the paramedic uttered breathlessly, pushing hard and fast on the lifeless young woman's chest as he knelt straddling her on the stretcher they'd brought her in on. At the same time, another paramedic urgently rolled the stretcher into an open trauma bay in the ER—the epicenter of the barely controlled chaos at Boston General Hospital—as the cries of other wounded patients echoed up and down every hallway.

"Call the OR and tell them we need a surgeon down here now—anyone they can spare," Dr. Erin Pryce told the nurse standing next to her. She gave the order in the same calm, controlled voice she always used, no matter the situation. And this one couldn't get much worse.

Erin quickly pulled on a pair of exam gloves, knowing there wasn't much help to be found. The ER was nearly at overflow capacity, despite all the efforts being made to keep beds open. Teams had been organized to manage the massive surge of walking wounded, and almost every department in the hospital was helping out in some way, but the number of seriously injured victims was staggering. And the trauma surgeons were all in the OR working as fast as they could. So at least for the moment, she was on her own.

There wasn't an act of terrorism, an insane gunman, or a hurricane that could be blamed for the catastrophe this time. Just fog and drizzle on an especially chilly May morning—which would have been perfectly harmless if everyone had stayed home.

Boston drivers were already well known for being some of the most aggressive, impatient drivers in the country on a good day. And with the dense fog and cold drizzle added to the mix, venturing out onto the roadways during the morning rush hour had become an especially dangerous proposition. But not enough people took heed of the warnings, unwilling to have their usual routines disrupted by the weather. As a result, ambulance crews from Boston EMS had soon been dispatched to accidents all over the city. But it was a crash on the interstate that precipitated the real mess, a disaster of epic proportions between Mother Nature and man.

A bus crash. At the worst possible moment. And in the worst possible place.

The bus, fully loaded with tourists, had spun out of control and flipped over on I-93 nearby, pinning several vehicles under it before bursting into flames. That horrific accident then triggered a massive pileup, the likes of which Boston had never seen before. At last count there were thirty-four people dead, with hundreds of others injured. Medical personnel at the scene were attempting to distribute the patients equally to all the local hospitals, but Boston General was the closest. It was also the best. Today, however, even its world-class resources were being stretched to the breaking point. Not even the Boston Marathon bombing had done that.

"She was an unrestrained driver who got T-boned in the pileup," the other paramedic said as he hauled the stretcher in, using one hand to intermittently squeeze an oxygen bag attached to the end of the tube they'd inserted into the woman's airway. "She was ejected from the driver's side door of her car and had a GCS of 7 when we picked her up—she'd moan once in a while and withdraw from pain. There was no one with her, and we couldn't find an ID. She had a pressure of 102 over 54 initially, with a pulse in the 120s. We intubated her at the scene and got two large-bore IVs in. She just went into cardiac arrest now."

The paramedics quickly transferred the woman to the trauma bed, and with CPR momentarily stopped, Erin looked at the heart monitor. A normal-appearing rhythm marched steadily, silently across the screen. She checked for a pulse in the woman's neck, but felt no movement against her fingertips. She was in PEA—pulseless electrical activity.

"Resume chest compressions, and switch positions with each rhythm check," Erin instructed the paramedics. Then she told the two nurses with her, "Give one milligram of epinephrine IV push. Run fluids wide open for now, and start TXA per protocol for hemorrhage."

Erin looked over at the only other person in the room, a young man she didn't know, who hovered near the doors. And when their gazes met she saw fear, bordering on terror, in his eyes. She glanced at his name tag. Danny O'Boyle, Pathology Assistant. "Call for blood," she said as gently as circumstances allowed. "Use the red phone on the wall near you. It connects directly to the blood bank. Tell them to activate the massive transfusion protocol. Then I want you to record everything we're doing."

Erin turned back to the bed, pulling a stethoscope from

the pocket of her white lab coat, and listened to the woman's chest and stomach while one of the paramedics continued to bag her and the other vigorously performed chest compressions. She heard good air movement in both lungs, and no gurgling sounds over her stomach to indicate the tube had accidentally been put into the esophagus instead of the trachea. It was one less problem, at least. A chest X-ray would still be needed, but they had more pressing matters to deal with at the moment.

"Can I hook her up to a ventilator?" the paramedic giving oxygen asked.

"No, they're all being used, so you'll have to keep bagging her for now," Erin responded grimly. The tourist bus crash alone had left dozens of people on ventilators, mostly due to inhalation injuries from the fire. And the shortage of mechanical ventilators meant they'd have to make especially tough decisions about who would get life support—a call she was going to have to make herself in the next few minutes.

Erin draped the stethoscope around her neck and took a penlight out of the breast pocket of her coat, then shined the light into each of the woman's eyes. They were brown. And both pupils contracted slightly in response to the light, indicating that at least some of her brain was still functioning.

Erin put the penlight away and started examining the woman for obvious signs of trauma, bleeding, anything they could fix immediately to improve her chances of survival, which dropped with each passing minute. There was some swelling and dried blood on her left temple, but no active bleeding. She'd obviously sustained a serious head injury, but that wouldn't explain such a rapid loss of blood pressure and pulse. Massive internal bleeding was almost certainly to blame.

"We've got to get her out of these clothes," Erin said, grabbing a pair of trauma shears. And with the help of one of the nurses, she cut off what was left of the woman's thick jacket first. After this morning it wouldn't be needed anyway, since warm weather was finally expected to settle into the Boston area.

Erin stopped cold when she had the woman's abdomen exposed, and her green eyes widened in shock. Then there was a flicker of fear. "She's pregnant..." The words came out barely above a whisper. In all her years of training and practicing medicine, this was the scenario she'd hoped she would never see. This was her worst nightmare come true.

Several of the staff present who knew Erin well—at least as well as anyone could, given her extremely reserved nature—looked up at her in surprise, not because the patient was pregnant, but because they'd never once seen Erin waver. She was well known, and well liked, for her even temperament: always calm, capable, and efficient in the face of crisis. Those attributes had gotten her through Harvard Medical School with honors, and had made her, at thirty-two, the youngest ER attending at Boston General.

Erin mentally shook herself. "Page overhead for an obstetrician to ER Trauma Bay 2 STAT," she told Danny. "Dial 1357 to get on the intercom." Thankfully, all the other lines of communication in the hospital were holding up fine—despite cell phone networks crashing as a result of the disaster—and the intercom was only being used when absolutely necessary. Experience had taught them well: The ability to manage a catastrophe of any sort was only as good as the quality of communication.

"Should I page someone in particular?" Danny asked.

Erin shook her head as she began palpating the woman's abdomen. "No. Call for any available obstetrician. Then have Radiology get an ultrasound machine in here immediately." There was a slight tremor in her hands as she felt for the top of the uterus. It was well above the belly button, which meant the woman was at least twenty-four weeks pregnant and the fetus had a chance of surviving outside the uterus. If it was even still alive.

She looked up at the clock. "Stop CPR for a second. It's been two minutes. Let's see what we have for a rhythm."

The paramedic ceased chest compressions, and they all looked anxiously at the cardiac monitor. They saw what no one wanted to see—a flat line.

"Resume CPR," Erin ordered. And to one of the nurses, she said, "Repeat one milligram of epinephrine three minutes from the last dose." She turned to the other nurse, willing away the fear that filled her. She knew what she had to do. There was no time to wait for an obstetrician, no time to wait for an ultrasound. This baby had to come out now. The clock was ticking. "We're going to do an emergency C-section. Call the NICU and tell them to get a team down here right away. In the meantime, we need to prepare for the baby."

Erin turned to Danny, who'd just picked up his clipboard after getting off the phone. "Don't bother recording anymore," she said. "I want you to stand by the patient instead and push her uterus over to the left. That will improve blood flow to her heart. It's a very important job. Don't stop until I tell you to."

Danny's eyes widened in shock at her request, the fear in them as bright as ever, and he didn't move.

He looks like a deer in the headlights, Erin thought. And she'd certainly seen enough of those deer to know, having spent many long years growing up in rural Wisconsin. You could never tell if they would move in time, or if they were truly going to stand right there and get run over. "You're part of our team now," she told him calmly. "And we need your help."

Danny opened his mouth as if to say something, then closed it again. Erin gave him a nod of encouragement, yet he still hesitated. But as she started to turn away, expecting he wasn't going to move, he did. He put the clipboard down, set his jaw in grim determination, and rushed to do as she said.

Erin didn't have time to give the moment another thought. She headed over to a cabinet that contained surgical supplies and quickly gathered what she would need for the C-section, placing everything onto a metal surgical tray nearby. Several more staff entered the room just as she was finishing, and she briefly looked up. Help had arrived after all, she was relieved to see. They were two surgical residents she knew well. Nick Olson was in his third year, and Jane Kinney was in her second. Both were already very good surgeons.

"Dr. Jones sent us down from the OR to help," Nick said. "What's going on?"

"Have either of you ever done a perimortem C-section?" Erin asked, pushing the surgical tray over to the bed.

There was no immediate response, and she glanced over at them again. They stood frozen, looking at each other in shock. She had her answer. "We have a pregnant trauma patient in asystole with a potentially viable fetus. Jane, I want you to manage CPR with the paramedics. Nick, you assist me with the C-section." She kept her voice calm, though her heart wasn't quite cooperating. "I'll cut."

"Yes, Dr. Pryce," Nick said in a voice that lacked its usual confidence.

Erin tossed her stethoscope onto a nearby counter and took off her lab coat, then hastily donned a sterile surgical gown, gloves, and mask. Nick did the the same, and they moved to opposite sides of the patient, with Nick standing next to Danny, who continued to push the uterus over to the left while the paramedics performed CPR.

"Should we do chest compressions during surgery?" one of them asked Jane.

"I—I think so," she said, looking uncertainly at Erin.

"Yes, we need to keep as much blood flowing to the placenta as possible until I get the baby out," Erin told them as she picked up a scalpel and handed Nick a pair of surgical retractors. "And delivering the baby might improve the mother's response to CPR. It's her only chance at this point."

Erin looked at Danny. "You can stop pushing now." Then she took a deep breath, and casting any doubts aside, quickly made a vertical incision from the pubic bone up to the belly button. She cut through all the layers of tissue, with Nick pulling the fat and muscle apart to help. She reached the abdominal cavity, and blood immediately poured out of the hemorrhaging patient.

"We need suction!" Nick ordered as he grabbed a stack of laparotomy pads—sterile surgical pads used to staunch the flow of blood—and urgently packed them into the woman's abdomen.

"I can see the uterus well enough," Erin said. "Just keep the bladder out of the way for now so I don't cut it."

Nick used a retractor to shield the thin sack overlying the lower part of the uterus, and Erin made another incision just above it, doing her best not to cut the fetus underneath. Amniotic fluid gushed out as she opened it up, mixing with the blood. She grabbed a pair of bandage scissors, slid several fingers into the incision to lift the uterine wall, and extended the cut upward. Then she threw the scissors aside and plunged her hands in, pulling the baby up out of the massive pool of blood and fluid.

It was a boy. And he appeared to be nearly full term. But he was blue and unmoving, as lifeless as his mother. Erin hastily suctioned his mouth and nose, then clamped and cut the umbilical cord. "You and Jane keep working on the mother," she told Nick. "I'll take the baby."

She ripped her mask off, intending to carry the infant over to the makeshift bed the nurses had set up. But as she turned, the obstetrician who'd responded to their page rushed into the room, and they came face to face. Dr. Peter Pryce—her ex-husband.

He stopped short, his brown eyes widening in horror at the sight of her standing there with the lifeless baby in her bloodied arms.

"Help Nick and Jane," she said briskly, and went over to lay the infant down.

One of the nurses was waiting with towels in hand, and they quickly dried him off. That usually provided enough stimulation to get most babies to breathe on their own if they weren't already. But he didn't respond.

"Go ahead and start positive-pressure ventilations," Erin instructed, then reached over and grabbed her stethoscope. She put the ends of the headset into her ears and placed the diaphragm on the baby's chest to listen for a heartbeat, holding her breath. And it was like music to her ears when she heard the soft, steady rhythm of his heart. She looked at the clock and counted for six seconds. "I'm getting a heart rate of 70," she said. For a newborn it needed to be faster—a lot faster.

The nurse had covered the infant's mouth and nose with an oxygen mask, and was now gently pushing on the bag attached to it, squeezing just enough for his tiny chest to rise slightly. Erin listened to his lungs, making sure oxygen was getting into both equally, and at the same time watched for improvement in his color, hoping to see movement in that limp body. He didn't appear to have sustained any obvious trauma. His mother had kept him safe within her womb.

"Come on now," she whispered, willing him to respond. They would have to begin chest compressions if he didn't improve within the next thirty seconds. But when she finished listening to him there was still no change. He was as blue and lifeless as before.

Erin set her stethoscope down, telling the nurse, "I'll get an IO line in. Let me know when it's been thirty seconds." The baby was going to need an IV, which would normally be placed in an arm, or sometimes through the umbilical cord in a newborn. But the best option at the moment was to put a line in through the bone in his leg instead, using an intraosseous drill with a needle attached to it. The rich supply of veins in the bone marrow would allow fluid and medication to get into his bloodstream quickly, and an IO line could usually be placed faster than a standard IV or an umbilical line. So she hurried back over to the cabinet and began pulling out the equipment she would need: the IO drill, a needle, syringe, tubing—

All thoughts of the procedure fled when she heard a faint cry. She turned to look at the baby, and saw he was moving his head a little now, weakly protesting the oxygen mask that covered his face. She came back over to the bed, and as she watched, the dusky blue of his skin rapidly faded away and a healthy pink color took its place. He let out another cry, stronger this time, and started flailing his arms and legs in a more vehement objection to his current treatment.

Erin felt her chest tighten with emotion at the sight. But it was with bittersweet joy she watched him come to life. "You can take the mask off now and keep it close to his face," she softly told the nurse. Then she picked up her stethoscope and checked his heart rate again. It was 130 this time, exactly where it needed to be.

The Neonatal Intensive Care Unit team arrived a moment later with an incubator, and Dr. Sam Coleman, the neonatologist, rushed over to her. "What have you got, Erin?"

She filled him in while he did a brief exam on the baby boy, who was now demonstrating a very healthy set of lungs.

"Everything's looking good for the moment," Sam said. "We'll take him up to the NICU for further evaluation."

A neonatal nurse placed the baby in the incubator and several members of the team rolled him out.

Sam looked back one last time. "Great job, Erin. Unbelievable job." He glanced grimly at the scene behind her, then rushed out of the room with his team.

Erin turned around, already knowing what she was going to find.

"I'm sorry," Peter said solemnly. "We couldn't save her."

Erin looked at the dead woman who would never get to hold her baby boy, then glanced at the faces of the staff members standing around the bed. Most were crying silently. A few couldn't hold back a sob. The surgical residents were at a loss, faces stricken with grief and shock.

She lowered her eyes to the blood-soaked gloves that still covered her hands, and her mind shifted to the familiar place in her brain that was devoid of emotion, where only logic and reason prevailed—the place that kept her sane. She'd needed that place more times than she could count in her life. "Unfortunately, we need to move on," she said quietly, peeling off her surgical gown and gloves and throwing them away. "We have other patients who need us."

She slipped into her white coat again. But as she turned to leave, Peter grabbed her arm. "Erin—"

She pulled free of him, not daring to look back. "I have work to do, Peter."

She left the room, trying to erase the scene inside from her mind. She'd seen death often, too often, in her thirty-two years. It was never easy to deal with in any form. But this one struck a particularly painful chord inside her. This one was personal.

ERIN DUMPED HER PILE OF PAPERWORK INTO THE out-basket with a weary sigh. So much for going paperless. She sat in a back office near the ER, where things were now eerily quiet after such an eventful day. Her dictations were done, and another disaster was finally in the books. Of course, it would never be over for some.

Laura…That was the name of the woman whose baby she'd delivered today. Erin had been the one to give Laura's family the heartbreaking news of her death, watching as the hope on their faces turned to utter despair and grief. In medical school they'd had lectures on how to give bad news. But she'd already learned that nothing made those moments any easier. And when Laura's brother had asked if it would have made a difference if she'd been wearing a seat belt, Erin had felt almost as bad telling him the truth—it might have. Unfortunately, pregnant women often didn't wear one because of the mistaken belief that it wasn't safe for the baby. And a significant number of those who did had never been instructed on how to position it correctly during pregnancy. Laura's husband had said she was on her way to an OB appointment when the accident happened. Maybe they would have reminded her then. *She'd probably been thinking about her baby while she was driving. Did she know she was going to have a boy?*

Erin let out another sigh and pulled her long, sandy blond hair free of the ponytail that had held it in place all day, tossing the elastic band onto her desk. She needed to go home. She just had one last stop to make before she could.

There was a rap on her office door, and she looked up. Dean Monahan, the hospital CEO, popped his head through the partially open door. She knew his face from pictures and an occasional meeting but had never talked to him in person before. "Do you have a moment, Dr. Pryce?"

"Of course." Erin was surprised he knew her name. She stood up and motioned to a chair next to the desk. "Have a seat." She sat down again after him and smiled wearily. "Should I be worried? It's not every day the hospital CEO tracks someone down in their office."

Dean shook his head, fatigue written all over his face as well. "What a day…"

Erin nodded, and for a moment silence fell heavily between them. There were just some things that couldn't be expressed in words.

"I heard you did an amazing job," Dean finally said. "Things wouldn't have gone as well without you. And it took real courage to go in and save that baby like you did."

"Some would argue that I shouldn't have done anything," Erin quietly responded, lowering her eyes to the desk. "We were dealing with a mass casualty incident. There were so many other seriously injured patients at that point, and our resources were spread so thin…It could easily have turned out that I spent them on two dead patients." She'd gone over that again and again in her mind. But in the end she knew she wouldn't have done anything differently, regardless of the outcome. Not when there had still been hope. "As it is, there's now a little boy in the NICU who has no mother."

"But he has life. You gave him the greatest gift he will ever get—a chance to live."

Erin said nothing, running her long fingers over the smooth wooden surface of the desk. The subject brought up too many emotions for her, exposed too many scars. She preferred to keep them hidden, so she said nothing.

Dean studied her thoughtfully. "In my experience almost anyone else would be patting themselves on the back right now. You made a tough decision today, one most doctors will never have to make, and you saved a child's life. You're the best we have at here at Boston General." He paused a moment, then said, "I understand you turned in your resignation a few months ago. What can we do to keep you here?"

Erin looked up at him in shock. He was the CEO of one of the largest and most reputable hospitals on the East Coast, and here he was in her office, asking her to stay.

"I've made some inquiries," Dean continued. "I gather you turned in your resignation because of some, uh, issues with your ex-husband?"

There it was, another scar she preferred to keep hidden. "I just think a change of scenery will be the best thing for me right now, that's all."

"What if we were to revoke Peter's privileges here? If I have to make a choice, I'll choose you, Dr. Pryce. No question."

Erin couldn't help but feel a little thrill of pleasure go through her with his words. He would probably send Peter's mistress over in the ICU on her merry way too, if she asked. She imagined them walking out of the hospital together with their personal effects and pink slips. There was definitely some satisfaction in that thought. But she let it go. "I truly appreciate the offer, Dean. And I'm sure I won't find a better place to work than Boston General. But this really isn't about Peter, so I have to stick to my decision."

"Are you planning to stay in Boston?" he asked.

"Yes. I couldn't imagine living anywhere else. Although I've been thinking about moving west into the suburbs, just to get a little more space."

Dean chuckled. "Please don't tell me Wellesley is luring you away. I play racquetball with their CEO every Friday, and I'll never hear the end of it."

"No, I don't think I'll go quite that far west," Erin tentatively replied. "But I haven't made a final decision yet." Several hospitals in the area were waiting for her to make that decision. And it was one she really needed to make soon, with only two weeks left at Boston General. But she kept putting it off. The truth was, she was coming to the realization that she needed a break far more than she needed a new job. It was time to take inventory of her life, and the thought scared her. She knew she wasn't going to like what she found—or didn't find.

She'd spent most of the last year buried in her work, trying not to think about anything else, trying not to feel anything. It was hard to believe that just last spring, barely a year ago, she'd still been trying to have a baby herself—until she'd come home from work early one day, sick with the flu, and caught her husband in bed with an ICU nurse from Boston General. So much for getting the flu shot.

She'd left him that day and never looked back, turning to the one true love of her life—medicine. But now she was exhausted, the kind of exhaustion that sleep couldn't cure. She really did need to take a break and figure things out. Something was dying inside of her.

Dean stood up. "Well, let me know if there's anything I can do to change your mind, Dr. Pryce. We'd love to keep you here at Boston General. But in any case, I need to get back to my office. There's still a lot of mess to clean up after today." He shook her hand. "Good luck to you, whatever you decide."

Erin expressed her thanks and watched him leave. Then she picked up her bag and headed out the door herself to make that last stop.

HE SLEPT SO PEACEFULLY ONE WOULD NEVER KNOW he'd just come into the world in such a traumatic way. He lay on his back, all bundled up in a blue blanket, with one tiny hand nestled against his cheek. The mitten that was supposed to be on it to protect him from scratching his face had come off and lay next to him. Erin smiled. He was already bucking the system.

She continued to watch him sleep for a while. She never tired of watching babies sleep. If the ER hadn't turned out to be such a good fit for her she would have gone into neonatology. *Babies are that little bit of innocence not yet disturbed by the world.* And she'd wanted one so desperately...But she needed to stop thinking about that. Every time her thoughts led her in that direction a piece of her never came back.

She lightly caressed the top of the baby's hand, and then couldn't resist the urge to hold it, gently lifting it up off his cheek. Dr. Coleman thought he was going to be fine. There were no signs of brain damage on his exam, and the scans had all looked good. They'd gotten him out just in time.

"I'm so sorry we couldn't save your mother," she whispered softly. "It's not going to be easy living without her." She knew that all too well.

The baby stirred slightly and wrapped his little fingers around one of hers, holding on tightly while he continued to sleep. A lump of emotion formed in Erin's throat, and her green eyes moistened. *I am not going to cry*, she willed herself. She remembered she used to say that all the time as a child, until one day she did stop.

"Erin."

She looked up and inwardly sighed when she saw Peter standing on the other side of the bed. She'd managed to avoid the man for months since their divorce, and now here he was again, twice in the same day. She regretfully let go of the baby's hand, slid the little blue mitten back on, and tucked the blanket snugly around him.

"I've been looking for you," Peter said. "One of the nurses told me you were here." He nervously ran a hand through his black hair and glanced down at the infant. "I understand he's doing well."

Erin took one last look at the sleeping baby, then headed toward the NICU exit without a word. Peter followed her anyway, and she didn't miss the speculative glances from the nursing staff. "Aren't you in the wrong ICU?" she asked dryly.

Peter grimaced. "Okay, I deserve that."

He deserved a whole lot more than that. But she didn't say it, just like she hadn't said so many other things, and they walked through the NICU in awkward silence.

"I've never done a perimortem C-section myself," Peter finally said. "It's kind of ironic that between the two of us it would be you who'd do one first."

"I'd hardly call it ironic that I did one first, Peter. In the ER I have to be prepared to do just about anything." Erin couldn't quite keep the bitterness out of her voice when she added, "But as far as real irony goes, there was certainly no lack of that in our relationship—when there was a relationship, that is."

Yes, the ironies…Like how she'd ultimately decided to marry him three years ago because she'd wanted a baby. She wasn't about to go the illegitimate route, as her mother had done. But then it turned out she was probably the only obstetrician's wife in all of New England who couldn't get pregnant.

And irony had definitely been in full bloom that day last spring when she'd been too sick to finish an ER shift for the first time in her life and had gone home early, only to find him in bed with a nurse. They'd been going at it like they were trying to rip each other apart, no less. She would never have guessed he was capable of such…enthusiasm. He'd certainly never displayed that kind of passion with her. Although if she was painfully honest, she knew she hadn't exactly given him much to be inspired about in the bedroom.

They left the NICU and Peter grabbed hold of her arm in the hallway, holding on tightly when she tried to pull away. "Please, Erin. I need to talk to you."

"Let go of me, Peter!" she vehemently whispered.

After a brief hesitation, he dropped his hand with a sigh. "I really am sorry about everything that's happened between us. I…I wish I'd done a lot of things differently."

Erin was surprised to hear the note of regret in his voice, and wondered if things weren't going so well between him and his mistress. "It doesn't matter," she said wearily. "I don't think we were meant to be together anyway."

Peter gazed at her for a long moment, then softly said, "It's always blown me away how you could be so smart and so beautiful at the same time."

Erin blinked in astonishment. He'd never said anything like that to her before. They'd always treated each other more like colleagues than husband and wife. And she realized with even more surprise that she would have liked hearing those words back then. But she certainly didn't want to hear them now. The only thing she wanted now was to end this conversation as quickly as possible and leave. She needed fresh air. Not to mention someone was probably already telling his girlfriend in the ICU what was going on here in the hallway. Neither of them was worth making a scene over. "I really need to go home, Peter. Goodbye—and good luck with your girlfriend."

With that she turned and walked away, leaving him standing there alone, watching her go.

CHAPTER

2

Peter still wanted her. She'd seen it in his eyes...

Erin sat down heavily on the living room sofa in her South Boston apartment and dropped her head back against the brown leather cushion with a sigh. So much had happened today, so many old wounds ripped wide open. And to top it off, Peter still wanted her.

Apparently he wasn't getting enough intensive care from his nurse. Erin smiled wryly at the thought and reached for the glass of Merlot she'd set on the coffee table in front of her. But all humor faded from her expression as she sipped the wine and thought about her years with Peter.

She'd been attracted to him once, with his tall, dark good looks. He was also an excellent physician and a gifted surgeon. She'd admired those qualities more than anything. But he didn't have the same appeal anymore, now that she'd seen such a different side of his personality. Funny how that worked.

They'd met at Boston General when she was an intern and he was a fourth year OB/GYN resident. She'd hardly ever dated before him, preferring to focus on her studies at Harvard. Math and science had always been her strong suits. She understood things she could define, preferred what was logical and concrete. The abstract was a challenge. And relationships fell into that abstract category for her. She'd never been good at them.

Life with Peter had been fairly uncomplicated, though, up until the end. He'd never been one to ask a lot of questions or invade her space. And with him she'd thought she could have the two things she really wanted—a new name and babies.

The first had been easy, of course. Changing her name from Harris to Pryce had felt like she was leaving another big piece of her past behind, as she'd worked so hard to do otherwise. Hearing her maiden name still made her cringe.

But the baby part, that was where things had gone wrong. She'd married Peter after her third year of ER residency, when her schedule had finally eased up a little. They'd started trying for a baby right away, and then continued trying for the next two years without any luck. Her period came like clockwork every month, and she'd eventually come to dread that time. She had been late once, and for a moment she'd never been so happy, thinking she was finally pregnant. But then she'd taken a test, and the negative result had cut especially deep.

They'd finally begun a fertility work-up, and when Peter's tests came back normal she'd known with devastating certainty that she was the problem. That wound had left yet another scar.

Erin wearily sighed and looked down at the now empty wineglass in her hand. Maybe she'd break her one glass rule and have another. She certainly deserved it tonight. But she knew she wouldn't. She was too good at maintaining control.

She set the glass back down on the coffee table and reluctantly stood up. She needed to go to bed and at least try to sleep. She had another twelve-hour shift to get through tomorrow—and the next day. And the day after that.

Wincing at the thought, she headed to her bedroom. But she abruptly stopped when she heard the faint vibration of her cell phone in the kitchen where she'd left it. She looked up at the clock and saw it was almost midnight. Someone really wanted to talk to her. It was probably a resident or another attending at the hospital with a question about how to treat a patient. She was used to getting calls like that at just about any hour. She had a reputation for always answering—and for always having the right answer when she did. But tonight she needed someone else to have the right answer, so she started walking to the bedroom again.

She didn't make it very far, though. With a defeated groan she turned and headed to the kitchen instead. It just wasn't in her nature to ignore someone who needed help.

The phone was still buzzing when she picked it up off the counter, and she looked down at the screen to see who was calling this time. Jenna. She blinked in surprise and immediately answered. "Jen, hello."

She and Jenna Godfrey had been best friends for twenty-six years, ever since the day they'd crossed paths in the woods just outside of New Dublin, Wisconsin, a small town north of Madison, during the summer that tragedy had first touched both their lives.

Erin had been sent to New Dublin to live with her grandparents after her mother died—grandparents she hadn't even met until then. And not long after that Jenna and her parents had moved into the house next door, the only other one on that lonely country road, hoping to make a fresh start after Jenna's younger brother died from a brain tumor.

Despite their misfortune, the Godfreys had treated Erin with the kind of love and affection her own grandparents had never given her, and she'd come to care for them deeply. But then tragedy ended up striking them all once again—Jenna's mother was diagnosed with breast cancer. And after a difficult, two-year battle, she died when Erin and Jenna were fifteen.

Erin had vowed never to go back to that miserable town once she'd graduated from high school. The problem was, Jenna never left. They'd originally planned to move to the East Coast together, but Jenna's father developed complications from diabetes, so her friend had stayed behind. She'd gotten a degree in education and worked in New Dublin as an elementary school teacher, all while taking care of her ill father. He'd died five years ago, but by then Jenna had made her life there. And Erin had never gone back.

They went on vacation together every year, and Jenna came to Boston whenever she could. But they hadn't been in contact much recently, and Erin knew it was her own fault. Jenna was probably calling now because she'd heard about the accident on I 93.

"Erin, it's so good to hear your voice," her friend said. "I wasn't sure you would answer this late."

"I was actually going to leave my phone in the kitchen and ignore it for once. But now I'm glad I couldn't go through with it," Erin responded with wry amusement in her tone. "I was shocked to see you were the one calling so late, though. Usually I'm the night owl, not you." She leaned against the kitchen counter, picturing Jenna on the other end of the line with her curly auburn hair and twinkling blue eyes, and the image brought a tender smile to her face. Jenna always made her smile. It was something she'd been forgetting how to do more and more lately. "I'm sorry I haven't called you in a while. I guess I kind of get lost in my own little world sometimes."

"You have nothing to be sorry for, Erin. I know how busy you are. I just hope I didn't pick a bad time to call now. With your schedule, I'm never sure. And I—I kept second-guessing myself about calling at all tonight."

"You can call me anytime, Jen. You know that."

"Yes, well…" Jenna's voice trailed off for a moment, and then she said, "I saw the news. That accident in Boston was horrible. Were you working?"

Erin's lips twisted into a grimace. "Of course. My black cloud never lets me down."

"I couldn't believe it when they showed all those cars piled up like that. And they said thirty-five people died. That's awful."

Erin hadn't stopped to think about it before. Laura had been the last one, number thirty-five…She mentally shook herself and headed back into the living room. "Let's talk about something more pleasant, Jen. I'm finished at the hospital in two weeks, and the school year should almost be over by then. Why don't we plan on meeting somewhere? I need a vacation, a very *long* vacation, and I'd love for us to get together. Maybe we can finally make it to Costa Rica."

"Oh, Erin," Jenna whispered.

Erin stopped short. There was a sadness and pain in her friend's voice that she'd never heard before. "What's going on, Jen?" she asked in alarm.

"I'm so sorry. This is really bad timing, but—but I've put off telling you for too long. I've dreaded having to tell you."

"What is it, Jenna?" Erin asked again, forgetting how to breathe. She knew it was going to be bad.

"I have cancer...Melanoma. I—I'm dying."

Erin stood frozen in the middle of her living room, and for a moment the whole world stopped. There was no sound, no movement, not a single thought in her head. Nothing.

"What?" she finally got out.

"I was diagnosed with melanoma," Jenna softly repeated. "Stage 4. I've had a bunch of tests done, and the oncologist gave me all the options for treatment, but the type of melanoma I have is especially difficult to manage, and it's spread to so many places." After another long pause she added, "I—I have a few months now, if I'm lucky."

The weight of Jenna's words finally hit Erin. "*No*," she whispered hoarsely. "*Jenna...No.*" Her legs started to go weak under her, and she managed to get over to a nearby chair and sit down. "How...how long have you known?"

"The first tests were done a couple of weeks ago. I'd been losing weight, which normally I wouldn't object to." Jenna laughed half-heartedly. "But I just didn't feel well in general. I was tired all the time and started having lots of aches and pains, especially in my back and hip, so I went to see my doctor. She did X rays, and they weren't normal. Then she ordered a bunch of scans, and those showed the extent of the cancer. She also took a biopsy of a mole on the back of my leg that didn't look right. I have so many moles and freckles all over, I never really noticed anything unusual... It was melanoma."

Erin sat there stunned, not knowing what to think, not knowing what to say. She finally went to the part of her brain that worked the best, the part she'd gone to earlier that day. Now she needed it more than ever. "I want you to come to

Boston and stay with me, Jenna. We have excellent cancer specialists here. We'll get all your records transferred and figure out what the best course of treatment is. I was going to hold off accepting another position here for a few weeks anyway, but I'll wait as long as it takes to get you better. We'll fight this."

"No, Erin. I'm not going to fight it, not when it's this far advanced," Jenna said. "I know as a doctor you always want to find a cure. That's your job. But sometimes there isn't one. Sometimes the best option is to do nothing. And right now I don't need you to be my doctor. I just need you to be my friend."

Erin couldn't accept that. "Jenna, there are clinical trials we can get you into—"

"*No*, Erin. I've made my decision. I'm not fighting this. I understand that there are really good treatments out there now for most types of cancer. But the fact is, they haven't found a good one for mine yet. And the options that are available can have serious side effects…No. I'm not going to spend whatever quality time I have left on this Earth feeling sick, all so I can cling to life a little longer and be sick some more. I don't want to live if I'm not really living. You were there when my mom went through all that with breast cancer. She tried everything right up until the end so she could hang on as long as possible for us. But she was so miserably sick, and in so much pain all the time. I can't do that. I won't."

Erin remembered how bravely Jenna's mom had battled cancer. *Shannon*…She'd been such a kind, gentle woman, just like her daughter. There had always been a sadness about her, though, even before she got sick. Erin understood that kind of sadness. Shannon had lost her own parents when she was young. And then there was Jenna's brother, of course. But Shannon would never talk about him. Some things were just too big and painful to push past the vocal cords. Erin understood that too.

She felt tears fill her eyes. This time she couldn't fight them off, and they spilled down her cheeks. She and Jenna had experienced so much pain, so much tragedy, in their lives, and now this...Jenna was the most kind-hearted person she'd ever known. Her friend didn't deserve this.

Erin felt that old anger, that old rebellion, rise inside her. "How can there possibly be a God, Jenna? I can't believe God could be this cruel."

"Oh, Erin," Jenna said. "This is not God's doing. It's just part of life. I know your horrible grandmother turned you against religion, but I truly believe in God and Heaven. I've been able to come to terms with all of this over the last few weeks, and I think it would have been a lot harder to do if I wasn't sure there was more than just this life here on Earth. There's a better place—there really is. And I know I'll be there with my family. I'm going to be fine...I'm really going to miss you, though."

Erin wiped her tears away with a trembling hand. "I don't know what I'll do without you, Jenna."

There was a long pause on the other end of the line, and Erin knew her friend was crying too.

"We'll see each other soon, okay?" Jenna finally said. "I would like to come to Boston. But first I have to do something I've dreamed about for a long time: I'm going to Ireland. My mom had always wanted to go there too, so I'm making the trip for both of us. I also found out we have some distant relatives in Dublin, ironically, and I'm planning to meet up with them. I just got a ticket yesterday, and the flight leaves in the morning. I thought I'd come home afterward, get a few last things in order here, then head to Boston."

Erin thought about her schedule, but there was no way she'd be able to get all her shifts covered in time to go along. "I wish I could come with you, but I'm working in the ER almost every day for the next two weeks."

"I wish you could come too, but I figured your schedule wouldn't allow it. And unfortunately, I can't wait. I want to go while I still feel well enough to enjoy this trip. I don't know if that will be the case even a week from now."

"You shouldn't be going alone."

"I'm not. Luke Mathis is going with me."

Erin was surprised. Luke Mathis. He was a police officer in New Dublin now, a detective. But after fourteen years she only had a vague image of him in her mind. Dark hair, blue eyes, quiet…They'd all gone to school together since first grade, but she hadn't known him well. Except for Jenna, she'd never really had any friends. She did remember Luke's father, though. She'd worked as a nursing assistant at the hospital through most of high school, and he was a surgeon there. In fact, he'd written her a letter of recommendation to Harvard.

"So you've finally hooked up with Luke, have you?" Erin asked, sniffing back her tears.

Jenna laughed softly. "He's like a brother to me. I've told you that before. He just didn't want me to go alone either. When he found out the police chief would let him off, he insisted on coming along. He's been a big help these last few weeks."

"Unlike me," Erin winced.

"No, you've always been a great friend—my best friend.

And I'm so sorry I didn't tell you sooner. But I knew this was going to be the hardest part, telling you."

"I really wish I was with you right now, Jen."

"I know. But I'll come to Boston right after this trip. I promise."

"No, you won't." Erin knew what she had to do. And it meant facing the demons she'd run away from for the last fourteen years. "I'm going to come stay with you in New Dublin as soon as I'm done here."

There was shocked silence on the other end of the line for a moment. "Are…are you sure?" Jenna finally asked.

Erin was scared to death at the thought of going back, that was for sure. She realized that despite fourteen years away, graduating from one of the best schools in the country, going through intense medical training, and getting married and divorced, there was still that same scared little girl inside her. "I want to be there for you, Jenna. It's my turn to come to you. I have to do this. I'll stay until…until the end."

"That could be months."

Erin sniffed back more tears. "I hope it's years."

"You're sure you won't mind staying at my house?"

Erin knew what Jenna was asking. Her friend still lived in the little house she'd grown up in, and the one next door was the old farmhouse Erin had spent many miserable years in. "My grandparents are dead. I need to get over it." They were in St. Mary's Cemetery in New Dublin, along with her mother. As for her father, she didn't want to contemplate where he was.

"Alright, Erin…If you're sure." The weariness in Jenna's voice was much more pronounced now.

"Yes, I'm sure," Erin gently told her. "Now go rest up for your big trip. I want to hear all about it, so text me every day, okay? And I'll call you whenever I can."

"Okay. I can't wait to see you," Jenna said. "I love you, Erin. Goodnight."

"You too, Jen. Goodnight."

With a shaking hand Erin set the phone down next to her on the chair, and tears started falling silently down her cheeks again. She tried to stand, but her legs wouldn't hold her, and she ended up sliding to the floor instead. She buried her face in her hands as the tears turned into sobs. And then she cried like she hadn't cried since she'd been a scared and lonely child locked up in the old farmhouse on the outskirts of that wretched little town.

CHAPTER

3

Police vehicles, with their lights flashing red and blue, blocked the highway going both ways.

Erin groaned and came to a stop behind several other cars in the northbound lane. She was almost to New Dublin—finally. It had been a long drive from Boston, with only her thoughts to keep her company. And her tears. Now that they'd started, she couldn't seem to stop them.

Things were becoming more familiar the closer she got to town, places long forgotten, like the horse ranch she'd passed a few miles back. The pasture was still there, fenced in next to the road, with several horses peacefully grazing inside. She'd always loved looking at them through the car window when she was a kid. They'd been like a dream, part of another beautiful world outside the window that was just beyond her reach…

Erin surveyed the scene before her now. There was dense forest on both sides of the highway, split only by a narrow gravel road to the right. Something was clearly going on down that way because the police cars were parked in the traffic lanes on each side of it. But the road disappeared into the forest after a short distance, so she couldn't see what was happening.

She glanced at the clock on her dashboard. She was going to be late if they didn't let her through soon. Jenna's class was getting out of school for summer vacation today, and she'd promised to drive her there to say goodbye. *Her last goodbye,* Erin thought sadly. And if it wasn't for an apparent bug in her car's navigation system she would already be with Jenna. But it had gone haywire about the time she'd passed the horse ranch, making her miss the next turn—which she probably would have remembered to make if the GPS hadn't been on in the first place. So now here she was, stuck in this mess instead.

A dark-haired man in a long-sleeved shirt and tie came out of the woods just then, running toward two uniformed police officers standing near the highway. A split second later she heard a high-pitched siren behind her and saw the red flashing lights of an ambulance in her rear-view mirror. It screamed past her, and the dark-haired man urgently directed it down the gravel road.

Erin didn't think twice. She eased her yellow Audi over to the side of the highway, then jumped out and ran toward him.

"A *DUEL?* ARE YOU KIDDING ME?" ONE OF THE PATROL officers asked in surprise.

Luke Mathis shook his head, not quite believing it himself. "I couldn't make this sort of thing up if I tried. Anyway, you can let traffic go through on the highway now. We're setting up a landing zone in the field for the chopper."

The two officers headed toward their vehicles, and Luke pulled out his portable radio. "New Dublin 28 to Comm Center."

"Go ahead 28," the dispatcher at the Communications Center responded.

"Can you get me an ETA for that helicopter?"

"Stand by 28." There was a momentary pause, and then she said, "Comm Center to 28. The ETA is six minutes."

"Ten-four," Luke acknowledged, and slid the radio back into its case on his belt.

"Excuse me, sir. I'm a doctor. Is there anything I can do to help?"

Luke turned around and looked down into dark-rimmed green eyes flecked with gold. They were eyes he remembered well, even after all these years. "Erin?" he asked in shock.

Erin blinked in surprise when he said her name, and briefly studied him. He was about six feet tall, with a lean, muscular frame. His face was boyishly handsome, and he had thick, slightly wavy, dark brown hair. His eyes were blue, azure blue, like a cloudless summer day. He wore civilian clothes, but had a holstered gun hanging from his belt, with a detective badge clipped on next to it. And as soon as she saw it she realized who he was. "Luke?"

He nodded, quickly shaking off his astonishment at seeing her. There was no time to contemplate those green eyes right now, or the warmth that filled him when he looked into them. A boy was dying.

"Yes, we can use your help. Come with me." He motioned her down the gravel road, explaining as they ran, "Two sixteen-year-old boys decided to skip the last day of school and have a gunfight instead—an old-fashioned English duel actually. They were standing about 80 feet apart, and both were injured. One has a minor wound on his arm. The other kid took a bullet to the chest. He's in bad shape."

There were thick woods on either side of them, but Erin could see the road opened up into a large field about a hundred yards ahead. "What kind of guns?" she asked, doing her best to keep pace with his longer strides.

"Both were handguns. The kid with the chest wound got hit with a .38 Special. The other was a .45. I guess they couldn't find any real dueling pistols around here." Luke glanced at her curiously. "Do you know much about guns?"

"I know what kinds of wounds some of them can leave. And usually the bigger the gun, the bigger the wound. But I guess better aim beats a bigger gun."

"Or just plain dumb luck."

They were almost to the clearing, and Erin was glad. She was out of breath. Maybe it hadn't been such a good idea to cancel her gym membership after all. She noticed Luke didn't look the least bit winded.

"We're pretty far from the hospital so we called in a medevac chopper," he said. "And it's a damn good thing, too, because the ambulance crew almost missed the party. They had some trouble with the coordinates and initially went too far north. But the chopper should be here shortly."

They reached the field a moment later, and Erin saw there were police and rescue vehicles scattered everywhere. A number of them were parked a little farther down the field with their lights flashing, where she presumed they were setting up the helicopter landing zone. The ambulance was parked in an area to their right, and Luke quickly led her around it to the injured boy on the other side.

He was lying on a stretcher that had been lowered to the ground, with an oxygen mask covering his mouth and nose. Two paramedics, a male and a female, were attending to him. One was hooking him up to a monitor, while the other was trying to get an IV into his left arm.

Erin knelt down next to him, tucking her blond hair behind an ear as she assessed the situation.

"She's a doctor," Luke told the paramedics when they looked up.

"We didn't hear any sucking sounds coming from the wound or see any air bubbles, and I heard breath sounds on the right," the male paramedic said, squatting down near the end of the stretcher to finish setting up the monitor there. "But we put a chest seal on just in case. And there wasn't an exit wound."

Erin noted they'd cut away the boy's T-shirt and placed the seal over the bullet wound lateral to his right nipple. The seal was made of a clear adhesive material with a plastic, one-way valve in the middle that kept air from getting sucked into the wound when he inhaled, but allowed any air that had already gotten inside to escape—that is, if clotted blood and damaged body tissues weren't blocking the way out. But even with the wound covered, air could still leak out from any part of the lung injured by the bullet and accumulate in the space between the lung and the chest wall. If that air couldn't get out through the valve, more and more of it would get trapped in there and push against the lung until it collapsed. Then, as the pressure increased further, the blood vessels to the heart would get squeezed shut. And if the air wasn't released immediately at that point, the heart would stop.

The boy was breathing rapidly, and Erin saw panic in his brown eyes. He weakly tried to pull at the oxygen mask on his face and gasped, "I…I can't…breathe…"

The female paramedic glanced up nervously. "I'm having trouble getting an IV in."

"His blood pressure is 81 over 45," the other paramedic said. "His pulse is in the 130s, and it looks like he's in a regular rhythm. The best oxygen saturation I'm getting is 83 percent—wait, now it's dropping into the 70s. I think we should intubate him."

"I need your stethoscope," Erin told him. She could see both paramedics were young and inexperienced.

He handed it to her, and she listened to the boy's lungs. There were no longer any breath sounds on the right side. His lung had collapsed. Too much air was trapped inside.

She set the stethoscope down and felt his trachea. It was being pushed over to the left by the trapped air. And she saw his neck veins were bulging because the blood couldn't get back to his heart. She checked for a pulse in his wrist. If his blood pressure was still above 80 she should be able to feel a pulse there. But there was no pulse. And his skin was becoming more bluish in color by the second. He was in serious trouble.

"I'm going to do a needle thoracentesis," Erin told the paramedics. "Get me a needle—at least 14-gauge and 3 inches long, some gloves, and an alcohol pad—quickly!"

She looked up at Luke. "I have to put a needle into his chest to get the air out, and there's no time to numb him up. Can you hold him still?"

Luke nodded, though his face visibly blanched as he knelt at the head of the stretcher.

Erin pulled on the gloves one of the paramedics handed her, then felt for the third rib on the right side, several inches below the middle of the boy's collarbone. She briefly swabbed the area just above it with the alcohol pad, keeping a finger there so she wouldn't lose her spot. And without hesitation, she grabbed the needle and plunged it into his chest.

The boy let out a moan and bucked with all the energy he had left, but Luke held him down.

Suddenly there was an audible *whoosh* when the needle hit the trapped air and released it. Erin was relieved to see no blood came out. That was a good sign.

The needle was surrounded by a thin plastic catheter tube, and she pushed the tube down all the way into his chest until only the hub was visible against his skin. Then she slid the needle out and held the tube in place with her fingers.

She felt for the pulse in the boy's wrist again with her free hand. There it was, weak but palpable. And within seconds it got stronger, and stronger. A healthy pink color returned to his skin.

Luke glanced up at the sky. "The chopper's coming."

Erin squinted into the sun and watched as the big blue and white bird headed toward them. Then she shifted her gaze to meet Luke's. Yes, there was definitely a perfect summer day in those eyes.

The boy groaned, and she turned her attention back to him. He wasn't struggling to breathe anymore, but was in obvious pain, thanks to the two holes in his chest now. *Better two holes there,* she thought, *than the one foot he'd had in the grave before. Another minute and that would have been two.*

"I'll need some tape to keep the catheter in place," Erin told the male paramedic. "And if his blood pressure is at least 90 systolic you can give him 50 mics of fentanyl for pain."

"Finally! I've got an IV in," the other paramedic said, looking up in relief. The color returned to her face, too.

Erin nodded, checking the cardiac monitor. "His heart rate is better, and as long as his blood pressure is stable, don't run fluids any faster than TKO. We don't want to blow open any blood clots with too much fluid."

While the paramedics carried out her instructions, she secured the catheter to the boy's chest. She could feel Luke watching her the whole time, and it set off an odd fluttering in her own chest.

A moment later the helicopter made a slow descent onto the field. The characteristic *whup-whup-whup* of its main rotor got louder as it came down, and it kicked up dirt and debris everywhere.

Erin grabbed the stethoscope, her hair whipping in the wind created by the aircraft, and listened to the boy's lungs again, covering one ear with her free hand to block out some of the noise behind her. She heard good air movement on the right side now.

She glanced back just as the helicopter was landing. "We've done as much as we can here!" she shouted to the paramedics. "Pull up the stretcher and get him to the helicopter!"

Luke jumped to his feet and reached down to help her up. Erin took his hand and instantly felt a rush of warmth flow through her. She tried to stand, but couldn't seem to get her legs to work right, and stumbled backward instead.

Luke immediately hooked an arm around her waist and pulled her up against him. Their gazes locked, and for a second Erin forgot about the chaos around them. It was just her and him and the infinite blue of his eyes.

He gave her a brief smile, attractive laugh lines forming at the corners of those eyes. "Are you okay?"

She didn't hear the question so much as she felt it, for some odd reason, and nodded in response.

Then the moment was broken. He let her go and turned to help the paramedics.

Erin stayed back, shaking off her embarrassment over acting like a total klutz in front of everyone—there was a good reason she'd never been in gymnastics—and watched as they rolled the boy toward the helicopter and quickly loaded him up. Within minutes the bird was flying again, and she marveled at the sight of it ascending into the cloudless blue sky. She'd never seen a helicopter take off or land, she realized. Plenty of helicopters came to Boston General, but she'd always been inside, waiting for the patient.

Luke jogged back over to her a few minutes later. "Do you think he'll pull through?"

"I think so," she said, ignoring the way his nearness stirred up those odd sensations inside her again. She was probably just feeling a little off-kilter because of what had happened with the boy. "There wasn't a lot of bleeding, so I doubt the bullet hit any major blood vessels. He's lucky."

Luke stared down at her with admiration in his eyes. "He's lucky you were here. That thing you did with the needle…" He shook his head. "I've never seen anything like it before. I just hope I'm never on the receiving end."

Erin laughed shortly. "I hope I don't have to do that again anytime soon. Are duels a common thing in New Dublin?"

Luke's lips twisted into a grim smile. "Before today the last duel on this side of the Atlantic probably happened over a hundred years ago. And I doubt it was anywhere near New Dublin, Wisconsin. I sure hope this doesn't become a trend."

Erin glanced up at the sky. The helicopter was just a tiny speck in the distance now. "Are they taking him to Madison? I would imagine the hospital in New Dublin is too small to handle that kind of trauma."

Luke remembered when Erin used to work at the hospital. He would go there sometimes under the pretense of visiting his dad, hoping to run into her. He'd been such an awkward teenager, though. If he did see her he would get so tongue-tied when he looked into those big green eyes that he would never be able to say two words. "Actually, they are going there," he told her. "The hospital's changed a lot over the years. They built a state-of-the-art surgery center, and my dad brought in a partner, Colin O'Reilly, who has experience in trauma. I think he came shortly after you left. He's originally from New Dublin. His dad had a family practice clinic here for decades until he retired a few years ago."

"Dr. Nolan O'Reilly—or Dr. O, as some of the staff liked to call him," Erin said with a smile. "Even after all these years he still sends me a card every Christmas and on my birthday."

Dr. O'Reilly had always been her idol. He was the smartest man she'd ever met, yet he had such a jovial personality, and his enthusiasm for life and medicine was infectious. The energy level immediately went up when he walked into a room. He would talk to anyone, and treated everyone with equal respect, whether it was Dr. Mathis, the chief of staff, or the cleaning crew. When Erin had shown an interest in pursuing medicine herself, Dr. O'Reilly took her under his wing. They'd had endless conversations on the subject, with him usually doing most of the talking. She would stay late at the hospital almost every shift, unpaid, to spend more time with him rather than going back to her grandparents' house. And he hadn't had anyone to go home to, either. One of the nurses told her that his wife had died from a massive pulmonary embolism while she was pregnant, causing the deaths of their unborn twin daughters as well. He'd never remarried, and his son, Colin, moved to Madison after high school to attend college and get a medical degree of his own. It was Dr. O'Reilly who'd written her first letter of recommendation to Harvard.

"How is Dr. O'Reilly doing?" Erin asked.

Luke chuckled. "He's energetic as ever. And as much as he complains about retirement, I think he's enjoying it. He likes to hang out at the Corner Café with all the other old timers in town and brag about his Irish ancestors."

Erin grinned at that. "I always thought he liked me because of my name. I told him I didn't have any Irish blood that I knew of, but he said I still had an Irish soul. Every time he saw me he used to say, 'Erin go bragh.' It's an Irish phrase that means Ireland forever."

As she spoke, the two paramedics walked up to them. "Should we take the other boy, Detective Mathis?" the female paramedic asked, her cheeks flaming crimson when she looked at Luke.

"It'll be easier for us to get him to the ER," Luke said. "It's only a minor wound."

The girl turned to Erin. "Thank you so much for your help. We've practiced putting a needle in like that, but I've never actually done it—or even seen it done on a real person before. You were amazing."

Erin shrugged off the compliment, uncomfortable as always with such praise. "I just did what I needed to do.

And now that you have seen it done, you'll be ready to do it yourself next time." She glanced down at the girl's name badge. Amy Duncan. "And another thing, Amy, do you have an intraosseous drill in your ambulance?"

"Yes, we have one," Amy answered with a wince. "I know I should probably have used it when I couldn't get an IV in the first few times."

Seeing her distressed expression, Erin smiled encouragingly. "Now you know that, too. And it wouldn't be unreasonable to use the IO drill right away if you've got a critical patient. Then you won't have to fiddle around with a peripheral IV when you need to get a line in fast."

"Yes, I'll remember that," Amy said. "Thank you again. And you too, Detective Mathis." She glanced at Luke before turning away, and another bright red blush stained her cheeks.

Erin's lips quirked up in amusement as she watched Amy leave with the other paramedic. "It looks like someone has a crush on you."

Luke laughed softly. "I like women, not girls."

Erin felt those strange, fluttering sensations start in her chest again, and she quickly changed the subject. "Do you want me to take a look at the other kid before you go?"

"Sure, if you don't mind. His name is Connor Murdock. He's the mayor's son." Luke motioned to two men standing near a sheriff's SUV and led her over to them. "Pete Thompson, one of the sheriff's deputies, has Connor in his vehicle. He and Scott Ripley were interviewing him. Scott's another detective on the force and a good friend of mine." A half-smile briefly crossed Luke's face. "He's the big, mean-looking guy in the Coldplay T-shirt. Obviously our dress code is a little lax."

Luke formally introduced her to the pair, and Pete opened the rear passenger door of the SUV.

Connor sat in the backseat with his hands cuffed behind him and tears streaming down his cheeks.

"Come on out, Connor," Luke said, helping him up. "Dr. Harris is going to look at your arm."

Erin opened her mouth to correct Luke about using her maiden name, but then closed it again. Suddenly it didn't seem that important.

"Is Jesse dead?" Connor asked, his voice trembling. "I wasn't really going to shoot him, I swear. The gun went off by accident when I turned around. I swear."

"Jesse's alive, and you can thank Dr. Harris for that," Luke told him. "She saved you from a murder charge, son."

Connor thanked Erin profusely, over and over, in the same ragged, anguished tone, and she soon had to look away, dropping her gaze to his bandaged left upper arm. He may have shot someone, but she still found that kind of pain difficult to witness.

She gently unwrapped the makeshift bandage and inspected the wound. Luke was right, it wasn't bad. Connor had a jagged cut on the outside of the arm where the bullet had grazed him as it went past. But it wasn't too deep, and there hadn't been much bleeding. A few inches over, though, and he would have been as bad off as the other boy— or worse. She didn't want to contemplate that scenario.

"He'll need a few stitches," she said, replacing the bandage. "Otherwise everything looks okay."

Luke nodded and turned to Scott. "Pete can take him to the ER. In the meantime, call Mayor Murdock and get him over there ASAP, and make sure one of our guys stays with the other kid. I'll work with the sheriff's deputies here and meet up with you in a little while."

"Sure thing, Luke," Scott said, glancing curiously at Erin before he headed to his own vehicle.

Luke sighed, rubbing a hand over his clean-shaven jaw. "We've got one hell of a mess to sort out. The Sheriff's Office has jurisdiction out here, but we offered mutual aid. The problem is, the sheriff, her chief deputy, and our police chief are all at a conference in Madison right now, and our assistant chief is on vacation in Mexico. Lucky me." He smiled wryly. "I'll give you a ride back to your car. I won't make you run this time."

Erin laughed. "I probably should. That little jaunt through the woods made me realize how much I need to start working out again."

Luke lowered his gaze to her body, clad in a T-shirt and jeans. "It looks to me like whatever you're doing is working out just fine." She was exactly as he remembered her, slightly above average in height, with curves in all the right places.

Erin felt her skin tingle wherever his gaze traveled. And when he looked back up at her there was an intensity in those blue eyes that made her knees weak and scattered every thought in her head. She was at a loss for words. She couldn't think. She couldn't move. So she just stood there like a deer in the headlights.

"I guess we'd better get going," Luke finally said. And much to her relief, he turned away, leading her over to his unmarked blue sedan.

He opened the passenger door for her, and she thanked him with a tentative smile before sliding in, though she couldn't quite meet his gaze after the foolish way she'd just acted—yet again. She wasn't any better than that twenty-year-old paramedic.

But almost as soon as he closed the door an entirely different sort of tension filled her—a tension she knew all too well. She felt her heart pick up speed. A deep sense of dread came over her, and she wanted to jump out of the car and run. She had no idea what would have triggered such intense anxiety in Luke's car, though, and hesitantly glanced around the interior, trying to reassure herself that she had nothing to be afraid of. It looked like a typical police car, or at least what she would expect one to look like. There was the radio, and a computer mounted above it next to the steering wheel. And behind the driver's seat was a rifle.

Then her gaze shifted to the metal and plastic partition that divided the front and back, and a memory flashed through her brain. It hit her like lightning…

"You just sit right here, Erin," the police officer said.

She reluctantly climbed into the back of his squad car, and he closed the door, leaving her alone inside. She looked out the window, but there were metal bars on them and it was hard to see. Then she turned forward and saw the metal screen between the front and back seats. It felt like he'd put her in a cage.

"Mommy!" she sobbed, though she knew her mother was dead. She'd seen her on the ground. But she cried for her anyway. "Mommy! Mommy!"

Luke got into the car and glanced over at Erin. She sat motionless, looking at the back seat, her expression transfixed in horror. He checked to see what might have provoked such a reaction, but nothing was out of the ordinary.

"Erin," he said, lightly touching her arm. When she didn't respond he lifted his hand to cradle her chin, turning her to face him. "Erin," he softly repeated.

She blinked, and her gaze came into focus again. But he could still see fear and pain darkening her green eyes. "What's going on in there, Erin?" he asked.

"I—I just remembered...the night my mom died," she managed to get out in a broken whisper. "I—remember what happened. They...they put me in a police car afterward."

Luke took her hand. "What do you remember?"

Erin didn't answer, unable to say more as unspeakable memories from the past continued to assail her—ones she hadn't even known existed. She remembered the fight...Her mother screaming. The terror she'd felt at the sound...The horrific image of her mother's broken body on the ground...

She leaned back against the seat and closed her eyes, trying to block out those images and sounds, trying to fend off the pain. She desperately searched for the safe place in her mind that had kept her sane so many times before, but it was nowhere to be found now, and she didn't know what to do. So she concentrated on Luke's hand and held on tightly until the storm inside her calmed a little, and she could at least breathe again.

"Talk to me, Erin."

She finally looked at him. And when their eyes met she saw more than just a summer day in his warm blue gaze, she saw the safe haven she hadn't been able to find in herself. "I...I don't know how much Jenna has told you about my family," she tentatively began. "My parents, they moved to Los Angeles right after high school, and I was born there... But I have very few memories of LA. And I couldn't remember anything about the day my mom died—until now. My grandmother never let me forget that they'd both been drunk and high that night, and that my father...he killed my mom in an argument. But I hadn't remembered I was there, or exactly what he'd done. And I never really wanted to know…I'd forgotten that he'd—he'd pushed her off the balcony of our apartment."

"Did you see it happen?" Luke asked, tightening his grip on her hand.

Erin turned to stare absently out the windshield. "No…I'm pretty sure I was in my bedroom when I first heard them arguing. I remember going into the living room and seeing them out there. I got scared and hid behind a chair, I think. But then my mom started screaming, and it sounded like she was getting farther away, so I ran out to her. My father was there, looking over the side. I looked down too, and saw her on the ground." She'd been lying face-down in a pool of blood on the concrete below, motionless, limbs askew. Erin wished she could at least put that image back into the cobwebs of her memory where it had been. But she couldn't, so she closed her eyes and focused on Luke's warm fingers again, not wanting to feel anything else but him.

Luke knew he had a lot of work to do. A shooting involving the mayor's son would mean hours, even days, of interviews and reports. But everything could wait. Erin needed him more at the moment. So he just sat there and held her hand. "I'm glad I was here with you when you remembered," he said softly after a while.

Erin opened her eyes. She looked down at Luke's hand and was amazed by her response to his touch. She should be uncomfortable with it. She always had an instinctive tendency to pull away when she was touched. But now she wanted it. She needed it. "My father…He—he's in prison for life, in California," she told him, stumbling over the repulsive words. "Seth Slater…I haven't said that name in forever. No one else knows except Jenna." She glanced at Luke, wondering if she would see the same disgust on his face as she felt. But she saw only concern in his eyes. "Has she told you about him?"

Luke nodded. Jenna had asked him to keep track of the man. He knew more about Slater than Erin did. And now that she was here, he was going to have to talk to her about him. But not today.

"I tell people they both died in an accident. It's easier that way—and a lot less ugly than the truth." Erin impatiently brushed a tear away. "They should never have had a child."

Luke let go of her hand, and she was sorry to see it go. But then he put his fingers under her chin and turned her to face him again. "Don't say that, Erin. Maybe they weren't the best parents, but they made an incredible child, a wonderful woman. And you're obviously a great doctor. I'm sure that kid would be dead today if it wasn't for you. And then another one would be going to prison for murder. You didn't have to help, but you did. And you saved two lives." He gently wiped away the tears sliding unheeded down her cheeks. "I'll bet there have been plenty of others too. No matter how it happened, a lot of people are grateful your parents had you. And you should be just as grateful."

"I'm sorry," Erin said miserably. "You'd think I was two instead of thirty-two. I've been a blubbering mess since Jenna told me she's sick. And now this."

"You can cry all you need to. Like I said before, I'm glad to be here for you." Luke found a tissue and handed it to her. "How is Jenna? She was pretty worn out after the trip."

Erin blew her nose. "I don't know. I haven't even gotten to New Dublin yet."

Luke stared at her, raising his eyebrows in surprise. "You were just getting into town when all this happened? Jeez, Erin! Jenna wasn't kidding when she said you have a knack for being around when shit hits the fan."

Erin made a weak attempt at a smile. "I doubt she said it quite like that, Luke. I haven't heard her swear once in twenty-six years. And what I have is a black cloud. A big, ugly black cloud. I hear it all the time."

Luke shook his head. "You won't hear it from me. I think you have a white cloud."

"I think that's a brand of toilet paper," she told him.

They looked at each other and grins split across their faces simultaneously. And in the next breath they were laughing.

"It's a good thing you're a white cloud then," Luke said. "You're the perfect person to be there when shit hits the fan."

Erin laughed again. "I'll have to remember that the next time I feel down in the dumps."

Luke's eyes dropped to her mouth as she continued to smile. God, she had such a beautiful mouth. He remembered being mesmerized by that mouth when they were in school. Of course, he'd been mesmerized by a lot of her parts back then. But she'd never really paid him any attention.

With an inward sigh he pulled his eyes away from her and started the car. He needed to put his fantasies aside for the moment. He still had a gunfight to sort out, and he was probably going to get a call from the mayor any minute. "If you'd like, I can call you tonight and let you know how Jesse is doing," he said, easing the vehicle up the gravel road.

"Yes, I'd appreciate that. Do you have a piece of paper? I'll write down my cell phone number."

"Just tell me. I won't forget." He had an exceptional memory. It had helped him excel in school and in his career. It just hadn't been very good for his love life—not when it left him forever haunted by green eyes flecked with gold.

Erin told him the number, then continued to study his profile. He was good-looking, very good-looking, but there was no pretentiousness about him. He had such an open and honest face. The combination was compelling. She hadn't realized until now just how single-minded she'd been about getting out of New Dublin. She couldn't believe she remembered so little about him. She especially couldn't believe she'd forgotten how blue his eyes were.

Careful, Erin, she told herself. *You're not here to get involved with him. You're here for Jenna. And then you're leaving this town behind forever.*

"Those boys in the shooting, do they get into trouble a lot?" she asked in an attempt to change the focus of her thoughts.

"Not at all. I know them both from football. I help coach in the fall. Connor is a wide receiver and Jesse Torres is our star running back—one of the best in the state actually. And we've never had a problem with either one of them. In fact, I thought they were good friends." Luke glanced at her, shaking his head. "Every time I think I've seen it all, something like this happens."

Erin nodded. "I know. I say that all the time in the ER. But the one thing there will never be a shortage of is ways people find to hurt each other—or themselves."

Luke grimaced. "Which is why I log so many hours at the hospital myself. And here I thought I was going to skip that family tradition."

"Did you ever think about going to medical school?" Erin asked curiously.

"No. My two older brothers went, and I saw enough to know it wasn't for me." Luke flashed her a grin. "Besides, I always thought guns were way cooler than stethoscopes. And I got a lot more respect from my brothers once they knew I might be carrying one."

Erin laughed softly in response, and a moment later they reached the highway. She saw her old, yellow Audi was still parked where she'd left it, but for some reason it looked different. *Probably because all the other cars are gone now,* she thought.

Luke pulled around behind it and walked with her over to the driver's side door. "You have a full load there," he said, glancing into the car. It was packed to overflowing.

Erin smiled sadly, turning to face him. "I never thought I would say this, but I hope I'm here for a while."

Luke took her hand again. "I hope you are, too."

Looking up into his eyes, Erin saw her own sorrow reflected there. And then she wasn't sure if he made the first move, or if she did, but suddenly they were in each other's arms. She laid her head against his broad chest and clutched his back, feeling the firm muscles under her fingers. She closed her eyes and breathed in his earthy, masculine scent. He felt so solid, so warm and safe. For just a second he made her feel like there really was hope.

They stood there holding each other, neither quite wanting to let go. But Luke finally pressed a kiss into her hair and reluctantly released her. "Tell Jenna I said, 'Hi', okay?"

Erin dropped her arms to her sides. "I will." She glanced at the spot on his chest where her head had rested. She wanted to lay it there again and keep listening to the steady beat of his heart under her ear. She must be losing her mind.

"If you can wait until tomorrow, I'll stop by and help you unload your things," Luke offered. "I'd help later, but I have no idea when we'll get this case wrapped up. I'm sure you and Jenna have a lot to catch up on today anyway."

Erin nodded. "Thank you, Luke."

"My pleasure." He gazed into her eyes, and it was far more than pleasure he felt. His chest tightened with it. "Well, I suppose I'd better get this mess sorted out. I'll call you later." After a brief hesitation, he turned and headed back to his car. But he knew there was a part of him that would stay right there with her. It had always been that way.

Erin watched him thoughtfully as he left. She'd grown up in the same small town as Luke Mathis, but hadn't really known him. And yet today she'd been with him for less than an hour and it felt like she'd known him forever.

She got into her car and leaned her head back against the seat to collect herself. So much had happened already, and she hadn't even made it to New Dublin yet. She could only imagine what was in store for her there. But Jenna was there. It was time to go.

CHAPTER

4

*E*RIN LOOKED LONGINGLY AT THE COOKIE THAT WAS sitting on the tree stump. She was sure the girl with the curly red hair had put it there.

She peeked her head around a tree. The girl was there now, where she often was, sitting on a blanket in her yard, playing with her dolls. Except she was even closer to the woods now. It seemed like she got closer every time Erin came to watch her play. The girl had tried to talk to her before, but Erin would always get scared and run back into the woods.

Erin eyed the cookie again, and glanced back at the path that led to her grandparents' house. Her grandmother wouldn't know. She'd started her prayers upstairs in the room with the rocking chair. Erin didn't know why she prayed up there, but she did it every day, and she stayed in there for a long time, sometimes until her grandfather came home from work at the factory. Erin was happy when she stayed in there.

Making up her mind, she quickly scooped up the cookie and stuffed it into her mouth.

"My momma says you shouldn't eat that fast."

Erin whipped her head around, green eyes wide with fright. The girl with the curly red hair was standing behind her.

"I'm Jenna," the girl said with a smile. When Erin didn't say anything back, she added, "We should be friends."

Erin remained silent. She was too afraid to say anything, too afraid to move. And her mouth was full of cookie.

"My little brother died, so my momma's sad and won't play. Will you play with me?" the girl asked.

Erin stared at her, and the fear went away. She felt bad that the girl's little brother died. She glanced back at the path again, then turned and nodded.

The girl grinned and took her hand. "Come with me. I'll show you some baby robins. They're in a tree behind the shed."

Erin hesitated, but finally allowed the girl to lead her out of the woods and into the green grass beyond.

THE LITTLE TWO-STORY HOUSE HADN'T CHANGED much, Erin noted as she stood in the driveway regarding it. The wood siding was still bright yellow with white trim that matched the porch railing extending across the front of the house. And roses were in full bloom all around it: large, elegantly beautiful blossoms in shades of deep burgundy, yellow, and orange.

A moment later the front door opened and Jenna stepped out onto the porch, waving to her with that familiar smile.

Erin started walking toward her. And then she ran. Taking the side steps two at a time, she rushed into Jenna's arms and they clung to each other wordlessly.

"Jen. Oh, Jen," Erin finally managed in a broken whisper.

"It's so good to have you here, Erin. I can't tell you how much I've missed you."

"I've missed you too, Jen. I'm so sorry."

They continued to hold each other close, not wanting the moment to end. Erin wished she could hold back time forever.

Jenna eased away first, pulling some tissues from the pocket of her cardigan. "I knew we would need these."

Erin took one and wiped her nose, sniffing back more tears. "I've been doing a lot of this the last two weeks."

"There's nothing wrong with shedding a few tears now and then. They're good for the soul," Jenna said. "While the length of one's life is measured in years, the depth of the soul is measured in tears."

Erin smiled. "Who did you get that from, Thoreau or Confucius?" Jenna was always quoting some philosopher or another, and those were two of her favorites. Erin was glad some things hadn't changed.

Jenna laughed softly. "You give me too much credit. That's just me—me and morphine, I suppose."

Erin studied her. Jenna's eyes were as bright a blue as ever, but there was a gauntness in her face that hadn't been there before, and her skin had taken on a slightly grayish-yellow hue. Erin knew that look well—it was the distinct look of a cancer patient. And to see it on Jenna broke her heart. More tears fell, and she brushed them away with a half-hearted smile. "Here I go again. I guess I do have some depth to my soul after all."

"Of course you do," Jenna responded in a gently chiding tone. "You've just kept all those tears dammed up in there for too long. They needed to come out."

"Well, damn them anyway," Erin said wryly, then grasped Jenna's hands in hers. "How are you feeling?"

"I'm doing okay. The pain's gotten a little worse, so my doctor put me on some long-acting morphine, which has helped a lot. And I went in for an injection to strengthen my bones the other day. I was pretty worried about it after they gave me a handout that listed about a million side effects the drug can cause. But I haven't had any problems so far, other than feeling a little more tired than normal." She glanced over at a wooden cane she'd propped against the porch railing nearby. "I bought that in Ireland. It takes some of the pressure off my hip. I guess I get to experience what it feels like to be an old lady for a little while anyway."

Erin didn't hear any anger or resentment in her words. Jenna was accepting this as graciously as she had everything else in her life. "Oh, Jen," she said desolately, unable to hold back her own tears.

Jenna hugged her again. "It's okay, Erin. We'll be okay. We have today, that's all we can ask for. And what a beautiful day it is." She leaned back and cupped Erin's face in her hands. "'You must live in the present, launch yourself on every wave, find your eternity in each moment.' That is Thoreau."

"You know I never learned how to swim, Jen. If I launch myself on *any* wave, you'll be giving me CPR on the beach."

Jenna threw her head back and laughed. "I'm not too confident in my CPR skills, so I think we need to teach you how to swim."

"Hah! That will never happen."

Jenna shrugged with a playful, slightly enigmatic smile pulling at the corners of her mouth. "Never almost never lasts forever, and forever tends to run out of time. So who knows?" Then she glanced at her watch, and her expression sobered. "But speaking of time, we don't have much left if we're going to make it to school before the kids get out. I hate to have us rush off when you just got here, but will you still take me?"

"Of course!" Erin said. "I can't wait to see your classroom."

They headed down the porch steps after Jenna grabbed her cane, and Erin discovered what a precarious venture it was for her friend. "We need to have a ramp built so you can avoid these stairs," she said, taking hold of Jenna's arm.

"I know. They're a pain—literally. But Luke already took care of it. He made arrangements for a mutual friend of ours to come over bright and early Monday morning to start building one."

At the mention of Luke's name Erin felt all those warm, fluttery sensations return. "I saw him today. That's why I'm late."

"Luke?" Jenna looked up in surprise. "He better not have given you a speeding ticket."

"No. Still no speeding tickets on my record," Erin said with a laugh. And as they walked to the car she told Jenna about the duel.

Her friend's eyes widened in shock. "Did you find out the names of the boys?"

"Yes. Connor Murdock and Jesse Torres."

"Oh no! I taught both of them. They were always such great kids, and so good at sports too. I went to all their football games last season."

"Connor was pretty shaken up afterward," Erin said, remembering the look on the boy's face. "I really don't think he'd meant for things to go that far."

Jenna slowly shook her head. "I still can't believe they shot each other. And you had to stick a needle into Jesse's chest? How awful! I hope it wasn't a very big one, at least."

"Just about as big as they come."

"Well, my hip doesn't hurt so much anymore," Jenna said, coming to a stop by the car. "Now my chest does."

Erin's lips quirked up into a half-smile as she opened the passenger door. "Luke probably felt the same way when he watched it go in. I don't think he ever wants to see anything like that again." Then she glanced inside the car and her half-smile gave way to a full-fledged grimace. "I guess I need to make some room for you in here or we won't be going anywhere."

Jenna chuckled. "It looks like you brought your whole apartment with you."

"Pretty much." Erin leaned in and started shoving bags into the back. "Luke said he'd come over tomorrow and help unload everything. He might be sorry when he sees the trunkload of books I have, though." She always brought a medical book or a journal with her wherever she went. And now that she would be in New Dublin for a while, she'd had a hard time parting with any of them.

She finished clearing off the seat and helped Jenna into the car, then walked around to the driver's side and slid in, fastening her seatbelt. "Are you ready?" she asked, noticing that Jenna hadn't yet buckled herself in.

Her friend said nothing, looking deep in thought.

"What's wrong, Jen?"

"Would Jesse have died if you hadn't been there?"

Erin hesitated, though she knew the answer. "Yes, I suppose he might have," she finally admitted. "The paramedics hadn't realized he'd developed a tension pneumothorax, and by the time I got there he was in pretty bad shape. If the air hadn't been released right away he probably would have gone into cardiac arrest before the helicopter even landed.

And it would have been hard to resuscitate him in the field after that." She frowned at the speculative look on Jenna's face. "I hope you're not thinking it's a good thing you got sick, so that I would be there today to help that boy."

Jenna shook her head with a rueful smile. "I'm not a saint, Erin." Then she fastened her seatbelt and quietly said, "I was just thinking that whenever my back, or hip, or anything else hurts, I'll think of him and remember he's okay, and it won't feel quite so bad, that's all. I have you to thank for that—along with so many other things."

Erin reached over and squeezed her hand. "I wish I could take more of the pain away for you."

"There's an old Swedish proverb that goes, 'Friendship doubles our joy and divides our grief.' You take some of the pain away just by being my friend."

Erin swallowed a painful lump in her throat and gave Jenna's hand one last squeeze before starting the car.

She briefly glanced to her left as she backed out of the driveway. Thick woods blocked the view, so she couldn't see her grandparents' old farmhouse. And she was glad for that. It was something she would rather face another day.

THEY MADE IT JUST IN TIME. THE KIDS HAD FINISHED packing up everything they'd accumulated over the course of the school year and were sitting with their bulging bags around them as the substitute teacher said a few last words of farewell, her tone touched with sadness.

But her face instantly broke into a smile when Jenna walked through the door in the back of the room, and the farewells were forgotten. "Class, look who's here!"

The kids turned around and chaos ensued. "Miss Godfrey! Miss Godfrey!"

Erin watched from the doorway as her friend was quickly surrounded by a sea of enthusiastic fourth-graders, all wanting to talk to her and give her a hug. Then the bell rang and students from other classes poured into the hallway. Word spread that Jenna was there, and before long a mass of kids wanted to come in as well.

Erin got out of the way, skirting around the growing crowd to the front corner of the classroom, and observed the melee from there.

Jenna's face beamed as she talked with the children, and for a moment she almost appeared like the Jenna of old. Erin pulled her cell phone out and snapped a few pictures, then took several more of the classroom. It was bright and cheerful, a perfect reflection of her friend. And above the blackboard at the front of the room, in large block letters, were the words:

> "IT IS THE SUPREME ART OF THE TEACHER TO AWAKEN JOY IN CREATIVE EXPRESSION AND KNOWLEDGE."
> —Albert Einstein

"Are you Miss Godfrey's nurse?"

Erin looked down in surprise. A little girl of about eight or nine stared up at her with big blue eyes. "No, I'm Miss Godfrey's friend," she said, slipping the phone back into her purse.

"Mrs. Thompson said she's very sick and won't be coming back again. But I want her to get better. She's my favorite teacher and she writes good poems."

Erin searched for the right words to respond to that, not sure there were any. "Miss Godfrey is very sick," she finally answered truthfully. "She won't be able to come back, but her heart will always be here in this school. I'm sure of that."

The little girl nodded, pointing to a large framed poem on the wall near them. "Miss Godfrey likes to write about hearts."

Erin went over to take a closer look at it. The poem was superimposed on a heart made up of small, variously colored squares that were patterned in a beautiful mosaic style, painted in watercolor. And the poem read:

If You Break a Heart

The heart was made to beat strong,
And for a lifetime to last,
Yet another can easily break it,
Like the most fragile kind of glass.

There are only so many pieces,
Only so many breaks,
That in a single lifetime,
Even the strongest heart can take.

So if you're going to break it,
Think hard before you do,
Because the pieces can't be put back
With stitches, tape, or glue.

The heart will lose more pieces
At times along the way,
So it might be needed tomorrow,
That piece you'll take today.

—Jenna Godfrey

Erin's eyes moistened. She was getting used to that.

"Jen—Miss Godfrey—made this?" she asked the girl, who'd come to stand beside her.

"No. Miss Godfrey wrote the poem, but Mr. Bidwell made the painting. He's our art teacher. They like each other a lot, but Mr. Bidwell got married to someone else."

Erin blinked in surprise at the statement. Jenna had never mentioned a Mr. Bidwell. But before she could ask more about him, the girl said, "My mom's here, so I have to go. It was nice to meet you, Miss Godfrey's friend."

"You too." Erin smiled as she watched the child walk away. Then she turned to inspect the watercolor again. A lot of time and effort had clearly been spent in composing the heart, and the elegant lettering of the poem must have taken almost as long to finish. It hadn't been painted for just anyone.

She eventually made her way back over to Jenna, who was talking to several teachers by the door. None of them turned out to be the mysterious Mr. Bidwell, though.

Everyone gradually trickled out, and Jenna had a happy, but tired smile on her face afterward. "I don't know about you, Erin, but I need to sit down and have some lunch."

"Jenna."

They both turned back to the door. A man stood there gazing at her friend, and Erin saw affection, sadness, and something more that she didn't want to guess at in his light brown eyes. He was pleasantly attractive, tall and lanky, with dark blond hair that was somewhat haphazardly styled. He had that air of an artist about him. This had to be Mr. Bidwell.

"Adam," Jenna whispered with just as much emotion in her voice. She took a hesitant step toward him, and he closed the rest of the distance between them, gathering her into his arms.

"I think I'll, ah, go for a walk," Erin said awkwardly after a moment.

Jenna withdrew from Adam's embrace. "No, I want to introduce you. This is Adam Bidwell. He's our art teacher. Adam, this is Erin."

He shook her hand warmly. "I've heard a lot about you."

Erin couldn't say the same, but that was definitely going to change later. "I saw your artwork," she said, glancing over at the watercolor on the wall. "It's very good. And that's a beautiful poem, Jenna."

Her friend looked over at it and smiled. "We had an anti-bullying campaign back a few years ago. That's why I wrote it. Adam read it and surprised me with the painting one day."

"I always knew you liked to write," Erin said. "But I had no idea you were such a poet."

Jenna laughed. "I'm no Shakespeare or Yeats, that's for sure. I just like to write simple poems."

"You don't give yourself enough credit, Jenna," Adam said, taking her hand. "You've written some beautiful poems. Ones I'll never forget."

"And you've made some lovely paintings," Jenna softly returned. "Ones that I'll never forget either."

For a moment they stood there and silently held hands, gazing into each other's eyes. Erin could see there was a lot being spoken in that silence.

"I—suppose I'd better get going," Adam finally said. "I just wanted to say…goodbye. It's—been great working with you, Jenna. I'll miss you."

"I'll miss you too, Adam." Jenna's voice broke at the end,

and Adam took her into his arms again.

Wanting to give them some privacy, Erin walked across the room and grabbed a few tissues, tucking them into her purse. Then she studied some of the children's artwork that Jenna had put up on the wall. And the sweet innocence of their imagination brought a smile to her lips.

But her expression sobered when she glanced back at Jenna a few minutes later and saw that she was now standing by the door alone, hastily brushing tears from her cheeks.

"Oh, Jen." Erin rushed over to give her a hug, feeling her own heart squeeze painfully in her chest at the look of sadness on her friend's face.

"That was the second hardest thing I needed to do," Jenna whispered against her shoulder.

Erin eased away after a moment, handing her a tissue. "Jen—" she started to say, but stopped herself. This wasn't the time or place to ask the questions she wanted to.

"It's a long story," Jenna said, dabbing at her eyes. "Let's get some lunch first."

"Do you need to bring anything home?" Erin asked.

Jenna shook her head and turned to leave. "No, I already have everything."

"What about your painting?"

"I told Mrs. Thompson I would leave it here."

Erin hesitated, contemplating the big heart hanging on the wall, painted in a hundred pieces. Then she followed her friend out the door.

Chapter

5

"You're in love with him, aren't you?"

Jenna didn't immediately answer. She'd been unusually quiet the rest of the afternoon. Her smile was still there, at the ready, when Erin tried to lighten her mood. But a faraway look had settled into her eyes after she'd parted ways with Adam, and nothing Erin said could dispel it.

They'd eaten lunch at the Shamrock Inn & Restaurant downtown. It had an Irish theme, like a lot of places in New Dublin. Afterward, they'd stopped to run a few errands, and everywhere they went someone knew Jenna. Erin hadn't said much during those encounters, though. She'd always been reluctant to socialize with people she didn't know in New Dublin, mostly out of fear that they would ask questions about her family or would recognize her because of her mother. She knew that aside from her green eyes they looked exactly alike. Her grandmother had reminded her of that all too often—along with a list of her mother's less redeeming qualities. And it still bothered Erin that someone else might remind her too.

Jenna had prepared one of the upstairs bedrooms for her at the house, and when they'd returned later that afternoon Erin brought in a few things she would need for the night. She was glad the master bedroom that Jenna used was on the first floor, as it meant fewer steps for her friend to worry about. But the house was still going to need some modifications, particularly the downstairs bathroom. Jenna made light of the issue, but Erin knew it couldn't be easy for her to get on and off the toilet or to use the shower anymore. So in the morning she planned to run back into town to pick up a few things that would help, including a raised toilet seat with side arms on it, a transfer bench for the tub, and a handheld shower sprayer. The bathroom would also be a lot safer then. Erin didn't want to contemplate how devastating it would be if Jenna fell and broke one of her fragile bones.

But the chaotic day was now drawing to a close, and the two of them sat together on a wooden swing in the backyard, facing an expansive green lawn that led out to a spring-fed pond in the distance. Jenna had loved swimming in that pond when they were kids. Erin had never gone in with her, though. She'd always been too afraid. She still was.

To the right of the lawn was a field full of wild flowers that Shannon had especially adored. Erin didn't know the names of most of the flowers, but the field was dominated by bright yellow—a common theme in the Godfrey household. Dense forest provided a backdrop to the scene all around, and the late afternoon sky was the same vivid blue as it had been earlier in the day.

"Adam started working at our school three years ago, and I think I fell in love with him the first time we met," Jenna finally said. "He was trying to turn a class full of kindergartners into little Picassos with finger paints. It was the most adorable thing I'd ever seen." A distant smile crossed her face. "I realized I'd never truly been in love before, not really, until him."

"What happened?"

Jenna turned to her, and the faraway look was gone. "Nothing. I never let anything happen. He asked me out eventually, but I said no. I think I gave him some lame excuse about not wanting to get involved with another teacher, and he respected that. We still became friends, but never anything more. And after a while he found the woman he's married to now."

"But why did you say no in the first place, Jenna? It doesn't make any sense. You love him, and he obviously feels the same way about you."

"That's exactly why I said no. I could tell right away that he felt what I felt, and I refused to break his heart. I knew if I said yes there would be no going back. And then one day he'd have to watch me die."

Erin looked at her in shock. "How could you possibly have known that back then?"

"Because it was written in my family history," Jenna quietly answered. "I found that out when I did some research years ago. I'd always wondered about my mom's side of the family. She would never talk about any of them. In fact, not even my dad had known she'd lost her parents so young until the day she told you." Jenna's expression softened. "You and my mom were a lot alike, you know. And neither of you did much talking. But then, I probably did enough for all of us."

Erin squeezed her hand. "I loved listening to your happy chatter when we were kids. It was very soothing."

Jenna laughed. "But not anymore?"

"Always." Fighting back the tears stinging her eyes, Erin gazed out at the pond as two trumpeter swans glided onto the surface of the water, the distinct, trumpet-like sound of their calls echoing through the air. They were a breathtaking sight, and it dawned on Erin how little she'd appreciated the beauty of this place before. Her mind had always been too caught up in leaving. Time couldn't go by fast enough then. Now all she wanted was to hold it back.

"What I found out was horrible," Jenna eventually continued. "My grandfather died of leukemia when my mom was seven. She had an older sister who died from bone cancer a few years later, and not long after that her mother committed suicide. My mom watched her entire family die, just like I did." She slowly shook her head. "But as far as the cancer goes, it went back for generations, parents watching their children die from it, children losing their parents…I knew there had to be something that was being passed on from generation to generation, some genetic defect. So I did more research, and it turned out there was. It's called Li-Fraumeni syndrome. When I read about other families with it I couldn't believe how similar many of their stories were to mine. I got tested for it, and I have the gene too."

Erin searched her memory, but couldn't recall anything about that particular syndrome.

"It's pretty rare," Jenna said. "It's a genetic mutation that prevents the body from destroying cancer cells. People who have it are almost always going to get cancer at some point, often as a child. And it's autosomal dominant, so there's a fifty-fifty chance of passing it on to your own child—if you survive long enough."

Erin was stunned. Jenna had known about this for years. "Why didn't you tell me?"

"I didn't want you to have to live with it too. So I decided not to tell you until I had to. I knew, I just knew in my soul that I was going to die young. I knew it even years before I got tested. Maybe I felt that way because my mom and brother had died so young, I don't know. But after I tested positive I decided I would never get married or have children. The odds have not favored my family over the years, and there was no way I was going to watch any child of mine die, or leave them without a mother. Not when I could prevent it."

"Does Adam know?"

"No. I didn't want to take the chance that he would change my mind."

"Oh, Jen," Erin whispered. "You should have told me."

"You had enough to deal with already. Plus I know you too well, Erin. You would have had me going in all the time for one test or another. And I would have been under the knife getting everything cut out or chopped off that I didn't absolutely need. I just couldn't live like that. I didn't want either one of us to have to live like that. As it was, I did have regular testing done. I thought I'd end up with breast cancer too, since I'd survived so long. But I had a breast MRI with a mammogram every year, and I was thinking about a mastectomy…I never expected it would be melanoma."

Erin winced. "I wish I'd stopped acting like an idiot and come here sooner. Maybe if I'd been around more I would have seen it."

"I don't think so," Jenna said. "I had a physical every six months, and my doctor hadn't noticed it before, either. I probably should have done better skin exams on myself, I suppose. But melanoma isn't even one of the usual cancers in the syndrome. I just happened to get the one that's fairly common in general, but rarely occurs in the rare disorder I have. Who would have guessed?" She gave Erin a rueful look, but there was still no anger or resentment in her tone.

Erin smiled grimly. "At least you figured out it was Li-Fraumeni syndrome. It's awful that your family went for generations without ever knowing why so many of them were getting cancer."

"My ancestors in Ireland thought it was a curse," Jenna said. "I found that out when I went to visit. They called it 'The Curse of the O'Callaghan Men.' O'Callaghan was my mom's maiden name. And for my family the syndrome probably started there with my great-great-grandfather. He and both his sons died from what was described as a mysterious illness that caused them to slowly waste away. I'm sure it was cancer of some sort. But before my great-grandfather died he'd already had two boys and a girl of his own. His oldest son passed away in a similar fashion, and my grandfather moved to the United States hoping to escape from the curse. He didn't, of course. But his sister stayed in Ireland and lived there into her eighties without any problems. She had six healthy children, five of whom were boys. I was told she spent most of her life fearing the curse would take her own sons as well. But it never did, so they assumed it had finally been broken. Their line is the only other one that's survived, and I'm sure the gene didn't get passed on to any of them."

"Did you tell them the truth behind this so-called curse?"

"No, I didn't see the point." Jenna's lips quirked up into a slight smile. "You know the Irish. They'd blame it on the curse anyway."

Despite her making light of it Erin knew why Jenna really hadn't said anything. She'd wanted to spare them the knowledge of what they'd all escaped from—and what she hadn't. "How are you dealing with this so well?" Erin asked her in amazement. "Why are you not screaming at fate and cursing life to Hell?"

"Oh, I've done my share of crying, believe me, Erin. But God and gratitude, those are the things that have gotten me through this. And I'm grateful, truly grateful, to have had the chance to live thirty-two years. I got to know you. I'm so grateful for that. And I'm grateful I got to teach. Most people never have a job they really love. I've loved every minute of mine for the last ten years—well, except for that time Johnny Tucker vomited all over the classroom floor." She made a face, and they both laughed. Then she softly added, "I'm also grateful I can end this thing in my family. So many generations of misery will end with me."

Erin thought about her own family history. "Generations of misery are going to end with me, too. In my family it was all self-induced. But in any case, it will also end with me. I can't be grateful that I'm childless, but it's probably for the best." She smiled sadly. "We're going to end generations of misery together, Jen."

"You don't know that for sure, Erin. Women get pregnant all the time with fertility treatment. If your ex-husband wasn't such an ass you'd probably have triplets by now."

Erin let out a laugh. "I just told Luke you never swear. I guess I have to take that back now."

"Well, I never did care much for Peter," Jenna said with a rare look of displeasure on her face. "He wasn't what you needed at all. There was certainly no way for you to swim in the depths of that shallow soul."

"Which is probably one of the reasons I married him," Erin said ruefully. And after a hesitant pause, she added, "I saw him the day you told me you were sick. I have a feeling things aren't going well between him and his girlfriend. He didn't seem very happy, and he was actually sincerely apologetic about what he'd done before."

"Good Lord, Erin! Please don't tell me you're thinking about taking him back."

"No, Jen. I have no interest in repeating that disaster—or creating a new one, either. I've put up too many walls to be in a healthy relationship. And if I haven't figured out how to get past them by now, how is anyone else supposed to? I think I'll probably end up dying alone behind them."

Jenna grabbed her gently by the arm. "No, you will not, Erin. Not if I have anything to say about it. And I do know how you can start breaking down those walls. I've wanted to say this for a long time, but I didn't think you were ready or willing to listen. You need to let go of the past. You aren't like your mother, or your father, or your grandmother. But you've let them dictate your life, and I don't think you even realize how much. It's time to let it be."

"That's easier said than done," Erin said tightly. "If letting it be means forgiving, I can't do that. I will never forgive my parents for what they did. And I will never feel anything but bitterness for my grandmother. She was a mean, vindictive woman who took pleasure in punishing a child for the sins of her parents, all in the name of God. I never told you this before, but she used to have me get down on my knees with a rosary and beg God to forgive me for being a bastard, and my mom for being a whore—among other things. And I did it at first because I was scared to death of her. But then I started to rebel against all her hateful words and wouldn't do it anymore. So she would lock me in the bedroom. It was punishment for 'entering the path of the wicked'—her favorite phrase." A ghost of a smile crossed Erin's face. "Until I rebelled against that, too."

She used to dread when her grandmother got into one of her moods, because she knew she would end up locked in the bedroom when stubbornness got the best of her and she inevitably rebelled. But it was there she'd found her first true love, and her first means of escape: books. Boxes full of books, stored in the closet and long-forgotten. She'd read them all, along with any others she could get her hands on, mostly from the school library. Books about the human body and illness had always been her favorites, though. By the time she'd finished elementary school she already understood more about how the human body worked than anyone she knew—even the school nurse.

It hadn't taken her long to discover that she could open the bedroom window and climb out onto the back porch roof. She would sit there and read for hours, always keeping her ears tuned in to the squeak of the floorboards in the hallway and scramble back in before her grandmother opened the bedroom door. By the end of elementary school no one had better hearing than her either. Or better reflexes.

But it all came to a head the summer after Erin turned eleven. She'd become especially rebellious by then and decided to climb down a tree alongside the porch one day. That was when her grandmother finally caught her. She'd gone into a rage like no other and dragged Erin into the house, spitting out random, broken verses from the Bible along the way, and locked her in the basement cellar.

The memory was as vivid and poignant as ever, and a cold, deep shiver ran through Erin. She'd thought for sure her grandmother was going to let her die down in that dark, airless little cellar. She would never forget the overwhelming sense of panic she'd felt, the fear that had reached into every part of her body and soul. It was something she never wanted to experience again.

But her grandmother's true intentions that day would forever remain a mystery, because it turned out there had been a means of escape from that horrid cellar after all. Erin eventually found a tiny, grime-covered window almost completely hidden from view behind the top of a wooden canning shelf. And in desperation she'd managed to climb her way up to it and crawl out. Then she'd raced over to the Godfrey's property and hid in their shed.

Erin glanced over at the old shed near the edge of the woods. Like the house, it was yellow with white trim, solidly built and well-tended. "I planned to stay in there forever, that day my grandmother threw me in the basement."

Jenna followed the direction of her gaze and grimaced. "I was so scared for you that day. When your grandfather came looking for you and no one could find you, I thought you were never coming back. And I remember screaming bloody murder—literally—when my mom called the police. I was sure your grandmother had killed you and buried you in the woods."

Erin laughed shortly. "She probably would have eventually if it hadn't been for your mom. She was the one who found me. I told her what happened, and she walked me back over to my grandparents' house. They were on the front porch talking to the police when we got there, and your mom marched right up to my grandmother and gave it to her like I'd never seen. I don't think I ever told you about that, either."

Erin smiled at the memory. Shannon Godfrey had always been so good-natured and soft-spoken. But she'd shown a different side of her personality during the confrontation. "She warned my grandmother that if I was ever mistreated again she would get every last God-fearing person in town after her, including the priest and the whole congregation of the church. And she told the police she would be more than happy to take me home with her, that I would be much better off in her house than in the Devil's." Erin shook her head and couldn't help but laugh, remembering the look on her grandmother's face afterward. Shannon had completely turned the tables on the old woman that night.

"The police said I had to stay with my grandparents, though," Erin continued. "And they didn't think anything else needed to be done since my grandmother promised not to lock me up anymore when I didn't listen. But your mom insisted they call someone in from Child Protective Services, and she waited with me until the woman showed up. I'd never seen my grandmother so submissive before. And she was never the same again. Of course, my grandfather had a stroke not long after that, which probably took the wind out of her sails more than anything. She was always at her worst when he wasn't around. Having him home all the time took the attention off of me." With a hint of venom in her tone, Erin added honestly, "I was happy he had a stroke. I remember wishing she'd be next."

But a stroke hadn't killed her. Ironically, it had been a fall down the basement stairs. Erin was the one who'd found her after coming home from work at the hospital one night during her senior year of high school. She would never forget her grandmother lying there face up at the bottom of the stairs with those hard gray eyes staring, but not seeing…

Her grandfather's health had quickly spiraled downward after that. Taking care of him by herself became increasingly difficult. Erin had finally told him that it might be best if he went to the nursing home. And to her astonishment the man who'd hardly ever said a word, much less expressed the slightest emotion, had cried. He hadn't even cried for her grandmother—although she could certainly understand that. But he'd begged her not to send him away, so she'd done her best to take care of him at home. Until one morning she found him dead too. He'd passed away in his sleep, dying as silently as he'd lived.

Jenna and her dad had helped her through those difficult times, and Erin didn't know what she would have done without them. But she'd soon been able to pay them back, when an extraordinary thing happened.

No one had ever told her that the old farmhouse and the dilapidated barn in back used to be part of a thriving dairy farm owned by her grandfather's parents decades ago, along with hundreds of acres of prime farmland and forest all around them—and that he'd inherited everything as their only surviving son. It turned out the quiet man who'd spent most of his life laboring in a factory had been a wealthy landowner, yet one who'd chosen to live in relative poverty, leaving all that valuable land untouched. He'd received countless offers for it in the past, but for whatever reason had refused to sell.

Those facts quickly came to light after his death, though. And when the land was sold Erin had become a wealthy woman in her own right. All her worries about paying for college had been lifted from her shoulders in an astonishing instant. But she'd also known that Jenna and her dad were struggling financially as a result of his worsening illness, so she'd insisted on paying off their mounting debt as well. Then she moved in with them until she left for college, staying in the very room she had now.

"Your grandmother used religion for all the wrong reasons," Jenna said. "It seems to me that people like her are really using it to cover up their own dark souls. God should be a source of strength and peace, not a dagger to be driven into the hearts of others." She took Erin's hand and held it tightly. "I hope you'll listen to me. I want you to let go of the past and start a new beginning for both of us, one that has a happy ending. I think talking about the past like this might help you come to terms with it, help you let go. But don't just talk about the past. Talk about the present, talk about the future—just *talk*, Erin. Open up and let people in, not for their sake, but for yours."

Erin stared off into the distance. "I've gotten really good at holding everything in, that's the problem. If things get even the least bit emotional or personal, I withdraw. I crawl into that safe place in my brain where I can't be touched. Like the day I walked in and found Peter with the nurse. I didn't say anything. I just packed up my things and left. I should have screamed at him. I should have kicked him out instead. I should have kicked *something* at least. But I didn't. I turned and ran. Just like I ran from here."

"Because it's easier to deny your feelings, to run from them, than to allow yourself to feel pain. The problem is, you can't be happy that way either. If you really want to live, Erin, you need to let yourself feel…You need to let yourself feel *everything*."

"I'm afraid to do that," Erin said painfully. "In fact, I don't think there's anything that scares me more. It's funny, I'm an ER physician. I make life and death decisions all the time, and I'm not afraid of that. But I'm afraid of so many other things." She sighed. "You've always been so much stronger and braver than me."

Jenna vehemently shook her head. "That is not true at all. I would never have made it out of that house alive—or at least not without a straightjacket on. I would have disappeared into that safe place in my mind you spoke of and never come back. But you have a stronger mind than that. You've survived because of it, and it's what makes you such a good doctor. It just hasn't been so good for you in other ways. There's a Zen proverb that goes, 'Be a master of the mind, not mastered by the mind.' If you don't remember anything else I say, please remember that."

"Yes, master," Erin responded with a faint smile.

Jenna briefly chuckled, and then eyed her speculatively. "Well, since you're being so agreeable, there are two other things I want you to do."

"Uh oh. Am I going to like this?"

"Probably not today, but maybe someday."

"Okay," Erin said hesitantly. "What are they?"

"I want you to go to church with me on Sunday. Just this one time."

Erin thought about that. She had a lot of painful memories associated with the church and hadn't been inside one since her grandfather died. She'd even chosen to marry Peter at Boston City Hall—something his mother had never forgiven her for. But she didn't hesitate now. "Yes, I'll go with you."

"That was easy."

Erin smiled at the surprised look on Jenna's face. "If it means that much to you, I'll go. Besides, I've always felt guilty that I couldn't come to your dad's funeral. I should've been there after all he did for me, and the least I can do is go with you on Sunday to make up for it."

"You have nothing to feel guilty about, Erin. You were in the middle of the hardest part of your residency training. I understood."

"I said I would never come back here. But I would have for him. Maybe if I'd pushed a little harder to get off—"

"Don't worry about it," Jenna cut in. And with a mischievous grin, she added, "But since you're feeling guilty, maybe you'll be more agreeable to the next thing."

Erin knew that grin didn't bode well for her. "Okay, lay it on me."

"I want you to learn how to swim."

Erin blinked in consternation. "What? Are you kidding?"

"No, I'm not. I want you to learn how to swim."

"Jenna, I'm thirty-two years old. I think it's a little late for that now."

"You can't learn anything at thirty-two? Why do you read medical journals then?"

Erin groaned, throwing her head back for a moment. "That's completely different, Jenna." She paused to think about it. She would rather get her teeth pulled. "How about if I go to church with you every Sunday instead?"

"How about if you think about going to church with me every Sunday and try swimming just once?"

Erin felt her heart race at the very thought. "Why do you want me to learn how to swim now?"

"Because there would be no better way for you to exercise—literally—that Zen proverb. I want you to master your mind." Jenna smiled at her tenderly. "I also know you're going to have children someday, whether you give birth to them, or adopt, or however they come along. I feel it in my soul. And I want you to be able to swim with them. Getting you to do this will be a gift I can give you long after I'm gone."

Erin's eyes misted with tears. She leaned her head back against the swing and looked up into the cloudless blue sky. It made her think of Luke again. "What exactly is Zen anyway?"

"It's a form of Buddhism that emphasizes personal enlightenment, finding harmony with the universe. Meditation is an important part of it. You should try it with me one of these days."

"I thought you were Catholic?"

Jenna laughed. "Yes, in a manner of speaking. But all religions that have a basis in love, peace, and enlightenment ultimately worship God, whether He's called by that name or not. Love is still love after all, no matter what language it's spoken in."

Erin smiled wryly. "I don't think your priest would like that answer."

"I think you're just delaying *your* answer, Erin."

"Jenna, it would be really embarrassing to get into a pool with a bunch of preschoolers for Swimming 101."

"I'm glad you said that, because I was just thinking we could have Luke teach you in the pond."

Erin's eyes widened at the thought of Luke with his hands on her, wearing nothing more than swim trunks. And the images that went through her mind did crazy things to her body. But then her gaze shifted to the pond, and fear drowned out any other thought. "I'm not sure I could do it, Jenna. You can't even see the bottom in there."

"We'll practice some Zen meditation techniques while you're in the water. Usually one is sitting in the lotus position. But we'll try a new one—the floating position."

Erin continued to eye the pond in trepidation. "I don't know…"

As if in answer, the calls of the swans filled the air again.

"I think they want you to go in too," Jenna said with a chuckle.

Erin watched the majestic birds and couldn't help but admire how peacefully they floated on the water together. "You'll be in there next to me?" she asked, turning back to Jenna.

"No, I think I'll stay on the shore and talk you through it."

That answer finally convinced Erin. She remembered all the times Jenna had tried to get her to go into the water when they were kids, but she would only sit on the beach and watch. "I'll do it if you go in with me."

"Erin, I haven't been in that pond in years. And now, in my condition, I don't think…"

"You don't think what?" Erin teased, grinning at the flustered expression on her friend's face.

Jenna groaned, then laughed. "All right, we'll go in together. You said Luke is coming over tomorrow. Why don't we do it then, before either of us has too much time to think about it?"

Erin's smile froze. "Wow, tomorrow." She took a deep breath. "Okay. I'll ask him tonight when he calls. But if he says no, we're done."

Jenna raised a brow inquisitively. "Oh really? He's calling you tonight?"

"I gave him my number so I could find out how Jesse is doing, that's all." Erin was going to leave it at that and change the subject. But she remembered Jenna's advice about opening up, and knew it was time to get out of old habits. "Okay, I'll admit that I think he's—well, attractive.

So why isn't he married with a houseful of kids by now?"

Jenna grinned impishly. "I may have had a little something to do with that—at least a few times, anyway. Women usually don't like it when their boyfriend is good friends with another woman."

Erin gave her a playful nudge. "Especially one so pretty and sweet."

Jenna rolled her eyes. "You're too kind." But her face beamed with pleasure at the compliment.

"So is he dating anyone?" Erin asked, telling herself she was just curious.

"He was until the day we left for Ireland. He and his girlfriend got into a fight, and he broke things off with her before he came to get me. I figured that would happen eventually, though. I never understood what Luke saw in her. The woman is about as warm as Antarctica in winter. I know she has a younger sister who's pretty sick with some sort of heart condition, and I feel bad about that, but it doesn't excuse her behavior. I think she has a serious heart problem of her own—if she has a heart at all, that is."

A droll smile pulled at Erin's mouth. "I'm guessing that was one of the relationships you got in the middle of."

"No, I don't think it was me who got in the middle of that one—or really any of the others, when it comes right down to it."

"Is Luke in love with someone else?" Erin casually asked.

Jenna chuckled. "He's always been in love with someone else."

Despite her efforts to remain indifferent, Erin felt an ache settle suspiciously close to her heart. "Who is she?"

Jenna shook her head with another chuckle. "*You*, Erin. The man's been in love with you forever. And I'm sure it was no coincidence that he broke up with his girlfriend right after I called and told him you were coming back."

Erin stared at her in disbelief. "I doubt I had anything to do with it. He never showed the slightest interest in me when we were in school. He certainly never asked me out."

"Because he was afraid to. All the guys were."

"He said that?"

"No, but I remember how he used to look at you. It was pretty obvious. Since you left he hasn't said much, but I've seen how he reacts when I mention your name. There's still a torch burning there. And when you got married he wasn't himself for months. I have a feeling that might have broken his heart."

"Really, Jen, that's ridiculous. I'd been gone for what, eleven years? There's no way."

"There is a way," her friend responded with a gentle smile. "It's called true love. And the bittersweet beauty of true love is that even when there's nothing to sustain it, it still lives on."

Erin sighed. "It doesn't matter anyway, even if I believed that. I'm not here to start a relationship with him or anyone else. I'm here for you."

"I can't expect you to be attached to my bum hip twenty-four hours a day, Erin. In fact, I don't want you to be, as much as I do love you. We need to find other things to occupy that mind of yours once in a while. I was even thinking it might be good for you to pick up a few shifts in the ER. Luke said they're pretty short-staffed right now."

"I don't need—"

"I know. Just think about it," Jenna interrupted mildly, patting Erin's jean-clad thigh. "When all is said and done, the only real certainty in life is that life goes on." And with an elvish twinkle in her eye, she added, "I also think you should give Luke the chance to warm you up a little with his torch. He'd be the perfect match for you."

Erin tried not to think about how much he'd already warmed her up. "It wouldn't be a good idea, Jen. He's part of this town." She was going to have to keep reminding herself of that too. "His family is here. His job is here. He even helps coach football. He belongs here. And I'm going back to Boston."

"I don't know that he necessarily belongs here. And not all his family is here either. His brothers moved away, and one of them lives out of state. If things worked out, Luke could go back to Boston with you. He would probably like the challenge of being a big-city detective."

Erin laughed at the absurdity of their conversation. "Do you already have our wedding planned out too?"

Jenna grinned. "Okay, I'm getting a little ahead of things. You haven't even kissed him yet—or have you?"

"Jenna!"

"Well, it would be best to do that sooner than later. How a man kisses will tell you a lot about him. And if he lacks skill there he probably doesn't have any in the bedroom either."

"I can't believe you just said that."

"I can say anything now. I'll just blame it on the morphine."

Erin chuckled, shaking her head. But when she thought about the issue Jenna raised, her expression sobered. She watched a rabbit race across the grass and into the woods, and stammered, "I—I'm—" She wasn't sure if she could get the words out, but finally managed, "I'm the one who would have problems in the bedroom."

Silence followed the statement.

Erin glanced at Jenna and saw a look of complete stupefaction on her face. "I think this is the first time I've ever seen you speechless in your life, Jen. But you wanted me to open up." She was too embarrassed to say anything more, though.

"Tell me what you mean about problems in the bedroom," Jenna said after a moment.

"You sound like my therapist. Or at least what they'd probably sound like if I had one. Maybe I should have one, I don't know." Erin sighed in resignation. "Besides Peter I've only been with one other guy…that way. We were chemistry partners during my senior year in college. You met him when you came to visit at Christmas that year."

"Yes, the science genius," Jenna said with a soft laugh. "I remember telling him my version of Newton's First Law: 'An object in motion stays in motion, and an object at rest tends to fall asleep.' He didn't seem to get it. But I think he was more into chemistry than physics."

"Well, our chemistry was definitely better in the classroom than in the bedroom. I think I only did it with him because I was almost twenty-two and figured I was probably the last virgin on campus—which sounds like the title of a really bad movie. But it was painful and awkward. I didn't care to repeat it."

"It was your first time, Erin. That was bound to happen."

"The problem is, I never got past that awkward and uncomfortable phase. I—I didn't like that part of my relationship with Peter. It never—I don't know…It never felt right. If I hadn't wanted to get pregnant so badly I would rather not have done it at all, to be honest."

Jenna looked at her thoughtfully. "Your problems with intimacy aren't surprising, given what you went through as a child. You lost both your parents at such a young age. And then you had to deal with your grandmother, who repeatedly punished you because of your mom's sexual behavior. I have a feeling that's always been there in the back of your mind during sex. The best thing you can do now is to forget about all the garbage she said, and not worry about who your mother was. Figure out who you are."

Erin hadn't considered any of that before. But then, she'd never spent much time looking inward. She'd dedicated all her time and effort to medicine. Maybe she did need a therapist. "I guess I picked the perfect career to avoid the whole introspection thing. I've spent so many years taking care of other people, I haven't had time to take care of myself—even if I wanted to. I feel like there's an expectation that as a doctor I shouldn't have any imperfections, that I should almost be superhuman. And I expect that out of myself most of all. It's probably one of the things that attracted me to medicine in the first place."

"Well, you're not superhuman. No one is. And you'll only wear yourself out by trying to be perfect all the time. But we can fix that." With a smile Jenna placed a hand over Erin's heart. "I officially anoint you human like the rest of us, Erin Pryce."

"Wow, I finally get to be human. I feel like Pinocchio."

Jenna dropped her hand back into her lap. "So how did Peter feel about what went on in your bedroom?"

Erin had contemplated that question before. "He never said anything, Jen. Until I found him in bed with another woman I had no idea he thought there was a problem at all. He'd never seemed particularly interested in that part of our relationship either. Of course, his schedule was even more brutal than mine was. He worked an insane number of hours at the hospital. When he was at home he usually needed to catch up on sleep. Or paperwork. Or the latest medical journal. There just wasn't a whole lot of time for, you know…that."

Jenna chuckled. "Sex, Erin. I think you need to say it."

Erin felt a blush warm her cheeks. "Really, Jenna."

"Blame it on the morphine. Now just say it."

"Fine. Sex." Erin rolled her eyes heavenward.

"You didn't say that with very much conviction."

Erin groaned. "Okay. Sex…Sex, sex, sex. There."

Jenna grinned. "Now didn't that get a lot easier every time?"

"I suppose," Erin admitted with a weak laugh.

"So did Peter at least try to work things out in the bedroom?"

Erin looked at her blankly. "How do you mean?"

Jenna raised an eyebrow. "You know, get you in the mood. Foreplay. That sort of thing."

Erin felt her cheeks get hot again. "Like I told you, our schedules were so busy there just wasn't a lot of—"

"Time, I know. But there's always time if you really want there to be. And if Peter wasn't much into foreplay, I'd imagine the rest of it didn't last very long either?"

"A few minutes, I guess," Erin answered, feeling her face burn hotter than ever. "Long enough to know I wasn't any good at it."

"A few minutes? That wasn't long enough to know anything," Jenna said, shaking her head in disbelief. "Whatever problems with intimacy you brought into your relationship with Peter, he and his two-minute quickies weren't going to solve them. They probably wouldn't get the job done for any woman. Maybe that's why he's having problems with his girlfriend now. Have you ever had an orgasm?"

Erin wondered if her cheeks were going to be permanently red. "If such a thing really even exists for a woman, then no."

Jenna's eyes sparkled with amusement. "Such a thing definitely exists. It just takes a woman some time to get there. Now I think I know what the solution to your problem is."

"Some Zen meditation technique, I suppose?"

"No, just the opposite really." Jenna grinned. "You need a vibrator."

Erin stared at her, completely dumbstruck.

"You do know what that is, don't you, Miss Harvard Graduate?

"Yes, I do, Jenna," Erin finally said. "And I can't believe you're talking about that."

"Once again, blame it on the morphine. But vibrators are commonly recommended by therapists as part of the treatment for a variety of sexual problems. In fact, it was an English physician who first invented one in the 1800s. And it's unfortunate they have so many negative connotations, because sexual dysfunction is a lot more prevalent than you probably realize. Like you, most people aren't comfortable discussing it. But sex should be a beautiful thing. It shouldn't be embarrassing, or painful, or feel like a chore. It's a celebration of life, and love, and creation—a celebration of God, really. And if a person needs to use a vibrator to experience the full glory of it all, more power to them." A devilish grin crossed Jenna's face. "No pun intended."

Erin raised an eyebrow. "So let me get this right, Jenna Godfrey. I've been here less than a day and you're already telling me to go screw myself?"

Jenna burst out laughing. "No, I'm telling you to go discover yourself, Erin Pryce." Then she schooled her features into a more serious expression, and added, "It's just something to think about, that's all. It might help you get over that 'awkward and uncomfortable phase,' as you put it."

Erin gave her a mystified look. "We've gone from talking about church to using vibrators. You've got my head spinning."

"Every head needs to be taken for a spin once in a while," Jenna said, reaching for her cane. "But right now my legs do, so let's go take a walk. Some baby robins were born the other day in a tree behind the shed. I'll show you."

ERIN NERVOUSLY HIT THE TALK BUTTON ON HER cell phone. Luke was calling.

"Hi," she said, sitting a little more upright in the overstuffed chair near her bedroom window. Moonlight streamed in onto the thick gray carpet in front of her, turning it to a light silver.

"Hi, Erin. How are you?"

The sound of his voice in her ear set off the butterflies inside her again. "I made it through my first day back in New Dublin in one piece. How about you?"

"I made it through my first duel in one piece," Luke responded with a dry laugh. "Jesse's going to be fine. Colin O'Reilly took him to surgery, and he told me the boy's recovering well. He was really impressed with what you did."

"How about Connor? Is he in a lot of trouble?"

"They're both in a lot of trouble. Connor was arrested and released on bond, but it could have been worse for him—a lot worse. We tracked down a couple of boys who were there when the shooting happened. You know how kids are these days; they record everything. I watched the video, and it was unbelievable, Erin. Connor really hadn't shot Jesse on purpose. When they walked the twenty paces and turned around, he never raised his arm to fire. The gun only went off after Jesse hit him in the left arm and he jerked that way. It was a one in a million shot, and clearly hadn't been intentional. But the real kicker is, if Connor had actually tried to shoot Jesse before the gun accidentally discharged, he probably wouldn't even have come close to hitting him. The only gun he'd ever used before today was a BB gun."

"That's crazy," Erin said, glancing out the window. She could see the pond in the distance, shimmering in the moonlight.

"Neither of the boys will say who or what they were fighting over, and no one else is talking. But the DA doesn't figure he'll go after either kid for attempted murder. He sends his thanks, by the way. You made his job a whole lot easier today. And Mayor Murdock wants to thank you personally." Luke briefly chuckled. "Not bad for your first day back. You've got the DA, the mayor, and our trauma surgeon all indebted to you. And you can add me to that list as well. Thank you, Erin. I don't know if I said that before."

"You didn't need to." She stood up and looked out the window again. "I guess I have to ask you for a favor in return, though. Jenna said I'm not supposed to influence you negatively, but it won't break my heart if you say no."

"What is it?" he asked with amusement in his voice.

"Jenna wants me to learn how to swim."

There was a pause at the other end of the line and Erin winced, waiting for the inevitable laugh that followed when someone found out she couldn't swim. It never came.

"You want me to teach you?" There was nothing but kindness in Luke's voice now.

Erin relaxed. "Jenna said you'd be a good choice. She wants us to do it in the pond. I agreed since I don't want anyone else witnessing the melodrama I'm bound to put on."

"I would love to help you learn," Luke said sincerely. And in a teasing tone, he added, "It's not every day a guy gets to teach a Harvard grad something. When do you want to start?"

"Tomorrow."

Luke did laugh then. "Sure. I can be there after lunch. I just have a few things I'll need to wrap up here at the station in the morning."

"You're still there now? It's almost ten o'clock."

Luke sighed. "Yeah. Not the ideal way to spend a Friday night, but I wanted to get some paperwork out of the way. Otherwise it'll be sitting in the back of my mind until it's done."

Erin smiled. "Ah, yes, I know how that goes." A lot of charts had spent time sitting in the back of her mind over the years. "Well, I guess I'd better say goodnight so you can finish up. You're going to need plenty of rest for tomorrow. But if you do change your mind about the whole swimming thing, I'll understand."

"I won't. I'm looking forward to it, Erin. Have a good night."

"Goodnight, Luke." She liked the sound of his name on her lips, and repeated it in a whisper after she ended the call. "Luke…" Then she mentally shook herself. *What has gotten into you, Erin?*

She set her phone on the windowsill and glanced out

at the pond again. Jenna had given her some breathing exercises to practice for tomorrow. Now would probably be a good time to do them, while there was still a window between her and that pond.

She sat down on the chair, keeping her back straight and her feet resting flat on the floor. *Don't think about anything but your breathing*, Jenna had said. *Clear your mind. Breathe in slowly. Feel the air reach deep inside you, then breathe all the way out. Inhale...and exhale. Let go of the tension in your body as you breathe...Inhale...and exhale...*

All of a sudden Erin felt a chill go through her. The hairs stood up on the back of her neck, and it had nothing to do with thoughts of the pond. She felt like someone was watching her. She looked at the doorway, expecting to see Jenna standing there. But she saw only the empty hallway beyond.

The feeling went away after a few seconds, and she smiled wryly. It had been a long day, and now she was delusional. The only breathing exercises she needed to do were in her sleep.

CHAPTER

6

Her mother had her head buried in the pillow, softly crying.

Erin crawled up onto the bed. "Mommy, are you okay?"

Her mother raised her head, quickly wiping her tears away. She smiled, though she still looked sad, and gently pulled Erin over to her. "Yes, baby. I'm okay."

Erin snuggled against her, and her mother pressed a kiss on her forehead. "I love you more than anything," she said. "Never forget that."

"I love you too," Erin answered with a drowsy smile, and fell asleep in her mother's arms.

Someone brushed a hand lightly over her hair, and she opened her eyes. Shannon Godfrey stood there smiling at her, looking radiant in a way Erin had never seen her look before. "Your mom wants you to know she loves you, Erin. She's so very sorry she left you like she did."

"Where is she?" Erin murmured.

"She's happy," Shannon said, touching her cheek. "Her soul is free and at peace. But she's always been with you. Heaven *isn't as far away as you might think..."*

Erin opened her eyes, and the heaviness in the air, the bone-chilling coldness of it, dimly registered in her brain. She pulled the bed covers higher and turned her head to the side, still half-asleep. That's when she saw it—a faint white haze next to the bed that rapidly faded away. For a split second it almost looked human. And after it disappeared the room became warm again, the air lighter.

She tossed back the covers and scrambled out of bed, her eyes wide with terror and her heart pounding in her chest. Grabbing her robe off the chair, she threw it on as she rushed out of the room and all but flew down the carpeted stairs to the kitchen. *Water*, she told herself in a panic. *I just need some water.*

She flipped the light on and hurried over to a cupboard that she remembered contained glasses, pulling one out. But it slipped from her shaking hand and fell onto the counter with a crash, shards of glass scattering over the laminate surface.

"Damn it!" she softly cursed.

Easing another glass from the cupboard, she filled it with water and took several long, slow drinks. But just as her quaking nerves started to settle she heard a strange sound in the hallway outside the kitchen. Terror filled her all over again, and with a pent-up breath she hesitantly turned around. A shadowy figure appeared in the doorway, and her breath escaped in a scream. The glass fell through her fingers—and shattered.

Jenna walked into the kitchen, her cane scraping across the wooden floorboards. But she came to an abrupt halt when Erin screamed and the glass hit the floor. "Good Lord, Erin! You look like you've seen a ghost."

Erin shrugged her shoulders helplessly. "If I wasn't sure there was no such thing, I'd say I just did." She glanced around, and added with a grimace, "I guess I owe you some new glasses."

"Don't move or you'll cut yourself. I'll go get a broom."

Erin felt her fear fade away now that Jenna was there, and she silently laughed at herself. She was acting like a fool, all because of a dream. Shaking her head, she carefully turned around and picked up the larger pieces of glass scattered on the counter, throwing them into the trash can under the sink.

"I was planning to get rid of those old glasses anyway—just not at 2:00 a.m. on a Friday night," Jenna said in amusement when they were done cleaning up. "But now that we're awake, why don't I make us some tea?"

"Yes, that sounds perfect." Erin sat down at the small breakfast table in the corner of the kitchen. "I'd help, but you'd probably be out a few teacups too."

Jenna chuckled, filling a kettle with water. "I do kind of like my teacups."

They had another visitor come into the kitchen just then. Wesley, Jenna's eighteen-year-old orange tabby cat, padded over to Erin, rubbing himself against her leg. "Mrroww," he said.

Erin hauled the large cat up onto her lap. "Did I wake you up too, Wesley?"

She brushed a hand over his soft, fluffy coat and he started to purr, affectionately licking her arm. She'd been so happy to see he was still doing well after all these years. The Godfreys had gotten him as a kitten the year Shannon died. She remembered he'd refused to leave Shannon's side toward the end.

While she continued to pet Wesley, her mind wandered back to her dream. She couldn't recall ever having a dream about her mother before, or one that seemed so real. Other details came back to her. The window had been open, and she'd fallen asleep to the noise from the busy street below. Earlier that night her mother and Seth had gotten into an argument again, and he'd stormed out. When Erin woke up the next morning he still hadn't returned. And she remembered seeing an empty wine bottle on the nightstand. That had been happening more and more too.

Erin's hand froze on Wesley's back. It hadn't really been just a dream, she realized with shock. It was part of another long-forgotten memory. "I used to call him Seth," she whispered, more to herself than to Jenna. "Why would I have called him that?"

Jenna eased into the chair next to hers. "Why would you call who what?" she asked.

"I remembered I used to call my father Seth. I'd forgotten that."

"You've hardly said two words about the man since I've known you."

"Like I told Luke, I don't remember a whole lot. Everything that happened in LA was pretty much a blank—until yesterday."

"You talked to Luke about that?" Jenna asked in surprise.

Erin explained what had happened in Luke's car, and then about the dream that wasn't a dream of her mother. Just as she finished telling her about falling asleep in her mother's arms the tea kettle whistled. "I'll get it," she said, setting Wesley on the floor. "I think your cups are safe now."

She prepared the tea and brought the cups over to

the table, along with a sugar bowl. "You should probably add your own sugar since I'm bound to put in too much." She slid back into her chair and smiled at the speculative expression on Jenna's face. "Uh oh. I don't think that look has anything to do with the tea. I hope we're not going to have another discussion about vibrators, Dr. Godfrey."

Jenna laughed softly. "No, you can do with that conversation what you will." She stirred her tea, and the speculative look returned. "I just wonder who your mom really was, Erin. I have a feeling your grandmother didn't tell you everything. And I'll bet a lot of the things she did tell you were skewed by her twisted way of thinking. It's interesting that your mom left here as soon as she finished high school and never came back, just like you did. I know you think your grandparents severed ties with her because she got pregnant and all that. But maybe it was really the other way around. Maybe your mom didn't want anything more to do with them because her childhood had been just as miserable as yours was."

Erin remained silent, wrapping her hands around her cup just as she tried to wrap her head around what Jenna was saying. She'd never thought about her mother in that light before. In fact, for most of her life she'd tried not to think of her at all. When she did, it was with the same resentment she felt for her grandmother. She'd put both of them into the same compartment in her mind—one she liked to keep shut. She'd never once considered that her mother might have experienced what she had, that she might have felt what she'd felt.

"I also find it interesting that she chose to live on the coast," Jenna added. "The same as you did. It's just that you went east instead of west."

Erin stared into her cup, stunned by Jenna's words. Was it possible she and her mother could be a lot more alike than she'd imagined? The East Coast had been her safe haven, an escape from the painful memories she'd left behind in Wisconsin. And despite her fear of going into the water, she'd always had an inexplicable fascination with the ocean. Maybe it was the freedom and strength she saw in the sea, the sheer vastness of it that made all her problems seem insignificant. Had her mother moved to California for the same reason?

Suddenly she felt something shift in her brain regarding her mother. She had to take her out of the old compartment in her mind and put her into a different one, one that wasn't well-defined. But she felt the beginning of an entirely unexpected emotion for the woman who'd given birth to her: empathy.

"You never said what happened in your dream after you fell asleep with your mom," Jenna said. "Or is that when you woke up?"

Erin shook her head. "Before it ended your mom was there instead of mine, standing by the bed. But she spoke about my mom as if she knew her. And then I really woke up." A chill ran through her at the memory, and she took a sip of her tea. "It was probably just my mind playing tricks on me, that I was still half-asleep…But it was strange, Jen. The room was really cold, and it shouldn't have been. I turned my head, and for a second I thought I saw…something. Then it disappeared, and the room warmed up again." She shook her head at how crazy she sounded. "I guess it must have been my imagination."

"I don't think you were imagining that at all," Jenna said with a soft smile. "I think you had a visit from my mom."

Erin looked at her in disbelief. "You can't be serious."

"I never told you this before because I didn't think you'd believe me—in fact, I'm sure you would have insisted I go in for a brain scan if I did. But I've felt my mom's presence here ever since she died. Sometimes I'll feel like she's watching me, or I'll hear footsteps when no one's there. I swear I've even caught glimpses of her a few times. And she definitely likes to move things. At first I thought it was all just my imagination, maybe wishful thinking. Then I asked my dad about it, and he said the exact same things had been happening to him. But he thought it would scare me, so he'd never brought any of it up before. That's when I knew it really was my mom. And lately her presence has become stronger than ever."

Erin's disbelief turned to outright shock. "You think your mom is haunting this house?"

Jenna chuckled. "Haunting seems like such a strong word, but yes. And no, I don't need a brain scan. I've already had one." Her expression sobered as she gazed down at the teacup in her hands. "The cancer hasn't spread there. That's another thing I'm grateful for. I'd like to keep my mind until the end."

Erin was dumbfounded. She'd heard stories about people seeing spirits, especially before their death. And staff members at Boston General frequently talked about strange things happening there that they attributed to ghosts. She'd never believed any of it was really true, though. She figured there were more logical explanations for such things. But what she'd seen tonight with her own eyes, what she'd felt, seemed all too real.

"I don't get it, Jenna. I've spent so much time here over the years—I even lived here for a few months. And nothing like that ever happened to me before."

"Maybe you weren't ready for it to happen before, sort of like you weren't ready to deal with some of the memories of your mom. The human mind can be funny that way. Despite our advanced intelligence—or maybe because of it—we have a rather perplexing ability to suppress information from our conscious awareness that we don't want to deal with. And we're often blinded by our preconceptions—literally and figuratively. As Ralph Waldo Emerson once said, 'People only see what they are prepared to see.'"

"I never imagined it was even possible…"

"Millions of people have had similar experiences, and I find it hard to believe that everyone is imagining the same things," Jenna said. "And those who argue that ghosts can't exist because they don't have a scientific explanation are really discrediting science itself, especially when ninety-five percent of the universe—dark matter and dark energy—can't be explained either, though no scientist in their right mind would deny they exist. And all the scientific advancements that have occurred throughout history would never have happened if someone hadn't made the effort to explain a thing that had previously been inexplicable. So I've come to the conclusion that ghosts are a very real phenomenon, yet another part of the universe that science simply hasn't been able to explain on paper yet, just like Heaven itself." She paused to sip her tea, then added, "Albert Einstein once wrote, 'Our limited minds cannot grasp the mysterious force that sways the constellations.' There is so much we don't know. Sometimes all we can do is believe."

Erin regarded her friend with new admiration, remembering the quote she had up on the wall in her classroom. "I would never have guessed you were so into Einstein."

Jenna laughed. "I didn't like him back when I was in physics class, believe me. But I've read some of the things he's written. He commented many times about how limited his understanding of the universe was. I find it fascinating that one of the most brilliant human beings who ever lived understood that he, too, knew so little. And scientists really haven't come up with many more concrete answers about the universe since his time—relatively speaking."

Erin smiled wryly. "I'll be the first to admit that I don't know everything—not nearly. But I feel like I knew a whole lot more yesterday than I do today. I certainly never dreamed that any of the ghosts I'd have to face here would turn out to be real."

"Oh my," Jenna said. "It almost sounds like Dr. Pryce might actually believe in ghosts now."

"I can't discount what happened. The more I think about it the more sure I am that it wasn't all just in my head."

"Don't discount it, Erin. And I hope someday you won't discount another ghost—the Holy Ghost." Jenna grinned. "That sounds like a poem I should write. I'd call it 'Holy Ghost.' Let me think how it would go…"

Erin couldn't help but laugh. "Oh Lord."

"Yes, He would be in there too," Jenna said, looking at her with a thoughtful and amused expression. "I think the poem would begin with:

> "The only life that ever existed for my friend
> Was in the mundane world she could comprehend.
> She aced chemistry, physics, and biology,
> But I'll bet she got an F in theology."

"Hey," Erin protested. "I would not have gotten an F in theology, if I'd taken it."

"Okay," Jenna laughed. "I'll make that: 'She aced chemistry, physics, and biology / But had no interest in studying theology,' since I'm sure you're right. You would have aced theology—while you sat there the whole time studying chemistry, physics, and biology."

"Now that might be true," Erin admitted with a grin.

Jenna's expression turned thoughtful again. "I think the next part of the poem would go something like:

> "Then one night she saw before her bed
> A wraith-like figure, quickly gone,
> But not all in her head."

"It was next to my bed, actually," Erin remarked in a droll tone. "And it's definitely in my head now."

Jenna nodded. "We can change the bed part to 'beside her bed.' But I have an idea about how the ending should go:

> "The room got strangely cold,
> And a shiver ran through her very soul.
> For what shook her heart and mind the most,
> Was if that was there, then so too could be,
> The Father, Son, and Holy Ghost."

Jenna's face split into a wide grin. "There you have it: 'Holy Ghost.' What do you think?"

Erin didn't immediately answer, taking a sip of her tea. She knew the question was Jenna's way of asking if she was open to the existence of God. And after their talk yesterday, she had a feeling her friend wasn't going to let her brush aside such sensitive topics anymore. But Erin realized she couldn't let herself do that anymore. Jenna had been right: She needed to open up—probably about this subject more than any other.

Setting her cup down, Erin finally said, "My grandmother always threw God's name in with the hateful things she would tell me. I think the only thing she really enjoyed was talking about how God was going to punish people for their sins and send everyone to Hell—except for her and a few other 'devout Christians,' of course. And she would inevitably rant on and on about the world ending according to the Book of Revelation and the horrible things God was going to do to people then. It was terrifying, and I would have nightmares about it all the time. So I guess at some point I decided I would rather not believe in God, that the worst thing there could possibly be was that God."

Jenna reached over and covered Erin's hand with hers. "As I've said in the past when you've let *me* rant on and on, a lot of things in the Bible shouldn't be taken literally. And that's especially true of the Book of Revelation. Chances are, if the world does end in such a horrible way, it will be humans who cause it. But God exists, Erin. Just not that God. People have a tendency to put their own likeness on Him. They see a God with attributes that are distinctly human and flawed, when He is, in fact, not human at all. He's the most loving and forgiving sort after all. And I'm glad for that, or I'd be pretty nervous about facing Him. I've got a lot to be forgiven for myself."

"Oh please, Jenna. There's not a better person around than you."

"I don't know about that. You're forgetting it was just yesterday I told you to go screw yourself."

Erin burst out laughing. "Yes, that is true. And you also spoke rather unkindly about men who aren't good at kissing."

"That wasn't very nice, was it?" Jenna said with a half-rueful smile. "I guess yesterday you were saving lives and earning a ton of frequent flyer miles from God, while I was earning a trip to the confessional. I'm jealous—and there I go again. I think I bought myself another trip."

Erin shook her head. "Now you're just talking crazy, Jenna."

Her friend laughed softly. "Ah, crazy. What an interesting word. It can mean anything from true insanity to absolute brilliance. And over the course of human history crazy has often turned out to make the most sense. But that's neither here nor there. And I think I'm just babbling now." With a whimsical smile she eased herself out of the chair and stood up, grabbing her cane. "I need to go back to bed before Wesley starts making more sense than I do."

Hearing his name, the big orange tabby got up from under the table and rubbed himself against Jenna's leg, purring loudly.

Erin bent down and scratched his back. "You are adorable, Wesley. I wonder what does go through your head?"

"Mrroww," he answered, brushing himself against her as well.

Jenna lightly touched Erin's shoulder. "You should get some sleep too. Just remember, you have nothing to fear here." Then she turned and hobbled out of the kitchen, with Wesley walking along beside her.

Erin continued to sip her tea for a while. But she knew she was only delaying the inevitable, so she finally forced herself out of the chair, put the teacups in the sink, and reluctantly went upstairs.

You have nothing to fear here, she repeated to herself. *You have nothing to fear here*…But as soon as she reached the bedroom doorway an image of what she'd seen earlier flashed through her mind—that translucent white mist, vaguely human in shape, hovering next to her before it faded into the darkness…

With a shiver running down her spine, she flipped the bedroom light switch on and peeked her head inside. Everything still looked the same.

She tentatively went in, leaving the door open just a crack in case Jenna needed her during the night. Then she glanced around the room for a lamp and softly groaned when she didn't see one. There was no way she would be able to sleep in the dark now.

She lingered indecisively by the door and almost headed back downstairs to sleep on the couch. But with a resigned sigh she eventually lay down on the bed, pulling her robe tightly around her. And under the bright, steady glow of the ceiling light, she hesitantly closed her eyes.

CHAPTER 7

Luke stood at the front door with a package of toilet paper in his arms, a big white bow on top. "For you," he said with a grin, and held it out to Erin.

She smiled, taking the package. It was economy size, no less. "Wow, this is the most—useful gift I've ever been given."

"I got it to remind you that you're a white cloud, so don't use it up too fast."

Erin met his gaze and immediately felt something electric pass between them. Those vivid blue eyes made her feel alive in a way she'd never experienced before. She opened her mouth to say more, but nothing would come out.

"Hello, Luke," Jenna said, walking into the little foyer as well.

Erin turned around, and Jenna's eyes dropped to the package in her arms. "Luke Mathis, that is not a very nice welcoming gift!" She shook her head and smiled at Erin. "I guess now you know why he's still single."

Erin bit her lip, not daring to look back at Luke. Now *he* knew she'd asked that question. She wondered if her friend had done that on purpose.

Luke didn't miss the meaning behind Jenna's statement either, and he briefly studied Erin from behind. Her sandy blond hair was pulled back in a ponytail, and she wore an airy short-sleeve white blouse and yellow capris—which highlighted the lush curves of her bottom nicely. He imagined slowly caressing her there, then sliding his hands around her waist and pulling her back against him. He'd brush his lips over her ear and whisper into it exactly why he was still single.

He'd been up half the night with her on his brain. Now that she'd returned, and he'd seen her and touched her, the glowing embers of what he'd felt for her before had reignited into a brightly burning flame. *Soon*, he promised himself. She wasn't going to leave this time without knowing how he'd always felt about her. He wasn't that awkward teenager anymore.

He set those thoughts aside for the moment, though, and told Jenna the story behind the gift.

"I see," she said, and slowly grinned as she glanced between the two of them.

Erin stood there hugging the package of toilet paper. She could feel the heat of a blush on her cheeks. Luke had moved closer to her. She didn't look behind her, and he didn't touch her, but she could feel him there, a breath away. "I…I'll go take this upstairs," she said awkwardly.

She made a beeline for the staircase, feeling like a bungling teenager as she went up to deposit the package in the bathroom. It was probably from lack of sleep after what had happened in the middle of the night. The very idea that Shannon could be there…Goose bumps rose on her arms at the thought, and she looked down the gray carpeted hallway in both directions before leaving the bathroom.

Luke and Jenna were still in the foyer when she walked back downstairs.

"I'll start unloading your car," Luke said. "I'm sure you'd like to get settled in."

Erin nodded, feeling some semblance of composure finally return. "I'll come with you and help."

"I think I'll go sit out back and enjoy the sunshine for a while," Jenna said with a rueful smile. "I wish I could be of more help myself."

"Don't be silly," Luke told her. "Go rest."

As they walked out of the house toward her car, Erin glanced at Luke. "Did Jenna ever tell you she has Li-Fraumeni syndrome?" She'd done some internet research on it before he'd called last night, and now fully understood what Jenna had been dealing with. It was a dreadful disorder to have.

Luke nodded. "She told me a few years ago—only because I kept trying to set her up with some of my friends and wouldn't stop pestering her about it. I told her you would want to know too."

"Yes, I would have. But I'm glad she wasn't dealing with it completely on her own all this time. You've been a great friend to her, Luke."

"I couldn't ask for a better friend myself. She's the nicest person I know." A guilty smile crossed his face. "Just don't tell my mom I said that."

Erin laughed. "I don't think I ever met your mom."

They reached the car and Luke turned to her. "I'm sure you'd like her. Everybody does—well, except maybe my brothers these days." He grinned. "My mom's come down with a serious case of grandmother fever, and neither of them has produced the cure. They're both married, so they're taking the brunt of her ire. It's kind of funny because they used to lay into me nonstop about being the baby in the family, and now they're the ones getting bombarded with the 'B' word. I love it. Although I wouldn't mind being the one to fix the problem."

Erin had felt like a deer in the headlights as soon as she'd realized where the conversation was headed. And his last words hit her hard, a poignant reminder that she couldn't get involved with him for either of their sakes—a reminder she shouldn't need. But it still hurt, more than she cared to admit. And not knowing what to say, she silently opened the rear passenger door of her car to start unloading the baggage inside.

Luke saw the wounded look on her face before she turned away, and he mentally kicked himself for talking about his mom, thinking he'd probably stirred up more painful memories of her own mother. "Erin—"

He abruptly stepped back to avoid getting hit by the suitcase she flung out of the car. A duffel bag followed, skidding across the driveway and into the grass, and he quickly grabbed hold of her arm. "Slow down, Erin. Let me help you."

She pulled her arm away as if his touch burned, and walked over to the suitcase she'd thrown out. "I'm going to take this inside," she said tightly, and rolled it away.

Luke collected a few more bags from the backseat, then grabbed the one in the grass, and headed after her, his brow furrowing with concern as he watched her disappear into the house.

Erin lugged her suitcase up the stairs to her bedroom. Luke's words echoed through her mind, and she could no longer fight off the maelstrom of emotions they aroused inside her—dejection, self-loathing, anger. And with no other outlet available, she released all that pent-up frustration on the suitcase, flipping it down hard onto the bed and pounding her fist against it, over and over, with a groan. She paused a moment afterward, closing her eyes as she tried to gather herself. *I'm not going to cry. I am not going to cry*...And when she felt like she was in control again, she swung around to leave—only to see Luke standing in the doorway watching her.

He dropped the bags he was holding and strode over to her, clasping her upper arms firmly in his hands. "We're not doing anything else until you tell me what's wrong. Did I upset you by bringing up my mom? I'm sorry, I wasn't thinking."

Erin shook her head, too embarrassed to meet his gaze. "No, please don't feel sorry about that, Luke. If I fell apart every time someone mentioned their mother I'd be in a mental institution by now...Babies, on the other hand, are a different story." She let out a sigh. "I can't have children. I gather Jenna never told you that."

"No, she didn't," Luke softly responded. Jenna would never have mentioned that Erin was trying to have a baby with another man. He was pretty sure she knew how he'd always felt about Erin.

"When you mentioned having babies it just brought up a lot of bad memories, that's all," Erin said, trying to downplay the issue.

Luke still heard the heartbreak she couldn't quite keep out of her voice. "Did you ever find out what the problem was?" he gently coaxed.

"I was the problem. Peter's tests came back normal."

"What about fertility treatment?"

"We never got to that point. By then Peter realized he preferred women who weren't broken."

Luke tilted her chin up. "You're not broken, Erin. Not unless you want to be. And I also happen to know a thing or two about infertility. My friend Scott—the detective you met yesterday—dealt with it for years. His wife ended up having in vitro fertilization done twice, and they got twins both times. I should take you over to visit them one of these days."

"But it's just as likely not to work," Erin said, still avoiding his direct gaze. "I've seen the numbers."

"Then you'll adopt and give some child out there a good home. You more than anyone should understand how important that is." Luke squeezed her shoulders affectionately. "But in any case, this can't be the same woman talking who just yesterday shoved a big ass needle into a kid's chest without batting an eye. You wouldn't give up on some boy you didn't even know, and yet you give up on yourself so easily? I find that hard to believe, Erin."

She smiled ruefully, studying the slight cleft in his chin that she hadn't noticed before. "I know. I'm pretty messed up."

Luke skimmed one hand over her shoulder to the side of her neck, and lightly caressed her jaw with his thumb. "I would just go with pretty."

Erin slowly lifted her gaze to meet his, mesmerized. The pain subsided, and his fingers started awakening entirely new sensations inside her. She watched his eyes drop to her mouth and felt him slide his thumb up to trace her lower lip. When he gently coaxed it down she knew he was going to kiss her, and her heart beat faster. She really wanted him to kiss her.

"Mrroww."

They both looked down at Wesley, and the moment was broken.

Luke laughed softly and bent over to pet the cat. "Do you want some attention too, buddy?"

Erin stepped away, still half-dazed by her reaction to Luke. "I—I guess we'd better go finish unpacking. Jenna's waiting for us."

Luke nodded, following her out of the room. She was right, of course. But there would be another time. He was going to make sure there was another time.

THERE IS NO WAY I'M GOING IN THERE.

That was Erin's first thought as she stood by the pond with Jenna and Luke.

It was a perfect day for swimming. The weather was warm, and the sky was once again cloudless, with the calm water in the pond reflecting the blue sky above.

"I'll go in first," Luke said with a grin.

Erin watched as he pulled his T-shirt up over his head and tossed it into the sand, giving her a brief glimpse of impeccably toned chest and abdominal muscles before he turned and ran toward the pond. Her gaze traveled over his broad shoulders and well-formed back, and lower to the firm, muscular backside outlined by his blue swim trunks, and the warm summer day suddenly got a lot hotter. But then he splashed full tilt into the water, letting out a whoop as he dove under the surface, and she grimaced at the sight.

After a few seconds he came up and turned toward them, brushing the wet hair out of his face while he tread water.

"Come on in, ladies! The water's perfect."

Erin and Jenna looked at each other doubtfully.

"I don't think this was such a good idea," Erin said.

Jenna laughed half-heartedly. "I guess that means I get to go in next."

Erin hugged her arms to her chest over the yellow swim robe she wore. "This was all your idea to begin with," she said, attempting a smile that ended in another grimace.

"All right, I'll do it." Jenna tossed her cane aside and hesitantly stepped into the water in the full-length black wetsuit she had on to keep out the chill of the water.

Erin had insisted she wear it, and a genuine smile crossed her face at the thought of their road trip down to Madison earlier in the day to buy it. She'd also gotten a swimsuit for herself, and the things she'd wanted for the bathroom—and a lamp for her bedroom, of course. The trip had been filled with lots of laughter, and she'd been reminded of all the other fun times they'd had there as teenagers, once they'd been old enough to drive. She was coming to realize that she had a lot of good memories of this place, memories she'd allowed to be overshadowed by the bad.

Jenna waded a little deeper into the pond, then rolled onto her back. "Oh, Erin, this is actually really nice," she said after a moment, closing her eyes in pleasure as she floated on the surface of the water.

Luke swam back in. "Your turn, Erin."

He came out of the water and Erin got an eyeful of his chest and abdomen this time. He had a light dusting of dark hair that tapered down over the sculptured muscles of his abdomen to the waistband of his swim trunks. Rivulets of water followed the same path as her eyes, and she watched them in helpless fascination as he walked toward her.

"Are you ready?" he asked, coming to a stop in front of her.

Erin glanced at the water and all thoughts of his washboard abs fled. "I don't know about this, Luke."

He reached out, gently easing her arms down to her sides, and tugged her robe tie loose. "You promised," he said with a roguish smile.

Erin looked up at him, and their gazes locked as he pulled the robe open and slowly slid it over her shoulders, letting it fall in a silent heap around her feet. She felt the electricity pass between them again, more powerful than ever, and it shocked her senses.

Luke couldn't resist the urge to let his eyes drop lower once he had her disrobed. She wore a one-piece swimsuit in a bright floral design, and the V-shaped neckline reached the hollow between her breasts, the cloth clinging to her curves and leaving nothing—and yet everything—to his imagination…He mentally shook himself before he lost control of his rapidly heating body and gathered her hands in his. "Come on," he said, stepping back toward the pond.

Erin's heart fluttered in her chest, and she wasn't sure if it was because she was about to go into the water, or because of the way he'd just run his eyes over her, leaving her feeling thoroughly discombobulated. In either case, her legs were wobbly as she followed him to the edge of the pond.

She hesitated there, and Luke lightly tugged on her arms with an encouraging smile. "Come on," he repeated. "You can do it."

"I feel like a baby learning to walk," she said, nervously eyeing the water. Then she took her first step in.

"Believe me, you look nothing like a baby."

Erin met his eyes again, and the heat she saw in them almost made her forget about the water at all. He started pulling her farther into the pond, holding her captive in the depths of his magnetic blue gaze, and she couldn't help but follow.

As they went in deeper, though, the sensation of her lower body being swallowed by the water finally registered in her brain. Fear began to surface again, and a jumble of emotions was soon warring inside her. Fear finally won over when her legs were completely submerged, and she resisted his pull.

Jenna swam back in and stood up next to her. "Work on your breathing, Erin," she instructed. "Remember, you're in control in the water. Clear your mind. Let go of the fear. Breathe in, and breathe out."

Erin nodded, taking slow, deep breaths, and Luke gently guided her forward. But she made it only a few steps farther.

"Keep going, Erin," he urged. "Just a little more."

"I don't know..." She looked at the water around her and felt her heart beat faster—and faster, and faster...Things started to become surreal. Everything looking distorted, out of proportion. The water seemed to go on forever, getting darker and deeper by the second. Her chest tightened painfully, and she lost control of her breathing. Jenna was talking to her, she knew, but she couldn't understand anymore. Her heart was pounding in her ears now. "I can't...breathe," she managed to get out. She couldn't think, she couldn't move. She was drowning. She was going to die...

"Luke, get her out of the water," Jenna said anxiously.

Luke lifted Erin's shaking body up against his, and she wrapped her arms and legs around him, burying her face in the nape of his neck. But he didn't take her out of the water.

He knew if they gave up now she would probably never go back in. "It's okay," he murmured soothingly, lifting one hand to shelter her head. "Just breathe against me."

Erin clung to him. Somewhere in the back of her mind she knew she was going to be embarrassed later, but right now she didn't care. She needed the support of his solid body more than anything else in that moment, more than she'd allowed herself to need anything—anyone—in a very long time.

She kept her face buried in his neck, and the trembling in her body gradually subsided, along with the pounding in her ears. She was able to get her breathing back under control, and her racing heart slowed down. "I told you this would be a melodrama," she finally whispered against him.

Luke brushed his hand tenderly over her hair. "We just did a little too much too quickly, that's all."

Jenna touched her arm. "Are you okay?"

Erin turned her head, keeping her cheek nestled against Luke. "Yes. Sorry, Jen. I'm such a baby."

"I'm the one who needs to apologize," Jenna said. "I shouldn't have made you do this."

"No, you were right. I needed to do it."

Erin leaned her forehead on Luke's shoulder for a moment, then finally lifted her head to meet his gaze. And as she looked into his concerned blue eyes all the rest of her fear melted away. Something else took its place, something deep and powerful that filled her heart and reached down into her soul. She felt her chest tighten in an entirely different way than it had a few minutes ago. "Thank you," she whispered.

Luke affectionately tucked several stray blond hairs behind her ear. "It's my pleasure, Erin."

She hesitated, then said, "Will you take me in a little farther?"

"Are you sure?"

She smiled ruefully. "Don't worry. I think you've already seen me at my worst."

Luke shook his head and started wading deeper into the pond. "You're facing your fear. That's seeing someone at their best."

"You sound like Jenna." Erin tightened her arms around his neck as she felt her legs sink into the water again. Her heart sped up a little, but she kept her eyes steady on his.

"Hey, that better be a compliment," Jenna facetiously retorted.

"Of course, Jen," Erin said, though she didn't dare look at her.

Luke grinned. "I hope I've learned a thing or two from Jenna after all the quotes she's rattled off to me over the years."

"Do you have a favorite one?" Erin asked, trying to take her mind off what was happening in the water.

Luke stopped, seeing the fear return to her eyes. She was also going to strangle him soon—or send all his blood flowing in a completely different direction with the way she was pressed so tightly against him. He was glad the water was a little cool, or he'd be in a real predicament. "Hmm, my favorite quote," he said, making a conscious effort not to think about what she was doing to his body. "I would have to say it's one from Thoreau—"

"Of course," Erin said at the same time he did, and they both laughed. She couldn't believe it. She was partially submerged in a pond and was actually laughing.

"Okay, I'll admit that I'm in love with Henry David Thoreau," Jenna said in amusement. "But he was such a great writer and philosopher. And so much of what he wrote applies today more than ever."

"And he went to Harvard," Erin added. She risked looking over at her friend, and was relieved that she felt fine as long as she didn't look directly at the water. "You were probably hoping his ghost would join us when I took you on a tour."

"Who knows? Maybe he was there," Jenna said with one of her whimsical, somewhat mysterious smiles.

Erin chuckled in response and turned back to Luke. "So what is your favorite Thoreau quote?"

A look of embarrassment briefly crossed Luke's face. "I can't believe I'm admitting this, but I'd have to say it's 'There is no remedy for love but to love more.' At least a man came up with it." He gave her a lopsided grin. "Don't ever repeat that to the guys at the station, though. I'd lose my man badge."

Erin softly smiled. "Jenna never told me that one. I like it." Her gaze dropped to his full mouth, and then to that enticing cleft in his chin. She imagined running her finger over it...

"What's your favorite quote?" he asked.

Erin blinked out of her reverie and looked up into his eyes again. "Oh, I don't know. I've never been good at repeating Jenna's quotes. I always mess them up. Like one day I was working in the ER and this little black girl came in with a cut on her arm. She hadn't really looked at it until I took the bandages off, and when she saw the wound for the first time she just stared at it in shock. I told her it wasn't that deep, that I could close it with skin glue and wouldn't have to poke her with a needle. But she said she wasn't afraid of the needle. She just always thought she was black inside, too."

"Now we're even," Jenna said. "You never told me that one before, either. I always get to hear the ER stories that involve a lot of blood and guts." She grinned at Luke. "You should take her out to eat if you really want to hear some of those. That's when they always seem to come up. Don't order anything expensive off the menu, though, because your food might come up, too."

"I think you're exaggerating there a little, Jen," Erin said. "But the point of the story is that I tried to repeat your quote about everyone being the same inside, like bubble gum lollipops. But I bungled it, of course."

"'Humankind is like a big box of bubble gum lollipops, with all the flavors on the outside, but inside all the same.'"

"Yes, that's the one. But I ended up just saying everyone looks the same inside. I did add that she should never start smoking, because then her lungs would turn black inside."

Jenna chuckled. "I can see you saying that."

"Based on how wide her eyes got, I think I convinced at least one child never to smoke."

Luke could feel Erin's body relax against him as she talked, and he slowly waded deeper into the pond. "So tell me another interesting ER story," he said. "And I don't mind the ones with blood and guts, by the way. I'm sure I've heard them all at the dinner table already—and my food never came up once."

"That's enough for me," Jenna said. "I'm going to swim a little—preferably out of hearing range." She looked appreciatively at Luke. "Your methods seem to be working better anyway." Then she squeezed Erin's arm. "Are you sure you're all right?"

Erin nodded, and her lips curved up into a slow grin. "Maybe I'll tell him about the case of the missing donut. Or the stuck plunger. We'll see if he really has heard it all."

"Oh, good Lord," Jenna groaned. "I am so out of here." And with a laugh she swam away.

"A missing donut? It sounds like a cop's worst nightmare," Luke said, coming to a stop in the water. He had Erin in up to her chest now, and her body was still relaxed against him.

"It happened a few years ago. A 500-pound woman was brought in by ambulance. She was having abdominal pain, and when I examined her belly there were all kinds of things stuck in between the folds of fat. Under one layer I found her missing inhaler and some money. But otherwise it was all food. It turned out she would hide snacks in there from her mother because she was supposed to be on a diet. I found mostly gummy bears and melted chocolate. Then I lifted another fold of fat and found the donut—or at least what was left of it. It had obviously been there awhile, and caused the skin under it to break down and get infected. She had a massive abscess that extended deep into her belly. That's why she was having the pain. When I first exposed the area the smell was horrendous. The nurse who was in the room with me turned green and had to leave. I think she deposited her lunch in the bathroom."

"Wow. A donut actually ate its way into someone's belly," Luke said with a grimace.

"Hey, you stole one of my punch lines," Erin jokingly chided.

"One of them?"

"Yes. And it left a donut hole."

Luke shook his head with a laugh.

"I told the surgeon on call he had a real treat in store for him," she added, tongue-in-cheek.

He let out another laugh. "You have a wicked sense of humor, Erin. I had no idea."

"You need to have a strange sense of humor to work in the ER. Otherwise you'll get eaten alive—by more than donuts."

"I'm going to have to tell my dad that one. He'll eat it up." Luke grinned, prompting her to laugh. And then he conceded, "But you're right, I haven't heard it all until now."

"You'll never hear it all, really. People always manage to find new and interesting ways to end up in the ER."

"You mentioned a plunger before. I gather someone found an interesting use for one?"

"Yes, that's one way to put it. A guy was trying to convince his wife to have anal sex. She wasn't going for it, so he grabbed the toilet plunger from the bathroom and used the handle to demonstrate on himself. He was standing while he did it, but then stumbled back and fell right onto the plunger."

"Oh Jeez, Erin!" Luke groaned.

"Anytime someone has a penetrating injury like that the object should be left in place until the person is brought to the hospital—usually to the OR—because there could be serious bleeding when it's removed. So in this case the paramedics put the guy on a stretcher on his belly and brought him in with the plunger sticking out of his backside. Everyone had a punch line for that one, believe me. But when I told the trauma surgeon what he had stuck up there, his response was, 'A plunger is supposed to unclog your plumbing, not plug it up.' I really liked that one."

Luke chuckled. "See, you're good at repeating some quotes."

Erin's lips quirked up into a wry smile. "I guess so."

"I don't think that guy did a very good job of convincing his wife to have anal sex, though."

"No, she probably decided it wasn't up her alley."

Both their faces split into grins. And for a long moment afterward neither of them said anything else, lost in each other's eyes. Luke traced the fine curve of her cheekbone with his thumb, then slowly ran his fingers along the side of her face to her neck. "Are you still feeling okay?" he finally asked.

"Yes," Erin answered a little breathlessly. She was feeling more than okay. Now that she was getting used to the water, and he was looking at her like that, touching her like that, other sensations were beginning to register in her brain. Like the way his hand gripped her bottom on one side as he held her cradled against him. And how his hard body rubbed so intimately between her thighs. Her breasts tingled where they touched his chest, and she wanted to push even closer. She felt a heat flow from him and seep through her, filling her down to her core. An aching need blossomed there, a yearning she'd never felt before.

She wanted him.

It hit her like a bolt from the blue sky above. She wanted him. She was stuck in the middle of a pond, submerged in water she'd been terrified of half an hour ago, unable to swim. And now she truly desired a man for the first time in her life.

She dropped her forehead back down against his shoulder and softly groaned at the irony of the situation.

"What's wrong, Erin?" Luke nuzzled his face in her hair, then brushed a light kiss on her ear.

The touch of his lips on the sensitive skin of her ear sent waves of sweet sensation running rampant through Erin's body. He was overwhelming her senses. Her heart raced. She couldn't think.

"Do you want to get out?" Luke asked.

Erin shook her head. She was drowning in him now, but she didn't want to get out of the water, not after the progress she'd made. She needed to work out what was happening between them later, when logic and reason hopefully returned. But right now she was going to have to choose the water.

"I—I think I'd like to try floating," she told him, lifting her head from his shoulder. But she didn't dare look directly into his eyes again.

"Okay. Just remember, I'm right here with you." Luke eased her up to float on the surface of the water, splaying his hands underneath her for support.

A pair of geese flew over the pond, and Erin watched them, willing herself to relax. It was cooler now that she didn't have Luke's warmth against her. She closed her eyes as the sun started to warm her instead, and she felt the tension gradually ease from her body. "This isn't so bad," she said after a while, daring to move her arms a little, skimming them lightly through the water…

She remembered then, the last time she'd gone swimming. She saw it all vividly in her mind. It was the day her mother died.

She stopped moving and looked up at Luke in shock.

"What is it, Erin?" he asked, pulling her closer.

"My mom…She used to take me swimming in the ocean. And we'd gone the day she died—I'm sure of it. I remember she got me a new beach towel before we went, and it was out drying on the balcony that night. It was pink, with a mermaid on it. I've seen that image in my mind so many times over the years. I just could never place it until now."

Erin looked up at the sky and concentrated on relaxing her body again as she floated, wanting to remember this time. "It was windy that day, and the waves were higher than normal. My mom held my hand and we waded out a little ways. I was afraid because the waves were so high. But she told me not to worry, that she wouldn't let me go. And when the waves came in we floated up into them together, then come back down again, over and over. Pretty soon we were both laughing. I'd never seen her laugh like that before. I'd never seen her look so happy."

Tears filled Erin's eyes. "Here I go again," she said with a sigh as they slid down her cheeks. She impatiently tried to wipe them away, but the water on her fingers only wet her face more.

"Why don't we get out of here and sit on the beach? I think you've had enough for one day."

Erin nodded, and without thinking she started to turn her body and lower her legs into the water, intending to stand up.

Luke quickly gathered her back into his arms. "Let's not have you try that here, Erin. You'll be up to your neck in water—literally. I don't think you're quite ready for that yet."

He carried her a little closer to shore and eased her down there. The water barely reached her chest, but even so, when her feet hit the sandy bottom of the pond it still took her a moment to get her bearings, now that she was standing on her own this time.

"I'm like the reverse of a beached whale in here," Erin ruefully quipped. "What would you call that? A ponded human?"

Luke smiled down at her, lightly resting his hands on her hips to keep her steady. "You remind me of a newborn filly I saw not too long ago. She was all legs when she got up for the first time and tried to walk. It was the cutest thing, watching her figure it out. I don't know how many times I thought she was going to fall. But pretty soon she was galloping around like she'd been doing it forever." He gazed searchingly into her eyes. "I'd love to help you figure this out, Erin. And if you do fall, I'll be there to catch you."

Looking up at him, Erin realized she might already be falling. "Luke…" she said uncertainly.

He took her hands in his, giving them a reassuring squeeze. "One step at a time," he said, and pulled her gently toward the shore.

Erin glanced back to make sure Jenna was okay as they got out of the water, then wrapped a towel around her shoulders and sat down next to Luke in the sand. "Do you ride horses?" she asked, watching him dry his hair. She wondered what it would feel like to run her fingers through that thick hair.

"Yeah, I do. It's kind of a hobby of mine."

Erin opened her mouth to ask more about that, but he started rubbing his chest with the towel, and she couldn't remember what she was going to say. Yearning filled her all over again as she watched him, and she imagined her hands on his chest instead. And then her lips. Her tongue. Tasting him…She forgot how to breathe for a second and looked away, pulling her own towel closer.

Luke finished drying off and turned to her. "Colin O'Reilly, the surgeon I told you about, bought a horse ranch south of town when he moved back here. I go there to ride pretty often." He debated whether or not to tell her that Colin's wife, Sophia, was also a fertility specialist, the same one Scott and his wife had gone to. But he decided to save that for another day. "Do you ride?" he asked instead.

Erin hesitantly glanced at him. Much to her relief, he had his arms folded over his bent knees, reducing at least some of the bare skin her wandering eyes could behold. "I've never even touched a horse before. But I think I know the place you're talking about. It's probably the one I drove by yesterday." *Which seems like a lifetime ago*, she thought.

"If you'd like, I can take you over there one of these days and teach you how to ride. I'm sure Colin and Sophia wouldn't mind. In fact, if Colin is there he would probably insist on teaching you himself. He's more into horses than anyone I've ever met. But it's a great way to forget about the rest of the world for a while—or at least I think so." Luke flashed her a grin and lay back on his towel, blissfully closing his eyes. "Hopefully we'd get a day like today. This is perfect weather for riding."

Erin slowly smiled as she regarded him, realizing how much she did want to ride a horse. "Yes, I would love to learn." Maybe that world wasn't quite so far out of her reach after all.

Still smiling at the thought of riding a horse, Erin gazed back out at the pond—and her smile instantly vanished. Jenna was wading in, and something was wrong. She was moving a lot more tentatively than normal and had a dazed look on her face.

Then all of a sudden she staggered and appeared on the verge of falling over.

"Jenna!" Erin cried. And without a second thought she threw off her towel and frantically splashed into the pond. It didn't even register in her brain that she couldn't swim. Her only concern was Jenna.

Fortunately, her friend wasn't in too deep, and she managed to grab hold of her before either of them went under.

"I—I think I may have…overdone it…a little," Jenna whispered, her face ominously pale.

Luke reached them a split second later and scooped Jenna up into his arms. "Let's get you out of here."

"Really, Luke. This isn't necessary," Jenna feebly objected as he carried her toward the beach.

"Bring her to the house right away," Erin said. And when they got back to shore she grabbed a bottle of water and opened it. "Drink this, Jenna. I'm going to run ahead and get my medical bag."

"Erin, I'll be—"

"*Drink*, Jenna." Erin gave her the bottle, then picked up her swim robe and dashed to the house, throwing the robe on as she silently chastised herself. She should never have asked Jenna to go into the pond with her.

She retrieved her medical bag upstairs and came back down just as Luke was carrying Jenna in through the kitchen patio doors. "Take her into the bedroom," she said.

Jenna shook her head in distress. "No, I'd rather lay on the couch. Please."

"Okay, Jen. That's fine," Erin reassured her.

Luke brought Jenna into the living room and carefully laid her down. "I'll go grab a towel."

Erin put her medical bag on the floor and set Jenna's water bottle aside, then helped her out of the wetsuit. And with her friend stripped down to the swimsuit she had on, a pang of sadness hit Erin, seeing just how thin Jenna had gotten.

"I'll spare your eyes," Jenna said with a weak smile, pulling a blanket off the back of the couch to cover herself.

Erin sat down and smoothed the wet hair away from Jenna's face. "We have to work on your diet. And you need to start drinking more fluids."

Luke returned a moment later with the towel and handed it to Erin. "How are you feeling, Jen?"

"I'm fine. The two of you are making this out to be a bigger deal than it is."

"You nearly passed out in the water," Erin said as she unfolded the towel and tucked it under Jenna's head, using the ends to dry her hair. "I'm so sorry I made you go in there. I'm definitely giving myself the worst friend ever award for that one."

"No, I'm glad you did." A soft smile crossed Jenna's face. "It brought back a lot of great memories. And being in the water took so much pressure off my bones. I haven't felt that good in a long time…Thank you."

Erin finished drying Jenna's hair and handed her the water bottle. "Well, I'm still giving myself the worst friend ever award. I deserve it anyway."

Luke put his hand on Erin's shoulder and gently squeezed. "No, you don't. I was pretty impressed with how you jumped right into the water to help Jenna. You were halfway to her before I even knew what was going on."

"She needed help. That's all I was thinking about." Erin grimaced. "I'm just glad she wasn't in deeper. That would not have been a good time to find out if I'd literally sink or swim."

Luke squeezed her shoulder again. "Another reason we need to have more swimming lessons."

Erin nodded. After the way she'd jumped heedlessly into the water, there was no longer any question that she needed to learn how to swim. But another idea occurred to her as she regarded Jenna. "I think we should get a hot tub. It would be good for you, and I don't want you swimming in the pond anymore."

"A hot tub sounds wonderful. But if you don't go in with me, I will go back in the pond," Jenna said, the sparkle returning to her eyes. "Although a hot tub might not be the best place for swimming lessons."

Luke grinned devilishly. "I'm sure there are plenty of things I can teach her in there."

Erin felt her heart skip a beat with his words. Jenna gave her a knowing smile, and flustered, she pulled her stethoscope out of the medical bag on the floor. "I need to check you over, Jen."

"No you don't. I'm fine now."

"I'll be the judge of that." Erin placed the buds of the stethoscope into her ears and pressed the diaphragm against Jenna's chest. Her heart rate was a little fast, but the rhythm was regular, with otherwise normal heart sounds. Then she listened to her lungs and heard the air move smoothly in and out. No rattling or wheezing anywhere.

Jenna grinned, watching Erin hang the stethoscope around her neck. "Do you realize, after all the years we've known each other, this is the first time I've actually seen you with a stethoscope? I always imagined you doing your job in scrubs, not in a swimsuit."

Erin laughed shortly. "I never imagined myself doing anything in a swimsuit." She took a blood pressure monitor out of her bag and wrapped the cuff around Jenna's arm, checking her pressure. "It's 90 over 54. That's too low," she said with a frown.

"Oh, blame it on the morphine," Jenna responded mildly.

Erin removed the cuff and packed her equipment back into the bag. "You still need to rest. And I'm not going to let you get off this couch for the rest of the day. That's an order."

Jenna opened her mouth to object, but Erin cut her off before she could start. "I know you don't want me to be your doctor, but just humor me once in a while, okay?" She smiled ruefully. "It's about the only thing I'm any good at, after all."

"I will on one condition," Jenna said.

Erin groaned. "Your conditions have gotten us both into trouble so far."

"Everything's gone rather swimmingly, if you ask me," Jenna quipped. Then she touched Erin's arm, and her expression sobered. "I'd like you to talk to Luke's dad about picking up an ER shift here and there. I think it would be good for you."

"I didn't take another job in Boston because I needed a break, Jen."

"You were planning to take a break for a few weeks, not months. And this would be a complete change of pace from Boston. You'll get a chance to experience a small town ER for the first time. I think it would at least be interesting."

Erin reluctantly smiled. "Are you trying to get rid of me already?"

"No, I just want you to be happy. And if all you can do is check my blood pressure once in a while or listen to my lungs, you won't be. I know you, Erin. You need medicine as much as it needs you."

"I'm sure the shifts would be long. Even if I would only fill in here and there I don't want to leave you alone for extended periods of time like that."

"I'll stay with her when I can," Luke offered. "And we'll make sure someone else is available otherwise. There are plenty of people who'd be willing to help."

Erin sighed. "Okay, fine." She turned to face Luke—and then wished she hadn't. She'd forgotten he was still only in his swim trunks. And now she was at eye level with his groin. She blinked, forgetting what she was about to say. "I, ah…Will your dad be around Monday?"

Luke misinterpreted the pained expression on her face. "Why don't you think it over a little more first, Erin? And if you're still interested, you can talk to my dad about it after church tomorrow. Jenna said you were going with her, so we'll look for you there."

Erin tried to ignore the little thrill that went through her at the thought of seeing Luke again so soon. "As long as Jenna is feeling up to it." She turned back to her friend, and a slight smile curved her lips. "Now I have a condition for you, Jenna Godfrey. If you don't do everything I tell you to for the rest of the day, we won't go to church tomorrow."

"Okay, Dr. Pryce, I'll follow your orders," Jenna conceded.

"I'm going to head upstairs and change," Luke said, giving Erin's shoulder one last squeeze before he left.

Jenna laughed softly. "One question has been answered today: There is definitely some serious chemistry between you and Luke. The sparks I've seen flying should have set this house on fire by now."

Erin smiled weakly in response, smoothing the blanket out over Jenna. "Yes, there's a whole lot of chemistry. But I just don't see how it could possibly work out."

Jenna covered her hand. "Confucius once said, 'Life is really simple, but we insist on making it complicated.' Don't overthink this, Erin. Just let it happen."

Erin sighed in frustration. "But what if I can't get past my inhibitions, Jen? They've destroyed every relationship I've been in, including my marriage. I'm sure Peter's infidelity was just the end result. Even if I'd gotten pregnant it probably would have happened eventually anyway. There was so much of myself I never gave him, either emotionally or physically. And I don't want to make the same mistakes with Luke. I feel things for him that I've definitely never felt before, and we connect on so many levels. But knowing me, there's still a really good chance I'll screw things up, especially…well, especially the sex part."

"You sound more comfortable saying the word, at least."

"I need to do a whole lot more than say the word." Erin smiled wryly, remembering their conversation yesterday. "Maybe I should get a vibrator. It would at least be a start—a jump start with a handheld power tool." As soon as she said it they both burst out laughing.

"What's so funny?" Luke asked, walking back into the room.

Erin's eyes widened, and she continued to look down at Jenna, not daring to turn her head.

Jenna grinned. "We were just talking about how to jump start Erin's car."

"*Jenna*," Erin whispered, though she couldn't help but smile at the mischievous expression on her friend's face.

Luke sat down on the arm of the couch. "Is something wrong with your battery, Erin?"

Trying not to laugh, Jenna answered for her. "Oh, I think her car just needs a really good tune-up, that's all." Then she gave Erin another impish grin, and before long they were both choking back laughter.

Luke eyed them with a raised brow. "It might be funny to the two of you, but in my experience women often don't think hard enough about taking care of their vehicles. No offense, but guys usually pay more attention to theirs. A woman tends to forget about things like her battery, and then she ends up stranded somewhere. I've seen it happen more times than I can count. The good thing is, they make these portable jump starters now that are handy to keep in your vehicle—"

Both women started laughing hysterically before he could finish, and he slowly shook his head. "I'm obviously missing something here."

"Luke…Dear Luke," Jenna said between laughs, wiping tears from her eyes.

"I think I have enough room—for one of those—in my trunk now," Erin managed to get out, and they laughed even harder.

"Oh, Erin," Jenna said after a while. "I don't think I've ever laughed this hard in my life."

Erin smiled down at her. "You're forgetting about that time we were in Virginia and I was attacked by an ostrich. I think you laughed just as hard that time."

"How do you get attacked by an ostrich in Virginia?" Luke asked curiously.

"Call yourself Erin Pryce," Jenna said with another laugh.

Erin finally glanced back at Luke and saw he'd changed into a T-shirt and jeans. But when that inquisitive blue gaze collided with hers she felt the heat of a blush creep over her cheeks. "We went to a drive-thru zoo there, and an ostrich put its head through the open window while I was driving. It scared me to death, and I ended up swerving off the road and almost hit a buffalo."

"I still say it was trying to kiss you, not peck your eyes out," Jenna said, breaking into more helpless laughter.

"Okay, you need to settle down, my friend, before you overexert yourself with laughter this time," Erin told her. "And you haven't had enough to drink. I'll go make you a glass of chocolate milk since we need to get more calories into you, too." She also needed to make a quick escape before Luke asked any more questions about her battery.

She headed to the kitchen, contemplating what she

would say if he brought that up again. She could just imagine him offering to pop her hood and check things out. Jenna would probably have a lot to say about that.

After making the chocolate milk, Erin returned to the living room and saw that Luke was giving Jenna a hug goodbye. It meant she didn't have to worry about him asking any more questions that would make her blush, but she wasn't as relieved as she thought she would be. In fact, she wasn't relieved at all.

Luke stood up and turned to face her, sensing she was there even before he saw her. "I know you want to make sure Jenna gets some rest—we both do—so I think I'll head back to the station. I still have a few loose ends to tie up." His eyes dropped to her swimsuit-clad body. The robe she wore over it gaped open temptingly, and he silently groaned. The first thing he was going to do was stop at home and take a cold shower.

But he couldn't resist the urge to torture himself a little more anyway, so he closed the distance between them and pulled her against him, whispering into her ear, "I'll see you tomorrow, Erin." Then he pressed a kiss on her cheek, letting his lips linger there, longing to taste more of her. *Another time*, he reminded himself, and reluctantly released her. For now he needed to take a really long, cold shower.

Erin watched him leave, lightly touching the spot on her cheek where he'd kissed her. She'd come back to this town for Jenna and starting a relationship had been the last thing on her mind. But Luke had lured her in too far, and now she didn't want to get out. She really hoped she could learn how to swim.

CHAPTER

8

She did believe. Deep down, she'd always believed. Erin came to that conclusion as she sat next to Jenna in the pew at St. Mary's Church. She remembered sitting there as a child and always staring straight ahead at the priest, not daring to look away for fear of being punished. Yet she would never hear anything. She'd always found better places to go in her mind during those long Sunday services.

This time she was present in mind as well as in body, though. She listened to the priest, but also let her eyes wander around the inside of the church. All the windows were made of stained glass: beautiful, colorful, intricately designed works of art that ran the entire length of both side walls, gleaming brightly in the morning light. And the high, sloping cathedral ceiling was just as awe-inspiring with its elaborate architectural design and ornate decorations. The ceiling also provided an incredible sense of spaciousness within the church, a hint of the infinity beyond.

She no longer felt the oppressive burden on her soul, the heavy weight of condemnation that had always filled her when she'd been inside the church before. Now she wanted to believe in God, she needed to believe. Not in the dark God her grandparents had worshipped—that stern, unforgiving, humorless God who allowed bad things to happen to good people—but in the God of hope, love, and peace, the God who was the shining light at the end of the dark tunnel of life. Jenna's God.

She glanced at Jenna. There was no one she knew who'd been through more hell than this beautiful, wise, warm-hearted woman who refused to stop loving, who smiled through the pain and lived every moment with joyful gratitude anyway, even now as she was dying.

The thought struck Erin then that maybe there was no other hell than this. Maybe it was all right here on Earth, even if it was a beautiful hell at times. But the only thing that could make it beautiful was to love. And to remember that Heaven wasn't too far away.

The church service ended, and they followed the stream of parishioners toward the church lobby. They'd arrived just as Mass was about to begin, so there hadn't been time to meet up with Luke and his parents beforehand.

"Was the torture as bad as you thought it would be?" Jenna asked as they waited for them in the lobby.

"It was surprisingly no torture at all," Erin responded. "In fact, I'm glad I came. It was an entirely different experience being here with you."

A teasing grin crossed Jenna's face. "Does that mean you'll come back next Sunday?"

"I knew that was coming," Erin said with a chuckle. "And yes, I'll—"

"Hey, you."

Erin jumped as those words were spoken from behind

her, close to her ear. She turned and saw Luke standing there, looking stylish and more attractive than ever in a suit and tie. And her heart leapt as it did every time she was near him. "Hi, you," she softly returned.

He leaned toward her, and for a heart-stopping moment she thought he was going to kiss her right there in the church lobby. But he brushed past her face and dropped his head lower until he was just a breath away from her neck. Then he inhaled for a second before straightening up. "You smell amazing," he said with a slightly devilish smile. "Just like you look."

Erin could only stare at him, speechless yet again. He shook her, right to the foundation of her soul. How he managed to do it was utterly beyond her. But he did it so effortlessly.

Jenna gave her a subtle nudge, telling Luke, "I think Erin would agree with me in saying that you clean up very nicely yourself."

Luke affectionately squeezed Jenna's arm. "I see you're recovering well."

"Yep, good as new, and ready for round two in the pond whenever you are."

"No," Luke and Erin said simultaneously.

Luke grinned at her. "One of these times I'm going to say—"

"Jinx," she finished with him, and they all started laughing.

Luke's parents walked up to them a moment later, and his father hugged Erin warmly. "It's good to see you after all these years, Erin."

"You too, Dr. Mathis." Erin guessed he was in his early sixties now. His previously dark brown hair was peppered with gray, but he still had the same boyishly handsome face as his son, with a few more laugh lines around the eyes.

"Please, call me Greg," he said. "And this is my wife, Joanne."

Erin looked into a mirror image of Luke's azure blue eyes as she shook his mother's hand and they exchanged pleasantries. Joanne was attractive, with mahogany brown hair that was elegantly cut in a long bob around her face, and she had a general air of sophistication about her. But there was also a kindness in her eyes and in her smile that softened the sharpness of her style, and Erin liked her immediately.

Greg and Joanne greeted Jenna, and while they were talking, Luke moved closer to Erin and softly said, "I told my dad your story about the missing donut right before Mass started. And when Father Burnett announced the bake sale next month, it took everything we had not to laugh."

"Was that all the coughing and choking I heard?" Erin asked in amusement. "I thought maybe I needed to give someone the Heimlich maneuver."

Luke chuckled, whispering into her ear, "You still can if you want. I'd be happy to volunteer. Or for any other maneuver you want to try on me."

Erin looked up into his heated blue gaze, and a nervous fluttering started in her chest. He was outright flirting with her again, and she'd never been good at that sort of thing. Not that she'd ever really tried—much less attempted any of the maneuvers he probably had in mind. And now they were inside a church of all places. She had no idea how to respond.

"Why don't we all head over to the Corner Café?" Greg asked, saving her from her ineptitude. "Luke tells me you might be interested in working some ER shifts, Erin. We can talk about that over lunch."

"If Jenna is up to it," she said uncertainly, turning to her friend.

"Yes, I would love to go," Jenna responded with an enthusiastic smile.

"All right then, we'll see you at the café," Erin told Greg. She could feel Luke's eyes on her the whole time, but she made a conscious effort not to look at him, so far out of her element with the man she didn't know what to do.

"Luke, you're coming too, aren't you?" Jenna asked.

"Yeah, that sounds good. I'll meet you all there."

Luke glanced at Erin as they left the church, trying to catch her gaze, but she continued to ignore him. And with a sinking feeling he wondered if he'd gone too far with his comments a moment ago. Maybe this amazing connection he felt with her was mostly in his mind. Maybe he was wrong in thinking there was anything brewing between them at all. He suddenly felt like that awkward, insecure teenager again, not knowing what to say to her, unsure how to act around her. Where she was concerned, he was clueless.

"JEN, THIS IS BEAUTIFUL."

Erin stood in front of a painting with a poem overlying it that hung on the far wall of the small café. It was another watercolor, this one of an elderly man and woman sitting at a table in the café, sharing a secret smile. Jenna's name was printed at the bottom of the painting, and Adam had scrawled his own in the corner, but Erin recognized his art style as soon as she saw it, and the poetry as soon as she started reading.

A Moment at the Corner Café

That cute old couple comes to the Corner Café,
   Walking hand in hand almost every day.
   They move along at a slow, unhurried pace,
While around them the younger generations race.

He holds the door open with a twinkle in his eye,
   And she conveys her thanks with a lovely old smile.
   Then they sit at a table by the window together,
A delightful display of rare antique treasures.

They're long past worrying about a watch or a clock;
   They simply take pleasure in the moments they've got.
   But for those who look closely it's clear to see,
They have more than a moment, but all of eternity.

—Jenna Godfrey

"Adam and I did this one together last year. The owners of the café helped our school out with a fundraiser, so we made it for them," Jenna said, standing alongside Erin. "I wrote the poem years ago. It was inspired by a lovely old couple who used to come in here all the time. They've both passed away since then. I guess they found their eternity."

Erin thought of Jenna and Adam together as she looked at the couple in the painting. This would be the only place they would get to grow old together, to share their own eternity. "Are you sorry you fell in love with him?" she asked.

"No, I'm not," Jenna said, turning to her. "As Tennyson would say, 'Tis better to have loved and lost than never to have loved at all.' Though I suppose if my mind had any say in the matter I would have chosen differently. But love is a choice the heart makes after all. And not even the strongest mind can withstand the most stubborn heart." She smiled ruefully. "Not that I have the strongest mind, as much as I do admire Einstein."

"I love your mind. And I'm sure Einstein would agree with that."

"We'll see. I have every intention of meeting him one of these days. It will no doubt be a very enlightening conversation."

Erin was still amazed at how Jenna could say something like that with such serenity, and even a touch of humor. She had a feeling her friend was going to help her through these next months more than the other way around. Her eyes misted with tears, but she attempted a smile. "I'm sure he's going to fall in love with you. And who knows? You might end up ditching Thoreau."

Jenna laughed softly. "Having to choose between two such great minds would present quite a dilemma indeed. But I'm sure we'll all get along just fine." She gave Erin's arm an affectionate squeeze. "And I love your mind too, by the way. You're without a doubt the smartest person I really do know."

"Then you admire a mind with a lot of imperfections."

"Confucius would say, 'Better a diamond with a flaw than a pebble without.' And every mind has flaws of some sort. I'm sure Einstein would agree with that, too."

"Well, I'd say mine are definitely multifaceted."

Erin heard the jingle of the café door opening as she spoke, and knew without even looking that Luke had just walked in. It was like he could touch her skin with his eyes. She turned her head and their gazes met across the room. Jenna was right. The heart certainly had a mind of its own, and hers never failed to do crazy things when he was nearby.

He started walking over to them, and she saw the questions in his eyes as he got closer. She knew what he was asking without him having to say a word. He wanted to know what was going on in her head. They needed to talk. Alone. She thought about the last time they'd been alone together, when he'd almost kissed her, and the fluttering in her chest went wild.

Erin didn't exactly know what she was going to say to him. On the way to the café she told Jenna what had happened in the church lobby, and once her friend stopped laughing, she'd repeated her quote from Confucius: *"'Life is really simple, but we insist on making it complicated.' So stop worrying about it. Just laugh and love instead, and you'll find out how simple life really is."*

When he reached them, Luke glanced up at the painting and smiled at Jenna. "I see the town poet is here with her poetry. Are you signing autographs?"

Jenna snorted a laugh. "I'm hardly the town poet, Luke. And since nobody's bound to ask for my autograph, I think I'll go sit and chat with your parents. I see they found a table." She grinned impishly at Erin. "I'll leave the two of you to contemplate the décor here—or anything else that catches your fancy." And with a wink she slowly walked away.

Erin tentatively faced Luke, who was now regarding her with the same questioning look as before. Once again, she had a hard time putting two words together in her mind when it took all her effort just to keep from drowning in the blue of his eyes. But she finally managed to get out, "Luke—"

"Erin—" he said at the same time, and they laughed, breaking some of the tension between them.

"Ladies first," he told her.

Nerves got the best of her, and she couldn't say what she wanted to. "No, you go ahead."

Luke took her hand lightly in his. "Erin, I was wondering if maybe I could—"

"Janey Mac! If me old eyes don't deceive me, it's Erin Harris!"

Erin turned in surprise, remembering well that voice with the melodic Irish lilt. And a thrill of pleasure went through her. "Dr. O'Reilly!"

Nolan O'Reilly smiled at her in delight. "Erin. Erin go bragh! As pretty as ever, like the land I was born in, with eyes just as green." He enveloped her in an enthusiastic hug. "And I think it's time ye call me Nolan, lass." He held her at arm's length for a moment, shaking his head. "My, how the time has flown by. It feels like just yesterday ye went off to Harvard to become a doctor yerself. And now here ye are back again. It's wonderful to see ye, Erin. Welcome home!"

"Thank you, Dr.—Nolan," she corrected herself. "It's good to see you again too."

Nolan greeted Luke, and Erin continued to happily drink in the sight of the man who'd been her idol for so many years. His blue eyes were as bright as ever, and he still had the same thick, white hair. His face had aged some in the decade and a half since she'd last seen him, but time had been kind overall, and he wore his seventy years well.

"Luke told me you retired from practice," Erin said.

"Och, I did. Retired but not tired, and now with perhaps a little too much time on me hands. A dangerous combination to be sure—as Colin will attest to. We don't exactly see eye to eye on the definition of retired." He chuckled. "But I amn't quite ready for the rockin' chair yet, though he has threatened to tie me down to one a few times."

Erin smiled at him teasingly. "And to think, you used to talk nonstop about how much you were looking forward to Colin coming home for good."

"I did mention that once or twice, didn't I?" Nolan chuckled again. "But there are no unmixed blessins' in life, as we Irish like to say. And aside from the whole rockin' chair business, it's been a real joy havin' him home. I wish he were here now so ye could finally meet him, but he's over at the hospital reducin' the world by one appendix as we speak. And Sophia's still at church, organizin' the summer bake sale."

Luke gave Erin a grin. "I think you and Jenna should help out with that."

"And I'm sure you'd want me to make donuts," she returned dryly. "But I suppose, it would be a crime if there weren't any."

"Yes, it would be." Luke's grin turned devilish. "And then I'd have to put you in handcuffs."

There it was, the flirting again. "Well, I have no idea how to make a donut, so that's bound to happen," Erin said, trying to keep her voice steady, though her nerves certainly weren't. "I hope you won't get too rough with me, Detective. I've never been in handcuffs before."

She watched the smile disappear from Luke's face and his jaw sag open a little. He stood there staring at her, dumbstruck, and she had to bite her lip to keep from laughing. She just might get used to this whole flirting thing after all.

"I see the two of ye know each other," Nolan said with a look of amused speculation in his eyes that reminded Erin of Jenna.

"Are you here by yourself?" she asked him.

"I am. I thought I'd stop in and have a bite to eat before I take me grandson, Sean, out for a drivin' lesson." A wry smile crossed his face. "I'm hopin' the food is especially good today because it may be me last meal."

"You should have lunch with us—especially if it's your last meal," Erin facetiously responded. "And you can tell me all about this grandson of yours before he takes *you* out."

"Ah, a lass after me own humor," Nolan laughed. "And that would be lovely, Erin. I hadn't realized until now how much I've missed our little talks. A few cards and texts here and there just aren't the same." He turned to Luke for approval. "I don't want to be a fly in the ointment, though."

"No, of course not," Luke told him, motioning to their table. "We're here with my parents and Jenna, so come join the party." His conversation with Erin would just have to wait until later, when he could catch her alone. At least she'd given him a glimmer of hope.

Nolan looked over at Jenna and softly sighed. "Such a dear girl. She comes to visit the nursin' home all the time, and the residents adore her. She always brings a special kind of sunshine with her, even on the gloomiest day. It saddens me somethin' fierce that she's got cancer."

Erin nodded, swallowing a lump in her throat. "Yes, me too."

Nolan patted her arm. "Forgive me for turnin' so heavy-hearted. We should never forget that all will be set right in the end. And if it isn't right, it isn't the end." His usual radiant smile returned, chasing away the clouds that had gathered on his brow, and he led them over to the table, announcing, "Lunch is on me—if ye're all willin' to put up with a crass old Irishman."

"Crass is an awful big word for an Irishman," Greg quipped. "Did you mean to say 'ass' instead?"

"Greg, really," Joanne said, though she couldn't hide a smile.

"If oid meant arse, oid have said arse," Nolan answered in an especially thick Irish brogue, his blue eyes twinkling with merriment.

Greg chuckled. "Fair enough, Nolan. But 'arse' or 'ass,' you can only park yours here if I pay for lunch."

Greg and Nolan continued their friendly argument over who was paying while Erin sat down next to Jenna. Luke took a seat across from them, joining the conversation with the other two men.

"So, did anything interesting come up over there?" Jenna softly asked Erin.

"Yes," she whispered back, grinning helplessly when she thought of her conversation with Luke. "I'll tell you about it later."

Lunch was an enjoyable affair, with plenty of lively conversation and laughter. Erin had attended many dinner parties in Boston over the years, especially after she'd married Peter, who came from a wealthy and socially prominent family in Boston. But she'd never quite been able to fit into that world, no matter how hard she'd tried. And when someone would invariably ask a question about her past, she'd hated telling her well-rehearsed lies. With this group she didn't have to pretend to be someone she wasn't, though, and the weight it lifted from her shoulders left her feeling unexpectedly at ease—even with Joanne, who knew the least about her. In fact, Erin felt a familiarity with Luke's mother that was hard to explain. Joanne and her son definitely had more in common than just the color of their eyes.

Her own eyes strayed to Luke again, as they always seemed to do when she was around him. She watched, entranced, as he slid a forkful of pasta into his mouth. He glanced up, feeling her gaze on him, and she dropped her eyes back to her plate in embarrassment, hastily taking a bite of her sandwich. She really was just as bad as that twenty-year-old paramedic who'd looked at him with such adoration the other day.

Much to her relief, Nolan started talking to Luke just then. But as she put her sandwich down, Jenna leaned closer to her and whispered, "You and Luke look like you want to eat lunch straight out of each other's mouths."

"Jenna!" Erin felt her face get hot. Now it was official—she was worse than the paramedic.

Her friend smothered a laugh. "Blame it on the morphine."

"Erin, would you be interested in taking a tour of the hospital?" Greg asked. "A lot has changed since you left. And you can see what you'd be dealing with in the ER." He grinned. "We're a little different here than Boston."

"Yes, I'd like that," Erin said, covering the remnants of her sandwich with a napkin.

"How about this evening? It sounds like the ER has been pretty quiet all weekend, so tonight would probably be a good time to go."

Erin agreed, and they firmed up the details of their meeting. "What happened that you're so short-staffed right now?" she asked.

"Two of our prior doctors were a married couple, and they decided to take jobs in Madison. That's one of the difficulties in staffing a small town ER like this. Some like the slower pace, and some find they don't. We're not typically part of the knife and gun club, as you've been in Boston—although you seem to have brought it here with you."

"Remember now, you're a white cloud," Luke teased.

Erin sent him a wry smile. "How could I forget after the way you reminded me yesterday?"

"I'll have to keep bringing you more of those reminders," he said in the same teasing tone. "Just to make sure you always have plenty on hand."

"My cup—or I should say my bowl—will be overflowing with your generosity," she returned with a grin.

Luke grinned back. "Like I said before, don't use it up too fast. That'll keep you in the clear." Then he gave her the devilish version of his grin again. "I wouldn't want you to have to stick a plunger into your bowl. They can be dangerous."

Erin couldn't help but laugh. "I have no rebuttal for that."

Greg glanced between them with a bemused smile and told Erin, "By the way, you did a nice job treating that boy with the pneumothorax. Colin was quite impressed, and that's not easy to do—believe me." He chuckled. "And now he wants me to do everything short of kidnapping to keep you here for good. But it goes without saying, I would love to see that happen. In fact, Chase McKellar, one of our ER docs, should be working tonight, and maybe he can help us convince you to stay. He grew up on a dairy farm near Madison, but lived in Chicago for a while. You'll probably find his perspective especially interesting."

"Along with just about every other woman in town," Jenna quipped. "He's very good-looking, not to mention single. But from what I hear, he doesn't socialize much."

Greg lifted a brow in his wife's direction. "So are you in the majority who find his 'perspective' interesting?"

"Well, I used to be a social worker," Joanne deadpanned. "I've learned to take everyone's perspective into consideration."

Jenna and Nolan promptly broke into laughter, while Greg shook his head—though not without a glint of humor in his eyes—and turned back to Erin. "In any case, Chase took the job here because he felt like he was getting burned out in Chicago. Unlike the two who left, he discovered the big-city way of life wasn't for him. And everything seems to be working out well so far—except for some of the women in town, I gather."

Erin smiled half-heartedly at his jest, feeling a little guilty that they hoped she'd also stay. But then the conversation turned to other subjects and she was able to relax again. Until she realized she had another problem. A much bigger problem at the moment.

"Jenna," she whispered uneasily when everyone else was engaged in other conversations. "What's the bathroom like here?"

Concern immediately filled Jenna's eyes. "Oh…I think I'd better go with you."

They excused themselves, and Erin silently cursed herself for being so absent-minded this morning and forgetting to use the bathroom before they left the house. She was usually so careful about that, always fearful of exactly this scenario. Today wasn't the first time she'd been caught in it.

Jenna led her around a corner to the bathroom, and Erin hesitantly opened the door—and blanched. There was a single toilet in there, and the lighting was dim. No stalls. No windows. It was the smallest bathroom she'd ever seen. And she was severely claustrophobic.

She quickly closed the door and leaned against the wall, dizzy at the very thought of locking herself in there. "Such a simple, stupid thing. It would take me a minute and I'd be done." Humiliation and despair filled her eyes as she spoke. "But I can't do it."

"Let's go home, Erin," Jenna softly urged.

"No. You've been enjoying yourself. I'll make some excuse about running an errand, then come back."

"We were pretty much done here anyway." Jenna touched Erin's arm sympathetically. "Please. Let's go."

After a brief hesitation, Erin nodded and followed her back to the table.

"Lunch was wonderful, but we have to get going," Jenna announced.

Luke didn't miss the change in their demeanor, especially Erin's. Though she tried to hide it, he could tell she was upset about something. And with worry furrowing his brows, he turned his attention back to Jenna. "Are you feeling okay?"

"Yes, I'm fine," she responded, waving off the question. "Just a little tired."

Luke stood up. "I'll walk you out—"

"No, please don't," Jenna interrupted. "There's no need."

Erin was beyond mortified that everyone looked so concerned about Jenna. And with a hasty goodbye to the group, she made a beeline for the door, desperate to get out.

Luke watched in confusion as they exited the café. Everything had seemed fine just moments ago, and now Erin was back to acting as uncomfortable and distant as she had when they'd left church.

With an inward sigh he sat down again, completely disheartened.

CHAPTER

9

"Not what you're used to, I know."

Erin turned from her survey of the ER and looked up at Chase McKellar. Jenna was right, he was good-looking. He was probably a few years older than her, with finely chiseled features, golden blond hair, and bright, baby blue eyes. And he was very tall. He looked like he came straight out of a magazine ad.

"No, it's not what I'm used to at all." Erin glanced around her again. Two empty trauma bays faced a central workstation, and there were a handful of smaller rooms down the hallway on either side, most of which were also vacant. She was used to the constant flurry of activity at Boston General, with its forty-five ER beds that were rarely empty. Even at the slowest times it was never this quiet.

"Oh God, she's coming! She's coming *now!*"

The cry came as the main ER doors burst open and a nurse pushed a very pregnant patient through them in a wheelchair. The woman's face was contorted with the pain of a contraction, and she continued to moan as she was rolled toward them, clutching the arms of the wheelchair in a death grip.

"Dr. McKellar, she's about to deliver," the nurse said. "I didn't think we could make it up to the OB floor."

Chase immediately turned to the unit clerk sitting at the desk behind them. "Lois, call OB and let them know what's going on. We'll take her to the GYN room in the meantime." Then he and the nurse rushed down the hallway with the patient.

Erin looked at Greg Mathis, who'd been standing with her and Chase. "Is there an OB provider here right now?"

"Probably not. Our family docs do most of the deliveries, and Colin and I back them up for C-sections. I doubt anyone would be here this late unless there happened to be another woman in active labor."

"The on-call doctor isn't upstairs," Lois said as she got off the phone. "I'll page him right away. And there aren't any postpartum patients on the floor tonight either, so I'll have to call in the OB nurse too. But I know she can be here in less than ten minutes."

Greg smiled at Erin. "It looks like things just got busy. Shall we lend a hand?"

"Of course," she said, hurrying with him down to the GYN room.

The nurse had already gotten the woman into a hospital gown and was helping her up onto the bed. Sweat matted the patient's hair, and she was breathing in short, rapid bursts. "I'm finally—getting—a girl," she said between breaths. "Please—let her be—okay."

"We will," Chase reassured her, now wearing a sterile gown, gloves, and mask.

"Lois is calling the OB staff in," Greg said. "We'll stay

and help until they get here."

Chase nodded. "That would be great. Thanks." And while Greg and Erin quickly put on sterile attire of their own, he introduced them to the patient.

"Have there been any problems with her pregnancy?" Erin asked.

"No," Chase responded. "She's right at forty weeks and just saw her OB doctor Friday. She was three centimeters dilated then, so they had planned on an induction tomorrow. It's her fourth baby, and the other three were all normal vaginal deliveries." He turned back to the patient after the nurse placed her feet into the stirrups, and examined her to check the baby's position. "She's crowning."

No sooner did he say that than the woman let out a piercing cry as another contraction came, and the baby's head emerged. Chase made sure the umbilical cord wasn't wrapped around her neck, then waited for the rest of the body to slide out. It didn't.

"I need you to push hard," he told the woman, grasping the baby's head and applying gentle traction to finish the delivery.

But the baby wouldn't move. Her head retracted back against her mother and her reddened cheeks puffed out. It was the classic turtle sign. And for a second Chase froze.

"She has a shoulder dystocia," Erin said, immediately coming around to the far side of the bed. It was something she'd dealt with more than once during her training. The baby's anterior shoulder was stuck behind the mother's pubic bone, keeping her lodged in the tight space of the birth canal. As a result, the umbilical cord was being squeezed shut, so blood couldn't return to her body from the placenta, depriving her of oxygen. And she wouldn't be able to breath on her own until the delivery was complete. Even though her head was out, she was suffocating.

Erin looked up at the clock. They had five minutes to free her before irreversible brain damage began to set in, with death not far behind.

She quickly let the patient know what was going on, then turned to the nurse across from her. "We need to push her legs back against her body, with her knees flexed. That will increase the space in the birth canal and hopefully dislodge the baby's shoulder. And watch the clock. Call out the time after each minute has passed."

Erin glanced at Greg, who'd lost a little color in his own face as he stood there regarding the infant's reddish-purple one. "Can you push on her abdomen with your fist clenched, just above the pubic bone on my side? The baby is facing the other way, so if you push downward and somewhat laterally in that direction it can help force the shoulder out."

Greg nodded and came over to stand beside her, pressing his fist down low into the woman's protuberant belly.

Erin turned back to Chase for further direction, and he gave her an appreciative look, saying, "We'll go all out with the next contraction."

The woman uttered an anguished moan as it came. Erin and the nurse pushed her flexed knees as far back as they could, while Greg applied downward pressure on her abdomen. Chase pulled on the baby's head at the same time, though not with too much force. Damage to the brachial plexus, the nerves that ran through the neck and controlled her arms, was a common thing to have happen in these cases, and doctors were often sued for it—by people who had never stood where he stood now.

The baby didn't budge.

"It's been one minute," the nurse announced.

"Let's get her on her hands and knees," Chase said. "That might increase the pelvic diameter enough to free the shoulder."

They rolled the woman over, and with the next contraction he gently pulled on the baby's head again, with no luck.

"I'll try to rotate the posterior shoulder." Chase quickly slid the fingers of his left hand into the part of the birth canal closest to the rectum and pushed against the back of the baby's shoulder.

But she still wouldn't budge.

He then tried to work his right hand in on the opposite side to reach the stuck anterior shoulder. But after a moment he shook his head, grimacing. "I can't get in."

"Two minutes have gone by."

"I—I need to lay down," the woman said.

They turned her back over just as the obstetrical nurse walked in and observed the scene with wide-eyed surprise.

"Get the Broselow bag," Chase told her. It contained all the supplies they would need to resuscitate the baby if it came to that. "And bring me 10 mls of 1% lidocaine and sterile scissors. I need to cut an episiotomy so I can get in there and turn the baby."

He looked somberly at Greg. "We should start preparing for an emergency C-section." If there was no other way to get the baby out they would have to try pushing her back up into the uterus as a last resort, and then take the mother to the OR for a C-section. It was called the Zavanelli maneuver—and carried a high risk of injury to both of them.

"I'll call in the OR crew," Greg said, making a beeline for the door.

"I can do the internal rotation maneuvers," Erin offered. "I have smaller hands."

Chase nodded, switching positions with her. "Let's get this baby out now, Erin."

"We're at three minutes," the nurse announced.

"Is she going to be okay?" the mother cried, trying to lift herself up to see what was happening. But she moaned and fell back when another contraction wracked her body.

"She's just being a little more stubborn than most, but we'll get her out," Erin said, squeezing the fingers of her right hand into the birth canal between the baby's neck and the mother's pubic bone. It was a tight fit, but she was able to reach the back of the stuck shoulder and push on it in a counterclockwise direction while Chase and the nurse flexed the woman's legs against her body. Chase also used his other hand to apply downward pressure on the abdomen as Greg had been doing.

But the baby remained lodged.

Erin then slid her left fingers into the bottom of the birth canal and simultaneously pushed on the front of the lower shoulder and the back of the top shoulder in an attempt to rotate the baby.

Still nothing.

"Four minutes have passed."

One minute left. Erin felt her heart start to pick up speed. *You can do this*, she told herself. *You will do this.* She'd never considered failure an option before, and she wouldn't now. In medicine she expected to succeed, had prepared to succeed. It was what had always made her especially good at her job.

"I'm going to try delivering the posterior arm," she told Chase. She'd never attempted the maneuver before, but she knew how to do it. She also knew there was a risk of breaking the baby's arm or collarbone. But at least those could heal. And she might have to break the collarbone on purpose anyway, if the posterior arm maneuver didn't work. Breaking the collarbone would reduce the width of the baby's shoulders to help get her past the mother's pubic bone. And if that failed, they would be forced to use the Zavanelli maneuver.

Erin pushed her left hand into the bottom side of the birth canal again, all the way into the woman this time, and slid it down along the baby's arm. She found the elbow, and then the forearm, gently bending the elbow and raising the forearm up against the baby's chest toward her head. There was some resistance when she attempted to pull the arm out, and she winced, afraid she was going to hear the sound of breaking bone—or worse, feel it. She held her breath as she had to pull a little harder…But suddenly it came free. She felt the rest of the body sink down slightly, and then the baby slid out and into her arms.

Erin immediately began drying her off. And a few seconds later the little girl realized she'd been born. She let out a loud wail of protest.

Erin felt her heart swell with love at the sight of the baby taking her first breath of life in her arms. And in that moment she knew without a doubt: She would have a child of her own someday. One way or another, she would make it happen. Luke was right. She was good at fighting for others, but not for herself. It had been a long time since she'd really even tried. In medicine she expected to succeed, yet in the rest of her life she expected to fail. But it was time she started fighting for that, too. Otherwise she would eventually fail at everything. She'd already been walking down that dark road for a while now. She didn't want to contemplate what might have been at the end of it.

"Is my baby okay?" the woman asked.

"Yes," Erin told her. "Dr. McKellar is just waiting to clamp the umbilical cord so more blood gets to the baby since it wasn't flowing when she was stuck. But she's doing fine."

Chase glanced up at Erin with admiration and interest in his baby blue eyes. "Yes, absolutely fine," he said.

Erin missed the innuendo as she continued to hold the newborn, watching her closely for any signs of distress. Her breathing remained unlabored, though, and her skin quickly lost its purplish hue. She was also flailing both arms around without any trouble. Either one of them could easily have been injured during the delivery.

A minute later Chase clamped and cut the cord, and the nurse wrapped the baby in a warm blanket.

"I'll bet you want your mama," Erin softly murmured, carrying the infant up to her mother. She'd stopped crying and was blinking her eyes open now, getting her first glimpse of the world.

The woman took the tiny bundle into her arms with a joyful sob and cradled her lovingly against her body. "Oh, my precious baby girl. You're finally here."

Erin smiled, even as her eyes misted with tears. "She's a stubborn one. But I guess she'll need it with three older brothers."

The woman reached out and squeezed Erin's hand. "Thank you, Doctor. You have my eternal gratitude."

"I'm just glad I was here to help," Erin said, meaning that in so many ways.

It struck her then how much she truly had to be grateful for herself. And she knew that if she was going to begin her journey back to life, gratitude was one of the things she would need to bring with her the most. And love, that was the other. Jenna was teaching her well, more than any Ivy League school possibly could in a lifetime.

There was a flurry of activity in the room after that, when the woman's family doctor arrived, followed shortly by her husband. Erin stepped back, not wanting to interfere with the happy reunion. She disposed of her wet gown and gloves and turned to leave. But Chase lightly caught hold of her arm, and she looked back at him questioningly.

"Thank you, Erin," he said. "I hope I'll see you here again soon. Maybe it'll be a little quieter next time." A sardonic chuckle escaped him. "Although I should warn you, I tend to have a bit of a black cloud."

Erin smiled, covering his hand with hers. "Think of it as a white cloud." And with that, she headed out of the room.

Greg Mathis was standing just inside the door and followed her out. "I've never been so happy to call off the surgical team," he said dryly as they started walking down the hallway. "And today might be first time I'll enjoy holding a good, strong drink in my hand more than a scalpel. I had called Colin, though, and he was on his way in to help. I figured with his experience in trauma it would be a good idea to have him here—not to mention he was the one on call. But I told him what you did in there, and he almost came in anyway, just to meet you. I think you have nerves of steel, my dear."

Erin laughed. "Coming from a surgeon that's quite a compliment." Then she remembered what had happened earlier at the café, and her expression sobered. If he knew why she and Jenna had really left he'd be saying quite different things about her nerves. In fact, he probably wouldn't even want her to work there. As it was, she was sure Luke thought she was a total head case. But she vowed those fears were no longer going to get the best of her. They were in for a fight now.

"Erin, I'd like to get you privileges here at the hospital as quickly as possible after what just happened," Greg said. "The baby seems fine now, but if she has any problems later on, even years from now, every aspect of her delivery will be analyzed for a possible lawsuit. And it wouldn't look good if one of the doctors involved wasn't credentialed here." He smiled wryly. "When I said we should lend a hand, I didn't know you were going to take me literally."

Erin couldn't muster up a smile of her own in response to the quip. Even though he was making light of it, she knew the hospital would have been put in a really bad position if she'd failed with that last maneuver. Once they were forced to use more drastic measures, the baby would probably have suffered significant brain damage by the time they got her out—if she survived at all. And then everyone would be looking for someone to blame. Which still might happen. "I'll take full responsibility if there's ever a lawsuit. I didn't think about—"

"No, you did exactly what you should have done," Greg interrupted. "And the day I worry more about being sued than saving a baby's life is the day I need to stop practicing medicine."

"I'll bring in the paperwork you need tomorrow," Erin said. "And I would like to fill in once in a while. But when—when Jenna passes, I'm planning to go back to Boston. I've lived there for the last fourteen years, and it's where I consider home now."

Greg nodded. "I understand. But if you change your mind, we'd love to have you join us permanently." He pushed the button to open the ER doors, and they walked into the central lobby of the hospital. "I'm going to run upstairs and check on a patient of mine since I'm here—before I go home and have that drink." He grinned and gave her a brief hug. "It's good to have you back, Erin."

She wished him a goodnight, then headed toward the main entrance.

"Erin!"

Chase McKellar burst through the ER doors, and Erin turned around in surprise.

"I'm glad I caught you," Chase said, walking over to her with that long stride of his. "I was wondering if you'd like to meet for a drink or two later, since we didn't get much of a chance to discuss the ER. I'll be done in an hour or so, and the Shamrock has a nice bar. It's usually a pretty low-key place to talk."

Erin was about to say no, but then stopped herself. She thought of Luke, and how her problems with intimacy had gotten in the way of every relationship she'd ever been in. It was time to take that head-on as well. The bar was at the Shamrock Inn…

A plan started to form in her mind, one that just a few days ago she would have thought insane. "Yes, I'd like that," she told him with a slow smile. "I'll meet you there."

CHAPTER

10

"Erin's not back yet?" Luke asked as Jenna let him in. "I see her car's not here."

"Ah, no…" Jenna answered, nervously twisting one of the rings on her fingers.

Luke's brows furrowed with concern. "What's wrong, Jen? Where is she?"

"I don't think she's in her right mind at the moment, Luke. She was so upset about what happened at the café. And then she called and said she'd had to help deliver a baby in the ER. I think it was all too much for her."

"Where the hell is she?" He'd come tonight because he needed to find out how Erin really felt about him—and he'd broken almost every traffic law in the book to get there as fast as possible. But he couldn't wait a minute longer. She was literally driving him out of his mind.

Jenna chewed on her lip. "I think I might have to go with Socrates on that one—'One thing only I know, and that is that I know nothing.' That is true, in a way…"

"You're not making any sense," Luke said impatiently.

"Let's start with what happened at the café. The two of you ran out of there like your pants were on fire."

"Well, in a way that was kind of true, too."

"Tell me what's going on here, Jenna." Luke wasn't sure he wanted to hear what she had to say, though. He had a bad feeling about it.

Jenna sighed. "Erin's really claustrophobic. It usually isn't a problem, except when it comes to small rooms without a window, or elevators. We've gotten a lot of exercise taking the stairs over the years, that's for sure."

"What has that got to do with the café?"

"She needed to use the bathroom, and the one there is really small, with no windows. She couldn't go in, so we left. She was pretty upset about it on the way home."

Luke stared at Jenna in astonishment. He would never have guessed…But now he was beginning to see things a little more clearly. "And you think she was upset about the baby because of her situation."

Jenna's expression turned almost as surprised as Luke's had a moment ago. "You know about that?"

"She told me yesterday."

"Really? She almost never talks about it. She hasn't been the same since all that happened."

"So what did she do, go off somewhere by herself?" Then a shocking thought occurred to Luke. "You don't think she'd hurt herself, do you?"

"I don't think so. At least not the way you mean." The lines of worry on Jenna's forehead deepened. "But then, I don't know what she's thinking right now. She didn't sound like herself on the phone, and she was so vague…"

"Where did she say she was going?"

After a pause Jenna reluctantly admitted, "To the Shamrock."

Confusion filled Luke's eyes. "Alone?"

Jenna remained silent.

Luke could tell by her expression that he wasn't going to like the answer to his next question. "Who is she with?"

"Chase McKellar," Jenna softly responded.

Luke felt like she'd just kicked him in the gut. "She's with Chase McKellar at the Shamrock *Inn*. How convenient."

"Go after her, Luke, before she does something stupid. She's not thinking straight right now."

"How am I supposed to compete with a guy like that?" he asked, unable to hide the despair in his voice. "She still bears the name of the first doctor she married. I wouldn't be surprised if she's still in love with him. And I'm sure McKellar is just her type."

"I really don't think so. And I know she has feelings for you."

"She told you that?"

"Yes. Now please go after her. Don't let her get away again without at least putting up a fight."

Luke would like to put up a fight—and knock out all of Chase McKellar's pretty teeth with his fist. But Jenna was right. He had to settle this with Erin once and for all. And if she did reject him maybe he could finally get those green eyes out of his head. "Okay, I'll go talk to her," he said, running a hand through his hair in agitation. "I'll call you later and let you know what's going on."

He turned to leave, but Jenna grabbed hold of his arm with a half-hearted smile. "Please don't do any permanent damage to Chase. The rest of the women in this town wouldn't be too happy about that. And I don't want to have to come visit you in jail."

"I can't make any promises there," he told her grimly, and headed out of the house.

Jenna eased the door closed behind him. Wesley came up and rubbed himself against her leg, and she looked down at the cat, shaking her head. "What has our friend gotten herself into this time, Wes?"

"Mrroww," the cat responded, and started to purr.

LUKE WALKED INTO THE BAR AND DINING AREA AT the Shamrock and saw no sign of Erin there—or McKellar. But he had seen her car in the parking lot. That bright yellow was hard to miss. And it could only mean one thing.

He headed out of the restaurant to the hotel lobby. Cody Winkler, one of the town's newly minted high school graduates, was standing behind the front desk.

"Hey, Detective Mathis," Cody said with a grin. "Is there a drug bust or something going down?"

Something might end up busted, and someone could definitely go down, Luke thought malevolently. "Did an Erin Pryce check in tonight?"

"I don't think so, and I've been here all night. But I'll double check." Cody looked her name up on the computer. "No, sir."

"How about a Chase McKellar?" Luke gritted out.

Cody's smile disappeared, and he quickly looked that name up as well. "Sorry, Detective Mathis. No Chase McKellar either."

"Did you see a woman come through here—blond hair, green eyes, attractive, about five foot six?"

"Yes, I remember her. She checked in a little while ago." Cody got back on the computer. "Sally Ride. Room 201." A puzzled look crossed his face. "Now that I think about it, her name sounds familiar. But she paid in cash—including a deposit since she forgot her ID—and got a room with a Jacuzzi."

Luke had heard enough. A Jacuzzi…So now Erin was going to literally test the waters with someone else. "Thanks for your help," he said, and headed out of the hotel.

He made it halfway to his truck before he stopped. Cursing softly, he told himself to keep going. It was over. But his legs wouldn't move forward another step.

"Damn you, Erin," he whispered, turning around.

He walked back into the hotel past the surprised clerk and took the stairs two at a time to the second floor. He had to finish this face to face.

ERIN SAT ON THE BED AND TOOK ANOTHER SIP OF her drink. It was her third, and she was starting to work up the nerve to do it now. Liquid courage certainly did wonders for the faint of heart. She just hoped she wasn't sorry for it later, like so many of her patients had been over the years.

She heard a knock on the door and got up to answer it, setting her nearly empty drink down on the nightstand. She'd timed that just right. But when she opened the door she blinked in surprise. There stood Luke Mathis, seething like a beast.

"Hello, Sally Ride."

Erin was glad she was a little tipsy or she probably would have fainted dead away. "Luke. How—how did you know I was here?"

"Jenna told me." Seeing her there in the flesh further inflamed his jealous rage, a rage he hadn't even known he was capable of until now. And he pushed past her into the room, his normally ironclad self-control crumbling.

Erin tentatively closed the door and followed him, stunned by this sudden and entirely unexpected permutation of events.

"Where's McKellar?" Luke demanded, glancing around the room. There was a king size bed with a black plastic bag on it to his left, and a large Jacuzzi in the far right corner. But no Chase McKellar.

Erin looked at him in confusion. "Who?"

Just as she asked the question, someone else knocked on the door.

"That must be him now," Luke said darkly. "Isn't he in for a surprise?" Then he strode back and ripped the door open.

A wide-eyed waiter stood there with a drink in his hand. "Ah, I have your order."

Erin came over to them and reached around Luke, taking the drink with a shaky smile. "That's for me, thanks." Now she was really going to need liquid courage.

Luke closed the door after the waiter left, and turned to face her. Their eyes met over the glass as she tilted it to her lips, and his desire for her burned hotter than ever. But she wasn't there for him. She wanted someone else. And so his mind completely surrendered to the jealous, lustful beast that had come to life inside him. He grabbed her arms and pinned her up against the wall. The glass flew out of her hand, its contents splashing over them, and fell to the carpet with a thump. "Where is McKellar?" he growled.

Erin could only stare up at him, shocked speechless by his behavior. And for a long moment they stood there facing each other in silence, just inches apart, with him holding her hostage against the wall. A veritable thunderstorm was brewing in the depths of his blue eyes, and she had no idea why.

Until it finally dawned on her. He thought she'd gotten a room with Chase McKellar, and he was crazy with jealousy. She felt a warmth start to fill her that had nothing to do with alcohol. "Chase is probably at home, Luke. I had a few drinks with him at the bar and left to come up here." Her eyes strayed to his lips, and she unconsciously wet her own with her tongue.

Luke was momentarily hypnotized by that tongue as it slid over her lips. And then his expression darkened even more. "Who are you meeting here then?"

Erin slowly looked up at him. "Myself."

Luke gripped her tighter, holding her gaze imprisoned in his just as completely as he held her body captive against the wall. "I want to know who he is. Tell me the truth."

Erin was especially glad for those three drinks now or she never would have been able to give it to him. "It's just me...and a vibrator."

It was his turn to blink in surprise. "What?"

"I couldn't use it at the house. Not with Jenna there." A ghost of a smile crossed Erin's face. "And apparently her mother, too."

"But why, Erin?" Luke asked, pressing nearer.

She could feel his breath on her skin now. Her eyes fell back to his lips, so close to hers, and the heat continued to spread through her. "Because of you. Me. I...I need to figure myself out—that way. In so many ways." She hesitantly met his gaze again. "I want to feel…something. I want to feel everything. I've never…" She didn't know quite how to get the words out then, even with those drinks running through her veins. "I haven't…"

Her voice trailed off completely, and Luke let go of her arms, cupping her face in his hands. "Erin," he whispered, and slowly lowered his head until his mouth hovered just over hers, nearly grazing it. He paused there, inhaling her breath and giving it back again, then finally closed that last bit of space between them, gently touching her lips with his in a tender kiss. Part of him wanted to press harder and devour her mouth right then and there. But another part of him wanted to savor the moment—a moment he'd dreamed about for most of his life and hoped to remember for the rest of it. So he reined the beast in, sampling her sweetness, wanting more but waiting. Reveling in anticipation of the repast to come…

He'd conquered her defenses. Erin knew it as soon as he kissed her. The walls surrounding her heart and soul that had seemed so impenetrable before came crashing down around her, disintegrating into dust and leaving her nowhere to hide. But she didn't want to hide anymore. "Luke," she softly pleaded against his mouth. And then she couldn't hold back a second longer. She wrapped her arms around his neck, pulling him closer, and slanted her lips hungrily over his.

Luke did devour her then, kissing her back with all the desire he'd kept pent up inside him for far too long, easing off at times to redirect his assault on her mouth, and then pressing even deeper, again and again. And Erin met him kiss for ravenous kiss, unable to get enough. She'd been starving, she realized—starving for something she'd never tasted before him.

His tongue found hers, pushing against it, then around, and she eagerly pushed back. He led, and she followed, in a feast between their mouths that turned the warmth inside her into a fever of need. He was teaching her how much she could feel, just in a kiss.

Luke finally slid his mouth off hers and skimmed his lips over the side of her face to her ear. "Let me help you find yourself, Erin," he whispered into it, and leisurely traced the ridges and rim with his tongue. Then he lightly blew on the wetness he left behind, and she grabbed hold of his shoulders, feeling her knees go weak with the dizzying pleasure of it.

"I want to help you feel everything," he murmured, blazing a path of heated kisses down her neck. "And I want to feel every part of you."

"Yes," Erin breathed. There was no longer any question of awkwardness. There was only need, a need she felt with every fiber of her being. "*Yes.*"

Luke needed no further invitation. He swiftly pulled her shirt up over her head, tossing it aside. And in the next breath he undid her bra, tugging it down and letting it fall between them to the floor.

"God, you're beautiful, Erin," he said in a voice raw with emotion, and cupped her breasts in his hands, kneading them slowly, reverently, for a moment. Then he stroked her nipples with his thumbs, circling around and over, gently coaxing them to life.

Erin's breath caught as pleasure, wild and sweet and unlike anything she'd ever known, rippled through her with every stroke, settling deep and hot inside her. She urged his head back down to hers, wanting more, and their lips met in another long, feverish kiss while his warm fingers continued to work magic on her breasts.

Luke eventually ended the kiss and lowered his mouth to the juncture of her neck and shoulder, sinking his teeth into her skin there, though not hard enough to leave a mark. And he heard her approval in the whispered moan of pleasure she let out just above his ear, the sound adding fuel to the fire of his own passion.

He gradually moved downward, brushing his lips seductively against her skin. And when he reached one of her breasts, he cradled the underside in his palm and pressed soft, teasing kisses over it, getting ever closer to her nipple. "You taste sweeter than honey," he whispered, and slowly circled her areola with the tip of his tongue. "I want to feel every part of you, but I want to taste every part of you even more."

A second later his hot, hungry mouth descended onto her hardened nipple, and Erin helplessly groaned, fisting her hands in his hair as his lips and tongue awakened sensations there that set her body on fire from her fingertips down to her toes. Then he finished the amorous assault by grasping her nipple in his teeth, lightly biting, tugging. "Luke!" she managed to get out in a strangled cry.

He moved to her other breast, making love to that one just as thoroughly, while he slid his hands down over her belly until he reached the waistband of her pants. He deftly undid the button and lowered the zipper, then plunged a hand inside. His searching fingers found the throbbing, swollen center of her need, and he gently caressed her there.

"Luke!" Erin repeated in a gasp, clenching him tightly as wave after wave of exquisite pleasure flooded her.

"You're so warm and wet," he whispered, skimming his lips back up over her skin to her mouth. He traced it sensuously with his tongue as he continued to massage her below, and she opened it wider in pleasure, moan after moan escaping from deep in her throat. Then he kissed her with renewed hunger, stroking harder, faster.

Erin tried to return the kiss, but sensation soon overwhelmed her, and she finally had to tear her lips from his and lean her head back against the wall. "Oh God, Luke!" she cried, letting go of him and bracing her hands there as well. She was held captive once again, this time by the invisible bonds of passion.

"Move against me, Erin. Dance with me," Luke softly urged, and cupped her bottom with his other hand, leading her in the dance.

Erin moved her hips to the rhythm of his demanding fingers, and the fire down low inside her burned even hotter, and hotter, until she felt ready to explode with it. "Luke… Oh God…Luke!"

"I want you, Erin," he said tightly into her ear, kissing her there again. "God, I want you so bad it hurts."

"I want you too," she groaned. "Now, Luke. Please!"

He swooped her up into his arms with the words still hanging in the air and carried her over to the bed, tossing the plastic bag sitting on it to the floor as he eased her down. Then he quickly sent the rest of her clothes to join it and all but tore off his own.

Erin's need only deepened as she watched him undress. The sight of his arousal stirred up something completely raw and elemental inside her, and after he kicked away the last of his clothes she urgently pulled him down on top of her, sliding her legs up around his hips without hesitation. He shifted over her at the same time, guiding himself to her entrance, and she closed her eyes as he slowly pushed into her, savoring the sweet sensation of his body filling hers.

"God, you feel so good, Erin." Luke dropped his head down on her shoulder, trying to rein in the pleasure that threatened to overwhelm him. And once he had control of himself again, he drew back and started thrusting into her, swiveling his hips upward to stroke the places she would feel him the most.

"Luke…" Erin clutched his back and needed no prompting to move against him this time, letting natural instinct take over as she met his thrusts, propelled by a greater need that she didn't quite understand.

"Yes…God yes, Erin, keep doing that," Luke murmured thickly, thrusting harder, faster.

Erin matched his pace, welcomed it, and was soon driving her hips up to meet his with abandon. Any remaining inhibition she had got lost in a sea of full-bodied sensation, and she let her unrestrained cries echo loudly through the room, over and over again.

Then pleasure took on an entirely new meaning. It became stronger, deeper, more exquisite than anything that had come before it. And with each thrust of his body into hers it heightened even more, and more…She felt like she was losing control of her senses. She didn't know what was happening. She didn't know what to do. "Luke!" she cried desperately, digging her fingers hard into his back. "*Luke…!*"

She was ready to come. He heard it in her voice. But there was something else in there too, so he lifted his head to look into her eyes. Pleasure was mixed with uncertainty—and fear. And in that moment he knew exactly what she'd been trying to tell him. She'd never been where he was taking her, and his heart exulted. "Just let it happen, honey," he whispered. "Let yourself go…"

And so she did. She threw her head back and let out a deep, guttural cry that came straight from her soul, arching up against him as her body convulsed and breathtaking sensations burst inside her, flooding her with a pleasure that was like nothing she'd ever imagined was possible. It soared past the boundaries of flesh and blood, taking her to a limitless place…a place where there was only sweet ecstasy.

Luke quickly followed her to that place. His own pleasure exploded violently inside him, and he uttered a moan of near anguish as he came, his body shuttering again and again in the aftermath of his release. Then he collapsed on top of her, still inside her, not ready to break the connection between their bodies, and leaned his head against hers on the bed.

Neither of them said anything for several long moments after that, the only sound in the room the heaviness of their breathing.

Erin felt herself drift gently back to earth, and turned her face into Luke's hair, catching the subtle smell of citrus and mint. She ran her hands leisurely over the muscles of his back and shoulders, loving the feel of him, the touch of his bare skin against hers, on top of her, around her, inside her. He'd kept his word. He'd helped her feel everything.

Luke finally lifted his head and looked down at her with a smile. "Sex with you is out of this world, Sally Ride."

Erin slowly smiled back. "It's the first name I thought of when I checked in, probably because Jenna and I were watching some show about astronauts last night. But it made sense. I felt like I was visiting another planet when I went into the adult entertainment store to buy the vibrator."

Luke laughed softly. "And how do you feel now?"

"Like I just took a ride to Heaven and back."

"I was on that ride with you," he whispered, and lowered his mouth to hers.

The kiss was slow and gentle, sweet and searching. It wasn't a kiss inspired by lust. It was a kiss inspired by love. And Erin knew without a doubt—she was falling in love with him. Hard. And fast.

The kiss ended and Luke eased off of her, turning to lie with his head propped up on an elbow. His eyes fell to her mouth, and he slowly ran a finger over her lips. "I'm sorry I flipped out on you earlier. The thought of McKellar here with you sent me off the deep end for a minute."

"You were very jealous, Detective Mathis," Erin teased, lightly biting his finger. "So much for 'There is no remedy for love but to love more.'"

"I see now you have no problem repeating Jenna's quotes," Luke said dryly.

"That one's pretty easy to remember. Maybe not so easy to put into practice." Erin giggled, and then laughed at herself for doing it. She'd never made such a sound in her life.

Luke smiled down at her, loving the carefree look on her face. It was a look he'd never seen before. Then it occurred to him that he might not entirely be the cause of it, and his smile faded. "How much have you had to drink, Erin?"

"You should know, Detective. You gave me a very thorough breathalyzer test." Erin let out another helpless giggle and wrapped her arms around his neck, urging his head back down to hers. "But you're more than welcome to double-check."

He wouldn't budge, though. "How much, Erin?" he repeated.

She looked up into his unwavering blue gaze and giggled. "Well, I had two at the bar, then I brought one up here that I didn't quite finish. And the last one is over there on the floor." She giggled again. "And it's also on the wall. And all over our clothes. I think it might even be in my hair." Another giggle bubbled out of her.

Luke's brows furrowed. "Erin, I don't want you to wake up with a hangover tomorrow and be sorry about what we did here tonight."

Seeing how concerned he looked, her expression sobered. "I'm not that drunk. And I promise, I won't be sorry about this tomorrow. What I feel has far more to do with you than the alcohol, believe me." She grinned. "But I'd be happy to perform any sort of sobriety test you want me to, Detective. Just don't ask me to do a handstand or a cartwheel because I would fail at those anyway—although maybe I wouldn't now. You did get my hips to do things they've never done before, either."

Luke didn't resist this time when she pulled him down. The kiss was light, tender and undemanding at first. Then it deepened as the embers of passion ignited into another full-fledged blaze between them. When they finally came up for air, he breathed, "God, you're intoxicating."

Erin rubbed her cheek against his, liking the rougher texture of his skin on hers. "Make love to me again," she whispered into his ear, and dared to run her tongue over it as he'd done to her before. "Is it even possible to do it again so soon?" She blew lightly on his ear. "I don't remember learning anything about that in medical school."

Luke groaned and slid on top of her, fully aroused. "I just found out it is from my end. We'll have to see about yours." He kissed her briefly. "But first I need you to do that sobriety test."

It was Erin's turn to groan. "What do you want me to do, Detective?"

"Just tell me something smart—like one of your doctor things."

"Hmmm. Let me think." But then he started kissing her neck, and she couldn't think at all. "You're going to have to stop that if you want me to pass," she told him with a soft laugh.

Luke lifted his head, grinning down at her. "And I really want you to pass. So tell me something that sounds smart."

Erin paused in thought. "How about the five H's and T's of cardiac arrest? It's a memory aid for the things that usually cause it."

"Yes, that sounds very smart. So what are the five H's and T's?"

"Well, the five H's are hypovolemia, which means there isn't enough fluid in the body because of severe bleeding or dehydration. Another one is hypoxia, or a low level of oxygen in the blood. And then there's hydrogen. Too much hydrogen makes the body dangerously acidic, and can be caused by things like sepsis, or kidney failure, or—mmm…" He'd lowered his mouth back down to her neck, and she felt him stroke her throbbing pulse with his tongue. Any other thought died in her head.

"Go on," Luke said, continuing his sensual exploration of her neck. He didn't tell her she'd already passed the test with flying colors. He was just going to play with her now.

"You're not being fair, Detective," Erin murmured, even as she slid her hands into his hair and pulled him closer. "I hope this isn't how you conduct all your sobriety tests."

"No. This is a very unique situation." Luke dropped one last kiss on her neck, then gave her a devilish smile.

"Now where were you? I think you told me three of the H's. So you're thirty percent of the way there." He had her legs pinned between his, and rubbed his thick shaft slowly, erotically between her thighs.

Erin moved restlessly under him, need pulsing wildly inside her. "Luke, please," she begged.

"What are the last two H's?"

She groaned, unable to recall either one of them. "I normally know this stuff cold."

Luke's devilish smile widened. "I don't think you're cold right now." Then he stopped moving.

"No, I'm not—oh, and that is one of the H's. Hypothermia. And the last one is hyperkalemia, or hypokalemia. Either one. They mean a person's potassium level is way too high or low."

"Very good. Now you're fifty percent of the way there." Luke skimmed his lips back down her neck to her chest. "So what are the five T's?"

Erin started searching her mind for them—until his seeking mouth found one of her aroused nipples, and she forgot what she was even searching for. "I—I can't…remember," she breathed. All she wanted to do was feel.

"Yes, you can, honey," Luke whispered against her breast. But when her only responses were soft moans, he ended the love play and rested his chin on her chest, waiting for an answer.

Erin looked down at him. He had that devilish grin on his face again, and she couldn't help but laugh. "You are relentless, Detective."

"It's what makes me good at my job."

"You're good at more than your job. But I don't think drunk people like you."

Luke chuckled. "We're trying to establish that you're not one of them."

Erin let her head fall back with a smile. "Thrombosis," she said, staring up at the ceiling. She could concentrate better when she wasn't looking into his eyes. "That counts for two. Cardiac thrombosis is a blood clot in the heart—a heart attack. And pulmonary thrombosis, that's a blood clot in the lung."

"Now you're up to seventy percent." Luke slid down her body, trailing a path of kisses along the way. And when he got to her belly button he swirled his tongue around it, then thrust in and out.

Erin closed her eyes with a murmur of pleasure and felt logic and reason start to slip from her grasp again. She needed to come up with the last three T's—and fast. "Tension pneumothorax—like that boy had. And…and tamponade, which is a fluid build-up around the heart."

"One more." Luke drew her legs up, easing them open. "You're almost there."

Erin scrambled for the last one in her mind. "I know it," she gasped. "It's—it's on the tip of my tongue."

"I want you on the tip of my tongue," he said, and dropped his head down between her thighs.

It was all over then, and her mind completely surrendered to sensation when she felt the warm tip of that tongue touch the most sensitive spot on her body. She cried out and arched up against him, clutching fistfuls of the bedspread as he mounted an assault on her senses like no other with that tongue. Then he slid his fingers inside her, finding the second most sensitive spot she'd never known she had, and stroked her there as well until she was delirious with sensation, every touch, every movement more exquisitely pleasurable than the last. She knew where he was taking her this time and finally grabbed his head to bring him back up to her, wanting him inside her before she got there.

Luke blazed a path of fiery kisses over her belly, her breasts, and her neck as she led him up. Then he thrust into her, hard and deep, closing his eyes in rapture as he felt the sweet, wet heat of her body surround him completely. "God, Erin," he groaned, trying not to climax right then and there. He hadn't expected control would be a problem again, but it was. She affected him, body and soul, in a way no other woman could, and he had to fight hard for that control.

Erin had long since let him free her of the invisible bonds of restraint, a slave to pleasure alone. She slid her hands over his buttocks and urged him to move, then pleaded for more when he did, her body demanding its own release. And she found it without any prompting, riding pleasure to its apex and letting out a cry of uninhibited bliss as it splintered into a thousand fragments of heavenly sensation inside her.

Luke felt her let go and couldn't help but follow. He dropped his head down against her shoulder with the mind-blowing pleasure of it, moaning her name as their bodies convulsed together, again and again…and again.

"Sweet Jesus, Erin!" he breathed when it was all over, and collapsed backward onto the bed.

Erin turned and nestled against him. Then another new sound escaped her—a purr. She giggled when she heard it, and looked up at him in amusement.

Luke chuckled. "You never did get that last T, honey."

Erin purred again. "I like how you say that." No one had ever called her honey before. She slid all the way on top of him and buried her face in his chest. There was a fine sheen of sweat on his skin, and she dipped her tongue down to taste it. She thought of Wesley and how he would sometimes lick her as he purred. She felt like a cat at the moment.

Luke groaned. "You're going to break me, woman."

"Well, at least you've got a doctor here." Erin rested her chin on his chest and gave him a Cheshire cat smile.

"A doctor who's possibly drunk and doesn't remember the last T of cardiac arrest," he teased.

It came to her then. "Toxin. Or tablet. They both fall under that T, and refer to either a poison or a drug."

Luke grinned. "Like alcohol."

"Mmmm." It came out as another purr. "More like you."

"Am I a poison or a drug?"

"Definitely a drug." Erin slid up higher, and their lips met in a slow, lingering kiss.

"I'm addicted to the taste of you. I want more," Luke murmured against her mouth. "And more."

"I know." Erin lifted her head and looked down at him in wonder. "I never imagined it could be like this, Luke."

"Neither did I," he said, smiling up at her affectionately. "Even in the million fantasies I've had about you, I could never come up with anything this good."

"So you've thought about us in bed together before, have you?"

"Ever since I was six. Although I wasn't exactly sure what we'd do in bed until my brothers filled me in a few years later."

Erin smothered a laugh. "Why didn't you ever say anything? You hardly said two words to me back when we were in school." But she wondered if he would have been able to get through to her all those years ago. He probably wouldn't have, given how closed off she'd been, and then she might never have gotten a second chance with him. She found the thought disturbing and put it out of her mind. All that mattered was that he was here with her now.

"You'd be surprised how insecure a guy can be when it comes to a girl, especially one he really likes," Luke said, running his fingers through her hair. "And the more he likes her, the harder it is for him to talk to her. That's why I could barely get two words out when I was around you."

"You've said a whole lot more than two words recently," Erin teased. "Does that mean you don't like me as much?"

"No. Now I know you at least like me back a little."

"I like you back a lot more than a little."

For a moment neither of them said anything else as they gazed into each other's eyes. Then Luke slid his hand out of her hair and cupped her face. "Erin, I—" But before he could finish her cell phone started buzzing on the dresser.

"It's probably Jenna," Erin said.

She got up to retrieve the phone and saw that it was indeed Jenna. "Hey, Jen. Is everything okay?" she asked.

"That's the question I was going to ask you," her friend said with relief clearly in her tone. "Luke didn't call, so I started imagining all kinds of things, and none of them ended well."

Erin smiled wryly, coming back to sit down on the edge of the bed. "Such as Luke finding me in the hotel with Chase McKellar, and then killing him?"

"Yes, that was one of the more concerning scenarios," Jenna responded with a sheepish laugh. "You didn't sound like yourself on the phone, Erin. After what happened at the café, and then with the baby, I was worried you might do something, well… that you normally wouldn't."

Which was, in fact, true. Erin glanced down at the bag on the floor that contained the unopened vibrator. "Did you tell Luke what happened at the café?"

"Yes, I did, and I'm sorry. I know it wasn't my secret to tell. But I was worried about you."

"No, it's okay. You saved me the embarrassment of having to tell him myself."

Luke sat up behind her, wrapping her in his arms. "You have nothing to be embarrassed about." Then he leaned closer to the phone and said into it, "Hi, Jen. Sorry I forgot to call."

"That answers another one of my questions. Is Chase there too—and in one piece?"

Erin grinned. Considering she and Luke were sitting in the hotel room quite naked, Jenna had no idea what she'd really just asked. "No, but he's in one piece as far as I know. He left before Luke even got here. We really did just meet for drinks. And I also told him right from the start that I was interested in someone else."

"Who?" Luke quipped.

Jenna chuckled at the other end of the line. "I'd better let you go so you can answer that. As for me, I'm going to bed, now that I won't be dreaming of murder and mayhem amongst my friends. I'll leave the front door unlocked since we haven't made another key yet—if you even come back tonight."

"Of course I will. I'll be home in a little while."

"Take your time then. Goodnight to the both of you."

"You too, Jen." Erin smiled, laying the phone down on the nightstand. Luke pulled her back against him, brushing light kisses over her neck, and she closed her eyes with a soft sigh of pleasure, murmuring, "I think you might know all my secrets now, Detective."

Luke froze for an instant. He knew one of her secrets better than she did. But now wasn't the time to tell her, at least not without casting a very dark shadow on the best night of his life. It could wait. "There's nothing you can't tell me. I want to know everything about you, Erin Harris." He pressed a kiss on her cheek. "Do you mind me calling you that? I know it's not your legal name, but I can't seem to get myself to say that one. Although I'm also kind of partial to Sally Ride now, too."

Erin laughed softly. "You can call me whatever you want."

"Then I'm going to call you beautiful," Luke said, kissing her shoulder. "And sweet." He slid his hands up over her breasts. "And most definitely sexy."

"Mmmm. I've never been called that before, either."

"Then the men you've known have been fools." Luke dropped his hands back down to her waist. "And your ex was the biggest one of them all."

Erin shook her head. "I'm the one who's been a fool. Things have happened in my life that were out of my control, but I've let them control me ever since. Jenna made me see that. I've spent most of my life hiding from who I am, hiding the scars and hoping they'd go away. But they won't. It just doesn't work like that."

"You couldn't have grown up in the environment you did without there being scars, Erin. They were inevitable."

"I know, and I have to accept that I'll never be perfect. But I guess the world would be a pretty boring place if everyone was."

Luke wrapped his arms tightly around her. "Whatever imperfections you think you have are perfect to me. They make you who you are."

"Well, I still don't want to be quite so imperfect," Erin

said. "Today when I delivered that baby I realized you were right—I have been giving up on myself, in so many ways. And it's time I start fighting just as hard for me as I do for other people. I guess I could go see a shrink and sit there for months on end rehashing my past and how it affects my life now—Jenna did say I need to talk about it. But I'm not sure a therapist is the best thing for me. In medicine I've always been better at doing something—taking action—rather than talking. So I decided to apply that to the rest of my life, starting tonight…with sex."

A half-smile crossed Erin's face. "I couldn't even say the word without feeling awkward about it until Jenna made me repeat it the other day. I've always been uncomfortable with sex, and I was afraid if we became intimate the issue would come between us. So I…Well, I bought a vibrator and hoped I might be brave enough to use it after a few drinks. I was planning to imagine you here with me." Despite her embarrassment over admitting all that, she couldn't help but laugh. "Then you actually showed up in the flesh and made my adventure to the adult entertainment store quite unnecessary."

Luke nuzzled his face in her hair. "I'm curious to see what my fill-in looks like."

"I don't even know myself," Erin said with embarrassment returning to her tone. "I called ahead and told the woman who answered to put their top-selling brand in a bag and leave it at the checkout for me to pick up later."

Luke chuckled. "Did you frame Sally Ride for that, too?"

"I probably would have if she'd asked."

"Okay, now I really have to see what you got." Luke leaned over and picked up the bag.

Erin felt her cheeks get warm. "Luke, really…"

He grinned and reached into the bag, pulling out a clear plastic box containing a purple vibrator. "Wow, waterproof, multi-speed, with massaging beads to boot."

"Luke, please, put it back," Erin implored, averting her gaze in mortification.

He didn't listen, and instead opened the box.

Despite her chagrin, Erin's eyes strayed back to the vibrator after he took it out, and she inspected it with reluctant curiosity. "That thing looks like some kind of alien weapon. And why is there a piece sticking out like that?" She leaned closer. "Is that a bunny?"

"Yes, it is," Luke told her, doing his best to keep a straight face. "I believe they call it a rabbit."

Erin glanced up at him. "I know you're laughing at me, Luke Mathis."

He did laugh then. "It's a clitoral stimulator, Erin. When a woman inserts the shaft, that part rubs against the clit for "extreme stimulation," as the package says right here—if you'd bothered to look." He grinned and twisted the bottom open. "Let's put some batteries in and see if this thing actually works." He fished through the bag. "Where are they?"

"Don't they come with it?"

"No, you have to buy them. What about lube, did you get that?"

Erin stared at the vibrator blankly for a moment, and then understood. "Oh."

Luke shook his head and laughed again. "Honey, I don't think you were going to get very far with my replacement tonight."

"I probably would have chickened out anyway."

"I believe the operative word is rabbit, not chicken."

It was Erin's turn to laugh. "Touché, Detective. But in any case, that's why I requested a room with a Jacuzzi. I figured if nothing else, I could at least get used to being in the water. I'd rather not recreate yesterday's melodrama in the pond anytime soon."

"I wouldn't mind recreating at least some of that," Luke murmured, kissing her ear. "Minus the swimsuits, though."

Erin smiled. "Some of that is actually what started all of this, you know. When you went upstairs to change after we brought Jenna in yesterday, I told her how I felt about you, and mentioned getting a vibrator." She laughed shortly. "I thought I was joking at the time. But that's what we were talking about when you came back downstairs, not jump starting my car—at least not the way you were thinking." She looked up at him and a helpless giggle bubbled out of her.

Luke remembered what he'd said to them, and a crooked smile tugged at the corner of his mouth. "Ah, it all makes sense now. I thought both of you were suffering from heat stroke." Then he turned his attention back to the vibrator. "So what do we need to power this thing up? It looks like three double-A's."

"Luke, we don't need to use that. The problem I bought it for has definitely been fixed."

"But there's another problem we might be able to fix," he said thoughtfully. "You have some powerful emotions associated with water, and we need to replace them with other ones, feelings that you aren't likely to forget either. And I think I know a way to do it—if we could just get a hold of some batteries." Then a possibility occurred to him. He set the vibrator down on the nightstand and picked up the alarm clock next to it. "Or maybe we do. There could be some in here as a backup in case the power goes out." He opened the battery compartment in the back. "Damn! Only one."

He set the alarm clock down and looked speculatively around the room, then up at the ceiling, and a slow grin broke across his face.

Erin followed the direction of his gaze. He was looking up at the smoke alarm installed in the ceiling near the end of the bed. "Luke, you wouldn't…"

"It's probably hardwired, but I'll bet there are backup batteries in there, too." Luke eased away from her and stood up on the bed. "Maybe we'll get lucky and find some double-A's."

Erin watched in amused disbelief as he walked across the bed and reached for the smoke alarm. "Detective Mathis, I can't believe you're going to steal smoke alarm batteries from the hotel."

"I'm not going to steal them. I'm just going to borrow them." Luke laughed at himself as soon as he said it. How many times had he heard that line before? Then he twisted the cover off. "Bingo! Two double-A's." He pulled them out and replaced the cover, grinning down at her. "Hopefully they work because you should've set this thing off by now."

He turned toward her, still standing on the bed, and she got a full view of him from head to toe. "No, I think it should've gone off for you."

Luke sat down, tossing the batteries onto the bedspread, and cupped her face in his hand. "Is your smoke alarm going off, Sally Ride?"

"Oh, yes," Erin answered in a low, seductive tone. It was yet another new sound, and she liked it. "But I'm not alarmed, just very turned on."

"There's no question *your* battery is working fine," Luke murmured, and lightly kissed her mouth.

Erin slid her hands around his neck, wanting more. But he eased away with a smile and stood up, pressing a kiss on her head. "Let's save that for the water."

He went over to the Jacuzzi, and her eyes were drawn to his naked backside as he bent down to close the drain and start the faucet. Then he turned around and walked back toward her, and she unabashedly studied other well-proportioned parts of him. In the past her fascination with the human body had always been purely scientific, how all the systems functioned together in such an amazing way to sustain life. She'd never thought of the human form itself as a work of art, a thing of beauty, until now.

The vibrator, however, did not look like a work of art in any way, shape, or form. And when he picked it up and sat down next to her again, Erin eyed it with trepidation. "So what exactly is this idea of yours?"

"We're going to have a swimming lesson, and the rabbit and I will be your instructors." Luke installed the batteries and turned it on. "Jackpot!"

Erin watched the rabbit ears vibrate, not quite sure what to make of it. Then he hit more buttons and the ears quivered wildly, while the shaft gyrated faster and faster. And her eyes widened in shock.

Luke chuckled at the look on her face and turned the vibrator off. "We'll save this for the water too."

"Luke, that thing looks like it belongs in a science fiction movie, certainly not…there." Erin knew she was blushing again. She'd done that more times in the last few days than she had in her entire life.

"You don't have to do anything you don't want to," Luke said, flashing her a grin as he set the vibrator on the bed. "It would just be a shame if you made that trip to the toy store for nothing."

"I probably wouldn't have even bought the thing if I'd seen it first," Erin admitted weakly. "It reminds me of all the sex-related injuries I've dealt with in the ER. Just a few months ago I took care of a woman who came in with severe vaginal bleeding that had started during sex. She told me they hadn't done anything unusual—of course, that's what they all say, even the guy who had a light bulb stuck in his rectum that showed up on an x-ray."

Luke shook his head. "The things that turn people on."

"You have no idea—or I guess you do. But anyway, this woman had a huge tear inside her vagina that had to be fixed in the OR. And she ended up needing a blood transfusion too. It wasn't any normal man that could have done that. Either she was having sex with someone who should be put in a museum someday, or they'd been using something that probably looked just like that. And I do not want to end up in the ER myself under similar circumstances, Luke Mathis. I would never be able show my face there again—and your dad would not be happy."

"No, he'd kill me," Luke said with a laugh. "If my mom didn't get to me first. But I promise, if you try it there will be no permanent damage done. And no blood transfusions will be necessary."

"I don't know…But in any case, I need to go use the bathroom." Erin smiled half-heartedly. "After seeing that thing I just might be able to lock myself in there tonight."

Luke's expression sobered. "Do you want me to go with you?"

"No, I'll just leave the door partway open." Erin stood up with a blush of embarrassment creeping across her cheeks. "It's yet another thing I have to work on."

"I'll be right here if you need me."

Erin nodded, feeling her face get even hotter. Then she headed to the small bathroom and closed the door as far as she could without panic rearing its ugly head. She thought of Luke sitting out there waiting for her—how his eyes were like windows to the most beautiful summer sky—and she pushed the door closed a little farther. Her heart began to race, and her chest tightened uncomfortably, but she took slow, deep breaths and thought of Luke again. The image of him standing naked on the bed stealing batteries from the smoke alarm floated through her mind, and she couldn't help but smile. Panic eased its grip on her, and she was able to close the door almost all the way.

Luke was sitting on the edge of the Jacuzzi with his legs dangling in the water, and appeared deep in thought when she came out of the bathroom. But as soon as she started walking toward him he looked up and smiled at her appreciatively. "Everything okay?"

Erin came up behind him and slid her arms tightly around his chest, burying her face in his neck and inhaling the musky, masculine scent of him. "Everything is more than okay." She dropped an affectionate kiss on his shoulder. "And what were you thinking about so seriously? I hope it's not that rabbit again." She saw it was now sitting on the tile surface next to him.

Luke swung his legs out of the water and turned to face her. "I was thinking about you," he said, pulling her onto his lap so she sat straddling him. He was thinking about all the things he felt for her and wanted to tell her, but wasn't sure she'd want to hear. She might think he was crazy. "Are you ready to get in?"

Erin looked over his shoulder into the Jacuzzi, the water now filled to the brim and bubbling turbulently, and felt a frisson of fear run through her. "Can we leave the jets off?"

"Of course." Luke reached down and pressed the button to turn them off.

Erin glanced into the Jacuzzi again, attempting a smile. "This should be a breeze after being in the pond."

"Let's do it then." Luke swung around and slid into the warm water, holding her firmly on his lap.

Erin buried her face in his neck and wrapped her arms around his shoulders in an iron grip, feeling panic rush through her as the water rose over her chest and they settled to the bottom of the Jacuzzi. It wasn't as bad as the pond, but she still struggled to maintain control of her emotions.

Luke eased her head back and looked into her eyes, seeing the fear there. "Remember, I won't let you go," he softly said, and drew her mouth to his.

Erin closed her eyes and concentrated on his lips as they brushed tenderly over hers, and it wasn't long before she was kissing him back. The tension in her body began to subside, and she loosened her grip on his shoulders, deepening the kiss. He slid his hands down to massage her breasts under the water at the same time, and his arousal swelled between them, teasing her belly. She instinctively pushed closer, and they moved against each other in a slow, sensual dance. All the rest of her anxiety melted away, turning into white-hot desire, heightened all the more by the fear that had come before it. And with passion giving rise to a new tension inside her, she broke the kiss and reached down for him. "Make love to me, Luke."

He intercepted her hand and eased her off his lap instead. "I want to bury myself inside your sweet heaven, honey, more than I want to breathe. But first we're going to have that swimming lesson."

"*Luke!*" Erin groaned.

"Turn around and hold on to the edge of the Jacuzzi," he commanded in a mild tone.

Erin glanced at the water uncertainly, feeling some of her anxiety return. But after a moment she did as he said.

Luke knelt behind her and lifted her up to the surface of the water. "Relax and let yourself float," he whispered, trailing a path of kisses down her back. "I just want you to feel. You, the water, and pure sensation." He reached her bottom and feathered more soft kisses over it, then lightly sank his teeth into her skin.

Erin let out a faint exclamation of surprise, though her body responded in an entirely different way, with delicious sensations flowing straight to her core, fanning the flames of desire again. And he used his free hand to further incite the fire, sliding his fingers downward between her thighs, gently probing, stroking.

"Luke," Erin uttered in a low moan, kicking her legs out to move harder against him.

"That's it, honey." Luke smiled. He just might teach her how to swim yet. Then he kissed his way back upward until he reached her ear, murmuring into it, "I think the rabbit wants to play too."

Erin nodded, not caring anymore, once again a slave to sensation. She watched him reach for the rabbit, heard him turn it on behind her, and felt him slowly push the vibrating shaft into her. The rabbit with its wildly twitching ears slid over her, and she immediately cried out as electrifying pleasure surged through her.

"Don't stop kicking your legs, honey," Luke urged, holding her steady with one hand while he moved the vibrator back and forth with the other, gradually increasing the intensity. "Feel this. Remember it every time you look at the water."

Erin kicked her legs out, and pleasure inundated her until she almost couldn't breathe. She was dizzy it. She was soon drowning in it. She finally couldn't take it anymore when sensation became so acute it was almost painful. "That's enough, Luke," she gasped. "I want you—I want *you* inside me." And without a second thought she let go of the Jacuzzi.

Luke caught her back against him, swiftly withdrawing the vibrator. He shut it off and set it on the tile surround, then hit the button to start the jets up again, creating vibration of a different sort.

Erin turned in his arms, her fear of the bubbling water long gone. "Now, Luke!"

"Over here," he said, pulling her with him to a seat built into the corner of the Jacuzzi.

Erin climbed up onto his lap, straddling him, and didn't think twice about the new position. As he started to push into her she sank down hard on top of him and urgently began to move, desire raging hotter than ever inside her.

Luke cupped her bottom in his hands and thrust back with just as much need. "God, honey, I love how you feel," he whispered tightly, spreading heated kisses on her skin. "I love touching you, tasting you. I love every part of you."

Erin moaned his name and drove against him harder, faster. "Oh God, Luke!" She clutched his shoulders in a white-knuckled grip, feeling sensation start to spin out of control. Then it exploded inside her, and she threw her head back with a helpless scream, the pleasure so exquisite, so powerful, that for a moment she thought she might actually pass out. He came with her, and their cries commingled in the room as they rode wave after wave of orgasmic sensation together.

Erin collapsed against him with a groan afterward. "I hope I can at least swim now because I'm not going to be able to walk tomorrow."

Luke lifted her up and sat her across his lap. "Well, you may have just broken me, Sally Ride."

"You know that can actually happen," Erin said, giving him a slightly impish smile. "When I was a resident this guy came in on New Year's Day. He and his girlfriend broke in the New Year by—"

"Okay, stop right there," Luke interrupted. "I guess there is something I can't handle hearing about after all."

"Oh well. My punch line was pretty soft anyway."

"I have no idea how to respond to that."

"You're probably thinking too hard," Erin said, tongue-in-cheek.

Luke's face split into a grin. "Anytime I'm near you I start thinking hard."

"And I like how you think," Erin playfully responded. "Your head is quite remarkable."

Luke chuckled and drew her mouth to his, murmuring against her lips, "I didn't know such a dirty mind went along with that wicked sense of humor."

"Neither did I." Erin pressed a deep, sensuous kiss on his mouth. "You bring it out of me."

"I seem to bring a lot out of you," Luke said, easing back. "I would never have guessed you'd be such a noisy lover either. Sex in the library is definitely out of the question."

Erin couldn't help but laugh, though she felt the telltale heat of another blush on her cheeks. "I honestly never understood what all the fuss was about with sex. But I get it now. And I can see why all these people keep showing up in the ER with injuries because of it. A woman even came in once claiming she had a seizure during an orgasm, and I didn't really believe her. You wouldn't like that story, though. Her husband also needed treatment. They were performing oral sex on each other at the same time—they called it something, but I can't remember what. Anyway, she had a seizure and bit down—"

"*Enough!*" Luke exclaimed, and then let out a dry laugh. "I can't believe I'm telling a woman to stop talking about oral sex. But you got me again. And they were in the 69 position, by the way. But you are officially banned from bringing up anything that has to do with the ER for the rest of the night."

"You better decide what we'll talk about then, because I'm bound to get myself into trouble."

Luke's expression sobered. "There is something we should talk about: We haven't been using protection."

Erin smiled ruefully. "You picked the right woman to make that mistake with. The chances of me getting pregnant naturally are somewhere between slim and none—and I'm pretty sure slim died of starvation." It was another first for her. Joking about such a painful subject was something she would never have imagined being able to do. And it was surprisingly therapeutic.

"Well, if it turned out slim wasn't dead, I wouldn't consider it a mistake," Luke said. "But that's not really what I was thinking about. I just want you to know you don't have to worry about catching anything from me. I've always been careful about that. Maybe even too careful, I guess. But my dad's idea of sex education was taking me and my brothers into his office and showing us pictures of every STD in the book. The one that really got to me was a picture of what looked like hunks of cauliflower stuck to the guy's parts. I'm surprised I'm not still a virgin after seeing that."

"Genital warts," Erin said with laughter in her tone. And then curiously, she asked, "What do you mean about being too careful?"

Luke's lips twisted wryly. "I guess I'd better take that back. A person can never be too careful—like that guy in the book should've learned. But until now I've always used a condom. Every time. Even if it was probably safe not to."

Erin grinned. "So in a way I did kind of take your virginity, didn't I?"

"Saying that kind of puts my man badge in jeopardy again. But I guess you're right—in a way."

"Mmmm. I think I like that idea," she said, nestling her cheek on his shoulder.

"Putting my man badge in jeopardy?"

"No, taking your virginity." Erin ran her hand slowly over his chest, enjoying the feel of his firm muscles under her fingers. "And you don't have to worry about me either. After Peter's infidelity I was tested for everything, and there's been no one else since."

Luke didn't want to think about her with anyone else but him, so he changed the subject. "How are you feeling?" he asked, wrapping his arms tightly around her.

"With my fingers." It was the response so many patients had given her over the years.

"I mean about the water," Luke said in amusement.

Erin lifted her head off his shoulder and smiled up at him. "You definitely accomplished your goal, Detective.

I'll never look at water the same way again. I think if they started having swimming lessons at the community pool like the one you just gave me, every woman in town would pretend she couldn't swim."

Luke chuckled. "I'd like to have more lessons like that with you."

"I'll sign up for whatever lessons you want to give me. Although I'll drown for sure if we have any more tonight. I can barely move a muscle."

"I'm in the same boat," he said with a grin. "What I'd really like to do now is go lay on that bed over there and hold you. Do we have some time yet?"

"Yes, a little while. But I need to be there for Jenna, so I can't—"

Luke gently pressed a finger to her lips. "I know. I'm just not quite ready to let you go yet." But then, he knew he never would be.

He turned off the Jacuzzi as they got out, then grabbed a towel and wrapped it around her from behind. "I'll do the honors," he whispered into her ear and slowly rubbed her dry.

Erin enjoyed every moment of it. She would never have guessed such a simple act could make her feel so good, so cared for. And when he was done she picked up the other towel and started kneading it leisurely over his chest. She felt his nipples harden under her fingers and lowered the towel, giving in to the urge to taste one of them.

Luke groaned, easing her away. "That's enough, or you really will break me, woman. And then I won't be able to show my face at the hospital again." He took the towel as she laughed, and quickly finished the job. Then he led her over to the bed, and they slid under the covers together.

Erin snuggled against him, closing her eyes with a contented smile. She wished she could suspend time forever. She was here with Luke, Jenna was doing fine for the moment, and she'd made huge strides in dealing with some of the issues that had tormented her for years. Maybe she really didn't need a shrink. She had Luke and Jenna. They were her therapists and love was her therapy. The best therapy. All was well with the world.

"Are you comfortable?" Luke whispered.

She didn't respond, and he tilted his head to look down at her face. She was sound asleep.

He smiled and tenderly pressed a kiss into her hair, then eased back and let his own eyes slowly drift closed.

HE CREPT QUIETLY THROUGH THE BUSHES AND peered into the bedroom window behind the house. There was a lamp on next to the bed that cast its dim light over the figures writhing against each other there. So it was true, he thought. She was screwing him, too. And in her condition… It made him sick.

The window was closed, but he could still hear them. And he watched, spellbound, as they went at it, even as anger burned deeper and hotter inside him. By the time the bastard left he could taste it on his tongue.

He waited in the shadow of the trees as the other man pulled out of the driveway. And when the car's rear lights disappeared into the darkness he walked up to the front door with a duffel bag on his shoulder. Pleasure, ever so elusive, coursed through him in anticipation of what was about to happen.

He checked the door, and his lips curved up into a cynical smile. She'd left it unlocked—an invitation for anyone to come in.

He slowly opened the door and started to walk inside. But he came to a halt a few steps later, suddenly having second thoughts. And then after a moment he quietly backed out, easing the door closed again...

He rang the doorbell instead. It would be more fun to make a grand entrance.

She opened the door, and he watched the look of pleasure on her face turn to one of surprise. He could tell she thought the bastard had come back again, and now was disappointed that it was just him. It fueled his rage.

"Why are you—?" she started to say, but he slammed his gloved fist into her mouth before she could get another word out.

Later, when it was all over, he walked casually out the back door and disappeared into the woods. He let the demons slither back down to hide deep inside him, and was disappointed. It hadn't been as good as he'd imagined it would be. And now there was only the dark emptiness in his soul again, the black void that couldn't be filled.

He slid his hand into the front pocket of his jeans and caressed the ring he'd taken from her, feeling some of the satisfaction come back for a moment. But it wasn't enough. He wondered what else he could have done to the slut that would have made it better, that would have made it last longer.

CHAPTER

11

Luke woke up to the pleasant sensation of Erin's naked bottom nestled against his groin. It brought a lazy, satisfied smile to his lips, and he propped himself up on an elbow and looked down at her. She was still sound asleep.

He lowered his head toward hers, intending to brush a kiss on her cheek. But the alarm clock caught his eye, and he stared at the display in confusion. 5:02 a.m. He glanced up, and as soon as he saw the faint light of dawn behind the curtains he realized there was no mistake—he and Erin had spent the night together.

Just as that sank in, he heard the muffled buzz of his cell phone in the pocket of his pants on the floor, and concern immediately filled him. If someone was calling at this hour it had to be important. Jenna came to mind, and he hoped it had nothing to do with her. Erin would never forgive herself—or him.

He eased away from her and got up off the other side of the bed to retrieve the phone. By the time he fished it out of his pocket it had stopped vibrating, but he saw there was a missed call notification from Jeff Kilbride, the Chief of Police. There was also a voice mail notice with it, and when he listened to the message his concern turned to dread. The chief requested he call him back right away. It was urgent.

He walked into the bathroom, not wanting to wake Erin until he had to, and made the call. "Hey, Jeff, what's going on?"

"I'm at Frank Murdock's house," the chief responded grimly. "I need you here as soon as possible."

"The mayor's place? What happened?"

"He came home this morning and found his wife dead—murdered. It's—it's pretty bad."

"*Jesus*," Luke whispered in shock. "I'll be there right away."

He left the bathroom and quickly threw his clothes on, then sat down on the edge of the bed next to Erin. She was lying on her belly now, with her face turned toward him. She'd slid her left arm up over the pillow behind her, where his head had been only moments ago, and her right hand was curled up against the side of her face, tangled in her hair.

He smiled tenderly down at her. He wished he could just sit there and enjoy the sight of her sleeping for a while. But he knew he couldn't, so he gently squeezed her shoulder. "Erin."

SHE WAS STANDING ON THE CONCRETE PARAPET OF Zakim Bridge over the Charles River in Boston. She gripped one of the steel cables that ran upward near her head, and held her hair away from her face with the other hand as she looked down into the water. She was making a scene, she knew, and that was so unlike her. But today she didn't care. Today she felt…nothing. Jenna was dead and buried, and now she was back in Boston. Back to her empty, barren life.

Blue eyes the color of a summer sky floated through her mind. Luke Mathis. She'd felt an instant connection with him the day she returned to New Dublin and looked into his eyes for the first time in fourteen years. But while they were in his police car after the shooting, he told her about his wife and three daughters. His love for them had been obvious, and her heart had ached with longing when he'd shown her their pictures.

But right now nothing hurt. She was numb.

She continued to stare down at the water, and for the first time in as long as she could remember, she wasn't afraid of it, even though she couldn't swim. But then, that was the point, wasn't it? It looked so peaceful down there, so welcoming, and she was tired of being alone. The last person who had ever really loved her was dead.

"Erin."

She felt someone touch her shoulder, and turned her head in surprise. Luke Mathis stood there behind her, his blue eyes filled with such tenderness that it took her breath away. She looked back down at the water and was afraid of it again. Hope blossomed inside her.

"Erin, honey, we've got to get going."

She turned around with a smile, ready to go—and her smile died. Luke had disappeared, and Peter was there instead. He leaned forward, cupping her face in his hand, and lightly kissed her mouth.

"Peter," she whispered in quiet despair.

He stepped back and held his hand out to her. She stared down at it, and pain tore through her, more agonizing than anything she'd ever felt before. Jenna and Luke were both gone.

She finally let the numbness envelop her again. She knew what Jenna would say—she was taking the easy way out. But she was just so tired of the pain. And God, she missed her friend. So she didn't take Peter's hand. She closed her eyes instead, and let herself fall back...

ERIN'S EYES FLEW OPEN IN TERROR, HER HEART pounding in her chest. Then she saw Luke sitting there next to her on the bed, and overwhelming relief flooded her. She'd only been dreaming. But she quickly realized something was wrong. He was fully dressed, and there was a look of such anguish on his face... "What is it, Luke?" she asked, shaking off the last remnants of sleep. "What's happened?"

You just ripped my heart out with a single word, he wanted to tell her. *That's what had just happened.* So he'd been right after all—she was still in love with Peter Pryce.

He remembered calling the man a fool last night, and how she'd shaken her head, calling herself one instead. She'd been defending the bastard, even though he'd cheated on her. And she'd probably been thinking of him the whole time they were making love. It made him sick inside. But right now he had another mess to deal with. "The police chief just called. The mayor found his wife dead this morning, and it looks like murder, so I have to go. I'll walk you to your car."

"That's horrible." Erin glanced at the alarm clock as she started to sit up, and blinked in surprise. "Oh no. I left Jenna alone all night."

She threw the covers back and scrambled past him out of bed, grabbing her phone off the nightstand. Then she hastily gathered her clothes and headed to the bathroom. "I—I'll be ready in a minute."

Luke stood up, scratching his stubble-roughened jaw in frustration. He hadn't missed the way she'd avoided meeting his eyes before she fled the room, or the chagrined look that had been on her face—it was the same one he'd seen yesterday when she left the café. And now she'd rather be in the bathroom of all places than get dressed in front of him.

Picking up the empty black bag lying on the floor, he walked over to the Jacuzzi and threw the vibrator into the bag with a little more force than necessary, not bothering to take the batteries out. He'd stop by the hotel with new ones another day. Then he opened the drain to the Jacuzzi and couldn't help but remember last night. He hoped to God she wasn't going to tell him she was sorry about it all, because he was sure that would take care of what was left of his heart.

ERIN THREW HER CLOTHES ON THE FLOOR AND leaned over the bathroom sink, fighting another wave of nausea. The world had started spinning as soon as she'd gotten out of bed, and she'd thought she was going to lose whatever contents were left in her stomach right then and there. She just hoped Luke hadn't seen it in her face, which looked almost as green as the color of her eyes. He seemed distressed enough about the mayor's wife. She didn't want him to think she'd been drunk after all—although she probably had been more than a little drunk. She'd never had one Long Island Iced Tea before, much less three "extra longs," as Chase had called them. And now she was paying for it with the first hangover of her life.

Groaning softly, she turned on the faucet and splashed her face with cold water until the nausea and dizziness let up some. Then she briefly dried off, moving her head as little as possible, and sent a quick text to Jenna, feeling equally sick that she'd left her alone all night. She could just imagine her friend falling and breaking one of her fragile bones, and then lying there in pain, with no one to help her...

Erin let out another groan at the thought and bent down to grab her clothes. But that made the spinning worse, and the nausea hit her harder than ever. Bile rose in her throat, and she dropped to her knees in front of the toilet, sure she was going to be sick this time. But nothing came up, and so she just knelt there, hovering over the toilet in helpless misery.

Then she heard the brief ding of an incoming text on her phone. Jenna.

After a moment she tentatively reached for the phone and read the message:

> *Just about to sit on the porch and watch the sunrise. I figured you were still with Luke. Can't wait to hear all about it!!!* ☺☺☺

Erin almost smiled, despite her misery. The nausea eased a little and she finally managed to stand up and get dressed.

Luke stood near the bathroom with Erin's things, waiting for her to finish. The door was mostly closed, but he'd still heard her muffled groans. And each one cut through him like a knife. There was no question in his mind now that she was indeed sorry about everything.

When she eventually came out, he handed her the bags without meeting her eyes, and they left the hotel in silence.

Erin's head throbbed as they walked to her car. She needed water and aspirin badly. It figured the best night of her life had to end with murder and a hangover. She was glad Luke seemed too preoccupied with the murder part to notice that she was even hungover.

They reached her car, and Erin opened the driver's side door, tossing her bags inside. Then she turned back to him, pasting a smile on her face that ended up looking more like a grimace.

Luke flinched when he saw it. "Go home and get some sleep, Erin," he said irritably. And without another word, he walked away.

Erin stood there, stunned. She watched him head across the parking lot to his truck, sure he'd turn around and say something more. But he didn't.

She finally slid into the driver's seat and stared out the front window, still in shock. He hadn't said goodbye, or anything about seeing her again, despite everything that had happened between them last night. He wouldn't even look at her.

She suddenly knew a lot more was wrong than either murder or a hangover could explain. She remembered the expression on Luke's face this morning, the wounded look in his eyes…That look had nothing to do with news of a murder, she realized. And she couldn't believe he would have acted the way he just did over a hangover. No, she must have done something else, something that had hurt him deeply. But what?

She went over it all in her mind. When she'd fallen asleep in his arms last night everything had felt so right, so perfect. Had she said something in her sleep? She knew she had a tendency to do that. But she couldn't imagine saying anything that would have upset him so badly.

Then she remembered the dream. And that's when it hit her. There was something she could have said when she'd been caught in that muddled state between dreams and consciousness. And the more she thought about it, the more certain she was that she really had said it.

"Oh God," she groaned, closing her eyes as another wave of nausea came over her. She'd ruined the best night of her life by saying her ex-husband's name in a dream—no, in a nightmare. And one that had even ended with her choosing death over him. But Luke didn't know that.

She wanted to chase him down now and tell him, but she knew she couldn't. He had more pressing matters to deal with. And how was she supposed to put something like that into a text message or a voicemail? She would have to wait until she could talk to him directly and explain. If he would ever talk to her again, that is.

She let out a dispirited sigh and started the car. "Leave it to you, Erin." Then she began the long drive home, stopping for water and aspirin at a gas station along the way. But nothing was going to help her heart at the moment.

"HELLO THERE, STRANGER."

Erin looked up as she started to climb the porch steps. Jenna was sitting in a chair near the top grinning down at her.

"Hey, Jen," she responded bleakly.

Jenna's smile immediately faded. "Oh no. What's wrong?"

Erin eased herself into the chair next to Jenna's. "I screwed things up big time."

"Oh, Erin." Jenna reached over and squeezed her arm. "You're dealing with a really complicated issue. You and Luke probably just need to take things a little slower, that's all."

Erin reluctantly smiled at the misunderstanding. "The problem you're referring to is about the only one I don't have at the moment. Twenty minutes in a hotel room with Luke took care of that. And then he made sure it was fixed a few more times afterward."

"Oh my…" Jenna's eyes widened in surprise. "Well…"

Now Erin couldn't help but laugh, even though it hurt to do it. "I can't believe this is the second time I've said something to make you speechless in a matter of days. It's kind of ironic that the first time was when I told you I had a problem with sex, and now the second time is when I tell you I don't."

"That's because you *really* don't."

"I think you mean I really, really, *really* don't."

They looked at each other and burst out laughing. Then Erin groaned again. "Oh, my head, Jen. It hurts too much to laugh. I hope the aspirin kicks in soon."

"You're hungover," Jenna said with a grin. "I've never seen that before, either."

"Chase introduced me to Long Island Iced Tea last night. And now I don't think I'll ever be able to drink again. My parents would not be proud."

Jenna looked at her in astonishment, and another laugh grudgingly escaped Erin. "Wow, I've made you speechless for the third time. This whole 'opening up and letting people in' business is proving to be very interesting. But I just figure if I can't ignore my past I might as well find the humor in it—what little of it there is to find anyway."

Jenna nodded. "That brings to mind one of my favorite quotes from Mark Twain: 'The human race has only one really effective weapon, and that is laughter.'"

"I don't think he knew about nuclear missiles back then."

Jenna chuckled. "No, I suppose not. But laughter still is the best medicine, Dr. Pryce."

"Not for a hangover, though. Believe me."

"Is that what you were referring to when you said you screwed things up?"

"I wish that's all it was," Erin said, her voice filled with self-reproach. "I hadn't meant to fall asleep last night. But I haven't gotten much sleep lately. And then with the alcohol and, well—anyway, Luke woke me up this morning, and I'm pretty sure I said Peter's name before I was completely awake."

"Oh, Erin…You still have feelings for Peter, don't you?"

"*No*, Jen," Erin groaned. If Jenna would ask the question, there was no doubt Luke would think it. "I was having a bad dream—and now I'm living one. Luke wouldn't even look at me when he left this morning…I don't know if he'll ever forgive me."

Jenna gave her a reassuring smile. "The man's been in love with you as far back as I can remember, Erin. Nothing is going to change that. Not even your marriage did, so saying Peter's name when you were half-asleep certainly won't. Yes, Luke was probably hurt by what you said, but he'll get over it."

"I don't know. I keep thinking about that poem of yours—how there are only so many times a heart can be broken. What if he decides enough is enough?"

"Don't let it be enough. Talk to him. Fight for him." Jenna laughed wryly. "I feel like a broken record here. That's exactly what I told Luke to do last night when he showed up at the front door looking for you."

Erin's expression softened. "He certainly came to the Shamrock ready for a fight. It's a good thing Chase wasn't there."

"Why on earth did you go out with Chase to begin with?"

Erin told her what had happened the night before, minus a few of the more intimate details. She had no intention of opening up about those—she couldn't even think about them without blushing, despite her hangover.

"Well, you certainly can't say you've been bored since you came back here," Jenna said in amusement afterward. "And to think, I was worried about that."

"I could never be bored with you here, Jen. In fact, I wouldn't mind if things slowed down a little." Erin's lips quirked up slightly. "I know you said every head should be taken for a spin once in a while, but now mine is quite literally spinning."

"It looks like I get to nurse the doctor back to health today," Jenna teased. "But we'll get you all patched up, I promise. And once you're feeling better, I'll have Luke come over, and you can patch things up with him. By tonight this will all be water under the bridge."

"More like Long Island Iced Tea under the bridge," Erin said with a grimace. "And I doubt he's going to come over any time soon. The police chief called him this morning. The mayor found his wife dead, and they think she was murdered."

"Oh no." All the color left Jenna's face.

"I'm sorry, Jen. Did you know her?"

"Yes, but not very well…Why—why do they think she was murdered?"

"I don't know. Luke didn't say. But then, he didn't say much of anything to me this morning."

"I can't believe Tina's dead," Jenna whispered. "Some friends of mine just went to her fortieth birthday party a couple of weeks ago."

"I feel bad for Connor. First the gunfight, and now this." Erin turned to gaze at the horizon. The vivid yellow, orange, and red hues of a beautiful sunrise were bursting across the sky. *Oh, what a beautiful hell indeed.*

"Tina was Connor's stepmother," Jenna said. "And from what I've heard, she barely tolerated him. It's sad, because I don't think his real mother treats him any better. Her name is Meredith Armstrong. She's a lawyer in town and a real you-know-what. Luke can't stand her. In fact, I wouldn't be surprised if she had something to do with this. It's a well-known fact that Tina broke up her marriage to Mayor Murdock."

"Was Tina a lawyer too?"

"No. Before the mayor was elected to office, he and Meredith ran a law firm together, and Tina was their legal secretary."

Erin closed her eyes and leaned her head back against the chair, unable to bear watching the sunrise any longer. "I guess her promotion isn't looking so good now."

Jenna didn't respond, and for a while neither of them said anything else.

Erin eventually peeled her eyes back open and glanced over at Jenna, sensing something was wrong as the silence grew heavy between them. And when she saw the anguished look on her friend's face, she knew something was seriously wrong. "What is it, Jen?" she asked, sitting up straighter in her chair.

Jenna remained silent at first, nervously wringing her hands. "There's—something I've been meaning to tell you," she finally said, avoiding Erin's direct gaze. "I know this is really bad timing, but—but with this murder…I'd rather you hear it from me. I'm so sorry. I should have told you this long before now. But I knew how much it would bother you, and I—I just couldn't tell you. And I never expected you would come back here…"

Erin watched Jenna struggle to find the words she wanted to say, and it brought back memories of that awful night in Boston when she'd told her about the cancer. Erin knew that whatever her friend was trying to tell her now wasn't going to be pleasant, and dread stirred up the already sick feeling in her stomach. "Just say it, Jenna," she urged, bracing herself for the news.

"Erin, your father isn't in prison anymore. He lives here in New Dublin."

Erin stared at her in shock. "But that's impossible. He's in prison for life. My grandmother said…" She realized her mistake then. She'd never thought to second guess her grandmother about that—she would never have wanted to. It hadn't once occurred to her that her father might get out of prison someday, that she should have checked to make sure.

"His sentence was twenty years to life," Jenna hesitantly explained. "There's a big difference. I asked Luke to find out more about him years ago. It turned out he'd already been released on parole by then. He finished that last year and moved back here. He lives with his mother."

For a moment Erin was in such a state of horrified disbelief that she didn't know what to think or say. Her stomach finally said it for her. "Oh God!" She shot to her feet and ran to the far end of the porch, then leaned over the railing and vomited into the rose bushes.

Jenna came up alongside her and held the hair away from her face until the heaving subsided. "Erin, I'm so sorry," she whispered. "I should have told you when I first found out."

Erin folded her arms on the railing and lowered her head onto them. She felt like her world had just spun completely out of control, and she took several slow, deep breaths, trying to calm herself. Her father was here—her mother's murderer. He was walking the streets, and she could run into him at any moment. Then she remembered there had just been another murder. "You don't really think the mayor's ex-wife killed her, do you?" she asked, looking up at Jenna. "You think he did it."

Jenna shook her head in distress. "No, it's just that after Tina married the mayor, they bought the Irish Waters Restaurant in town. Seth is a cook there, so his past is bound to come up if they don't arrest someone else right away. But that doesn't mean he did it. Who knows? Maybe Meredith really was involved. She certainly keeps plenty of criminals on the streets. She could have hired one of them to do it."

"Why would she risk everything to get involved in something like that, Jen? No, Seth Slater has got to be a prime suspect. He worked for Tina. And no matter how many petty criminals are out there roaming the streets, I'll bet he's the only convicted murderer." And if he had done it, that would make her the daughter of a serial killer. *Oh God.* Now she really was living a nightmare. Bile rose in her throat, and with a soft moan she dropped her head back down, willing herself not to vomit again.

"I don't know what motive he would have for murder," Jenna said. "Luke's been keeping an eye on him, and he hasn't caused any problems here. He also had a clean prison record in California."

"That's reassuring," Erin murmured dryly, keeping her head buried in her arms. And after a pause, she asked, "Does anyone else here know he's my father?"

"Only Luke and I. No one else needs to know."

"Oh God, Jenna." Erin abruptly stood up and pushed away from the railing. "I can't deal with this right now. I need to go inside." But as soon as she turned toward the door, she let out a startled gasp and stepped back, seeing a man standing at the top of the stairs on the other side of the porch.

Jenna looked that way in alarm, and then lifted a hand to her chest, breathing a sigh of relief. "It's only James, Erin. Luke asked him to come today to build the ramp for the porch. He's Father Burnett's nephew."

"I made these for you last night, Jenna," James said in a somewhat bashful tone, walking over to them with a plate of cookies. "I know chocolate chip is your favorite."

"How thoughtful of you, James. Thank you," Jenna responded, smiling half-heartedly as she took the plate from him. "This is my friend, Erin. She's—"

Erin took one look at the cookies and spun around,

vomiting into the roses again.

Jenna winced. "She isn't feeling very well right now."

Erin eased herself up and turned back to them after a moment, clutching her stomach. "So much for the aspirin kicking in. And I don't think I'll be eating cookies anytime soon." She glanced painfully at James. "Sorry to meet you under these circumstances."

Feeling too miserable to be embarrassed about those circumstances, she headed inside. But just as she started climbing the stairs she caught sight of someone else out of the corner of her eye: a woman with long red hair standing between the dining area and the living room beyond. She stopped short and looked directly at that spot, but no one was there. *Shannon.*

Erin felt another wave of nausea hit her. And with a groan she rushed upstairs to the bathroom.

In the meantime, Jenna retrieved her cane and gave James an apologetic, flustered look. "I'm sorry. I need to go in too. Thanks again for the cookies—and for working on the ramp, of course."

She left him standing there scratching his head in bewilderment and hurried into the house, setting the plate of cookies on the foyer table. Then she grabbed her cell phone and quickly sent a text to Luke:

CALL ME ASAP. URGENT!!!

CHAPTER 12

The chief wasn't kidding. They had a real mess on their hands.

Luke looked over at the body on the bed again in disbelief. He'd never seen anything like it before. He'd never *heard* of anything like it before.

Tina Murdock was lying naked in a spread-eagle position on the bed. Clearly her killer had wanted her displayed like that. She had multiple stab wounds over her lower abdomen, and a knife was buried in the middle of her chest. There was very little blood, though. The stab wounds had probably all been inflicted after her death.

But above that was where things got especially bizarre. It appeared she'd been strangled with barbed wire. And then her head and neck had been wrapped in it, leaving her barely identifiable. The mayor said he didn't own any barbed wire, which wasn't surprising. He lived in an affluent subdivision on the edge of town. It was a heavily wooded area, which allowed for a lot of privacy, but wasn't a place where barbed wire would be of any use. So her killer must have brought it along. This was definitely premeditated murder, executed in the most barbaric fashion—literally.

Everyone working around Luke was eerily quiet, and no one wanted to go near the bed if they didn't have to. Several of the other officers still looked green, and the chief was especially reserved. Luke knew he was good friends with the mayor and his wife. The mayor himself was outside, walking around in a daze. And they still hadn't been able to locate his son, Connor.

The crime scene response unit was processing the scene—a meticulous task that would probably take a few days to finish—and the medical examiner was there as well. She figured the time of death had been somewhere between 9:00 p.m. and 1:00 a.m.... Right around the time he and Erin had been making love. Or it could have happened while she was sleeping in his arms. He remembered the look on her face last night... But then the sound of her ex-husband's name on her lips this morning when he'd kissed her echoed through his mind all over again, slicing into his heart like a freshly sharpened dagger, and he forced himself not to think about her anymore. He couldn't afford to be distracted right now. He had a murder to solve.

But a moment later the text alert on his phone went off, and he read the frantic message from Jenna. *So much for not being distracted.* And with a resigned sigh he walked into an unoccupied room to call her.

"Luke, please tell me this murder has nothing to do with Erin's father," she immediately said.

"I don't know, Jen," he answered wearily, running a hand over his unshaven jaw. "In fact, there's not a whole lot I do know right now. But he's certainly a person of interest at this point."

"Erin knows he's here. I told her this morning."

Shit. "How did she take it?"

"She started throwing up over the side of the porch. I've never seen her so upset before."

Luke winced. The vomiting probably had more to do with a hangover. So Erin had been drunk and in love with another man when she'd slept with him last night. His day was getting better by the minute.

"You need to talk to her," Jenna continued. "You're wrong about Peter. She doesn't—"

Scott Ripley walked into the room as she was talking. "We have a major problem, Luke," he said at the same time.

"Jen, I'm sorry, I have to go," Luke interrupted her. "I'll come by when I can."

He ended the call and looked up at Scott as he put his phone away. "What is it?"

"Dispatch got a call from the hospital. Jesse Torres escaped. Someone drugged Ben Watkins while he was on shift last night and helped the kid get out. A nurse found Ben handcuffed to Jesse's bed this morning."

"Jesus Christ!" Luke softly cursed. Ben Watkins was a deputy fresh out of the police academy, and he'd been assigned to sit outside Jesse's room overnight.

"It gets worse, Luke," Scott said in an especially somber tone. "Ben's alive, but he's in pretty serious condition. Someone stuck a chest tube in him—the one that was supposed to be in Jesse."

"What the hell do you mean by that?"

"When Torres had surgery the other day Dr. O'Reilly put a tube in his chest and attached it to a machine they use to keep the air from building back up. Last night either Torres, or whoever was with him, pulled the tube out. Then they cut Ben's chest open and stuck it in him instead, probably to make it look like Torres was still there. Dr. O'Reilly is taking Ben to the OR as we speak."

For a moment Luke wasn't able to speak. And when the full impact of Scott's words hit him, rage thundered through his veins. His fellow officers were like brothers to him. He would put his life on the line for any one of them. And for something like this to happen…He felt like his own chest had just been cut open.

"We need to get an APB out on Jesse Torres right away," he finally said, shaking off his anger. There was no place for emotion right now.

"Already done," Scott responded.

"Does the chief know?"

"Yeah. He's outside right now making sure everything's secure. As if we don't have enough to deal with, there's a storm coming in. I'll help him with that, and then we're going over to the hospital. He wants you to keep working this case."

Luke nodded. "Once I wrap things up here I'll have Frank Murdock meet me at the station for a formal interview. I told him to track Connor down and get him over there too. I don't think it's any coincidence that he and another kid had a shootout yesterday and now his stepmother is dead today."

They walked out of the room and Scott motioned to the master bedroom down the hall. "There's going to be a media frenzy over this, you know. I wouldn't be surprised if it makes national news."

Luke didn't even want to think about the level of chaos that would ensue then. "It'll help if we can keep some of the more gruesome details quiet. But the chief will have his hands full with the press no matter what. I hope he pulls it together. He's not taking this too well."

"Do you think DCI will get involved?" DCI was the Division of Criminal Investigation—sort of like the FBI at a state level.

"That'll be up to the chief," Luke said. "But we could use the help, that's for sure."

"What we could really use are a few more cops in our own department—and a decent raise for once. But I'm beating a dead horse there." Scott's lips twisted into a sardonic smile. "Anyway, I'd better get going. The chief is waiting."

After he left, Luke headed back to the master bedroom to do one last inspection of the body before the medical examiner had it removed. And he soon caught something he'd missed the first time around: She wasn't wearing a wedding ring.

He leaned down, picking her stiff hand up to take a closer look. There were multiple bloodless wounds over the second knuckle of her left fourth finger, which meant the killer had probably ripped the ring off post-mortem.

He stood up and slowly shook his head, murmuring to himself, "We've got one hell of a monster in our midst."

No sooner did he say that than lightning flashed through the bedroom windows, followed by the deep rumble of thunder.

LUKE SAT IN THE INTERVIEW ROOM AT THE POLICE station a few hours later, oblivious to the storm still raging outside, and wondered if he wasn't looking into the bearded face of that monster—the man who'd always reminded him of a younger, slightly less rotund version of Santa Claus, with gray hair instead of white: jolly old Frank Murdock.

A day ago Luke would never have thought the mayor capable of such an atrocity. But then, a lot of things had happened in the last day that he never would have expected. And the statistics already pointed to Frank: Most female homicide victims were killed by someone they knew—more often than not by a current or former male partner.

Frank hadn't said or done anything in particular that was overtly incriminating. In fact, he'd gone out of his way to cooperate with them and hadn't even requested another lawyer be present. But there were subtle things in his behavior and speech that raised plenty of red flags.

The story Frank gave was that he'd gone to City Hall late yesterday afternoon to work on some issues with the budget in preparation for a city council meeting today. He'd ended up working longer than expected and had decided to sleep in his office, something he'd been doing a lot lately because of the budgetary issues. Then he'd headed home early this morning, exiting from the back entrance to the parking lot where he'd left his Cadillac all night.

Frank had mentioned early on in the interview that video surveillance would be able to confirm his whereabouts—the first red flag. His responses had also been subtly evasive at times, with an uncertainty in his tone that he hadn't quite been able to hide. And when Luke had asked more detailed questions about the problems with the city budget, he'd been especially ambiguous, taking way too much time to answer them. If he'd really been working so hard on the budget last night, he shouldn't have had any trouble answering those questions.

He'd shown other signs too: frequently clearing his throat or covering his mouth with his hand—almost like he was covering up a lie. And he'd smiled way too often, even attempted to joke around here and there. The mayor was well known for his jovial personality, but that kind of behavior was completely inappropriate under the circumstances.

Luke could smell lies from a mile away, and the mayor reeked of them.

A moment later there was a brief knock on the interview room door, and a uniformed officer popped his head in. "Meredith Armstrong is here with Connor."

"Okay, send them in," Luke said. Connor had apparently been at his mother's house last night, making her his alibi—and his attorney.

She'd been with him Friday for the interrogation at the Sheriff's Office after the shooting as well, which Frank hadn't bothered to attend, despite the fact that his son's future was at stake. He'd said he was letting Meredith handle Connor's legal matters herself, since her area of expertise was banking and finance, not criminal defense. But everyone knew the truth: He just couldn't stand being anywhere near his ex-wife.

Luke had insisted Frank stay for this interview, though. And it was for one specific reason: Getting the three of them in the room together was the best way to throw them all off their game.

"Connor, Meredith," he said in greeting as they sat down at the interview table across from him, with Connor taking a seat between his parents.

"Good morning, Detective Mathis," Meredith briskly responded. "I hope you haven't forgotten that this is an informal interview, and we need to keep it brief. I have other business to attend to this morning."

"I haven't forgotten," Luke said, making a conscious effort not to let her condescending tone get to him. He should be used to it by now anyway. But nothing about Meredith Armstrong was easy to get used to.

Some might consider her attractive with her medium length brown hair and deep-set brown eyes. But the perpetual scowl on her face completely detracted from any beauty. And her intense, unwavering stare was enough to make any man want to run from the room. Luke thought maybe next time he would wear his bulletproof vest.

He shifted his gaze to Connor. "My condolences for the loss of your stepmother."

"Thanks," the boy muttered, not quite meeting his eyes.

"How are you doing?" Luke probed.

Connor shrugged. "Fine, I guess."

"You've had an eventful few days."

Another shrug and no answer.

"Where were you around nine o'clock last night?"

"He was with me," Meredith answered for him. "All night."

"What did you do at your mom's house?" Luke asked Connor.

Meredith didn't get the hint and answered for him again anyway. "We watched a new show on TV. It's called Vengeance." Her lips quirked up slightly. "You should check it out sometime. It's very good."

The blatant arrogance on her face irked Luke to no end, but he kept his own expression impassive. "What time was that on?"

"It was the season premiere," she easily responded. "A two-hour event from eight to ten. Then we went to bed."

"Ten o'clock is pretty early for a sixteen-year-old to go to bed," Luke said to Connor.

"There's nothing wrong with that," Meredith responded yet again. "'Early to bed, early to rise,' as they say."

"Is it possible he could have left while you were sleeping?" Luke asked her.

"The alarm system was on all night, which the security company can verify. And only I know the code."

Luke knew there were plenty of ways to get around a security system, and he turned back to the boy. "I need you to answer some of these questions, Connor. Were you supposed to be at your mom's house last night?"

Connor paused before answering, glancing at his mother. "No, it's my dad's week, but he said he was going to be working late, so I went over to my mom's."

"Do you do that much?"

Another pause. "Sometimes."

"When was the last time you stayed at your mom's house when it was your dad's week?"

Connor didn't respond, glancing at Meredith again.

"It doesn't happen often. We try to keep a strict schedule," she said coolly. "But I think the boy is getting tired of Frank being gone all the time."

"So when was it decided that he would stay with you?"

"He called just before six and asked if he could stay, then came right over."

Luke directed the next question at Frank. "Did you know Connor would be with Meredith last night?"

"Of course," Frank answered with a good-natured smile, giving Connor's shoulder a squeeze. "He called and asked me first. And he wasn't upset at all that I was working last night. He knows it's part of the job."

Luke turned back to Connor, who continued to appear disinterested in the conversation. "Where were you before you went to your mom's house?"

"I was at my dad's."

"Was Tina there?"

"Yeah."

"Did you talk to her?"

Connor shrugged. "Not much. I just said I was going to my mom's. She didn't care."

"How did she seem last night?"

The boy shrugged again. His shoulders were certainly getting a workout. "Normal, I guess."

"Was she upset that your dad was at work?"

"She didn't seem like it."

"Did she say what her plans were last night?"

"No. She was just about to go down in the basement to work out. I don't know what she was doing after that."

"Did she and your dad argue much?"

Another shrug. "Not really."

"Is there anyone you can think of who might have wanted to hurt her?"

"No."

Luke turned back to Meredith. It was time to stir the pot a little. "Frank mentioned that you and Tina didn't get along very well."

There was an immediate spark of anger in those deep-set brown eyes at the implication. "I hardly think that's surprising, given the circumstances," she said shortly. Then her lips twisted into another mocking smile. "But I have to wonder how Frank and his dearly departed wife really did get along when there was no one around to see."

"What do you mean?" Luke asked.

"I can't imagine Frank was very happy about his wife's gambling problem—her very *serious* gambling problem. Or that his restaurant has been losing money hand over fist." Meredith's contemptuous smile widened. "Of course, the two are probably related."

Luke looked over at Frank, who'd lost a little color in his face, and waited for him to respond.

"Things weren't as bad as she's making them sound," he said, pulling at his tie. "We were managing just fine." Luke noted how he unconsciously shook his head as he spoke.

Meredith laughed. "I have my sources, Frank. Tina had you on the fast track to bankruptcy." She shifted her gaze back to Luke. "And Connor told me he spent the night at his office. Now isn't that a coincidence? He just so happens to be away all night when his good for nothing wife gets murdered."

Frank glared at her. "You'd like to point the blame at me, wouldn't you? I'll bet you had—"

"Didn't your wife do enough betting for the both of you?" she interrupted with another one of her malicious smiles.

Frank's face turned as red as Santa Claus's jacket. "Don't mock me, Meredith. I know you probably had a hand in this. And I swear I'll hunt down all of your good-for-nothing criminal friends and find out which one of them helped you. This was revenge, plain and simple. You hated Tina because she loved me."

"Oh, please," Meredith said, all amusement gone as she shot daggers at him. "Tina did me a favor by spreading her legs for you. It's a chore I do not miss, that's for sure. Hell would have to freeze over before I'd subject myself to that again."

"You always were a frigid bitch—"

"Shut up!" Connor yelled, closing his eyes tightly and

fisting his hands in his hair as he leaned over the interview table, rocking back and forth. "Just shut up, both of you! Shut the fuck up!"

Luke knew he had an opening then. "Did you kill Tina, Connor?"

"Give me a break, Detective," Meredith immediately cut in. "You watched the video just as well as I did on Friday. The boy probably wet his pants when the gun went off. There's no way he would have the guts to commit a murder like that."

"Did you kill Tina, Connor?" Luke repeated, ignoring Meredith.

Connor opened his eyes—a deeper shade of blue than his dad's—and they glittered with anger. "No."

"Why did you shoot Jesse?"

"Like I told you before, it was an accident."

"You said Jesse started it. Why?"

Connor briefly glanced at Frank. "Because I called him a bastard and said he should go back to Mexico."

"Why did you say that?"

Connor shrugged, and the blank mask returned to his face. "He was being a jerk and I just said it. Jesse is a hothead and things went too far, that's all."

Luke intentionally made his own feelings very apparent, staring at Connor with cold, hard fury in eyes. "Someone helped Jesse escape from the hospital last night, and in the process they nearly killed a police officer. Do you know who helped Jesse?"

A look of surprise, along with a hint of fear, crossed Connor's face, and he gave his father another surreptitious glance. "I...I don't—know."

Meredith stood up. "I believe this interview is over,

Detective Mathis. My son has told everything he knows. Come along, Connor."

"I'll be in touch," Luke said in his usual, impassive tone.

Frank laughed weakly. "Sorry things got a little heated there. Meredith is always a handful, as you know."

Luke chose not to comment on that, pulling out a packet of paperwork and handing it to Frank. "These are some financial disclosure forms I need you to fill out, along with a list of documents we'll need: bank and credit card statements, life insurance—"

"Luke, you can't possibly think I killed Tina?" Frank interrupted, his expression filled with disbelief.

"It's all standard procedure," Luke responded mildly. "I'll give you a call tomorrow. I'd like to have everything by the end of the day."

The mayor didn't raise any objections, but he wasn't looking so jolly when he left.

Luke called Scott afterward. "Are you and the chief still at the hospital?"

"Yeah. And we've got a lead on who Jesse's accomplice is. Get this, Luke: It's probably Wayne Raabe. Just when we thought he'd gone straight. It turns out he got a job working as a nursing assistant here and was on shift last night until midnight. He was the last one to check on Jesse before the nurse found Ben this morning. And the unit clerk up there has seen Jesse stop by and talk to Wayne quite a few times lately. We're in the security office right now pulling up video surveillance. If you hang on a minute we might have an answer for sure."

Luke wasn't surprised to hear Wayne Raabe's name come up. The kid was probably about nineteen now, but they'd already been dealing with him for the better part of a decade. He'd quit school at sixteen and had been in and out of jail several times on drug-related charges. But he'd kept out of trouble lately, so they'd figured he was finally getting his life together. More than likely, though, he just wasn't getting caught. And his lawyer was none other than Meredith Armstrong. Maybe she was paying him this time.

"Sure as shit, Luke," Scott said on the other end of the line. "Wayne is pushing Jesse out the back entrance in a wheelchair. Neither of them is even trying to hide their identity. Another camera covers the parking lot back there, so we should be able to ID the car they're using and get an APB out."

"What's the time on the video?"

"12:09 a.m."

"Within the window Tina Murdock was killed," Luke noted.

"Yeah, I wouldn't put murder past Wayne Raabe. Especially after what he and Jesse did to Ben. I wonder if the crime lab will find Ben's blood on the knife that ended up in Tina Murdock's chest."

Luke grimaced. "That would answer some of our questions and leave a whole lot more. When will you and the chief be back so we can compare notes?"

"I'd say we should be done here in about half an hour. The chief's putting out word that he wants all hands on deck at the station for a meeting at one."

"I'll be there," Luke told him. "In the meantime, I'm going to run over to Seth Slater's place. I'd like to know where he was last night."

"You should have backup, Luke. Why don't you wait until after the meeting and I'll go with you?"

"No, it'll be fine. I've talked to Slater before and haven't had any problems. I'll see you at one."

Luke ended the call and looked at the time on his phone. Exactly noon. High noon.

THE HOUSE WAS ON A DEAD END ROAD JUST OUTSIDE of town. And Slater was definitely home.

Luke parked his unmarked sedan behind Seth's beat up gray truck in the weed-festooned gravel driveway. Stepping out, he unconsciously rested his hand on the gun in his holster as he surveyed the property. It was eerily quiet there. No sound. No movement. The perfect calm after the storm…Or maybe it was the eye of a hurricane.

The yard was ragged and overgrown, and the ramshackle two-story house probably hadn't been painted in decades. Bits of peeling, light green paint stubbornly stuck to the weathered gray wood in places, and the few remaining shutters were a darker shade of peeling green.

Luke stepped up onto the porch, littered with all kinds of junk, and caught the slight flick of a curtain in the window to his right. Knocking hard on the door, he announced, "New Dublin Police."

He waited, watching for any further movement, keeping his ears tuned for any sound. But there was nothing. Only stillness. Silence.

He waited another minute, then knocked again. "I know you're in there, Slater," he said loudly. "This is Detective Mathis. I have a few questions for you."

There was no response.

"This will only take a couple of minutes. It'll be easier

on all of us if you cooperate."

Still nothing.

"I'll talk to you eventually, Slater."

Luke waited another minute. Then another. And when it was clear there would be no answer, he sighed in frustration and finally left.

So much for a showdown.

CHAPTER

13

The dam burst, and a river of pain raged through Erin, wild and unstoppable, washing away all the barriers to its flow in her mind. The river was filled with years and years of unacknowledged pain and grief that had slowly built up behind that dam, pushing against it, wearing it away, waiting to be set free.

And she thought she had set it free with all the tears she'd cried over the last few weeks. But they'd just escaped from a crack in the dam. Now the whole thing was collapsing inside her.

Erin felt her body shake with the force of it as she sat in the sand by the pond with her arms wrapped around her legs, blindly watching the sunset. And when it became too much to bear, she dropped her forehead to her knees and helplessly sobbed, from the very bottom of her soul.

After a while she felt a hand gently squeeze her shoulder. "Everything is going to be okay," Jenna softly said. "Luke will call."

Erin lifted her head, letting the tears continue to fall

unheeded down her cheeks. "It's not just Luke. It's every-thing—*everything* that's happened to us. To me. To you. To your mom. My mom…Oh God, Jenna, I miss my mom." She buried her head in her hands and continued to cry. "I need her. I've needed her so many times…It's not fair. I want—I want my mom back."

"Erin…" Jenna sat down and gathered her into her arms. "I know. I know."

"It's so wrong. She shouldn't—she shouldn't have died like that. And I hate my father for what he did. God, I hate him…I can't believe he's free. He's free, but my mom is dead. And I—I have to spend the rest of my life without her."

Jenna didn't say anything, just held her close until the deep, wracking sobs subsided. Then she fished some tissues out of her sweater pocket. "Here, I think we need these again."

Erin sat back and blew her nose. But she couldn't stop the tears from flowing. There were just too many things she'd never let herself cry about before. "It's because of me that a child in Boston doesn't have a mother, either. And I think about him all the time, wondering if he's going to be okay." She briefly paused, drawing in a shuttered breath. "I never told you about that. It happened the day of the pileup in Boston. A pregnant woman came in, and I had to do an emergency C-section to save the baby. But I couldn't save her. She died at about the same time her baby let out his first cry just a few feet away."

"I heard about that on the news," Jenna whispered. "They never said who the doctor was, and I had really hoped it wasn't you."

"Oh, it was me all right," Erin said, brushing away the tears on her cheeks. "And an hour before that I was right there when they brought in some of the survivors of the bus crash. One of them was a woman who'd been on vacation with her husband and daughter. They'd taken the trip as a gift to their daughter—one last vacation together before she started college. But the woman's husband was killed instantly and their daughter died in her arms while other people trampled over them trying to save themselves. When the ambulance crew brought the woman in she had severe smoke inhalation and was struggling to breathe and completely overwhelmed with grief. She told me she wanted to die too, and refused to have anything done at first. But I finally convinced her to accept treatment, that her family would want her to live. I had to intubate her, and I'll never forget the look in her eyes before I put her to sleep. It's another thing on a very long list of things I wish I could forget—and another thing I'll always second-guess myself about. Maybe I shouldn't have said anything to change her mind. Maybe she would have been better off dying. I can't even imagine what it must have been like for her to wake up later and have to relive that whole nightmare all over again—and again every day for the rest of her life."

"I'm so sorry, Erin," Jenna said. "But please don't second-guess yourself. You did the right thing."

"I don't even know if there is a right thing anymore," Erin bitterly responded. "I think I realized that about a year and a half ago. It all started the previous summer when I was on the night shift and a mother brought her ten-month-old daughter in. She said the basement door had been left open by accident, and while she was in the kitchen cleaning up, her daughter fell down the basement stairs in her walker onto the concrete floor below. The child was somewhat lethargic and didn't cry or protest much when I examined her, which was the first sign that something was seriously wrong. And there was obvious swelling over the back of her head. I immediately ordered a trauma workup, including CT scans, and did a quick ultrasound to check for internal injuries. But before she was taken over to the CT scanner she became even more lethargic and had spells where she would stop breathing. Her symptoms were consistent with a rapidly worsening brain hemorrhage, and I paged the attending neurosurgeon on call while we were getting everything ready to intubate her. He'd had a long day and wanted to wait to come in until the senior resident finished his evaluation and all the CT scans were done to completely rule out other major injuries. But I knew, I knew with absolute certainty, that the child was bleeding into her brain and that every second mattered. I'd seen her, I'd examined her, and I'd already learned that training, experience, and common sense were more important than a CT scan. So I insisted he come in right away. And he ended up taking her right from the CT scanner to the OR when the scans confirmed that she was bleeding into her brain—badly—and that every second really had mattered. They did a craniotomy, and by the next day she was completely back to normal."

Erin smiled painfully. "Sounds like the perfect happy ending, doesn't it? I certainly got a lot of congratulations for what I'd done, let me tell you. And if ever there was a case that I thought validated all the years I'd spent studying and practicing medicine, it was that one." She slowly shook her head. "Until the child came back nine months later. Once again, I was there. And once again, her mother brought her in. But this time there were obvious signs of child abuse, and this time the mother had waited too long. The CT scans showed another brain bleed, and the same neurosurgeon did another craniotomy. But the child died on the OR table during the procedure. Afterward, the neurosurgeon told me it was the first time his team had ever given a child her first haircut, and her last one."

Erin unfolded the tissue in her trembling hand and wiped her nose. "Big surprise, there were no congratulations that day. And for the first time in my career I wondered if medicine was really even worth it. Why bother? Sure, when the child was brought in the first time no one else had suspected she was being abused either. There hadn't been any history of it, and the mother had given a good story. But the fact is, I helped save a child's life, all so she could be subject to God only knows what kind of abuse for nine more months until she was finally, brutally, beaten to death. It turns out the mother's boyfriend had been doing it. And now he's in prison for murder. Just like my own father had been. And it kills me that however unwittingly, I contributed to the pain and suffering that little girl had to endure, even though I'd give my life to protect any child from harm like that. Now there's real irony for you."

Jenna didn't respond, looking thoroughly shaken as tears slid silently down her cheeks.

Erin winced when she saw her expression. "These are the kinds of stories I don't tell you about, Jen," she said, impatiently wiping away her own tears. "It's easy to talk about the funny cases, or the ones that really do have a happy ending. But there are a lot more stories like these. Pages of them. So is it any wonder that I would question the existence of God when I see this stuff happen all the time? I keep hearing how God works in mysterious ways, that everything happens for a reason, and that it's all part of God's greater plan. Well, do you know what I think? The plan sucks." She turned her face up toward the sky, brushing away more tears, and yelled, "Do you hear me? Your plan sucks! It really, really sucks!" And with an exasperated sigh she wrapped her arms around her legs again and stared broodingly out at the pond, which had turned a fiery red in the light of the blazing sunset.

After a moment Jenna quietly said, "I think I understand now why you really do need to take a break from medicine."

"Because I'm carrying on like a raving lunatic, crying for my dead mother and yelling at God?" Erin's lips quirked up into a ghost of a smile. "Maybe it wasn't such a good idea to get me talking about Him after all."

"Oh, Erin…" Jenna said with deep sadness in her voice.

Erin let out another sigh. "Don't worry, I do believe in God, and I won't change my mind about that now. But when we were at church the other day it occurred to me that the fire and brimstone Hell my grandmother used to preach about probably doesn't exist. I think Hell is actually a very cold place—and it's probably all here on Earth. But what I don't get is how God can possibly be this kind and loving, divine entity, and yet it doesn't feel like His presence is very strong here. Tell me, Jenna, why is God so weak?"

"God isn't weak, but people are," Jenna responded. "And God, like the Devil, can only work through people. I think God is too often blamed for the inherent weakness of human beings."

Erin sniffed back her tears and smiled wryly. "You always have a good answer for everything. It's very irritating sometimes, you know."

Jenna chuckled. "As I've told you before, I really don't know much—just enough to make life bearable. But I have done a lot of thinking since I found out I had cancer, especially about the meaning of life. I think the most important thing all of us need to do in this lifetime is to understand what makes us who we are, to learn our strengths and weaknesses in the face of our own trials and those of others, so that we can become the best, most loving version of ourselves that we're capable of being. And the farther along we get in achieving that in this life, the less work we'll have to do in the next one. Progress to achieve perfection—I believe that's what God's goal is for everyone and everything. And isn't that the goal of every science on Earth? It just might turn out that God has been a scientist himself all along—the master scientist of the universe, one with knowledge of scientific principles and laws that are far beyond our comprehension. As it is, there is a theory in physics, supported by data, that would suggest there are alternate worlds, and that they interact with ours. I'm certain Heaven is one of them. And Hell is probably another."

"So are you saying God is some kind of mad scientist who creates things in our world like cancer that serve as obstacles for people to overcome in order to make it to Heaven—or to go down in flames if they don't get it?"

"No, Erin, just the opposite. I don't think God would intentionally create obstacles for us—He wants to eliminate them. A lot of those obstacles are created by our own lack of self-awareness, our own weaknesses, or the weaknesses of others. And those are the things we can fix, or at least work on improving. We'll never be perfect in this lifetime after all. But things like cancer, they're just another part of our imperfect world—imperfect science, imperfect biology. And they're things that neither God or the Devil can magically create or make disappear. They're not punishment.

They're not put here on purpose. They're not anything. They just happen. Like a calf with two heads."

"What?" Erin asked with a bemused smile.

Jenna laughed softly. "No, it's not the morphine talking this time. I actually saw a picture of a calf with two heads not long ago, and that's when it really hit home for me. There's imperfection everywhere in nature—in humans, in animals, in plants, in the weather. There's no intention in it. God certainly isn't going to punish a calf by giving it two heads. And I don't see any other purpose for it either. I doubt having two brains is going to help a cow any more than having one. I've seen how dumb those animals can be."

A bubble of laughter escaped Erin. "Okay, now that has got to be the morphine talking."

"No, it's only me justifying why I should be able to eat a hamburger."

Erin laughed helplessly, and then shook her head in amazement. "Twenty minutes ago I thought I would never laugh again, and now I can't stop. I don't know how you do it."

Jenna affectionately patted Erin's leg. "Here's another quote from Mark Twain: 'Against the assault of laughter, nothing can stand.'"

"Especially not a cow," Erin said, laughing again. "But tell me, how do you really know if cows are that dumb? I've never seen you get anywhere near one—probably because you'd scream bloody murder if you stepped in cow manure."

"That is true," Jenna responded with a sheepish smile. "Just to be fair to cows, though, if one considers how little anybody—even the smartest person on Earth—actually knows about the universe, none of us is really that much smarter than a cow. But I wrote a poem about cows that will answer your question. Let me think if I can remember it."

"Uh oh, another poem," Erin teased.

"It's called 'Seeking Shelter,' and it's really about how people can be as clueless as a cow. Just keep in mind, it isn't Walt Whitman or Robert Frost type of material."

"That's okay, because I wouldn't know their poetry anyway." Erin chuckled. "And I didn't mean for that to rhyme."

"Most people don't anymore. It's not en vogue to rhyme in poetry these days. But as for me, I feel like the English language sounds too cacophonous without rhyme, so I do it anyway. It's not like I'm trying to make a living at it or anything." Jenna grinned. "It's just for my own enjoyment, and now for yours. So here's how 'Seeking Shelter' goes:

> 'A shelter was built on top of a hill
> Where cows were kept in a farmer's field.
> It was put up there for them to come
> To seek shelter from the rain, snow, and sun.
> But a storm came through the field one day,
> And the whole thing was utterly blown away.'"

Erin snorted a laugh over the last line, and Jenna paused to laugh too. "Now you've thrown me off," she said. "Where was I? Oh, yes:

> 'Yet every day those cows still came
> To huddle on the hill as if nothing had changed,
> And I would drive by and shake my head
> At their simple, bovine intelligence.
> Until one day it occurred to me
> That we, Mother Nature's prodigies,
> Do the same thing all the time:
> Seek shelter in things where shelter exists
> Exclusively in our minds.'"

"So we're Mother Nature's prodigies, are we?" Erin said dryly. "I'm not so sure Mother Nature would agree with that." Then she looked out at the pond and her smile faded. "You probably had me in mind when you wrote that poem."

"No, Erin. It applies to everyone in some way. So many of the things we believe, and the ways we behave, are based on illusions—shelters that exist only in our minds. And more often than not, we're just as clueless about it as those cows were."

"Me more than most…I don't know, Jen. I wonder if I'm too messed up to ever find real happiness. Yesterday I was so sure it was possible. But today I wonder if it will always be out of my reach."

"It's only out of your reach because you choose to keep it there. You need to let yourself be happy."

"That's a whole lot easier said than done."

"For someone who's accomplished so much in her life, you sure do say that a lot, my friend," Jenna gently chided. "And nothing in life is easier done than said."

"But that's just it: Nothing *is* easy. Life feels like a never-ending battle, and I don't know if I have enough strength to fight." Erin grimaced. "I mean, look at me. I'm in worse shape today than I was when I got here. And I was a wreck then."

Jenna shook her head. "You're wrong, Erin. I think you've made more progress today than you have in the last twenty-six years. You just don't realize it yet. And you will fight. You have to fight, because you care so much. It's not just medicine that needs you: The world needs you. As Dr. Seuss would say, 'Unless someone like you cares a whole awful lot, nothing is going to get better. It's not.'"

Erin smiled ruefully. "It figures you're quoting me a line from a children's book right now."

"Everyone should read Dr. Seuss books. And the people who think they're too old for them are probably the ones who need to read them the most."

Erin grabbed hold of Jenna's hands. "The world needs you, too. I need you. Come back to Boston with me and let's fight for you. Please."

"Oh, Erin. You know I can't."

"Please, Jenna. I need you to fight this cancer. Fight it for me."

"If you were in my shoes, is that what you would do? Tell me honestly, Erin. Would you fight this, knowing what you know?"

After a moment's hesitation, Erin responded, "It's different with you."

"No, it's not," Jenna said. "And the reason I'm not fighting isn't that I've given up. I've chosen not to fight because I've accepted something I can't change. And you need to accept it too. But I want you to fight. I need you to fight, because you can have a happy ending here. I want you to do that for both of us."

Tears welled up in Erin's eyes again. "I wish I could trade places with you, Jen. I'm the one who should be dying, not you."

"Please don't say that, Erin. And I'm glad it's me and not you. I would do anything for you."

"I would do anything for you, too," Erin whispered brokenly.

"Then accept what can't be changed and live for me."

"I don't know if I can. This shouldn't be how it ends for us."

"This won't be the end for us. It will just be a new beginning. I promise you." Jenna motioned toward the setting sun, which had now almost completely disappeared in a fiery glow on the horizon. "The sunset will tell you that too. Doesn't it look exactly like the sunrise this morning? You wouldn't know the difference except we're facing west instead of east. It's just a matter of perspective. *Everything* is a matter of perspective. And in every sunset there is a sunrise. Don't ever forget that." She took Erin by the shoulders. "Promise me that you're going to fight for every sunrise; that you'll live every day with hope and gratitude, no matter what—and I'll know if you're lying when you answer, because you're a terrible liar."

Erin looked at her in shock. "I have never lied to you."

"Oh yes you have. All those times over the years when you said you were fine and you weren't, I knew you were lying. That makes about a thousand times you lied." Jenna reached up and gently brushed the tears from Erin's cheeks. "And do you remember when I got that neon pink dress with the poofy skirt in tenth grade, and you said it looked good? You definitely lied about that."

Tenderness filled Erin's eyes, chasing away some of the heartbreak, and she pulled Jenna into her arms. "Okay... Okay, I promise. I'll fight every day for the rest of my life. For you."

"And promise to love, even when you'd rather hate," Jenna said as they clung to each other. "And laugh, even when you'd rather cry. Or just laugh at yourself for crying, because you still need a good cry every once in a while."

Erin did laugh then, even as she cried. "Yes, I promise."

"And if you feel overwhelmed, pray. Pray anyway, every day. And don't forget that I'll always be there for you. So talk to me, too. And think of me every time you watch the sunrise or the sunset."

"I will," Erin whispered.

Jenna drew back and looked into her eyes. "Yes, I think you're telling the truth."

Erin wiped away more tears. "I wasn't lying about the dress, you know. I did think it looked good." A crooked smile crossed her face. "In a way."

Jenna chuckled. "See, you are a bad liar. Which is why I could never tell you I'm the one who let Billy Rodgers' mouse escape when we were in sixth grade."

It took Erin a moment to register what she was talking about, and then her mouth fell open. "*You* did that? Miss Ankey spent the whole year trying to figure out who it was." She let out a laugh. "I'll never forget when the mouse ran across the room and she jumped up onto her desk screaming, and split her pants wide open. She hated our whole class after that."

Jenna bit her lip. "I did feel bad about her pants, and how she treated everyone the rest of the year. And I guess I should bring that up in confession next time. But if I'd told you it was me who let the mouse escape, I thought Cranky Ankey would probably have figured out right away that you knew. So I never said anything."

"Why did you let the mouse out in the first place?"

"Billy said he was going to feed it to his cat. He might have been teasing, but I wasn't going to take any chances, so I set it free."

"Oh, Jen." Erin shook her head with a smile. "Is there anything else you haven't told me?"

Jenna grinned impishly. "No. At least nothing I can think of at the moment."

"Well, I hope not."

They sat there and did think of a lot of things they hadn't

talked about before, though. Dusk eventually faded into darkness, and Erin smiled sadly at Jenna. "I wish I'd come here years ago and we'd been able to talk like this. We've never really known each other, not completely, until now. And it's all my fault. I'm so sorry about that, Jen."

"No, Erin. We're both at fault there. And it's mostly because we've tried to spare each other from grief. But sometimes the things we do to protect those we love end up being the things that hurt them the most. Remember that someday when you have children." Jenna gave Erin's arm an affectionate squeeze, then looked up at the sky. "The stars are out. Why don't we set our problems aside for the moment—let God do the worrying, as Martin Luther would say—and look for some constellations?" She eased back into the sand and continued to gaze up at the stars with a distant smile on her face. "Remember how we used to come out here and do that all the time when we were kids?"

Erin lay down next to her and regarded the sky. "You were always a lot better at it than me—like almost everything else."

Jenna laughed softly. "That's utter nonsense, Erin, and you know it. I wouldn't have done half as well in school if it wasn't for your help all the time. But hopefully I can at least find a few constellations for you now." She gazed back upward and pointed to an area in the northern sky. "There's the Big Dipper. It got that name because it looks like a bowl with a handle on it. The bowl is made up of those four stars there, shaped in a rectangle—or more like a trapezoid. And then if you look farther up to the left, three more stars form the handle. Can you see it?"

"Yes, I can," Erin said, and turned to look at Jenna in amazement. "I think this is the first time I've ever really seen a constellation."

Jenna grinned. "I think this is the first time you've ever really paid attention when I've tried to show you one."

Erin grinned back. "Aren't you going to give me some quote about that? I know there's one you've told me before that would apply here—something about a student finding a teacher."

"Yes, it's an ancient proverb: 'When the student is ready, the teacher will appear.'"

"The student is ready, teacher, so show me another constellation."

Jenna looked thoughtfully up at the stars. "How about Ophiuchus? It's also called the Serpent Bearer. It's harder to see than some constellations, but it depicts a man holding a snake. In Greek mythology, it represents the god of medicine…"

CHAPTER

14

Erin needed to go to the police station, and she needed to do it now. She felt it in her bones.

Quickly stopping her car, she made a U-turn and hit the gas hard before she could second-guess herself.

Jenna clutched the passenger door handle and eyed her in bemusement. "Did you forget something in town?"

"Yes, I forgot to hunt down a detective. I need to find him, and I can't wait any longer. It's driving me crazy. Do you mind if we go to the police station and see if he's there?"

"No, I don't mind at all," Jenna said. "I'm glad you're taking my advice about fighting for what you want."

Erin winced. "I just hope he'll talk to me." Since Luke had left her in the hotel parking lot two days ago she hadn't heard a word from him.

"Of course he'll talk to you. It's just that one of you needs to break the ice, and I'm sure he's up to his ears in work because of this murder. He doesn't take his job lightly. It's another thing the two of you have in common."

Erin turned off the main street and headed to the police

station down the block. When they arrived, there were numerous media vehicles parked in front, and a lot of people milling around.

"Oh boy, it's busy here," Jenna said, grimacing.

Erin found a parking spot across the street and nervously looked out her open window. "I think I see Luke's car, so he must be here too."

A moment later there was no question that Luke was there. He walked out the front doors of the police station, not with any of his fellow officers, but with a fashionably dressed and very attractive woman.

"Oh dear," Jenna whispered, biting her lip.

"Who is that?" Erin asked in confusion.

Jenna paused, then hesitantly told her, "It's Lexi Hightower. She's the one Luke broke up with the day we left for Ireland."

Erin watched as the two of them continued their conversation in front of the building. Lexi was tall, with long jet-black hair, and there was a cool sophistication about her that was obvious even from across the street. "Does she work for the police department?"

"No. Her father owns Hightower Industries, and Lexi runs the factory in town."

"Really?" Erin said in surprise. "I would never have guessed she works in a factory."

"She is smart, I'll give her that," Jenna grudgingly admitted. "She has a degree in engineering, and Luke said she's pretty well known for designing screws."

"Screws?" Erin asked with a raised brow.

"Yes, they manufacture screws and nails and other things like that. I guess she designed some special screws they make there, and even has patents on them. At one point

Luke tried to explain what they're for, but it all sounded too complicated. And it's not really my thing. I mean, I can barely handle a normal screw."

As soon as the words left her mouth they both started laughing, despite themselves. "Okay, that didn't come out right," Jenna said.

"So Luke's ex-girlfriend is a screw expert," Erin commented dryly, watching them through the window again. "That's not very reassuring."

Jenna's expression sobered. "Lexi can be pretty difficult, Erin. Why don't we leave, and you can call Luke later?"

"Really, Jen?" Erin asked, turning back to her. "You of all people are telling me not to fight now?"

"I'm not saying that…exactly," Jenna responded, wringing her hands in agitation. "But I know her. And I'm just afraid she'll—"

"Afraid?" Erin interrupted. "What about all those quotes I'm always hearing? Apparently you forgot that it was Thoreau who wrote, 'Nothing is so much to be feared as fear.' And how that inspired Franklin D. Roosevelt's famous words, 'The only thing we have to fear is fear itself.' Or that Eleanor Roosevelt once said, 'You gain strength, courage, and confidence by every experience in which you really stop to look fear in the face.'"

Jenna stared at her in amazement. "I guess you've paid more attention to me over the years than I thought."

Erin smiled wryly. "I think everything's been there in my mind all along. I just never took any of it to heart before." A spark of determination lit her eyes. "But do you know what I think now? I've spent so many years running from demons, for once I'd like to have one run from me." She got out of the car and leaned down to look at Jenna through the open window. "You can quote me on that."

"I will," Jenna said with a laugh. "And now I think I might be a little afraid for Lexi. I never thought the day would come when I'd say that."

Erin stood up and took a calming breath, then headed over to Luke and Lexi, who were still deep in conversation. Luke had his back to her, and as she approached them she heard Lexi say, "We can discuss this a little more over dinner if you're free tonight—"

"No, he's not free," Erin told her. "Not tonight or any night."

Luke immediately turned around. "Erin," he said, looking at her in shock. "What are you doing here?"

The moment their eyes met everything melted inside Erin. She didn't care if Lexi or anyone else heard what she had to say. "We need to talk, Luke. It was all a misunderstanding about Peter. When I said his name the other morning I was having a nightmare. You were with me in the dream, and then you disappeared, and he was there. It was awful—"

"It doesn't matter," Luke said, cutting her off. "I—"

"Yes, it does matter," Erin interrupted back. "It matters because we matter. And I'm not going to let you give up on us."

A slight smile pulled at the corners of Luke's mouth. "Good, because that's exactly what I was going to tell you later. And it really doesn't matter that you said your ex's name once when you were half-asleep. When I finally had a chance to go over everything that happened between us the other night, I could think of at least thirty-six times you said my name when you were awake. And I'll take my chances with thirty-six to one odds any day." His smile widened into a devilish grin. "And I figure I won't stop until that ratio is a million to one."

"Just a million?" Erin asked softly. "Then I'm going to have to call you something else so we never reach a million."

"I'm kind of partial to Neal Armstrong," Luke said, giving her another grin.

Erin grinned back, and for a moment they just stood there, lost in each other's eyes.

"Who exactly are you?" Lexi asked in an annoyed tone.

Erin reluctantly tore her gaze from Luke's and met Lexi's cold blue stare. "I'm Erin—um, Erin Harris." She suppressed a smile after she said it. "I'm Jenna Godfrey's friend. You probably remember her. She's in the car over there." Erin turned and waved to Jenna, who happily waved back.

Lexi rolled her eyes at Luke. "Okay, I've seen enough of this show. If you change your mind, call me." Then she brushed past Erin and walked away.

"Don't hold your breath on that," Erin said to her back. "Then again, hold your breath as long as you want to."

Lexi made a faint sound of indignation and kept walking.

"Jeez, Erin, I knew you had claws," Luke said in amusement. "I have the marks on my back to prove it. But—"

Before he could finish, Erin threw herself into his arms and buried her face in his neck. "I never loved Peter. I never even pretended to. I used him as an escape because I wanted to be someone else. But with you…with you, for the first time in my life, I want to be me."

Luke held her tightly. "I'm sorry I was such a jerk Monday morning, but I thought you regretted what happened between us, and it tore me up inside. Since then I probably picked up the phone a hundred times to call you. But every time I did, I would hear your voice in my head saying it was over, and I couldn't do it."

Erin leaned back and tenderly smiled up at him. "I never want it to be over. Not ever. And that night at the Shamrock Inn with you was the best night of my life."

Luke ran his fingers slowly, reverently, over her face. "God, Erin, I—"

"Hey, Romeo, we have to get going," Scott Ripley interrupted as he walked over to them. "You ready?"

Luke groaned, leaning his forehead against Erin's. "Can I stop by tonight so we can talk alone? It's probably going to be another long day, but I should be able to get there around nine."

"Yes, and you'd better come," she teased. "Otherwise I'll have to hunt you down again."

"I will," Luke promised with laughter in his voice. "I'll see you later." He pressed a kiss on top of her head and reluctantly turned to leave.

He didn't make it far, though. "Ah, to hell with it," he said. And much to Erin's surprise, he rushed back and pulled her into his arms, capturing her mouth with his in a long, sensuous kiss. Afterward, he cupped her face in his hands and smiled. "Your eyes turn a darker shade of green with passion. I want to see that color again tonight." He punctuated his words with another kiss, then finally left with Scott.

Erin headed back to her car in a happy daze, grinning at Jenna when she got inside. "We made up."

Jenna chuckled. "So I saw."

"Along with the rest of New Dublin, I suppose," Erin said lightly.

Jenna reached over and affectionately squeezed her arm. "I'm glad you're okay with that."

"Well, I can't exactly hide from demons if I want to keep

chasing them away." A gleam of satisfaction entered Erin's eyes. "And I really did enjoy watching Lexi run."

"So did I," Jenna said.

They looked at each other and tried not to laugh. But Erin broke first, letting out a helpless giggle. And before long they were laughing themselves to tears.

LATER THAT AFTERNOON LUKE SAT IN HIS OFFICE and read the preliminary autopsy report on Tina Murdock. As expected, the cause of death was asphyxiation due to strangulation. Motile sperm had been found, indicating recent sexual activity, but there hadn't been any evidence of rape, which was a little surprising given the way her body had been displayed on the bed. But it was another finding that completely threw him for a loop: Tina had been pregnant—almost four months pregnant. Far enough along that she'd probably known about it for a while.

Luke set the report down and mentally went over all the interviews he'd done in the last several days. Not a single person had hinted that Tina was even trying to get pregnant—including her husband. A baby would be about the last thing they needed.

Meredith had been right. The Murdock's financial situation was a mess. The restaurant was losing a ton of money, and credit card records revealed that Tina had been spending even more, mostly by taking out large cash advances from ATMs at a couple of casinos in the area. It was highly unlikely that they'd planned to have a baby under those circumstances. But it could have been a stressor—a major stressor—and another possible motive for murder. The mayor was looking more and more like his prime suspect.

DNA from the fetus would be processed by the State Crime Lab in Madison, which had all the other evidence collected from the crime scene. So far they hadn't found any incriminating fingerprints, and the only blood was Tina's—including the blood on the knife that had been buried in her chest post-mortem.

Luke was still waiting for results on any other potential DNA evidence. Normally that could take weeks—it wasn't like on TV, where tests came back instantaneously. But the lab was putting a rush on it, so he expected to have results within a week.

He had gotten a report on Tina's cell phone, and they'd struck out there as well—no suspicious texts, tweets, emails, photos, videos, calendar entries, map downloads, internet searches, Facebook info…It was unfortunate, because a cell phone could tell a person's entire life story these days. But if she had been engaging in any nefarious activities by phone, she'd either covered her tracks well or had also been using a burner phone that she'd payed for in cash and then disposed of. Hopefully data from their home computers would turn up something.

The barbed wire was also being processed, and Luke had spent a lot of time thinking about it. Barbed wire was an unusual murder weapon, to say the least. It was bulky and difficult to handle. The murderer had probably used it in some other capacity before, most likely on a farm, given their rural location. And if they could figure out where the barbed wire had come from, they'd almost certainly find the killer. The problem was, there were hundreds of farms in the area. It was going to be like literally trying to find a needle in a haystack.

And there were other possibilities too. Barbed wire was used by security companies, the military, and of course, prisons. It was something the inmates had to look at every day—a harsh reminder of their imprisonment—and Luke imagined the sight of it stirred up a lot of anger. And he was sure about one thing: The barbed wire reflected the rage that had prompted this type of killing.

Wayne Raabe had spent time in the county jail, not in the prison system, which left Seth Slater as their only person of interest with an actual prison record. And if no other solid leads developed soon, Luke had every intention of flying out to LA so that he could conduct face-to-face interviews with some of the people who'd known Slater there. No one in New Dublin seemed to know much about him, not even his coworkers, and he'd been just as closed off with Luke in the past. But a person doesn't spend twenty years in prison without talking to somebody. And if Slater had ever voiced any thoughts about barbed wire being used on people instead of on prison walls, then they'd have the evidence they would need to haul him in for questioning and get a search warrant for his property, where Luke presumed the man was holed up. No one had seen him since the murder.

But even if Slater had the means and opportunity, there was still the question of motive. And so far Frank Murdock was the man with the strongest motive, though his story about being at City Hall checked out. Security cameras had indeed recorded him coming and going as he'd said, and his car had been in the parking lot all night—his brand spanking new Cadillac.

Luke had asked him about that in a follow-up interview yesterday, and Frank had said he purchased the car with money he kept hidden from Tina. But that was an awful lot of cash, especially for someone so deeply in debt. And Luke had seen their tax returns over the last several years. He doubted Frank could have saved that much money based on his salary alone. So the question was: Where else was he getting it from? Maybe unreported income from the restaurant? And had he used some of it to pay a killer like Seth Slater? Or could he have hired Wayne Raabe? Unfortunately Wayne, along with Jesse Torres, had disappeared without a trace.

Luke stood up. He knew where Frank was, though. Despite the fact that his wife had been brutally murdered just two days ago, the mayor was back at work. It took his mind off things, he'd said.

The police station was connected to City Hall, so Luke headed over there to talk to him about the autopsy report.

The office door was open when he got there, and Frank was standing next to his desk talking to Stella Givens, the city treasurer. She was a petite woman in her mid-forties who'd worked there for as long as Luke could remember, and was well-liked by everyone.

"Sorry to interrupt," he told Stella. "But I need to have a word with the mayor."

"Of course," she responded in the warm, friendly tone she always used. "I was just about to leave anyway." She picked up some files from the desk, tucking a loose strand of her long, platinum blond hair behind an ear. And on the way out she squeezed Luke's arm sympathetically. "Have a good afternoon, Detective Mathis. I know you've had a rough time of it these last few days."

"Thanks, Stella. You too," he returned with a brief smile, and eased the door closed behind her.

The mayor sat down at his desk. "I gather this isn't a social call."

Luke took a chair across from him and didn't mince words. "I got the preliminary autopsy report back on Tina. Did you know she was almost four months pregnant?"

A look of utter shock crossed the mayor's face, and he didn't say anything in response.

Luke thought if he was faking the reaction he ought to get an Academy Award for it. "Was she trying to get pregnant?" he asked.

Frank's expression remained stunned. Finally, stumbling over his words, he said, "No. I…She…" And then his voice trailed off.

Luke was pretty sure he could fill in the rest of the sentence: She shouldn't have been able to get pregnant. "Have you had a vasectomy?"

The mayor remained silent for a moment, then weakly admitted, "Yes."

"How long ago?"

"Thirteen years," he answered with a grimace. "Meredith didn't want any more kids."

"Did you know Tina was cheating on you?"

"No, I didn't."

"Any idea who the father is?"

"No." Anger sparked in Frank's eyes, turning them an icy blue. "And if you want to continue this conversation I think I should have my lawyer present."

"No need. I'm done for now." Luke stood up. "I'll let you know if I have any more questions."

Frank didn't respond, staring straight ahead at nothing, and Luke thought better of saying anything else before he left. Something like Stella's "Have a good afternoon" probably wasn't in order.

He took the stairs down to the first floor and headed to a vending machine at the end of the main hallway. He could use a stiff drink right about now, but water would have to do. And with a bottle in hand he left the building through a side door to get some fresh air.

There was a break area with a picnic table nearby, and he sat down heavily, taking a swig of the water. This case was getting uglier by the minute. And to make matters worse, Jeff Kilbride had just gone home with a bad case of stomach flu, and the assistant chief wouldn't be back from Mexico until Sunday.

Luke watched a couple kids cross the street to the grocery store a little farther down the block. They were jaywalking, he noted with a wry smile.

Then he looked beyond them to the parking lot of the store, and his expression sobered when the significance of the location dawned on him. He could see the parking lot from this angle, which meant the security cameras there could have caught activity at the door he'd just exited—the only one to City Hall that wasn't under video surveillance itself. Frank's car had been there all night, but had Frank?

Luke threw his water bottle into the recycling container and immediately jogged over to the grocery store to check it out.

AN HOUR LATER LUKE FOUND OUT THAT FRANK hadn't left City Hall the night of the murder—but someone else had come in.

He sat in a back office at the grocery store and rewound the video, pausing on the frame when the person—most likely a woman—first walked into view. She was facing away from the camera, but he could see that she was petite, with long white hair—or maybe blond hair. Light blond hair.

It struck him then who the woman was, and he stared at her image in shock. *Shit…Stella Givens.* He was sure of it.

He hit play again and watched as someone opened the side door for her, though it was too dark to see who actually let her in. But he knew who it had to be.

"Shit," he said out loud this time.

He made a mental note of the timestamp on the video as she was about to go in. Exactly 11:00 p.m. Then he hit fast-forward until he got to the image of her exiting from the same door alone…1:35 a.m.

He sat back, running a hand through his hair as the full implications of the video hit him. So this was why the mayor had been so evasive in answering questions about the city budget. He hadn't been working hard on the budget—he'd been working hard on diverting money away from it. And it meant they were dealing with something that ran even deeper than murder. Now he was pretty sure they had fraud and embezzlement on their hands.

He thought about how upset Frank had looked after finding out about Tina's infidelity. The man really did deserve an Academy Award. While his wife had been cheating on him, he'd probably been carrying on an affair with the city treasurer and robbing the people of New Dublin in the process. A brand new Cadillac certainly wouldn't have been approved by the city council—or the whopping fee that Frank had likely paid for his wife's murder.

And Stella Givens, sweet-as-pie Stella Givens…She didn't own any Cadillacs, but the stables on her sprawling ranch were full of their four-legged equivalents—horses. Some of the finest Arabians Luke had ever seen. He knew she bred them, and otherwise spent most of her free time taking them to shows, so he'd figured she was financing her extravagant hobby that way. But the city had probably been footing those bills too.

Luke blew out a sigh and checked his watch. 5:54. He'd wait to discuss this new development with the chief tomorrow. They were scheduled to meet with the DA in the morning to review the murder case anyway, so they could figure out the best way to investigate this then. Hopefully the chief was up to it.

He also knew that if he called an emergency meeting now it would kill any chance he had of seeing Erin later. And after all the ugliness he'd uncovered at every turn these last few days, he needed to see her more than anything, to be reminded that there was still good in the world, that there was still love.

CHAPTER

15

Erin sat in one of the chairs on the front porch and waited for Luke, excited and anxious at the same time. She knew that after everything they'd already been through she had no reason to let anxiety undermine her happiness, but there were still so many unanswered questions between them that part of her couldn't help but feel anxious, no matter how much she abhorred the emotion. It was proof that she was human, she reminded herself. In fact, everything she'd ever felt—good and bad—was just proof that she was human. She didn't need to be embarrassed about the bad. Maybe she even needed to embrace it.

Her lips quirked up into a wry smile. Jenna was really getting to her now.

She thought about going back into the house to look for her cell phone in case Luke called. That would also keep her from obsessing over all those bothersome questions churning in her brain. She'd lost track of the phone earlier in the day and couldn't remember where she'd left it. She'd been doing that a lot lately.

But a moment later Luke's blue SUV came down the road, and he pulled into the driveway. Her heart started fluttering in her chest—though it had nothing to do with the questions she'd had, which suddenly didn't seem that important—and she waited at the edge of the porch as he headed up the walkway.

Then he saw her and smiled, and she couldn't wait a second longer. She flew down the steps and ran to him.

Luke caught her in his arms, gathering her tightly against him, and for a while they just stood there holding each other.

"God, you feel so good," he eventually whispered. "You have no idea how much I needed this."

"Oh, I think I do." Erin lifted her head from his chest and gazed up at him with a teasing glint in her eyes. "And you have no idea how glad I am that you're here and not at Lexi Hightower's house."

"I wouldn't be there anyway, even if you hadn't shown up at the station and chased her off." Luke chuckled and tenderly kissed her forehead. "We ran into each other by accident today when she was at City Hall on other business, and she asked if I'd be interested in doing some consulting work to improve security at the factory. That's all it was, and I told her I didn't have time."

Erin slid her arms around his neck. "Maybe that's all it was for you, Detective, but I heard what she said. When she asked if you were free tonight I really don't think she was worried about her screws being stolen."

Luke grinned, lowering his mouth so it hovered just over hers. "I see the claws are out again. But I'd rather have you use them on me."

Erin drew his head down the rest of the way, and their

lips met in a long, heated kiss, tongues joining in, stroking and circling the other's in an erotic dance that heightened the pleasure of the kiss even more.

Luke softly groaned when they finally came up for air. "We really need to talk, but right now all I want to do is rip your clothes off and make love to you." He cupped her bottom in his hands, pulling her up against the hard evidence of his arousal, and brushed his lips seductively over her ear. "Do you think Jenna would mind if I get a much more in-depth tour of your bedroom this time?"

Erin felt her anxiety return as soon as he asked the question, and she realized there was another reason for it, one she hadn't thought about before—or maybe one she hadn't let herself think about before. "Jenna's asleep. But Luke…"

Hearing the hesitancy in her voice, Luke eased back and searched her face. "What's wrong, Erin?"

She wasn't sure how to say it. "What if…What if it isn't, well, like it was at the hotel? I mean…I—I guess I was kind of drunk that night after all."

"So you're worried I might stink in bed if you're not drunk?" Luke asked with barely suppressed laughter.

Erin's eyes widened in horror. "Of course that's not what I meant!" She felt her face get hot with embarrassment and nervously fiddled with the collar of his shirt. "It's me I'm worried about. What if I'm not good at it—at sex—if I'm not drunk. Until the other night with you it wasn't—"

Luke pressed a finger to her lips. "I don't think you're going to have a problem, Erin. If there's one thing I've learned about alcohol, it doesn't turn someone into something they're not. Alcohol takes inhibition away, and tends to reveal a lot about who a person really is underneath it all." He grinned devilishly. "And I like what I found out about you. But let me also give you a little lesson in physiology I guess they never taught you in school. If anything, alcohol can make it harder to have an orgasm—for both men and women. And you, my sexy Harvard grad, did not have a problem with that at all. So I'm sure it will be a virtual slam dunk now that you're sober." His grin widened. "If you let me score, that is."

The worry in Erin's expression faded, and she gave him her own version of a devilish grin. "First you'll have to stop talking and start swinging the bat."

Luke chuckled. "I'm more of a football guy, so let's talk in terms of touchdowns. Like how I want a touchdown here." He pressed a slow, sultry kiss on her lips. "And a touchdown here." His mouth descended to the juncture of her neck and shoulder, and he sucked deeply there.

Erin closed her eyes in pleasure. "Mmmm, I think I might actually like football."

Luke reached under the back of her shirt and unclasped her bra as he trailed more sensuous kisses over her neck. "And I definitely want a touchdown here," he said, sliding his hands around to her breasts and lightly stroking her nipples, rousing them to hardened peaks.

Erin felt liquid heat flood her, and knew with certainty then that her problems with intimacy were a thing of the past. "You're very good at body checks, Detective," she breathed, clutching his shoulders. "They'll help get your puck in the net for sure."

Luke raised his head and looked at her in admiration. "Hockey references. Very impressive."

Erin softly smiled, though it was more in response to the heavenly sensations his fingers were eliciting. "I've lived in Boston for the last fourteen years, so I was bound to learn something about hockey."

"I think I'm going to like Boston," Luke said, tenderly kissing her mouth.

Erin's smile instantly vanished, and she stared up at him in shock. "Are you saying what I think you are?"

Luke tugged her bra back into place and refastened it. "I think we should go sit down on the back porch swing and talk about all that before I score too many touchdowns to think." He flashed her a grin and took her hand, leading her toward the back of the house.

Erin followed him, still not quite believing what he'd said. Going back to Boston was the biggest obstacle she'd thought stood between them. And now, apparently, it wasn't an obstacle at all. She felt like another huge weight had just been lifted from her heart, and it soared to the stars.

Then they turned the corner to the backyard, and her breath caught at the sight that met her eyes. "The fireflies are out," she whispered, coming to a halt. "I'd forgotten about them."

Hundreds and hundreds of fireflies filled the yard—little twinkling balls of light that flitted over the grass, the wildflowers and the pond, which itself was gleaming under the bright light of the full moon above.

"Come on." Luke pulled her across the yard to the field of wildflowers and stopped in the middle of it, gathering her close. "Dance with me."

Erin smiled up at him. "We don't have any music."

"Of course we do, and in a venue that can't be beat." He started swaying gently back and forth. "Thousands of crickets are playing in the band. There's a huge disco ball hanging up there in the sky. The floor is completely decked out with flowers, and our fellow dancers are fireflies. What more could you ask for?"

"Not a thing." Erin nestled her head on his shoulder as they continued swaying to the music of the night. "I never want this dance to end," she said after a while.

"Neither do I." Luke stopped moving and eased her head up, cradling her face in his hands. "That's why I don't want you to leave here alone. When the time comes, and if you're not sick of me by then, I want to go back to Boston with you."

Erin felt tears fill her eyes. "I'll never be sick of you, Luke. There's not a doubt in my mind that I want you in my life—forever. But are you sure? I don't want you to do something you'll resent me for later."

A look of pain briefly mixed with the tenderness in Luke's expression. "When you left here the last time you took my heart with you. And if that happens again I think it would kill me. You mean more to me than this town, or my job, or anything else. My heart is where you are. It always has been and always will be. I want to go back with you—I need to go back with you. I love you."

Erin looked into his eyes and knew that she loved him too, so much she ached with it. "Luke, I…" But she couldn't get the words out.

He gently put a finger to her lips. "I don't expect you to say anything back right now. I've known how I felt about you for as long as I can remember, but it's way too soon for you. I get that."

Erin shook her head. "It's just something that's hard for me to say, Luke. Jenna told me the other day that nothing is easier done than said, but for once she was wrong. I haven't even said those words to her. I've tried, and I freeze up every time. I know it's crazy. I can bring a dying person back to life, but a lot of things that are easy for most people have always been the hardest for me, like saying those three words…It should be such a simple thing to do, but when I try to say them I feel like I'm about to jump off a cliff. And jumping off a cliff would be crazy to most people."

"We're all crazy in our own ways, Erin. Some of us are just more willing to admit it than others." Luke bent down and plucked a wild purple petunia from the field and tucked it behind her ear. "I love you, and I won't expect you to say it back. I just hope one day you can, and you won't feel like you're jumping off a cliff anymore."

"Thank you, Luke," Erin whispered. "And I promise, if you're patient that day will come."

"And it will be the happiest day of my life." Luke smiled, lightly tracing her lower lip with his thumb. "But right now it's fine with me if we don't say anything at all."

Erin grinned devilishly and took hold of his thumb, running her tongue over it. Then she sucked it into her mouth, enjoying the look of desire that immediately tightened his features, the heat that filled his eyes and warmed her just as much. And when she finally let go, she asked in a low, seductive tone, "Don't you want to sit on the back porch swing and talk some more?"

"No," Luke answered, and hauled her up against him hard, capturing her mouth hungrily with his.

Erin grabbed the back of his head, pulling him even closer, and their lips met in kiss after amorous kiss, while the fireflies danced all around them.

"I feel like a man who's been walking in a desert all his life searching for water," Luke murmured, blazing a path of hot kisses over her face and down her neck, stroking the sensitive skin there with his tongue. "And now that I've found you, I can't get enough of you."

Erin rubbed her cheek against his and ran her hands over the back of his shoulders, luxuriating in the feel of him. "I've never wanted anyone to touch me the way I want you to. And your fingers, your lips, they don't just touch my skin, they touch my soul."

Luke lifted his head and smiled down at her. "You don't ever have to tell me you love me if you say things like that instead."

Erin tenderly smiled back, and then lowered her arms to his shirt and slowly undid the buttons. "As much as I want you to touch me, I want to touch you. I want my hands on your body. I want to feel you, your skin against my skin." She reached the waistband of his jeans and pulled the ends of his shirt out to finish unbuttoning it, then slid it off his shoulders so it fell amongst the flowers at their feet. "I want to take all your clothes off and ride you to the stars and touch the moon, Neal Armstrong."

"Okay, it's official," Luke said, undoing her blouse and bra and tossing them to the ground as well. "I don't ever want you to tell me you love me if you say things like that instead." He took a moment to enjoy the sight of her breasts in the soft light of the moon, running his hands over them, gently massaging. And then he kissed a sensuous path down her chest to one of her hardened nipples, sucking it deeply into the moist heat of his mouth.

Erin grabbed hold of his shoulders and gazed up into the night sky with half-closed eyes, letting out helpless moans of pleasure as he continued to make passionate love to her breasts. But the fire he was setting ablaze inside her with his lips and tongue soon burned hotter than she could bear. "Luke," she gasped, reaching down to unbuckle his belt. "I need you. Right now."

"God yes, honey." He bent lower and quickly stripped off the rest of her clothes, then branded her skin with feverish kisses as he made his way back up her body.

Erin urgently drew him up the rest of the way. "I remember when you first called me honey," she said tightly, unfastening his jeans and tugging them down, along with his briefs. "I found out what an orgasm was about three seconds later. And I think I'm already halfway there now."

Luke groaned, kicking away his clothes, and pulled her with him into the flowers. "Now you're just plain driving me crazy, honey."

Erin came down on top of him, her lips curving up into a grin. "I just might start to like crazy."

"Me too," he said with a soft laugh. "Me too."

All humor was gone after that. Their mouths met in a searing kiss, then feasted on the other's skin, hands exploring, bodies giving and seeking pleasure in return. And when desire turned to desperation, Erin lifted herself over him and took him inside her, letting sensation be her guide as she started to move. And it wasn't long before she got into the rhythm, rocking her hips against his with unbridled passion.

"Erin. God, Erin," Luke whispered, savoring the exquisite pleasure of her body moving on his, around his, with only the ground underneath them and the stars above, and the enticing smell of her and the wildflowers filling the air.

"Oh…Luke…" Erin managed to get out, her face contorting in ecstasy. "How…how is this even—possible?"

A smile briefly tugged at Luke's mouth. "Do you need a biology lesson, honey?"

"I just can't believe," she began, having to pause and gulp air as she felt her body drown even deeper in sweet sensation. "I can't believe…this can feel—so good."

"Now that's chemistry," he said, drawing her head back down for another kiss. "Pure chemistry."

Their lips met with the same wild passion as their bodies, both demanding more, and more, and more…

Erin finally tore her mouth from his and leaned back, feeling pleasure start to reach its glorious peak. And when it burst inside her she looked up into the star-studded sky, crying out her release, and no longer felt like she was on the ground. The fireflies all around her were stars, and the stars were fireflies. She was part of Luke, and he was part of her. She was still herself, and yet they were all one…And at that moment she knew what it felt like to be in harmony with the universe.

Afterward, she fell on top of Luke, fulfilled in a way she'd never been before, and they lay there in the field of wildflowers, basking in the warm afterglow of passion under the moon and stars.

Luke eventually pressed a kiss on her ear and teasingly murmured into it, "So was I any good, or do you need to get drunk again?"

"No, I don't need to get drunk again. Not when I have you to get me high." Erin nuzzled her face against his neck with a satisfied purr. "You definitely took me to the moon, Neal Armstrong. And you helped me touch the stars."

"It was my pleasure, Sally Ride."

Erin lifted her head and gazed into his eyes, shining such a deep, dark blue in the light of the moon, and so many emotions flooded her. She couldn't believe this man could make her feel so much, that he could make her love so much. And she wanted to tell him. "Luke," she whispered. "Luke, I—I…" But the words caught in her throat again.

He knew what she was trying to say, though. He saw it in her eyes. "I love you too," he whispered back.

Erin lowered her mouth to his, telling him in her kiss what she couldn't express in words.

"Keep doing that instead," Luke told her when the kiss ended, "and I'll forbid you to ever say you love me."

Erin knew he was teasing, but she still couldn't make light of it. "Luke, I want to—"

"It's okay, Erin," he interrupted. "I would rather have you show me in a thousand ways that you love me than to ever hear it even once in words alone—which sounds like something Jenna would say."

Erin immediately smiled. "Actually, you probably have heard her say something like that before. I've heard it many times myself: 'An ounce of action carries far more weight than a ton of empty words.'"

Luke chuckled. "Ah, yes. That is where my inspiration came from."

"And I remember she said her inspiration for the quote came from Ralph Waldo Emerson—a friend of Thoreau's, not surprisingly—who once said, 'An ounce of action is worth a ton of theory.'"

"You're just spitting out the quotes now, aren't you?"

Erin grinned. "Oh, you should have heard me let them fly earlier today when I saw you with Lexi and decided to take action."

"You took more than an ounce of action there, that's for sure," Luke teased. Then a devilish smile crossed his face. "But speaking of taking action, I have another thing in mind for you to do with me."

"I'm guessing it's something quite indecent by the look on your face," Erin said in amusement. "It just better not be illegal. I won't be the one stealing batteries from a hotel this time."

Luke's expression turned sheepish. "That's right. I still have to replace those."

"Don't worry about it, Detective. I'll cover for you and get them some new ones tomorrow."

"That would be much appreciated, Sally Ride. And then you can get your deposit back, too."

"I forgot about that," Erin said ruefully. "I was supposed to get it back the next morning. But I doubt I can now."

"Because you lost your Sally Ride ID?"

"Very funny," she responded with a grudging laugh. "But let's get back to the question at hand. What is it you really want me to do—if I dare ask?"

Luke gave her another devilish grin. "It's something that's always been on my bucket list. I want you to go skinny dipping with me."

Erin raised a brow at him. "Skinny dipping with me has always been on your bucket list?"

"Skinny dipping has. With you would be a bonus beyond my wildest dreams." Luke slowly ran his fingers through her hair, and his expression sobered. "But it's just a thought. We don't have to do it if you don't want to."

Erin was surprised that the very idea of swimming naked in the pond at night didn't give her a full-blown panic attack right then and there. But what surprised her more was the realization that she could do it. And even more shocking was that she really wanted to do it. Not just for him, but for her, too. "Okay, take me to the pond, Neal Armstrong, and I'll help you live out your wildest bucket list dream." She slid off him and got up to gather her clothes. "And we'd better hurry before I have too much time to think about it."

Luke didn't move, though. Instead he lay there with his hands behind his head, smiling up at her appreciatively as she stood in the moonlight. "I think I am dreaming. Either that or I just died and went to Heaven, and they sent their most beautiful naked angel to greet me."

"Well, I'm going to turn into a real angel if you don't come with me and I drown trying to skinny dip alone." Erin flashed him a grin and took off running toward the pond.

Luke grabbed his own clothes and followed her at a more leisurely pace, laughing softly as he watched her run, with the moon highlighting the voluptuous shape of her bottom. She'd probably never mooned anyone in her entire life, and now she was taking it to a whole new level.

Down at the beach Erin didn't let herself think twice, the exhilaration of the night driving away all inhibition. She dropped her clothes in the sand and raced full tilt into the water.

Luke's amusement instantly faded when he realized she wasn't going to stop. "Hold up, Erin!" he yelled. And throwing down his own clothes, he sprinted the rest of the way to the pond and splashed in after her, urgently closing the rest of the distance between them and swooping her up into his arms. "Christ, have you been drinking after all?"

Erin laughed and slid her arms around his neck, dizzy with a different kind of intoxication—and just a touch of nerves. "This is all your fault, Detective, after what you did to me in the Jacuzzi the other night."

"Then I think I've created a monster," Luke said dryly, willing his own nerves to settle down after watching her jump into the water like that.

"I'm not an angel anymore?" Erin teased, nipping his ear.

"No, you're a monster. A very beautiful monster." Luke

lightly brushing his lips over hers as he carried her farther into the pond. "One that tastes really, really good."

"Mmmm, so do you." Erin deepened the kiss and shifted in his arms, wrapping her legs around his waist and pressing her body closer to his, skin against skin.

Luke finally drew back when they were almost chest-deep in the water. "How are you feeling?"

"Really, really good," Erin responded in a sultry whisper. The heat of his body made her forget all about the coolness of the water, and she was getting hotter by the minute. She rubbed her breasts against his chest like she'd wanted to do the first time he'd taken her into the water, and softly moaned as pleasure, raw and yet deliciously sweet, rippled through her. "I would say I'm feeling with my fingers, but I'm definitely feeling with a lot more than my fingers right now."

Luke chuckled. "I really have created a monster." Then he eased her down to stand in the water and held her at arm's length. "But we'd better do some swimming before I drag you out of here and we have sex on the beach instead—which is on my bucket list too, by the way."

Erin gave him her devilish grin. "I think we've been in the pond long enough to check skinny dipping off the list." She stepped toward him. "I am so ready to hit sex on the beach."

Before she could get her hands on him again, though, he dove to the side and swam away from her a ways, then stood up and faced her with a devilish smile of his own. "Catch me first."

Erin let out a laugh. "Oh, I will." But as she gazed at him her amusement quickly turned to wonder, and for a moment she couldn't move. He stood in a pool of shimmering liquid light, and the moon cast a soft glow over his features. The stars sparkled in the background, and the fireflies flickered all around him. He looked...magical, and it took her breath away.

"Come on," Luke urged, holding his arms out to her.

Erin slowly waded toward him, enjoying the feel of the water against her skin now that the fear was gone. She leaned forward a little, fanning her arms out and pushing off with her feet, letting the buoyancy of the water propel her faster toward him. And in the next instant a memory clicked in her head...

Her mother stood in the water, giving her an encouraging smile. "You can do it."

Erin smiled back and started paddling toward her, emboldened by all the love she saw on her mother's face.

"That's it, baby," her mother said, holding her arms out. "Come to me..."

Erin looked up at Luke and lunged ahead. She allowed her feet to lose contact with the sandy bottom of the pond and floated on her chest, using her arms to crawl forward while she kicked her legs up and down.

Luke caught her when she reached him. "You were swimming," he said in astonishment.

Erin smiled up at him. "I'm pretty sure I've done that before."

"Well, you did an awesome job, honey."

He gathered her into his arms for a hug, and Erin lifted her gaze up to the stars and silently said, *Thank you, Mom.*

Luke let her go and waded backward. "Do it again."

Erin laughed and swam toward him, but he kept moving away, staying just out of her reach. And for a while they played a game of cat and mouse, though she felt more like a mouse trying to catch the cat.

Then he finally stopped, and she jumped on him, wrapping her arms and legs around him. "Caught you," she said gleefully.

"You did," he responded with an affectionate smile. "A long, long time ago."

Erin slid one of her arms from around his neck and ran her fingers slowly over his cheek, his lips, the dimple in his chin. Then she lifted her eyes to his and told him once again with her look that she loved him.

Luke tenderly brushed his lips over hers, saying it back in his kiss.

More kisses followed, and tenderness soon turned to passion. Erin felt his arousal tease the sensitive skin of her bottom, and she restlessly moved against him, murmuring, "I think it's time you dragged me to shore, Neal Armstrong."

Luke laughed softly and carried her toward the beach. But he stopped in the shallow water. "I want you right here," he said, sinking down into the sandy bottom of the pond with her straddling his lap. Then he captured her mouth with his in another torrid kiss, guiding her over him to join their bodies as well.

Erin broke the kiss with a low moan and tried to thrust against him when he was fully sheathed inside her. But he wouldn't let her move, holding her hips firmly in his grip.

"Let's take it slow this time," Luke whispered, and leisurely traced her lips with his tongue.

"Luke," Erin groaned in protest and tried to move anyway, her body throbbing with too much need to hold still.

He gave just a little, and she slowly rocked against him, letting out soft murmurs of pleasure. He sucked her lower lip in and out of his mouth at the same time, and then her tongue, intensifying the exquisite sensations that were already building inside her. Soft murmurs turned into deep moans, and she tried once again to go faster. But he held firm, continuing the torturously slow pace.

"Be patient, honey," Luke said with amusement in his tone, and lowered his head to her chest, making love to her breasts as leisurely as he had her mouth.

"Oh God, Luke, please," Erin begged, digging her fingers into the back of his shoulders. It felt like every nerve ending in her body was charged beyond capacity, all her circuits overloaded, smoking and ready to explode.

Then he gave a little more, and it was just enough. She threw her head back and cried out as pleasure splintered into sweet spasms of release, rocketing her up to the moon and stars, and taking him along for the ride.

When they finally came back to earth, Luke regarded her with a mixture of satisfaction and wonder on his face. "I don't care if it turns out you're an Olympic swimmer, honey. I see a lot more swimming lessons in your future."

Erin chuckled. "I have a long way to go before I'm an Olympic swimmer, so I'll need a lot more lessons for sure. And who knows? Maybe after enough of them we can do one of those cliff dives into the ocean—although the day I do that we'll probably see pigs flying with us. But maybe that can happen too. Jenna did say two-headed cows exist."

Luke shook his head in bemusement. "Two-headed cows? I'm not even going to ask about that. And I don't need to do any cliff diving when we can have midnight lessons here in the pond." His lips curved up into a wolfish grin. "Watching you howl at the moon when you climax is spectacular enough for me."

"I can't help it." Erin lightly sank her teeth into his neck.

"You make me wild. So beware."

Luke let out a tortured groan. "Okay, we need to get out of this pond before you eat me alive."

Erin gave his shoulder an enthusiastic love bite, and he hauled her up with another groan and led her out of the water.

They used a blanket draped on the back porch swing to dry off, then got dressed and sat down. Luke wrapped an arm around her, and Erin laid her head on his shoulder. The fireflies were still playing in the yard, and she smiled as she watched them. It had truly been a magical night, one she wouldn't forget for the rest of her life.

Luke gently rocked the swing, and they continued to sit in companionable silence for a while. Then he eventually pressed a kiss on her head. "I hate to say this, but I'll have to head home soon. We have a meeting with the DA about the murder case first thing in the morning, and I still need to prepare a few things."

Erin buried her face against his shoulder with a soft murmur of protest. She didn't want to return to reality quite yet. "I wish you could stay all night."

"Ah, honey, I wish I could too. But I've got to get ready for this meeting."

Erin lifted her head after a moment and tentatively asked, "Do you…do you have any idea who did it?"

Luke knew what she was really asking. "No, not for sure. I still haven't had a chance to question your father, but at this point there's no evidence that he was involved."

He didn't mention the barbed wire. So far they'd managed to keep some of the gorier details of the crime out of the press, and he couldn't discuss them with her or anyone who wasn't directly involved in the case. Not that he wanted to anyway.

"I'm sorry I didn't tell you about your father," he said in a tone filled with deep regret. "I was going to, but I knew you'd be pretty upset about it, and I kept putting it off."

Erin nodded. "Jenna said basically the same thing the other day. But yesterday she also told me this: 'Sometimes the things we do to protect those we love end up being the things that hurt them the most.' It's something we've all been guilty of."

Luke took her hands, kissing the back of each one. "The last thing I ever want to do is hurt you. There are a lot of things I can't talk about with respect to my job, just like you can't with yours. But outside of that I'll always be honest with you from now on, no matter what. And I need the same thing from you."

"Yes, I promise," Erin vowed, squeezing his hands. And with a grin she added, "Apparently I'm a bad liar anyway, according to Jenna."

Luke chuckled. "That's good to know." Then he reluctantly stood up. "But I guess the time has come. I've got to get going."

He helped her up, and they walked hand-in-hand back around the house to the front door.

"Make sure you lock everything up when I leave," Luke said, pulling her close.

Erin slid her arms around his neck. "Yes, Detective."

He gazed down at her with tenderness in his eyes. "Can I come over tomorrow night?"

"Mmmm, yes," she purred, drawing his mouth to hers for a kiss. And then another. And another.

Luke groaned. "I really have to go." But he didn't move.

Erin heard the conflict in his voice and knew she had

to make the decision for them. "Okay, I guess you should head home, Detective Mathis." She brushed one last kiss on his lips. "Sweet dreams."

She slipped into the house, resisting the urge to look back at him, and locked the door. Then she turned and leaned against it with a contented smile. Something tickled her ear, and she reached up. The wild purple petunia was still in her hair.

Laughing softly, she plucked it out and went to go put it in a glass of water.

ERIN TOSSED RESTLESSLY IN BED THAT NIGHT, unable to sleep. She finally threw off the blanket, feeling too hot to have the covers on, and turned onto her back. The ceiling was softly illuminated by the light of the nearby lamp, and images of Luke came to mind as she stared up at it: those deep blue eyes, the way he smiled, that hard body…

With a helpless groan she got out of bed and stood there uncertainly, not quite sure what she could do to settle her senses. One thing was definitely for sure: being in love made it almost as hard to sleep as thoughts of ghosts did. She glanced at the lamp and shook her head wryly.

Part of her still found it hard to believe that she'd fallen in love. Just a week ago she would probably have given more credence to ghosts. Letting the heart rule the mind had seemed like a foolish—even dangerous—thing to do. It was the last thing on earth she'd thought she needed or wanted. And now to have fallen for Luke so hard, and so fast…It defied every logical bone in her body.

"It is only when we forget all our learning that we begin to know..."

The quote was one of Jenna's favorites from Thoreau. And Erin finally understood it.

Smiling to herself, she grabbed one of her medical journals off the pile she'd set on the dresser and headed back to bed with it. She couldn't literally forget all her learning or she'd be permanently unemployed, so she might as well catch up on some reading. And the longest, most boring article she could find would hopefully do the trick and put her to sleep.

She stacked up a couple of pillows and reclined back on them, then started paging through the magazine. A title caught her eye, and she blinked in surprise: "Can Nipple Stimulation and Orgasm Help Prevent Breast Cancer?"

She flipped the journal back over to the front cover, holding her spot with a finger. Yep, no mistake. It was the same reputable journal she'd always read, not some trashy magazine that had been slipped into her bag at the adult entertainment store.

Laughing silently at the thought, she opened the journal up again. This wasn't likely to be the tedious sort of article she'd been looking for, but now she didn't care. She was wide awake and intended to read every word.

Interesting, she thought as she read. The article focused on oxytocin, a hormone that was produced by the brain during breastfeeding to stimulate the breast ducts to contract and release milk for the nursing baby. The authors discussed the fact that women who breast fed were less likely to get breast cancer, and theorized that regular nipple stimulation could have the same effect, as this also caused oxytocin to be released. They noted that nipple stimulation during sex often helped a woman achieve orgasm as well, and orgasm further increased oxytocin release. So both nipple stimulation and orgasm might help prevent breast cancer. And by increasing the likelihood of orgasm, nipple simulation could also reduce the risk of sexual dysfunction and improve a woman's emotional health.

Erin laid the magazine down on her lap and contemplated what she'd just read. The article made a lot of sense, and she was surprised she'd never heard the topic discussed before. Peter certainly hadn't mentioned it.

She thought about him explaining the importance of regular breast stimulation and orgasms to his patients, and the very idea made her laugh out loud. She imagined him putting up a sign in his office, maybe something like 'Breast Cancer Prevention Begins in Bed,' and she laughed even harder.

Then something hit her bedroom window.

She abruptly stopped laughing and sat still, listening.

A moment later she heard the noise again, and her heart beat faster. *Oh God, what now?* It didn't sound like a bug, and there were no trees near the window, so it wasn't a branch. She glanced around the room, wondering if she was going to have another ghost encounter. That would definitely kill any chance of getting sleep.

Then it happened again, making her jump. And she sat there, waiting for the worst…

But nothing came through the window except moonlight, so she finally went over to it and hesitantly peered out. And her breath caught. There was someone out there, standing below the window.

A second later it registered in her brain who it was. Luke.

Fear turned to surprise, and she quickly pushed up the window, along with the screen, and leaned out. "Luke? What are you doing?"

"I couldn't sleep," he said, grinning up at her. "Now that I've slept with you, I can't sleep without you."

Erin grinned back. "I couldn't sleep either, so I just read an article about how nipple stimulation and orgasms might reduce the risk of breast cancer. That didn't help."

Luke chuckled. "Let me come up there and I'll be your poster boy for breast cancer prevention."

"I don't know if I should," she teased. "Not after you scared me half to death by throwing rocks at my window."

"They weren't rocks. They were just pebbles. And I tried to call when I was in the driveway, but you obviously couldn't answer." He held up two phones.

Erin squinted down at one of them. "Is that my phone?"

"Yeah, it was in your car. And you should keep that locked up too, by the way."

"So that's where it was," Erin said, shaking her head ruefully. "But why didn't you just pick the front door lock to get in? I'm sure you know how."

"I didn't want to scare you or Jenna. You probably would've called the cops."

Erin's lips twisted into a half-smile. "As it is, I didn't know what to think when I heard strange noises outside my window. I've seen a ghost here several times already. If I hadn't lost my phone I might have called Ghostbusters."

"Come on, Erin. You of all people can't possibly believe in ghosts?"

"Oh, they're real all right. Either that or I'm crazier than I thought."

Luke raised his arms to her. "Rapunzel, Rapunzel, let

down your hair, and I'll come save you from ghosts."

"You're making fun of me. Now I really shouldn't let you up."

"Please, I'm dying of sleep deprivation without you," he said in mock seriousness. "How can I gain your mercy, Rapunzel?"

Erin propped her head on her hands and gave him a playful grin. "Well, Prince Charming, since you're standing down there like that, how about a serenade? If you can sing, that is. I wouldn't want you to offend the crickets."

"I can sing a little." Luke looked up at her thoughtfully. "And I have the perfect song for you. It's a country song."

"Okay, I'm listening."

He cleared his throat and started singing:

> "'I never did like Mondays,
> They put me in a funk.
> And the only way to fix it
> Was gettin' good and drunk.'"

Erin laughed shortly. "Now you're making fun of me because I got drunk the other night. If you think that's going to—"

"Just wait, it gets better," Luke interrupted with amusement in his voice, and continued singing:

> "'But it all changed that Monday
> I went to the liquor store.
> I was lookin' for a six pack
> 'Til you walked through the door.'"

He smiled up at her affectionately and started the chorus:

"'Now it's hello Monday,
My favorite day for sure,
'Cause I know every Monday
I'm gonna love you even more.'"

A soft sigh escaped Erin. "I wish we'd met on a Monday, then that could be our song."

"We did." Luke's smile widened into a grin. "Monday, August 24th, 1992. It was the day we started first grade. Both your front teeth were missing, and you were the most beautiful thing I'd ever seen."

Erin felt her eyes immediately get hot with tears. "Luke…"

"Are you going to let me up now, or do I have to keep singing?"

"Yes—I mean no, I'm coming."

Erin shut the window, then threw on her robe and flew down the stairs to the front door. Luke got there just as she opened it, and for a moment all she could do was stand in the doorway and stare up at him in amazement. "I can't believe you remembered that day."

"I wouldn't forget it any more than I would my birthday," he said, giving her a boyish smile.

Erin closed the rest of the distance between them and pulled his head down, pressing her lips to his in a deep, impassioned kiss.

Luke chuckled afterward. "I gather you liked my singing?"

"Yes, you have a very sexy voice." A slow, devilish grin crossed Erin's face. "And now I'm too aroused to let you sleep."

Luke swooped her up into his arms and carried her inside. "It must be the vibrato."

Erin laughed softly, nuzzling her face his hair. "You are a clever one, Detective."

Luke took her up to the bedroom and gently laid her on the bed. Then he sat down next to her, and an intense look entered his blue eyes as he gazed at her. "You don't know how many times I've imagined you in your bed like this," he whispered, easing her robe open and running a hand slowly over the white silk nightgown she had on underneath. "Or how many times it killed me knowing I wasn't the one with you."

"Oh, Luke." Erin took his hand and tenderly kissed his palm. "We both need to leave the past in the past and concentrate on what's right here, right now." She looked up past his shoulder, and her eyes widened in surprise. "Like that ghost standing behind you."

"What—!" Luke whipped around so fast he lost his footing and slid to the floor.

Erin clapped a hand over her mouth, smothering a laugh. "I'm sorry, Luke. I was just kidding."

He smiled at her in chagrin and stood up, kicking his shoes off. "I'll give you a ghost," he said, pulling the sheet out from under her. Then he threw it over his head and jumped on top of her, leaving the other ghosts behind him.

CHAPTER 16

Luke left early the next morning, and Erin had been half-asleep when she returned his goodbye kiss, falling back into blissful slumber afterward. But she would have given him a much better goodbye if she'd known they wouldn't see each other again that day because he had to leave town to hunt down criminals. And when he called later to tell her, she'd gotten her first taste of the worry that went along with loving an officer of the law.

Wayne Raabe's car had been found in Eagle River, a small town about three hours north of New Dublin, so he and Scott Ripley were driving up there to investigate. Erin had already heard about how Wayne helped Jesse Torres escape from the hospital, and what they'd done to the cop who'd been on duty. That and the murder were the talk of the town and all over the news. The media was speculating that Wayne and Jesse were the ones who'd killed Tina Murdock, and she hoped it wasn't true. She'd saved Jesse's life, and now Luke could be in danger because of it.

She wasn't going to think about that, though. She couldn't, or it would drive her out of her mind. Instead, she did her best to stay busy—and prayed that Luke was careful.

She stopped at the Shamrock Inn with new batteries after lunch and was glad the desk clerk hadn't asked any questions. She also decided to keep her Sally Ride alter ego a secret between her and Luke and hadn't asked for her deposit back, either.

From there she went to the hospital and started the process of getting privileges to work in the ER. Jenna hadn't wanted her to, but Erin explained that she was only doing it because of what had happened with the baby last Sunday. She wasn't committing to anything. And the paperwork would take weeks to get approved, so she wouldn't be able to pick up shifts for a while anyway.

But as soon as Erin walked into the hospital she'd felt a longing to work in the ER again. In fact, she would have started right then and there if they'd let her. Jenna had been right in the first place: She needed medicine as much as it needed her.

Greg hadn't asked why she'd failed to show up on Monday as originally planned, and it was another question Erin was grateful she hadn't had to answer. Telling him she'd been hung over and puking her guts out that morning wasn't a good way to get hospital privileges.

They'd gone down to the cafeteria for coffee after finishing her paperwork, and she told him that she and Luke were seeing each other. He'd laughed and said they'd all seen that coming on Sunday. She also hesitantly mentioned that she still planned on returning to Boston, and he'd assured her that it was okay—he and Joanne already figured there was a good chance she wouldn't be going back alone.

Later that day she made another trip to Madison with Jenna and ordered the hot tub, which would be delivered on Saturday and installed on the back patio. Then they'd done some serious grocery shopping.

Erin had always felt a little inept when it came to nutrition, even though Harvard taught it better than most medical schools. But in the ER she didn't need to know much about nutritional medicine. The focus, more than any other specialty, was on treatment—immediate treatment.

Bad nutritional habits had also been easy to develop in medical school and residency—not to mention in the ER. She'd always been eating on the run, grabbing quick meals from the cafeteria or stopping for takeout on the way home. And a lifestyle like that wasn't exactly conducive to the development of any culinary skills. Maybe if she'd tried a little harder she would have become more adept in the kitchen. But as things stood, she was a terrible cook.

Now, however, she was getting a crash course in nutrition and cooking. She had to learn because it was the best way she could help Jenna. Good nutrition was as important as anything in fighting cancer and improving a patient's quality of life.

A lot of food had been thrown into the woods over the last week courtesy of her cooking attempts, but Erin still felt like she was making a lot of progress with Jenna's help—she could actually prepare her own vegetables and boil an egg now without having to look up how. Jenna couldn't stand for long, but she was still an excellent cook and an amazing teacher. And she didn't mind that they were keeping the wildlife so well-fed.

Erin had also spent a lot of time reading about nutrition and cancer. Eating a variety of high-calorie and high-protein foods, along with drinking plenty of fluids, was imperative, as the cancer cells were basically eating the body alive. And cancer patients often lacked an appetite, even those not on chemotherapy, so it was an ongoing battle to avoid malnutrition and dehydration. Parenteral (intravenous) nutrition and fluids were sometimes necessary, and the question of when, or if, to give them to a terminal patient was a difficult one. But Erin planned to do everything she could to keep Jenna out of the hospital. And she knew the hospice program her friend was enrolled in would provide invaluable services as well—though she hoped they wouldn't need to do much for a while.

Erin had tried to find some good data on the best vitamin and herbal supplements for cancer patients, but the literature was surprisingly ambiguous. Unfortunately, most supplements hadn't been well-studied in large clinical trials. Pharmaceutical companies were often the ones funding research, and the majority of that research was focused on the synthetic drugs they could exclusively manufacture. That's where the money was. And medicine, like almost everything else in the world, was driven by money.

But in her literature search she'd also come across some very disheartening statistics about the health of Americans. Despite spending more per capita on health care and retail drugs than any other nation by far, the average life expectancy of people in the United States only ranked forty-third in the world according to 2017 data in the CIA World Factbook. And the U.S. had one of the highest rates of cancer. The numbers made Erin realize with startling clarity just how much more was involved in keeping people alive and healthy than could be found in a hospital, clinic, or pharmacy.

Diet certainly played a role, and Japan was one of the countries where people lived the longest, so she'd spent some time reading about their dietary habits. They ate more seafood, rice, and vegetables, consumed less red meat, dairy and processed foods, and drank a lot of tea. She'd also read that the incidence of most cancers in India was significantly lower than in the U.S., and it might be related to their dietary habits as well. They ate a predominantly plant-based diet, and like the Japanese, consumed very little red meat. They also used a lot of spices. In particular, turmeric, ginger, chili pepper, and cloves were some that did have a number of studies supporting their potential cancer-fighting benefits. There were studies that indicated green tea might be beneficial as well.

Garlic also had a lot of promise in the fight against cancer. When it was chopped or crushed an enzyme was released that initiated the production of a substance called allicin, which was responsible for many of the health benefits of garlic (and the odor too). But allicin deteriorated quickly and wasn't heat stable, so the garlic either had to be eaten raw or cooked at low temperatures soon after it was crushed to achieve the maximum health benefits. Another option was to buy an allicin supplement. But due to the lack of adequate studies and federal regulations, it was hard to really know what a safe, effective dose was, or which manufacturers were actually producing the allicin in reliable concentrations.

In any case, the kitchen was now stocked with plenty of seafood, rice, fresh fruits, and vegetables. And Erin planned to add plenty of herbs and spices to various dishes, soups, and teas. She knew none of these things would be a miracle cure, but maybe they could help give her a little more time with Jenna, and for that they would be priceless.

ERIN WAS IN BED CATCHING UP ON READING HER medical journals—one of the long, boring articles this time—when Luke called again, much to her relief.

"It's good to hear your voice, honey," he said.

Erin heard weariness in his tone and wished she could put her arms around him. "Yours too, Luke. Are you still up in Eagle River?"

"Yeah, we'll have to stay here tonight. So far we haven't got a clue where those boys are. Wayne's car was parked at a rest stop outside of town, and the woods are pretty thick around there, so we're going to do a more thorough search with a K-9 unit tomorrow. Wayne's got some family in town we've interviewed, but no one's talking. And as far as we can tell, Jesse hasn't shown up at any of the hospitals or urgent care clinics around here. What do you think? Can the kid survive without medical care?"

"He was in the hospital for two days with a chest tube, so his lung might have healed enough that he could get by without it. And Wayne probably knew how to close the chest tube incision site by tying up the stitches that were in his skin to hold the tube in place. But if air starts building up in his chest cavity again, he's in big trouble."

"Well, if we find the kid rotting in the woods tomorrow, I can't say I'll feel sorry for him."

"I don't know much about wilderness medicine," Erin

said thoughtfully. "But if you do find Jesse alive, and he looks like he did the day he got shot, the first step would be to put your ear against his chest and listen for air movement on the right side. If you don't hear anything, I suppose as a last resort you could take a knife and cut through his skin at the same spot where I inserted the needle before. I'm sure you'll still be able to see the wound. Then push the barrel of a pen through there until air comes out. He's thin enough, so it might work."

"Shit," Luke responded.

Erin couldn't help but laugh at his lack of enthusiasm for the idea. "It would be pretty ironic if you had to do that. At least you watched the procedure once—and on the same kid, too."

"God, I hope it doesn't come to that," Luke said. "And now I need another drink to get the thought out of my head."

"You're drinking on the job?" Erin asked in amusement. "Is that allowed in your profession?"

"As far as I'm concerned, we're off the clock right now. Scott and I just stopped at a bar near the hotel for a drink before we call it a night. And I needed something to help me sleep since I'm not there with you—although I probably wouldn't get much sleep if I was with you, either."

"No, you probably wouldn't, Detective," Erin said, using her best sexy voice. "And I'm getting warm just thinking about how much I'd like to be the one investigating you right now."

Luke groaned. "Okay, now it might be two more drinks. And I'd better get off the phone before this conversation goes any further, or I won't be sleeping much at all tonight."

Erin chuckled. "I'll have to read a few very boring

articles myself." But her expression quickly sobered, knowing their conversation was about to end. "Be careful, Luke."

"I will," he assured her. "Have a good night. I love you."

"You too," Erin whispered back.

But he'd already ended the call.

AT THE BAR IN EAGLE RIVER SCOTT STARED AT LUKE incredulously. "Jesus Christ, you're already telling her you love her? Man, you are totally screwed."

"That sounds good to me." Luke grinned and tossed back the shot of whiskey in his hand, feeling the heat travel down his chest and settle into his stomach.

Scott slowly shook his head. "You have no idea what you're giving up, Luke. You don't have any responsibilities, no one to nag you constantly and make up those goddamned honey-do lists. You can do whatever the hell you want. Why would you mess that up?" He took a long swig of his beer. "The best advice I can give you now is to run. Run like hell."

"What's going on with you?" Luke asked, his brows furrowing with concern. "You haven't been yourself lately."

Scott let out a frustrated sigh and ran a hand through his thinning, dark blond hair. "My life is a clusterfuck, that's what's going on. Nothing's what I thought it would be. Marriage, kids…Shit, I've got four kids and none of them are even completely out of diapers yet. The house is always a mess, and if one kid's not crying then another one is…It's madness. And just to go out to eat we have to pack up like it's a week-long goddamned vacation. Not that we can afford to do either one much anyway." He grimaced, finishing off his beer. "I have no idea why we didn't quit while we were behind after the first IVF. We knew there was a good chance we'd end up with twins again."

"Scott, I think you should talk about all this with one of the EAP counselors."

"Hah! If they'll change some diapers, clean my house, and put some money in my bank account, then yeah, I'll go."

"If money is a problem, I'll loan you whatever you need."

"No, I made my goddamned bed and I'll lay in it." Scott stood up, his blue-gray eyes sparkling with anger, and turned to leave. "Let's get out of here."

Luke shook his head wearily and headed to the hotel with Scott, completely baffled by his friend's behavior, but too exhausted to think much more about it.

CHAPTER

17

Luke didn't make it back the next day either. They still hadn't found any signs of the boys and were staying another night to continue the search—which could take even longer depending on what they did find, and where the trail might lead them.

By the following morning Erin had run out of ways to distract herself from the anxiety that was relentlessly gnawing at the pit of her stomach. And before it drove her crazy, she thought about following her new resolution to drive it away instead—literally this time—by driving up to Eagle River with Jenna. At least she would get to see Luke in person for a little while, and maybe he'd let them help out in some way, such as rechecking hospitals and urgent care clinics. But then she'd laughed at herself for even considering such a ridiculous idea. She could just imagine the look on Luke's face when she showed up, having dragged Jenna along with her to boot. He would probably tell her that she really had lost her mind.

But even so, an hour later she tried to convince Jenna

that it wasn't such a ridiculous idea after all.

Fortunately, before her arguments took them down a road that had trouble written all over it, Luke called to let her know they'd given up the search and were finally heading home. He had a pile of work waiting for him at the police station when he got back, but he promised that their next kiss would happen before sunset, come hell or high water. And he planned to stay with her all night this time instead of throwing rocks at her bedroom window later when he couldn't sleep alone.

Smiling at the thought, Erin looked out the kitchen window as she washed dishes from lunch. James Burnett had just finished building the ramp out front—which he hadn't been able to get done on Monday because of the storm—and was now tossing some scrap wood into a bonfire he'd started near the shed.

He was a small man in his late thirties, she guessed, with a wiry frame hardened by years of manual labor. She'd seen for herself in the last few days what a tireless worker he was. And even though he didn't say much, he also clearly had a crush on Jenna.

Erin glanced at the latest batch of cookies he'd brought and laughed softly. The man sure did like making cookies. But then her expression sobered when she recalled what Jenna had told her about his past.

James was originally from Springfield, Illinois. His mother was Father Burnett's sister, and he'd moved to New Dublin several years ago, after his wife and son had been killed in a gruesome car accident. Jenna said he never talked about it, though. She'd gotten the details from Father Burnett.

James had been working as a carpenter in New Dublin ever since. But then last year he'd fallen off a ladder and sustained a serious head injury. He'd developed significant brain swelling as a result, and medical treatment hadn't been effective, so he'd needed to have part of his skull temporarily removed—a decompressive craniectomy—until the swelling resolved a few months later. But after going through intense rehabilitation, he'd made a remarkable recovery. And now he was helping Jenna.

Erin winced when she thought about the long surgical scar on his head, extending from ear to ear over the top of it. He was going prematurely bald, and his remaining thin brown hair didn't do much to hide it. At least her own scars weren't there on the surface for all the world to see. But then again, maybe it would have been better if they were.

"A quarter for your thoughts," Jenna said, walking into the kitchen. "Since a penny doesn't buy much these days."

Erin looked at her in surprise. "I thought you were taking a nap?"

"I was about to, but I forgot to drink something first." A slight smile pulled at Jenna's mouth. "You've been a bit of a drill sergeant about that—and the fruit and veggie shakes. And the high-protein snacks. Before I know it you'll have me in the gym lifting weights."

Erin chuckled. "That's not a bad idea." Then she dried her hands off and filled a glass with lemonade. "I'll bring this into the living room for you."

She followed Jenna out of the kitchen and down the hallway, glancing at the open doorway to her friend's bedroom near the end of it. "I just don't get why you won't take naps in your room, Jen. If your bed isn't comfortable we should get you a new one. And I'm also going to pick you up an assist rail. That should make it easier to get in and out of bed."

"I never thought of that, and it would be helpful," Jenna said vaguely.

Erin came to a halt outside the living room. "What's really the problem?"

Jenna reluctantly stopped and turned around, letting out a resigned sigh. "Oh, it's just that the bedroom is so dark. There's only one window…And—it used to be my parents' room. I remember how it was for my mom, and I figure I'll be spending a lot of time in there myself soon enough."

"Oh, Jen," Erin whispered. "Let's go see what we can do."

"Really, Erin. It's not that big of a deal. I don't mind the couch, and at night it's dark in there anyway."

Erin went into the living room and set the glass of lemonade on the coffee table, then marched back to Jenna. "You know I'm going to keep nagging you about the bedroom until I can fix it, right? That's just how I am, so you might as well give in now."

Jenna reluctantly smiled. "Okay, fine. I was pretty impressed when I watched you install the shower sprayer. But I seriously doubt there's much you can do in there."

"We'll see."

Erin walked into the bedroom and was immediately assailed by many long-forgotten, painful memories. She hadn't stepped foot into this room since the day Shannon died…Then she mentally shook herself. She wasn't going to remember Jenna's mom like that. She was going to remember her just as she'd seen her in the dream: beautiful and radiant with so much love and happiness.

Feeling her heart lighten with the image, she thoughtfully surveyed the room. The small window on the far wall looked out into the backyard. There was a closet along the wall to the right, so another window couldn't be installed there, and a bathroom was on the other side of the wall to the left.

Jenna came in as well, glancing around with a grimace. "Do you see what I mean? It's kind of a dungeon in here. Maybe I should've asked you to pick up an extra lamp last weekend."

Erin smiled wryly and continued her inspection of the room. "We could make the window bigger, or add a second one on that wall." Then an even better idea struck her. "Or we can just build you a new bedroom."

Jenna immediately burst out laughing. "Where, pray tell, would we build that?"

"The back patio. The hot tub is going in one corner, but there's plenty of space to add a small sunroom off the kitchen, which could be your new bedroom."

"No, Erin, that's too much," Jenna protested. "And I wouldn't be using it long enough to—"

"Too late, you already said I could fix the problem," Erin interrupted, giving her a grin. "James can build it. I'm sure he would jump at the chance. And he'd probably bring you more cookies since he's so sweet on you. We've already gotten chocolate chip and oatmeal. Maybe the next batch will be peanut butter."

Jenna rolled her eyes. "We're just friends."

"If you say so," Erin teased. And after a contemplative pause, she said, "But the more I think about adding a sunroom, the more I like it. He can build it level with the kitchen so there won't be any steps, and another set of patio doors can lead out to a deck." She snapped her fingers enthusiastically. "That would solve another problem, too. We'll have James build the deck around the hot tub. And I'll order a swimming pool lift so we can lower you into the water. Then it will be even easier to get you in."

Jenna shook her head. "Now you're going completely overboard, Erin."

"No, it really won't be that hard to do. And I want the roof to be made of plexiglass so you can fall asleep watching the stars at night."

Jenna's expression softened, and her eyes misted with tears. "That sounds wonderful."

"All right then, it's a done deal," Erin said, fighting off her own tears at the look on Jenna's face. "But first thing's first: Let's get you into the living room so you can drink your lemonade and take a nap. Then I'll talk to James about the project. I'd like to get it started right away."

Erin turned toward the door with those objectives in mind. But she stopped in her tracks when a painting she hadn't noticed before caught her eye on the back wall. It was clearly another piece that Adam had done for Jenna, with a poem superimposed on an outdoor night scene.

Intrigued, she went over to take a closer look. And much to her astonishment, she saw that it was a watercolor of Jenna's backyard, painted exactly as it had looked for real the other night, her magical night with Luke, complete with the fireflies, the pond, the moon and stars, the wildflowers…

She reverently touched them and read the poem:

Fireflies

This field full of fireflies
Makes me believe in magic again,
A glowing gift sent to the earth,
A thousand lights from Heaven.

They're flickering little stars
As they fly around,

A capricious constellation
Right here on the ground.

And if they wouldn't mind,
I'd like to take one home with me,
A memento from tonight,
A miniature starlit memory.

But the magic of the night
Can't be captured in a jar,
So I'll hold on to the fireflies
Contained within my heart.

—Jenna Godfrey

"Adam's never been here, in case you're wondering," Jenna said, coming over to stand next to her. "I gave him some pictures of the backyard, along with the poem, and asked if he could paint a scene with the fireflies. None of the actual pictures I took of the fireflies were very good, so I was surprised at how well the painting turned out anyway."

"Yes, it's amazing…Perfect." Erin pointed to a spot amongst the wildflowers. "We were dancing right there when Luke said he loved me." And she would never forget how completely in tune with the universe she'd felt right there as well.

"I'd meant for you to have this one," Jenna said. "And now it looks like it will be the perfect gift for both of you."

"I'll cherish it always." Erin brushed a tear from the corner of her eye and smiled. "It will look really good in the sunroom too, so I need to get James cracking."

"Okay," Jenna chuckled, heading for the door. "And I think I'm ready for that nap now."

Erin helped her get settled on the couch with the glass of lemonade. Then she went outside and found James standing by the bonfire.

"Sure, I'll build a sunroom for Jenna," he quietly said after she explained the project. "It'll probably take me a couple of weeks to finish, but I might be able to start working on it tomorrow if I can get the go ahead from the building inspector. He's usually at the golf course every Sunday morning, and I don't mind interrupting his tee time if it means I can get the room built sooner for Jenna." A slight smile crossed James' face and he threw the last of scrap wood into the fire. "I'll take a few measurements and draw up some plans right now."

Erin remained by the fire after he left, watching sparks fly as the wood crackled and popped. But she soon got a little too warm and stepped away, looking around indecisively for something to do. She had about an hour and a half to kill before the hot tub arrived.

It was another beautiful summer day, so she headed down the driveway. A peaceful walk in the countryside would be the perfect way to occupy her time. And maybe afterward she would take a nap too.

At the end of the driveway she went left and started walking down the road. But it wasn't long before she realized there was something else she needed to do if she was ever going to have peace of mind. And without letting herself think twice about it, she turned around and went the other way instead…It was time to face another demon.

She walked about a quarter-mile past the woods and at first hesitated to lift her eyes from the road when she reached the gravel driveway that led to her grandparents' old farmhouse. But with a deep breath she finally looked.

She expected a lot of emotions would hit her right then: anxiety, fear, anger, disgust. But none of them did. The first thing she felt was surprise. And the second thing was, of all things unimaginable, admiration.

It was the same place in some ways, and yet totally different. The house was still white, but had been freshly painted. Cute, maroon-colored shutters now adorned the windows, and the front porch didn't look like it was about to collapse anymore. Someone had put a lot of care into the yard, too. The grass was thick and green, and brightly colored shrubbery had been planted in various places, along with flowers. Lots of flowers…

Erin slowly shook her head and laughed. The place looked pleasant, peaceful actually.

A moment later a woman about her own age with short brown hair came out the front door and headed down the porch steps, waving to her.

Erin paused uncertainly, but then waved back and walked up the driveway to meet her.

"You must be Erin, Jenna's friend from Boston," the woman said, holding out her hand. "I'm Meghan Carey."

Erin returned the handshake. "I was just admiring your yard. Did you do all this?"

Meghan nodded with a look of wry amusement on her face. "Yes, I've been working on it since April. My husband said I shouldn't have bothered since we're moving out later this fall. But I figured we'll still be here all spring and summer, and I love doing it, so why stop now? And I'll be leaving something nice for the next person to enjoy."

"Have you lived here long?" Erin asked curiously.

"No, we moved here in March after our house sold. We're in the process of building a new one, and it was either rent this place or stay with my in-laws until it's done. I chose this place."

Erin chuckled. "Well, you really will be leaving behind a beautiful legacy. Jenna must love your yard."

"She gave me ideas for some of it," Meghan said. "How is she doing, by the way? I wasn't able to stop by this last week. My husband has been working on the house whenever he can, so I'm pretty much on my own here, and it's just been one thing after another. Today it's a teething baby who won't sleep. I just laid him down before I came out, and I'm crossing my fingers that I get a little peace and quiet."

Erin smiled sympathetically. "Jenna's taking a nap herself at the moment. But she's been doing fine overall. In fact—"

"Mommy!" a girl suddenly yelled from somewhere inside the house.

Meghan heaved a sigh. "Well, there goes the peace and quiet. That's my other child, Bella. She's in the playroom upstairs having a tea party with her stuffed animals. I'm sure she hears us out here and is wondering what's going on."

Erin raised her brows in surprise. "Wow, she has really good hearing."

"Yes, she certainly does. But she's blind, so her other senses are a lot stronger."

"Oh, I'm sorry," Erin apologized. "I didn't know." Jenna hadn't told her anything about the family, probably because they were living here. And she guessed Meghan didn't know about her own childhood either.

"Don't be sorry. I'm not," Meghan said. "I developed a pretty bad blood infection when I was pregnant and ended up delivering her at twenty-six weeks. The doctors hadn't thought either one of us would survive, but here we are. And Bella doesn't feel sorry for herself because she ended up blind as a result, so I guess I can't either."

"Mommy!"

"I'm coming!" Meghan called out, then turned back to Erin. "Do you have a minute? Bella would love to meet you. We were down at the pond last week listening to the swans with Jenna, and she told us you were coming to stay with her. Now all Bella's been talking about is meeting the lady who's a doctor in Boston."

Erin laughed nervously and glanced at the house, not missing the irony of the situation—it was the story of her life. She couldn't have imagined any reason that she would willingly go into this house again. And yet here was one. "I would love to meet her," she said sincerely.

Meghan headed back up the front porch stairs, and Erin tentatively followed her inside. *It's just a house,* she silently reminded herself. *It's just a house...*

The front entrance led into a beautifully decorated dining room. To the right was the kitchen, which was cheerful and modern. Erin would never have known she was in the same house.

Then they went down the hallway and up the steep, narrow staircase to the second floor. And that's when memories started to flash through her mind in bits and pieces. She could hear her grandmother's voice just as clearly as she had twenty-six years ago. *You're even worse than your mother...You'll burn in the fires of hell for your sins if you don't repent...For the wages of sin is death...Get down on your knees and beg the Lord for salvation...Our Father who art in Heaven, hallowed be thy name. Thy kingdom come. Thy will be done, on Earth as it is in Heaven...*

Erin mentally squashed that angry voice in her head as she followed Meghan into the playroom—the room her grandmother used to pray in all the time. And the dark cloud that had settled over her on the way up there lifted when she got her first glimpse of the tea party going on inside.

A child-sized table and chairs had been set up in the middle of the room, and Bella sat in the one farthest from them. Erin guessed she was about seven or eight years old, with long brown hair and brown eyes. Two teddy bears and a baby doll sat in the other three chairs, and Bella was pretending to fill a teacup for one of the bears. But when they walked in she set the pot down and looked toward them with unfocused, slightly wandering eyes. "Who's with you, Mommy?"

"It's Jenna's friend." Meghan gave Erin an embarrassed smile. "I'm not sure what to call you. Would you prefer—"

"Dr. Erin?" Bella asked excitedly. "Is that you?"

Erin walked over to her. "Yes, and you can just call me Erin." She squatted down next to the child and squeezed her hand. "It's very nice to meet you, Bella."

The little girl shifted in her seat so they were facing each other. "I should call you Dr. Erin. And it's nice to meet you too. Can I touch your face?"

"Bella, where are your manners?" Meghan gently chided.

"No, I don't mind," Erin said, patting the child's forearm. "You need to put a face to the name after all."

Bella giggled, then reached up and began exploring Erin's face with both hands. "You have soft skin."

Erin smiled ruefully. "Hopefully I don't have bad breath. I made garlic shrimp for lunch today, and I went a little heavy on the garlic."

"No, you smell good, like flowers." Bella lightly brushed her hands over Erin's hair until she reached the ends. "You have nice hair, too."

"So do you." Erin ran her fingers through Bella's hair. "It makes me think of chocolate—rich brown and silky smooth."

Meghan chuckled. "Bella loves chocolate."

The little girl's expression became thoughtful, and she touched her own hair. "No one ever told me that before. I thought it was like dirt and tree bark." Then she slowly grinned. "My hair is like chocolate, too."

A moment later the baby started crying down the hallway, and Meghan groaned. "Oh boy, here we go again. If you need to leave, Erin, I understand. This might take a while."

"No, go ahead. If Bella doesn't mind, I'll join her tea party."

The little girl clapped her hands gleefully. "Yay! You can have Sunny Bear's spot, and he'll sit with me." She felt for the bear and put him on her lap.

Meghan left, and Erin tentatively sat down on one of the little wooden chairs, praying it held her weight. And when she was sure it wouldn't splinter into a hundred pieces and send her crashing to the floor on her backside, she smiled at Bella. "Okay, I'm ready for tea. Would you like me to pour a fresh cup for everyone?"

"No, I can do it, Dr. Erin. I won't spill."

Bella picked up the teapot and reached for the porcelain cup in front of Erin, pretending to fill it. Then she set the cup back on its plate and did the same thing with two more cups for the bears.

Erin was amazed at how well she managed without being able to see a thing. "What about your baby? Doesn't she get tea?"

An odd look crossed Bella's face. "She's too little to have tea, Dr. Erin."

"Of course. I don't know what I was thinking," Erin said sheepishly, lifting her own cup as if to drink. She had a feeling the child would call her on it if she didn't. "I'll bet you're a very good big sister."

Bella nodded. "I like to hold Oliver, but he's kind of boring. It's more fun having tea with you." She put a plastic cookie on a plate for Erin. "And I like you better than Miss Helen. She's not much fun either."

Erin froze with her cup in mid-air. "Hel—Helen?" That was her grandmother's name.

"Uh huh. Mommy thinks she's my imaginary friend, but she used to live here—well, until Walter pushed her down the basement stairs and she died." Bella pretended to feed a cookie to the bear in her lap. "That wasn't very nice, was it, Sunny Bear?"

Erin set her teacup down on the plate with a clatter and sat there in shock. Her grandfather…

She eventually gathered at least a few of her scattered wits and thought back to that time. Her grandfather hadn't been able to use his right arm because of the stroke, but he'd still managed to get around with a cane back then. It was possible he could have pushed her grandmother down the stairs.

"Don't you like your tea, Dr. Erin?"

Erin mentally shook herself and took another pretend sip of the tea. "It's very good. But Bella, who told you that Walter killed Helen?"

"Miss Helen did. She tells me stuff sometimes. But she'll only talk to me when she sits in the rocking chair in Oliver's room holding her babies."

Erin looked uneasily around the playroom. "There's a—a rocking chair in Oliver's room?"

Bella gave the other bear a drink of the invisible tea. "Mm-hmm. It used to be in here when we first moved in, but Daddy put it in Oliver's room."

For a moment Erin didn't know what to think. Was this all the vivid imagination of a child who'd overheard a conversation about how her grandmother had died falling down the basement stairs? Or was it the very real experience of a child who hadn't yet learned what should or should not be? And the fact that Bella had mentioned the rocking chair…No one else would have known how attached her grandmother had been to it. Erin hadn't even discussed it with Jenna.

Then something else that Bella had said struck her: *babies*. "Has…has Helen said anything about her babies?"

The child nodded, setting the bear's teacup down. "She talks about them a lot, and it makes me sad. They all died in their sleep."

"How many babies died?" Erin asked in surprise. Her grandparents had never mentioned any other children besides her mother.

Bella picked up the doll and put Sunny Bear in the chair instead, then held a fake bottle to the doll's lips as she cradled her. "She had one boy and two girls. She found the baby boy dead in his crib, and she kept the other two babies with her all the time and held them in the rocking chair every night, but they died anyway. Walter buried the second baby girl in the woods by a big rock 'cause he said people would think they killed her. And Miss Helen is still mad about that. She said God would have wanted Anne Marie in the cemetery with the others."

Erin stared at the little girl, completely stunned. Anne Marie was her mother's name. And there was indeed a very large rock deep in the woods. She'd discovered it herself years ago—along with a cross made of sticks right next to it. "Did Helen…Did she say anything else about Anne Marie?"

Bella set the bottle down and pretended to burp the doll. "Miss Helen said God helped her find another baby girl to replace Anne Marie. But that girl was naughty all the time and ran away and had a baby when she wasn't supposed to. Then the second Anne Marie died too, and Miss Helen's granddaughter came to live with them." A brief grin crossed Bella's face. "She had the same name as you—Erin. But she wasn't nice like you. Miss Helen said she was even more naughty than Anne Marie, and the police even had to come over one time. I feel bad that Miss Helen had to take care of her."

Erin's head spun. If that was true about her mother… "Bella, did Helen say where she found the second Anne Marie?"

The little girl shook her head and turned the doll to sit in her lap. "No, she wouldn't tell me. She was too afraid Walter might hear 'cause he told her never to talk about it."

Erin glanced hesitantly around the room again. "Where—where is Walter?"

"I don't think he's here like Miss Helen thinks. He hasn't ever talked to me, and Willy said he's learning lessons in Heaven."

"Who is Willy?" Erin dared to ask.

"He's Walter's big brother. But he fell out of the hayloft in the barn and died a long time ago. He sometimes talks to me over there. Miss Helen said she never liked him, but I do. He's funny."

Erin couldn't believe it—and yet she could. Another ghost. "Why didn't Helen like him?"

Bella started to pour tea for them all again. "Miss Helen said it wasn't fair that Walter loved Willy more than her, even after Willy died. She was scared of living in the country, but Walter wouldn't sell the farm 'cause he said it belonged to Willy. And he got mean if she talked bad about Willy. Miss Helen thinks God was punishing Walter 'cause he loved Willy too much, and that's why all their babies died." Bella set the teapot down. "You should drink your tea before it gets cold, Dr. Erin."

Erin lifted her cup. "Has Willy said anything about Helen?"

"No, he only talks about the farm and what he and Walter used to do when they were kids. He told me how they milked cows. It sounds really gross." Bella made a face—one Erin hadn't even known a child blind from birth could make.

Meghan walked into the playroom just then. "Oh, Bella, I hope you're not telling Dr. Erin about those imaginary friends of yours."

The child let out a mildly annoyed sigh and leaned toward Erin, whispering, "Some people just don't get it."

"Hey, I heard that, young lady," Meghan said, though there was amusement in her voice.

Erin awkwardly got up from her chair, still a little dazed by what had just happened. But she knew one thing for sure—she needed to find that rock in the woods again. "Bella was telling me some interesting things about this place. Do you mind if I look around outside a little before I go?"

"Of course not," Meghan told her. "Explore all you want."

Erin squatted down next to Bella and gave her a hug. "Thank you so much for the tea party. I'd never been to one before. Next time you'll have to come over to Jenna's house, and we can have a party there. You're welcome anytime. And I would love to sit by the pond and listen to the swans, too."

Bella clapped her hands. "Yes, I want to! When can we, Mommy?"

Erin smiled and stood up. "I'll leave the two of you to discuss that. I can find my own way out."

She gave Meghan a brief hug goodbye and left the room, glancing down the hallway in the direction of her old bedroom. The door was partially open, and she could see the end of a crib inside. Oliver's room. She thought about taking a quick peek at the rocking chair, but then goosebumps started to form on her arms, and she hurried down the stairs and out the door instead.

On her way to the woods she stopped by the barn, pondering it for a moment. Unlike the house, it had been left to war with the elements—and the elements were definitely winning. It was weathered gray, with gaping holes in places where the boards had either fallen off or were rotting, and parts of the roof were missing as well. It really did look like it had been through a war, and Erin felt a deep sadness for Willy.

She turned to face the house and looked up at the window to her old bedroom, remembering all the times she'd climbed out and sat there reading on the back porch roof. Had he been watching her from over here? Maybe those old books in the closet had been his.

Her eyes fell to the tiny basement window she'd escaped from so long ago, and a memory struck her. She'd only found the window because she'd heard a strange noise up there—a tapping sound. She'd thought it was a mouse, but at that point she hadn't cared. She would have eaten a mouse to get out of that basement. She'd never seen a mouse, though. And now she wondered if it might have been Willy who'd helped her.

Erin shifted her gaze back to the barn and quietly said, "If that was you, Willy, thank you. I owe you more than I can ever repay—and for the farm, too. But now I think you should leave here and go to Heaven. You deserve to be happy."

She started walking toward the woods again, laughing softly. Not only did she believe in ghosts, now she was talking to them.

Then a creaking noise made her stop. She turned around and looked up in the direction of the sound. The old rusted weather vane on the edge of the barn roof was spinning. She thought back, but couldn't think of a single time in all the years she'd lived there that it had ever moved. And there wasn't any wind.

She continued to watch it in amazement. And when it finally stopped spinning, she headed to the woods, determined to find that rock.

"SO WHERE DO YOU THINK WAYNE AND JESSE WENT?" Scott asked, sitting in the passenger seat of the police car as they drove back to New Dublin.

Luke shrugged, keeping his eyes on the road in front of him. "Your guess is as good as mine. But no one's reported seeing them in the Eagle River area, so they were probably picked up at the rest stop by someone they knew. And I'll bet it was Zeke Raabe."

Luke had interviewed Wayne's older brother Zeke, who was one mean son of a bitch. He'd said he had no idea where his brother was, but then had outright admitted that if he did know he wouldn't tell them. And the rest of the family hadn't been any more pleasant, much less helpful.

"I'll have to call it a day when we get back," Scott said. "The wife has another to-do list a mile long waiting for me, and I'll catch hell if I don't get some of it done today."

Luke glanced at Scott. Since the episode at the bar, his friend had been even more withdrawn and irritable than normal—or at least what had become normal in the last month or two. "Scott, I really think you should talk to someone, maybe a marriage counselor—"

"Jesus Christ, Luke, I don't need a goddamned marriage counselor!"

"Scott—"

"I can handle things on my own, Luke. Just give it a rest."

Luke mentally sighed, feeling increasingly helpless and frustrated. Scott's personal problems were yet another layer of ugliness this case had uncovered, and now he'd just lost two valuable days chasing shadows instead of investigating the murder, which was going nowhere otherwise.

On Friday morning the State Crime Lab sent him their latest report. They'd recovered DNA from under Tina Murdock's fingernails, as well as elsewhere on her skin and on the bed, and all of it belonged to one person—the man who'd fathered her baby. But they hadn't gotten any hits off CODIS, the national DNA database, so their new prime suspect was unknown.

To make matters worse, on Friday afternoon patrol cops in New Dublin reported that Seth Slater's truck was gone. But like Wayne and Jesse, he'd disappeared without a trace.

And to top it off, this morning the chief sent them a text message that he was going to Minneapolis for the rest of the weekend to visit his son, despite the fact that they had a murderer on the loose and two fugitive kids on the run.

Luke knew Jeff wasn't looking forward to Monday, when shit was really going to hit the fan in New Dublin. The DA had arranged for an independent forensic accounting team to come in and start the embezzlement investigation. The plan was for Jeff to break the news to the mayor and Stella Givens when the team arrived, and then they'd bring them to the station for questioning.

At the meeting on Thursday Luke had pushed for DCI, and even the FBI, to get involved. But the chief had been adamantly against it, arguing that they were doing good work on their own and didn't need too many cooks stirring the pot. But Luke had a feeling Jeff's friendship with the mayor—who also happened to be his boss—was affecting his objectivity. And the mayor answered only to the people, unless there was evidence of serious misconduct or a crime. But for all they knew he and Stella were just having an affair, which would hardly raise an eyebrow these days. And it certainly wasn't a crime.

CHAPTER

18

Erin was surprised at how easily she found the big rock, even though she had to go fairly deep into the woods to reach it. But she'd spent so much time in these woods as a kid, she'd become familiar with every tree, every path, every rock. And it was all coming back to her now, this piece of her childhood she'd left so far behind.

The dark, quiet mystery of the woods had always intrigued her as a child. She'd enjoyed roaming through them, making new discoveries, immersing herself in a world that gave her comfort, just as she'd found in her books. Jenna, on the other hand, preferred lots of sunshine and green grass, so she'd rarely come along—especially after her dad warned them about all the wild animals they might encounter in the woods.

Erin smiled at the thought as she walked up to the big rock and lightly touched its solid, moss-covered surface. It was slightly taller than her and somewhat rectangular in shape, with the edges having been whittled away over time by Mother Nature. There were a number of smaller rocks scattered about as well, and she'd always wondered how they got there—yet another mystery of the woods.

But as much as the rocks had fascinated her, she'd never stayed in this part of the woods for long because of the cross that had been pounded into the ground near the big rock. It made her think of her grandmother and cast a forbidding shadow on what might otherwise have been her favorite place.

She walked around to the other side of the rock and saw the cross was still there, standing slightly askew, made of two thick tree branches held together with twine. And without hesitation she went over to inspect it more closely. But nothing was inscribed in the wood, and there weren't any other obvious signs to indicate that it did indeed mark a grave.

Searching for other clues, Erin used her foot to push aside the branches, leaves, and pine needles that covered the ground at the base of the cross. She had no intention of trying to dig up a body, though. The cross was enough evidence for her. But much to her surprise, she uncovered a square, concrete slab several feet in width.

Squatting down, she brushed away more of the debris with her hand and discovered a crudely written inscription in the concrete:

Anne Marie Harris
August 20 to September 1, 1967
Rest in Peace

Erin stared at the inscription in shock. August 20th was her mother's birthday. Then she did a quick calculation in her head to figure out the year her mother had been born…1967.

"Bella, did Helen say where she found the second Anne Marie?"

"No, she wouldn't tell me. She was too afraid Walter might hear 'cause he told her never to talk about it."

Erin slowly stood up. So it really all hadn't been just the imagination of a child. With the proof she had here, there was no doubt about it: Helen and Walter had kidnapped her mother. But where had they stolen her from? Who had her mother really been?

Erin wondered if the answers might lie in her own childhood memories. Maybe there was a clue buried in the recesses of her mind. But before she could think about it any further, she was suddenly startled out of her reverie by the sound of footsteps coming from somewhere deeper in the woods to her right, soon followed by a male voice pleading, "I have to stop, Wayne. I'm dizzy…I'm gonna be sick." Then she heard the sound of vomiting.

"What the fuck, Jesse!"

Erin quickly crouched down on the other side of the big rock, her heart racing. Oh God. Wayne and Jesse were here. And she hadn't brought her cell phone along.

She desperately looked around for something she could use to defend herself and crawled over to a pile of branches that caught her eye. She picked up the longest, thickest one amongst them, hoping to God she didn't have to use it, then crept back over to the rock and huddled against it, waiting.

"Come on, we need to keep moving," Wayne said. "That hunting shack has to be around here somewhere."

Erin heard them start walking again, and they were getting closer.

"I can't make it," Jesse said a few minutes later. "I think I'm gonna pass out. I need to lay down." Leaves rustled as he collapsed to the ground somewhere near the group of stones.

"Fuck! Where is that goddamned shack?" Wayne said angrily.

Erin listened to the sound of his footsteps get closer and closer. Then he abruptly stopped, and all she heard after that was the rapid pounding of her heart in her ears. *Concentrate on your breathing, Erin,* she silently told herself. *Inhale and exhale. Inhale…and exhale…*

"Holy fuck!" Wayne suddenly exclaimed.

"What?" she heard Jesse ask.

"There's a cross here. It's a fuckin' grave," Wayne said. "And it looks like someone was just here. We need to get the fuck somewhere else. Now."

Erin heard him walk back to Jesse, and she leaned her head against the rock with a silent sigh of relief.

"I can't, Wayne," the other boy said weakly. "Just…Just leave me here."

Wayne sighed in exasperation. "I'll keep looking and come back for you."

The sound of his footsteps became more distant, and Erin dared to peek her head around the rock, just in time to see him disappear into a thicker part of the woods to the east—right in the direction of the Carey's house.

When she could no longer hear him, she got up from behind the rock and tentatively approached Jesse. He was lying on the ground next to one of the smaller rocks, and as she got closer she saw his eyes were closed and his face looked flushed. There was a duffel bag nearby, but she didn't see any sign of a weapon.

She took another hesitant step forward. A twig snapped, and in the quiet of the forest it almost sounded like a gun going off. She froze, not sure what to do.

Jesse immediately opened his eyes, turning his head in her direction. And a shocked expression crossed his face. "You…" he whispered, but made no further movement.

Erin rushed over to him and knelt down, setting her stick aside. She'd long ago learned to tell who was really sick and who wasn't the second she looked at a patient. And this kid was sick, though it didn't look like the cause was a pneumothorax this time. She felt his forehead with the back of her hand. He was burning up with fever. And his brown eyes were glazed over. He was septic.

"I must be hallucinating," the boy murmured through dry and cracked lips.

"I need to get you some help, Jesse. Do you have a cell phone?"

He nodded. "In the side pocket of the duffel bag."

Erin quickly found the phone and came back over to Jesse, sitting down next to him while he turned it on and unlocked it. He also had to show her how to use it since she wasn't familiar with that particular model. Then she punched in Luke's number, thankful she remembered it, especially now, with her mind racing in a thousand directions.

"Hello," he answered.

Erin felt relief wash over her as soon as she heard his voice. "Thank God you answered, Luke," she said in a rush. "I'm with Jesse Torres. We're in the woods behind the Carey's house—the place I used to live. Wayne Raabe is headed that way right now. You need to get over there as fast as you can. And call an ambulance for Jesse. He's really sick."

"Erin?…I didn't…Where…Something about…"

"Luke, you keep cutting out. Can you hear me?"

Silence followed, and Erin looked at the phone screen: Call Failed.

"Damn it," she whispered, turning back to Jesse. "I need to go—"

She abruptly stopped talking and whipped her head around, hearing the sound of footsteps approaching again. And when she saw who it was, her eyes widened in horror: Wayne Raabe was walking through the trees toward them.

He hadn't seen her yet, and she hovered in indecision… But there was really only one choice she could make. And with her heart pounding and her stomach clenched in a knot of fear and dread, she grabbed the stick and slowly stood up to face him.

Wayne shifted his gaze in her direction and halted in surprise. But then he looked her up and down, and his lips lifted into a slow, lascivious smile. "I came back for the bag, but I see we've got something a lot more interesting here now."

Erin knew exactly what Wayne Raabe was the moment she got a good look at him. She'd seen countless patients like him at Boston General: the gaunt face covered in angry-looking abscesses as a result of injecting; the bony frame and sallow skin with scabs all over from itching; the disheveled appearance and lifeless demeanor. He was a classic heroin abuser in the final stage of addiction. And now that he'd reached it nothing mattered to him except the next fix. Death didn't even matter. Not really. He'd already become one of the walking dead.

"This kid is really sick and needs to get to a hospital now," Erin said desperately, clutching her stick and hoping there was at least a tiny bit of humanity left in Wayne Raabe.

"Take your bag and go. I'll help him."

Wayne responded with another leering grin, then pulled a hunting knife out of its sheath on his belt and slowly walked toward her again. "I just took a ride on the white horse, so I'm feelin' pretty fuckin' good. But I haven't had much fun lately, and right now I'm thinkin' it would be a whole lotta fun to make you scream in ways you never have before." He laughed, and it sent a cold shiver running straight down Erin's spine. "Then I'm gonna cut you up into little tiny pieces and bury you in these woods." He was just a few feet from the end of her stick now.

"What are you talking about, Wayne?" Jesse said in distress. "Don't touch her."

Wayne met the boy's gaze and let out another laugh. "Didn't I ever tell you I go both ways? You're a good fuck, kid, but right now she'll be better."

Erin knew she should have tried to hit Wayne as soon as he got distracted by Jesse. It would have been her best chance. But she could only stand there, frozen in fear, her arms trembling as she held up her paltry weapon.

Wayne turned back to her and smiled tauntingly. "Are you ready for the party, baby? We'll make real good use of your little stick there."

He took another step toward her, and even though he was only a few inches taller than her, and way too thin, Erin knew by the look on his face that she was no match for him. She should at least try to defend herself, she thought in a panic. But she still couldn't move. Her heart pounded in her ears, and she could barely breathe.

And in that instant she realized she was as good as dead.

WITH RED AND BLUE LIGHTS FLASHING, LUKE SPED into Jenna's driveway and came to a screeching halt behind a delivery truck that had backed into it.

Both he and Scott immediately jumped out with guns drawn and approached the truck from opposite sides, cautiously looking into the cargo area.

"Luke, I'm so glad to see—"

Jenna came out of the garage, but abruptly stopped in wide-eyed surprise when Luke spun around to face her with his gun in hand.

"Jenna, where is Erin?" he urgently asked.

"I don't know," she answered in a worried tone. "I got up from a nap about half an hour ago and I can't find her anywhere. I thought maybe she took a walk. But she knew the hot tub was coming, and she still hasn't shown up. She left her phone here too. Something's wrong, I'm sure of it."

Luke turned to Scott. "Call for backup from the Sheriff's Office, and get the K-9 unit over here ASAP."

"What's going on, Luke?" Jenna asked, fear filling her eyes as she watched the other detective run to the car.

Luke holstered his gun. "Erin called me on Jesse Torres' phone as we were heading into town. We have the phone under surveillance, and the cell company alerted us as soon as it was turned on. The call dropped, but they were still able to pick up the GPS signal and localize it to a point less than a half-mile west of here."

"Oh no," Jenna whispered after a moment. "They have her in the woods."

"I only caught a few things she said before I lost her, but I'm pretty sure I heard the name Carey. Do you know who she's referring to?"

"Yes, the Careys. They're renting the old farmhouse Erin grew up in. Dear God, Luke—"

"Get in the house and lock the doors," he abruptly told her. "Keep your phone with you and call 911 for anything suspicious!" And on his way back to the police car he yelled to Scott, "I think they might be next door. Let's go!"

He jumped into the driver's seat and did a quick U-turn, tires squealing on the way out, and raced over to the Carey's house while Scott called in the new location. Then they sprinted up to the house, guns once again drawn.

"You take the front, I'll go in back," Luke said.

Meghan was hanging up laundry on a clothesline when he came around into the backyard, and as soon as she saw him she let out an involuntary scream, dropping the pants in her hand.

"I'm Detective Mathis, New Dublin Police," he told her. "Have you seen Erin Pryce here?"

"Dr. Erin?" Meghan asked in confusion. "She came to visit about an hour ago. Then she wanted to look around the property a little. I—I thought she went home after that."

"Is anyone else here?"

"Just my daughter Bella and her baby brother. She's— she's feeding him a bottle in the living room right now."

Luke ran to the back porch door and opened it, yelling in, "Scott, the house is clear! Come out back and help me search the property!"

Meghan rushed over to him with a look of panic on her face. "What's going on?"

"We think the two boys who've been on the run are nearby and have Erin with them," he explained as calmly as he could. "Gather your kids and lock yourselves in a room until the sheriff's deputies arrive. It shouldn't be long."

"Oh my God!" Meghan cried, dashing into the house just as Scott came out.

They quickly checked the garage and barn, then made their way to the edge of the woods, but found no signs of Erin or the boys.

Luke knew it would be foolish to go in and try to find them on his own, as desperately as he wanted to. But there were hundreds of acres of woods to cover, and he'd risk losing even more valuable time if he headed the wrong way. His best bet was to wait for the K-9 unit.

"Erin!" he yelled helplessly. "Erin…!"

DEEP IN THE WOODS ERIN WAS OBLIVIOUS TO HIS CRIES.

Wayne stood in front of her, still just beyond the reach of the stick. But he clearly knew it would do little to stop him. In fact, he seemed more amused by it than anything, though the amusement didn't reach his eyes. They were cold and empty, reflecting a much different illness than Jesse's.

"You ready to play for real, darlin'?" he asked.

Erin opened her mouth to say something, but she couldn't get a single word out. Terror had stolen her voice.

Then Wayne started to make a move for the stick.

But in the next instant it was the last thing on his mind.

A bear cub appeared from amongst the trees and ambled past Jesse, followed by the sound of a much larger animal crashing through the woods. And a few seconds later they all watched in horror as a full-sized black bear—presumably the mama bear—charged toward them.

"Holy fuck!" Wayne exclaimed.

Erin shook off some of the fear that had paralyzed her a moment ago. "Don't run," she said, pointing her stick in the direction of the bear instead. "If you run she's more likely to attack."

The words of Jenna's dad came back to her from years ago when her friend had asked him if there were bears in the woods. "Sure, there might be black bear," he'd said. "But they're usually more afraid of you than anything. They just want to be left alone. They're a lot like humans, though: They'd rather attack you when your back is turned. So never run if you see one. Face it with any kind of weapon you have, look as big as you can, and try not to show any fear. Let it know you're human and willing to fight, but don't step toward it or yell, unless it keeps coming at you." Then he'd chuckled and said, "Now grizzlies, they're a different story. They won't listen to reason. So if you ever run into one of those, your best bet is to play dead and pray." Jenna had never gone into the woods with her again after that.

The bear came to a halt about fifteen feet from them on the other side of Jesse. She pinned her ears back and swatted the ground with her front paw, revealing large, pointed teeth as she made a huffing noise that almost sounded like a growl. Then she clacked her teeth together, quickly lunged forward a step, stopped, and huffed at them again.

"Fuck this!" Wayne said.

Erin knew he was going to run, and this time she didn't freeze. When he started to turn away she drew her stick back and swung it as hard as she could. With a loud thwack it hit the back side of his head, violently jerking it the opposite way, and he crumpled to the ground unconscious.

Erin didn't stop to think twice about what she'd just done, though. She quickly turned back to face the bear, raising her stick again. Her heart pounded in her chest, but she knew she had a better chance with this bear now than she'd had with Wayne before. "If you're going to rip me to shreds, I won't make it easy this time," she told the bear. "You might not leave here with both eyes, so I'd suggest you just go and take care of your cub."

But the mother bear didn't listen. She got up on her hind legs and made a grunting sound, staring at Erin with her small, close-set dark eyes.

*Oh God. Oh God...*Erin readied the stick, grasping it firmly, but not too tightly, just the way she'd been taught to hold a scalpel. *"Keep your hand steady, Erin,"* the instructor had said. *"Don't hold it too hard or you won't have as much control."* But life had already taught her not to hold on to anything too hard.

The bear dropped down on all four paws, and Erin had to make a conscious effort to breathe. *Aim for the eye*, she told herself. *Just aim for the eye…*

But in the blink of an eye the bear gracefully turned and ambled off after her cub. And then she was gone, leaving only the stillness of the forest behind.

"Wow," Jesse whispered.

Erin quickly pointed the stick back in Wayne's direction, knowing she wasn't out of danger yet. But he still lay unmoving on the ground. She lightly prodded him, and when he didn't respond she squatted down to check for a pulse in his neck—and a small part of her almost hoped she wouldn't find one. But it was there, steady and strong.

"Is he alive?" Jesse asked.

"Yes," Erin said, tossing the stick aside and grabbing Wayne's knife instead. At least she had that now. And after facing the bear, she was confident she would use it if she had to.

"Wayne has handcuffs in the bag. He took them from the cop," Jesse told her softly. "You should put them on him."

Erin hurried over to the duffel bag, setting the knife down next to her. But when she unzipped the bag and saw what else it contained, she stopped cold and her eyes widened in shock. There were hundreds and hundreds of packets of white powder stuffed inside, and other small bags containing round, white pills. Drugs. Enough to supply the entire town—probably the entire county.

Shaking off her surprise, she carefully searched deeper into the bag. Her fingers made contact with metal a moment later, but she hadn't found the handcuffs, she soon discovered—she'd found a gun. And she gingerly pulled it out, never having touched a gun in her life before.

"It's loaded if you want to shoot him," Jesse said. "He deserves it."

"Do I just pull the trigger?" Erin asked. She had no intention of shooting Wayne now, but it would be a good idea to know how if he woke up anytime soon.

"Disengage the safety by pushing up the lever on the left side," Jesse said. "And if you do need to shoot, hold the gun with both hands, aim, and pull the trigger."

Erin pushed up the safety lever like he'd told her, and carefully set the gun on a rock. Then she found the handcuffs and hastily shackled Wayne's arms behind him. But it occurred to her afterward that he could still get up and run—if she didn't shoot him, of course.

She had no desire to find out if she had any skills with a gun, though—or if she would even try to shoot him—so she needed another way to keep him from escaping. And as she looked around for a solution, her eyes fell on the cross, and she knew in an instant what to do.

Grabbing the knife, she went over to it and whispered, "I'm sorry, Anne Marie, but I'll get you a better cross as soon as I can."

She cut the knot that held the cross together and quickly unraveled the twine. Then she used it to tie Wayne's legs up, and even had enough left over to secure his legs to the chain linking the handcuffs for good measure. She used surgical knots the whole time—the same type of knot she used when stitching people up in the ER. Patients were often impressed with her knot-tying skills and said she must be good at fishing or knitting. Men were usually the ones who mentioned fishing, and ladies the ones who brought up knitting, but she imagined fishing and knitting were probably the perfect combination of hobbies to have. She would never have guessed her skills would come in handy to tie up criminals, though.

"I thought you were a doctor?" Jesse asked with a faint smile as he watched her work.

"I'm dating Detective Mathis," Erin said wryly. "Maybe he'll give me an honorary badge."

The boy's expression turned somber again. "I'm sorry he has to deal with all this. He was always nice to me."

Erin finished with Wayne and knelt beside Jesse. "Can I take a quick look at your wounds?"

He nodded, and she gently eased his shirt up—and grimaced. There was a dirty bandage hanging from the pus-covered bullet wound, and the infection had spread over a large area of the surrounding skin.

"We need to get you to a hospital, Jesse. I know the way out of here, but's it's a pretty long walk. Do you think you can give it a try?"

"Just leave me here," he responded, looking away. "Maybe I'll die before anyone finds me again."

Erin gently touched his arm. "I'm not leaving you here. And you're not going to die if I have anything to say about it."

Jesse turned back to her, and the pain she saw in his brown eyes had nothing to do with the infection. "Why do you keep helping me? You shouldn't even want to after everything I've done. You don't have any reason to care about me."

"I care because I can see there's good in you, Jesse. I think you've let the world get to you. And believe me, I know exactly how that feels."

The boy stared up into the canopy of trees overhead. "I can't believe all of this is even happening. And Wayne…I thought I loved him—I did love him. He's the only guy I've ever been with, and…and he wasn't always like this. I know he got into trouble with the cops before, but he had it pretty rough as a kid. He was working to make things better, though. He took classes and got his GED so he could go to tech school to be a nurse. But he threw his back out around Christmas when some demented guy went nuts at the hospital, and his doctor gave him a prescription for oxycodone. He got addicted and then started using heroin. He said it was easier to get than oxy. And after that everything went to hell."

Erin nodded, having heard the same story over and over again in Boston. Prescription narcotic abuse had become a national epidemic. And many of those patients went on to use heroin, patients who would never even have dreamed they'd go down that dark and often deadly road. "I saw the drugs in the duffel bag," she said. "Are they Wayne's?"

Jesse shook his head. "No, they're the mayor's. Wayne's really smart and figured out it was the mayor who was supplying drugs to the dealers. He stole them from his house after he got me out of the hospital—which I didn't even know he was gonna do. And I told him to leave that cop alone. But I went with him because I wanted to get as far away from this town as I could. I hate it here."

Erin realized the implications of what the boy had just said. "The mayor is dealing drugs, and the two of you were at his house the night his wife was murdered?"

Jesse continued to stare up into the trees. "Only Wayne went in, and he said she was already dead. But now I don't know…He was gone a long time, so he could've killed her." Then he turned to her, and the glazed look in his eyes cleared a little. "Wayne stole a flash drive he found in the house too, and he called the mayor the next day to tell him he had his stuff. They were supposed to meet at Maguire Park on Monday at noon, and the mayor was gonna give him a million dollars for it. But he told Wayne he has a cop helping him, and if Wayne said anything about what was on the flash drive the cop would kill him. Wayne thought they might try to do something to him anyway, so he drove us up to Eagle River and asked his brother Zeke for a different car since Zeke sells cars as a side job. But Zeke wouldn't help him, and Wayne got mad and stole a car from him, and the gun too. He hid the car in the woods near the shack, and the flash drive is taped inside the trunk."

"What's on the flash drive?" Erin asked.

"I didn't look, but Wayne said he found a bunch of files on it. Some of them have to do with drugs, but he said there's a lot of other stuff on it too—like how the mayor has a ton of money in bank accounts in other countries. We were gonna leave this town for good, but when Wayne saw what was all on the flash drive he thought he could blackmail the mayor. I told him it was a bad idea, but he wouldn't change his mind, so we've been staying in a hunting shack near here until the meeting. Except we didn't bring enough food, and we got lost when we tried to find some."

Just then Wayne started to moan, and Erin quickly turned around, grabbing the knife. But he only made a few restless movements and was still again. "I've got to get help," she told Jesse. "Stay right here. I'll be back as soon as I can."

The boy shook his head, looking up at her in anguish. "I just wanna die. Please. I don't have any reason to live now. I'm going to prison, and I'm Mexican and gay, so I'd be better off going to Hell. My dad told me I'm going there anyway if I wanna be gay. The Bible says so. But I didn't choose this. I didn't. It's just who I am." His lips twisted into a grim smile. "You know what my real name is? Jesús. And six months ago I did everything exactly like I was supposed to—I was the perfect student, the perfect son. But I couldn't pretend anymore. I told my parents I was gay, and now they're fighting all the time because of me. And I told Connor, who was my best friend since kindergarten, and he hates me for it—he even said so. All he's done is bully me ever since, and now I hate him back. So I challenged him to a duel and told him if he didn't do it I would tell the cops his dad is as bad as the drug lords in Mexico. And I wanted to kill him too. Then no one would question I was a man. And I really would deserve to go to Hell for being gay."

Erin softly sighed. "My best friend, Miss Godfrey, was your teacher in elementary school, and she would know exactly what to say to you right now. She's much better at this sort of thing than I am. And she hasn't forgotten you, by the way. She even went to all your football games last season."

"I used to bring her candy almost every day in fourth grade." A look of affection briefly crossed Jesse's face. "Even gay boys can have a crush on a girl."

Erin gave him an encouraging smile. "Well, here's what I think Miss Godfrey would say: When people are faced with something that goes against the norm, or is different than what they've been taught to believe, they have a natural tendency to reject it rather than to understand and accept it. People strive for conformity. They feel more in balance when everyone does the same thing, thinks the same way, because it's a survival instinct that's been built into us. But all too often that instinct ends up being mankind's worst enemy. It takes a lot of strength and courage to be different. But it also takes just as much strength and courage for other people to embrace differences. If you stay positive, though, and you make yourself part of the solution and not the problem, no matter how much you want to fight back at those who hurt you, then you'll find out that there really are a lot of strong and courageous people in the world. And you can become one of them."

Erin lightly squeezed his arm. "Another thing Miss Godfrey would tell you is that no one is going to Hell just for being gay, and that when people use the Bible to make judgements against others, they're the ones committing the real sins. She's also mentioned a few things the Bible says about women, things that sound more like the words of men than the word of God—like how it's written that women shouldn't be allowed to teach men and should remain quiet and submissive. Those aren't exactly her favorite verses, believe me. And it also says that women will be saved through childbearing. So taken literally, it means God has condemned millions of women to Hell for not having a child, and Miss Godfrey and I will be heading there ourselves. But everything that ended up in the Bible was entirely written by men—a whole lot of men—a very long time ago. And even though they probably were inspired by the Holy Spirit, and I'm sure had very good intentions, what they wrote was still bound to be heavily influenced by their own experiences and beliefs—they were still human after all. The same goes for the men who chose what to include in the Bible. And just like everything else in life, the Bible will be interpreted very differently when people are motivated by hate and cynicism instead of love. But I think Miss Godfrey would say that if you do love, and you care about others more than anything, then it really doesn't matter if you're gay, straight, or sideways. You'll go to Heaven just the same." Erin chuckled. "Yes, that's exactly what she would say. And she would also tell you to go to church and pray about it."

The boy winced. "If I survive for even a day in prison."

"You're only sixteen, Jesse. I don't think they'll send you to prison." Erin studied him thoughtfully. "There might even be a way to get you out of this mess entirely. And I'll help with that. But I need you to give me your word as a man that you'll start getting your life back together after this, one day at a time. And swear to me that you won't use drugs. I've seen what drug abuse does to people and how badly it can end. I don't want you to be another statistic."

"I stopped using anything when I saw what was happening to Wayne. But there's no way you can get me out of this."

"Just swear to me. And that you'll go to church, too. You need to work your problems out with God for yourself, in your own time, but Miss Godfrey would tell you that praying with others is an especially powerful thing."

Hope sparked in the boy's eyes. "Yes, I swear."

Erin nodded. "Well, here's what I'm thinking: Right now you, Wayne, and I are the only ones who know where the mayor's flash drive is. And I'll bet the district attorney's office would be willing to do some serious negotiating with you to get it. They'll probably want you to testify against Wayne. But if you'll do that, you might not have to go to jail at all."

Jesse stared at her in amazement. "Are you sure you're a doctor?"

Erin laughed softly. "I'm finding out a lot in these woods today."

The boy shifted his gaze up toward the sky. "I'll testify against Wayne."

No sooner did he say that than the other boy started wiggling around, letting out his favorite word in a low groan, "Fuck…"

Erin leaned closer to Jesse and whispered, "I need to tell Luke they have a dirty cop and that Wayne was supposed to meet the mayor at the park on Monday. But I won't say anything about the flash drive. Do you have a lawyer?"

"No, my parents were gonna get one, but then I took off with Wayne."

"I'll find you one as soon as we get out of here," Erin promised. "In the meantime, don't talk to anybody about the flash drive either. And don't say a word to the police at all until you talk to your lawyer. Okay?"

"Okay," Jesse said, giving her another incredulous look.

"I still can't believe you want to help me."

Erin gently smiled. "I'm only doing what so many others have done for me."

But a second later she heard the deep bark of what sounded like a very large dog, and her smile faded. *Oh God, what am I in for now?*

Then she shot to her feet and grabbed the gun.

THE BIG GERMAN SHEPHERD BANDIT SNIFFED around excitedly and continued on through the woods ahead of Melinda Mann, the petite blond K-9 officer who loosely held his leash, while Luke, Scott Ripley, and several sheriff's deputies followed behind them.

Luke gripped his gun in both hands as he scanned the woods, knowing by the dog's behavior that they were getting close. He just hoped to God they got there in time. After what those boys had done to Ben, he didn't even want to contemplate what they might be doing to Erin.

Then Bandit raced around a huge rock, barking wildly.

"Bleib!" Melinda commanded, stopping the dog in his tracks.

Luke quickly came around after them, holding his gun at the ready. But when he took in the scene before him, he did a double take. Wayne Raabe lay on his belly, handcuffed and hogtied, squealing like a stuck pig who'd learned a lot of dirty English. Jesse Torres was sprawled out beyond him, looking sicker than a dog. And Erin stood next to Jesse, her eyes wide with fear, pointing a gun right back at them.

"Erin, put the gun down!" he ordered.

But she didn't move.

"It's okay, Erin," he said in a softer tone, slowly holstering his own gun. "You're safe now."

Erin blinked, and it finally sank in that he was there. "Luke," she whispered, her shoulders sagging in relief. "Thank God you're here."

Luke ran to her and eased the gun from her hand, tucking it into his belt after he engaged the safety. "Are you all right?"

"Yes, I'm fine," Erin automatically responded. But then everything that had just happened hit her all at once, and without another word she threw herself into his arms.

Luke gathered her against him, burying his face in her hair. "You scared the hell out of me, woman."

Erin closed her eyes and clung to him, taking comfort in his strength, his warmth. But as the tension that had built up inside her dissipated, she remembered there were more urgent matters at hand and forced herself to let go of him. "Jesse is really sick, Luke. He needs to be taken to the hospital right away."

Scott stood nearby and pulled out his radio. "I'll call for an ambulance."

Erin looked over at Wayne Raabe. "I guess he's going to have to be medically cleared too. I hit him with a tree branch and knocked him out for a while."

Luke shook his head in disbelief, watching as the two sheriff's deputies worked to cut Wayne free of the twine. "When all the dust settles, I want to know everything that happened here—and where in the hell you learned how to tie someone up like that."

Erin didn't comment, glancing furtively at the other officers. And seeing that everyone's attention was focused elsewhere, she whispered, "There are some things you need to know about right away, Luke." She grabbed his arm and pulled him over to the duffel bag. "Jesse told me the mayor is dealing drugs. Wayne figured it out. And after he helped Jesse escape last Sunday he stole this bag from the mayor's house, then blackmailed him. They're supposed to meet at Maguire Park on Monday, and the mayor said he has a cop helping him, and the cop would kill Wayne if he didn't keep quiet." She felt a pang of guilt for not telling him the whole story, but it couldn't be helped.

Luke knelt down and opened the bag wide. "Holy shit!" he softly exclaimed, examining the contents. Heroin. And the pills were probably oxycodone—the more dangerous street variety. Both were a huge problem in the area, with the number of overdose deaths having skyrocketed in the last few years. And the dealers always seemed to be one step ahead of them. It was one of the reasons a handful of good cops had left New Dublin. Watching the bad guys win all the time wasn't exactly fun.

But now it all made sense. The mayor was the drug kingpin, and his sidekick was someone on the force...And in a flash Luke knew exactly who that sidekick was. "Son of a bitch," he said, looking up at Erin.

"You know who the cop is, don't you?" she whispered.

Just then Scott came up behind them. "The ambulance is on the—" He looked down at the duffel bag and his eyes widened in surprise. "Damn!"

Luke quickly zipped the bag closed and stood up. "Mel," he called to the K-9 officer. "I need you to take charge of this bag. I think it's full of heroin and oxy. Radio in a report to the sheriff right away." He also knew that when Sheriff Gaines found out about the drugs she would get DCI involved for sure. And the sooner the better, because they had a bona fide disaster on their hands now.

He handed the bag to Melinda, and then he and Scott went over to pick Jesse up.

"I'm sorry, Detective Mathis," the boy said feebly. "I didn't have anything to do with hurting that other cop."

"You'll have to tell it to the judge, son," Luke responded in a dispassionate tone. "All I know is that one of my fellow officers—a good man and a friend of mine—almost died thanks to you."

Erin opened her mouth to defend Jesse, but thought better of it. Now wasn't the time. She caught the boy's eye, though, as they hauled him to his feet, trying to convey with her look that she would still help him. She had to—whether Luke liked it or not.

The two sheriff's deputies finished cutting Wayne free and pulled him up as well, then they all started back through the woods toward the Carey's house, with Erin leading the way this time.

But they didn't get far.

"I need to—stop…a minute," Luke said, bringing them all to a halt. He shook his head, trying to clear it, but felt dizzier by the second.

Erin came back to him. "What's wrong, Luke?"

He blinked at her, unable to think clearly. "I have to…sit down." He staggered, unable to hold Jesse up anymore, and then lowered himself to his knees after Scott grabbed hold of the boy.

Erin knelt down in front of him and took his face in her hands. He appeared drowsy. His gaze was unfocused and his pupils were constricted. It looked like he'd been exposed to something, and she urgently turned to Jesse. "What exactly is in that bag?"

"Heroin and oxy," the boy responded, staring at Luke in confusion.

Erin knew then with dreaded certainty what was going on, and she turned to the K-9 officer. "Put the bag down as gently as you can. I think there's fentanyl in there, and Luke got some of it on his skin or breathed it in. Do you have any naloxone?" It was the antidote for a narcotic overdose.

"Not on me," Melinda said, slowly lowering the duffel bag to the ground. "We keep Narcan spray in our vehicles."

"I think Wayne has some in the bag," Jesse told her.

"Erin," Luke whispered, but couldn't get any other words out. He felt like his whole body was shutting down. He collapsed backward to the ground, and as he lay there, everything around him became even more surreal, more distant. He thought he ought to be scared, but he couldn't feel a thing.

Erin took one look at him and didn't think twice about the risk she would have to take in retrieving the naloxone from the bag. She'd already played Russian roulette with it more than once. And now Luke's life was at stake.

She quickly opened it up, doing her best not to touch the packets of powder. Fentanyl was easily absorbed through the skin, or could be inhaled if the powder was disturbed, and it only took a miniscule amount to kill a person.

She found two vials of naloxone and some unopened syringes and needles—probably all stolen from the hospital—and tore open one of the packages containing a long needle. She quickly attached it to the syringe and drew up two milligrams of naloxone—the maximum dose—from one of the vials, then hurried back over to Luke. And without pause she stuck the needle straight through his jeans into his thigh, injecting the full contents of the syringe.

He didn't even flinch.

She glanced up at him as she put the cover back on the needle and set it aside. His eyes were closed. "Luke," she said anxiously, scooting up to touch his face. But then she realized her hands might be contaminated and pulled them back. "Luke, open your eyes. I need you to stay with me. Talk to me."

Luke forced his lids open and they felt like they weighed a hundred pounds. He tried to speak, but his lips wouldn't move at all now…And a second later he couldn't fight what was happening to him anymore. He closed his eyes and let himself be swallowed by the darkness.

"Luke!" Erin cried. Hastily wiping her hands on her pants—though she knew the effort was probably futile if she did have fentanyl on them—she unbuttoned his shirt to watch his breathing.

He took one shallow breath, and after that, all movement of his chest ceased.

"Oh God, no!" Erin whispered.

She quickly checked for a pulse in his neck, and released her own pent-up breath when it pushed slowly but steadily against her fingertips. She tilted his head back afterward by pressing a hand to his forehead, simultaneously lifting his chin up with several fingers of the other hand to keep his airway open. Then she covered his mouth with hers, giving him a breath. She watched his chest at the same time, making sure it rose as the air expanded his lungs.

"I'll take Bandit and get help," Melinda said, her amber eyes filled with fear. "We should be able to find our way out of here okay."

"Bring someone with you, just in case you have symptoms," Erin told her. And after giving Luke another breath, she added, "Some of the drug could've gotten on you while you were carrying the bag."

Scott lowered Jesse to the ground. "I'll go, and on the way I'll call in the hazmat team."

Erin briefly glanced up as they sprinted away, feeling utterly helpless and more terrified than she'd ever been in her life. "Please come back to me, Luke," she begged, and pressed her lips to his again.

But he didn't respond, lying there completely motionless, lifeless, with no signs that the naloxone was kicking in.

Erin continued to give him a breath every five to six seconds, and in between she loaded the syringe with more naloxone, completely emptying the remainder of the first vial and the entire second one into it. Fentanyl was at least fifty times more potent than heroin—or even hundreds of times more potent if this was a modified version of it—so the standard doses of naloxone might not be enough to reverse it. And if Luke didn't show any signs of improvement in the next minute, she was giving him all six milligrams in the syringe. She didn't care that there would be none left for her if she needed it.

The forest was eerily silent around her, and no else said a thing. The two sheriff's deputies looked on in horror as they held Wayne, who watched with an almost morbid fascination. Jesse lay on the ground nearby, but soon turned away with a look of despair on his face.

Luke still didn't show any response after another minute, and Erin plunged the needle into his other thigh this time. Once again, he didn't flinch at all. Then she rechecked his pulse with trembling fingers. It was still there, but felt weaker than before, and the pause between beats was way too long.

A raven flew down just then on wide, fluttering black wings, and settled on a branch high above them. Opening its long beak, it let out a harsh "Craa…Craa…Craa…" that echoed through the forest.

Erin glanced up, and a shiver ran down her spine when she saw the big, black bird. Then she continued to breathe for Luke, willing the naloxone to work.

Another minute went by, and it was over. The drug took effect—and quickly.

Luke opened his vivid blue eyes and looked up at her in confusion. "What happened?"

Erin had seen how well naloxone could work many, many times over the years. But she'd never appreciated the drug more than she did right then. And for a moment she was too overwhelmed to speak. It was truly a miracle…A miracle of modern medicine.

Luke slowly propped himself up on his elbows and looked around, blinking his eyes and shaking his head to clear the cobwebs. "Did I pass out?"

Erin finally found her voice. "I think you got fentanyl on your skin or inhaled it when you searched the duffel bag. I had to inject a bunch of naloxone in both your legs to reverse it. Fortunately, there was some of that in the bag too." And it was just as fortunate that she hadn't been exposed to the fentanyl herself when she'd searched the bag earlier, with only Jesse to help her. There probably wouldn't have been enough time for her to self-administer naloxone before the deadly effects of the fentanyl kicked in. How ironic it would have been to escape Wayne Raabe's threats of rape and murder, and then to stand up to a very disgruntled black bear, only to be taken down by a few tiny specks of white powder.

"Shit," Luke said, sitting up and running a hand through his hair. "I just read an article about that. I should've been more careful."

"I can't believe I didn't think of it either. Fentanyl is a really big problem in Boston," Erin told him. "But right now we need to get you out of these woods and to a hospital as fast as possible. Naloxone only lasts about thirty minutes to an hour, and the fentanyl can stay in your system for several hours, so you could start having symptoms again. Do you think you can walk?"

"Yeah, I think so." Luke gingerly stood up with her help. And after a few wobbly steps he got his bearings and managed to walk around on his own.

Erin turned to the officers holding Wayne. "Can one of you help me with Jesse? There's no way he'll be able to walk by himself."

"No, Erin," Luke protested. "I'm not letting you touch that kid."

"Luke, we need to get both of you out of here now. He's not a threat. He helped me—" She glanced at Jesse and abruptly stopped talking. The boy's eyes were closed, and he lay there as still and lifeless as Luke had looked moments ago.

She immediately rushed over to him and dropped down to her knees, shaking him. "Jesse!"

He didn't respond, and she pressed her fingers to his neck, checking for a pulse. And she said a silent prayer of thanks when she found one. It was weak, but at least it was there.

The boy opened his eyes then, and they were even more glazed over than before. "I…I'm probably not…getting out of here—after all…"

"Yes, you are, Jesse. You need to hang on. You need to fight." Erin felt her eyes get hot with tears, and it was like she was by the pond all over again, and it was Jenna fighting for her. "Please, Jesse. I'm not giving up on you, so you can't give up on yourself either."

The boy managed the barest hint of a smile as he looked up at her. "I don't think…anyone's ever…cried for me—before."

Erin hastily wiped away her tears. "Well, I'm going to cry a whole lot more if you give up now. So just hang in there for me, okay?"

Jesse let his lids fall closed, but nodded slightly and whispered, "Okay."

A moment later they heard Bandit barking, and then the sound of an engine. Shortly after that Melinda came running through the trees with the dog, followed by an ATV driven by a firefighter decked out in full hazardous materials gear—complete with a protective body suit, hood, respirator, and gloves. He was pulling a small trailer with wooden sides that probably belonged to the Careys, and in it were two men wearing similar gear.

Melinda came to a halt in front of them and stared at Luke in shock. "You're okay."

Luke smiled wryly. "I gather I wasn't looking okay when you left."

"No, I thought…Anyway, I'm just glad you're breathing, Mathis. Fortunately, the sheriff had already called in the fire department." And to Erin she said, "Two paramedics came along, and they brought more Narcan."

The firefighter pulled the ATV around, and the paramedics quickly jumped out of the trailer. They loaded Jesse into it first, which left only enough room for Luke and one of the paramedics. Luke didn't want to go with them, but the sheriff's deputies and Melinda all but tossed him in since no one wanted to see a repeat of the events they'd witnessed earlier.

As they prepared to leave Erin told the paramedic in the trailer, "I gave Luke two milligrams of naloxone initially, but he didn't respond, and I ended up giving him a total of eight. You should get an IV in as soon as you can, and have more naloxone ready in case he needs it. And Jesse is septic and dehydrated. He'll need two large-bore IVs and fluids pushed in both."

The paramedic gave her a thumbs up, and the other one hopped on the ATV, taking the place of the firefighter, and they raced off down the path.

"Why the fuck do I have to walk?" Wayne complained. "I have a fuckin'—"

"Brummen!" Melinda ordered Bandit.

The dog immediately lunged forward, straining at his leash as he snarled at Wayne, who jumped back in wide-eyed fear. Even the two deputies holding him eyed the dog apprehensively.

With a slight smile on her face, Melinda told Wayne, "That means shut the fuck up in German Shepherd. Keep talking if you want to learn more." Then she gave Bandit the command to stand at attention again.

Wayne took the hint and didn't say a word the rest of the way out of the forest. The firefighter was going to stay behind with the duffel bag until other members of the hazmat team came to get him, but Erin told him about the bear encounter, and he decided to go with them after all, keeping a safe distance with the bag—and cautiously looking around him the whole way.

When they finally exited the woods there were police and rescue vehicles parked everywhere. Erin felt like it was déjà vu from the day she'd arrived in New Dublin—except this time she was leaving the woods instead of going in.

There were two ambulances parked by the old barn, but before she could head over there another fireman came up to them, also wearing full protective gear, and said, "All of you need to go over to the decon area and get cleared."

Erin looked in the direction he was pointing and saw a long red trailer parked well away from everything else, with white block lettering on the side, labeled:

NEW DUBLIN FIRE DEPARTMENT
HAZARDOUS MATERIALS UNIT
DECONTAMINATION TRAILER

She reluctantly walked over to it with the group and couldn't help but grimace the whole way. She knew the basics about decontamination procedures, having practiced them occasionally at Boston General. She'd also dealt with numerous cases involving individual patients or a handful of workers who'd been brought to the ER after a chemical or gas exposure. But the incidents had all been relatively minor. Nothing like this. And now that she'd become a victim instead of the doctor treating them, it meant she was going to have to strip down naked, right here in her old backyard.

"Don't worry, I've got your back, Dr. Pryce," the K-9 officer said with a friendly smile. "I'm Melinda Mann, by the way. And you met Bandit, of course."

Erin glanced down at the big dog, glad he was on the other side of Melinda. "When I saw him come around the rock I thought I was a goner for sure. I think I'd rather have faced the bear again."

Melinda chuckled. "He's actually a big baby. We do school visits all the time, and the kids love him." They reached the trailer just then, and she told the firefighter in charge, "Let's put Dr. Pryce through first. I'll show her how it works and go next."

The firefighter nodded, and Melinda led Erin to an open door on the back side of the trailer. "We'll go in here. This is the dirty end. Anyone who can walk goes inside, and it's pretty private. You'll strip down behind the first curtain and throw all your clothes into the container. Then go through the next curtain to the rinsing station. The shower will go on automatically. Rinse off and move to the next station, where a cleaning solution comes out in the shower. Wash yourself from head to toe, and rinse off again at the next station. On the other side of that is an area stocked with towels, scrubs, and sandals. Dry off and get dressed, then walk out through the clean door. It's all pretty slick, and Bandit and I will be right behind you." A smile briefly pulled at the corner of her mouth. "At least I won't have to give him a bath tonight."

Erin went through the stations and did as Melinda had instructed, cleaning herself thoroughly. She knew how serious the situation really was. Trace amounts of the fentanyl powder could easily have gotten onto her clothes, sitting there like a ticking time bomb, waiting to reach her skin and get into her system.

She quickly dried off and put on a pair of gray scrubs—a new color for her—and black plastic sandals afterward. Then she exited the trailer, glancing down at her flimsy attire with a silent sigh of resignation. Going commando and braless in scrubs was another new experience, but there was nothing she could do about it now.

A firefighter stood waiting at the bottom of the steps, decked out in full protective gear like the others. "Are you feeling okay, Dr. Pryce?" he asked.

"Yes, thanks," she said, giving him an embarrassed smile. And after he assisted her down, she hurried over to the only ambulance still parked by the barn.

A group of police officers stood guard near it. She'd never met any of them before, but they all greeted her as if they knew her. The back of the ambulance was open, and Jesse was inside with the same two paramedics who'd taken care of him the last time. "Did they take Luke in the other ambulance?" she asked anxiously.

Amy Duncan was hanging a bag of fluids on a ceiling hook and smiled when she saw her. "Hi, Dr. Pryce. Yeah, they left a few minutes ago, and Detective Mathis was doing fine. They put an IV in and took him through decon, but he didn't need any more naloxone before they left." A weak chuckle escaped her. "I hope we don't keep running into each other like this. It's crazy."

"Yes, I know," Erin said, shifting her gaze to the stretcher. "How is Jesse doing?"

The boy raised his head, and his eyes weren't nearly as dull as before. "I'm all right. They stuck a needle in my leg this time, but it didn't hurt as much as I thought it would."

Erin looked down at his left lower leg, and saw they'd put an intraosseous needle into the tibia, a few centimeters below and medial to his kneecap.

"I put the IO line in him," Amy said proudly. "After he went through decon his pressure was only 78 systolic, so I got it in right away and pushed fluids while Jimmy worked on starting another line."

"Hey, Dr. Pryce," the other paramedic said, jumping out of the ambulance. "We've got the second liter of fluids running now. His last pressure was 104/58, and his pulse is better too, around 110. We're ready to take off."

Erin looked into the back of the ambulance again. "Jesse, don't forget what we talked about."

"I won't," he promised.

The paramedic closed the doors, and Erin watched them head out, lights flashing and the high pitch of the siren renting the air. Bella's poor ears were certainly getting a workout. She glanced toward the house but didn't see any sign of the family. She imagined Bella was taking everything in stride, though. Blind or not, the child wasn't easily intimidated.

Then a thought struck her. *Maybe Bella is so brave because of her blindness. A limitation is only as limiting as one lets it be. And it can even become a person's greatest strength.*

Erin smiled to herself. Jenna would love to hear her repeat that later.

"Dr. Pryce!"

Erin turned around, and a middle-aged man with short gray hair walked up to her in civilian clothes. "I'm Pat Connolly, Fire Chief. I was hoping I'd get a chance to meet you." He held out a hand in greeting. "How are you?"

"I'm fine, thanks," she told him, shaking his hand. "Is everyone else doing okay?"

He nodded. "Yep, no one else has had any symptoms." And with a look of gratitude on his face, he added, "I sure am happy we've got the decon trailer. Hightower Industries donated the funds for it this spring. I'll have to let them know we've already put it to good use."

Erin mentally groaned. *Oh, great. Lexi is going to find out about this. Maybe it hadn't been such a good idea to tell the woman to stop breathing after all.* But to Pat she said, "If everything is under control, I think I'll head home. I'm staying with Jenna Godfrey next door." Her lips twisted into a half-smile. "I'd only intended to go for a short walk when all this happened."

"You're walking back over my dead body," Pat said. "Hop in my truck. I'll give you a ride." He motioned to a big red pickup marked with his title, then yelled to a group of firefighters nearby, "I'm taking Dr. Pryce home! I'll be back in a minute!"

Erin climbed up into the truck after he cleared the front passenger seat off for her. And as they backed out of the driveway she saw that the firefighters were standing there watching her with big grins on their faces.

The chief chuckled. "It's a good thing I'm getting you out of here. My boys won't be able to do their jobs otherwise."

Erin felt her cheeks get hot. They all probably knew she had nothing on except the scrubs.

Pat started down the road toward Jenna's house and briefly glanced at her. "I heard you're from Boston, and yet you look familiar somehow." He shook his head in bewilderment. "It must be my imagination. I've never been to Boston, though I'd like to visit someday. It's one of the few places this side of the Atlantic that's anywhere near as Irish as New Dublin."

Erin looked at him and realized that she'd finally been recognized because of her mother. But it didn't make her want to jump out of the truck and run. Instead, it made her smile. "I went to school here, but I don't think we've ever met. You probably knew my mom, Anne Harris." Or at least that's the name he would have known her by.

Pat raised his brows in surprise as he pulled into Jenna's driveway. "You're Annie Harris's daughter?" Then he parked the truck and turned to stare at her. "My God, you do look just like her. Annie and I went to school together. Class of '85." A distant smile crossed his face. "Boy, I'll never forget how talented that girl was. She could draw, paint, or make anything in the art room. I was more of a shop guy myself, but I always looked forward to checking out the latest thing she was working on. If you wanted to find Annie, you only had to go to the art room." He laughed softly. "But I shouldn't call her Annie. She never did like that."

"I didn't know she was an artist," Erin said in amazement. But almost as soon as the words left her mouth another memory stirred...

They were near the beach. Her mother was standing at an easel drawing a picture of a man and woman posing in front of it.

Erin sat cross-legged on the ground by her feet, watching in admiration as she recreated their images on paper with precise, confident strokes.

"How's your picture coming along?" her mother asked after a while, glancing down at the sketch pad in Erin's lap. "Ah, another ocean scene. Very nice."

"I'm drawing a mother and daughter mermaid and their pet dolphin. They're swimming to Hawaii."

Her mother chuckled. "Wow. I can't wait to see it."

Erin smiled up at her, and then they both happily went back to work...

Sadness filled Pat's hazel eyes. "It's a real shame what happened to Annie. Seth should have rotted—" He stopped abruptly and gave her a pained look. "I'm sorry. I shouldn't have brought that up."

Erin shook her head, tucking away the latest memory of her mother. "No, you're right. He should have rotted in prison."

She opened the door to leave, but Pat stopped her with a gentle hand on her arm. "Luke's a lucky man. I'll be sure to remind him of that. And if you ever need anything—anything at all—you just let me know." He grinned, revealing years of laugh lines around his eyes. "You have me and the entire New Dublin Fire Department at your service, ma'am."

Erin smiled back and climbed out of the pickup. "Thanks, Chief."

She stood there a moment, waving briefly as she watched him leave, and wondered how one little walk could have led her down so many unexpected roads. Then she headed up to the house.

Jenna was waiting at the door for her. "Erin, thank God you're okay!" she exclaimed. "I've never heard so many sirens in my life! What happened?"

Erin walked inside, running a hand through her wet, tangled hair with a grimace. "It's a really long story, and I'll tell you about it on the way to the hospital. Luke was taken there by ambulance."

Jenna gasped. "Oh my God! Was he shot?"

"No, Wayne Raabe had a bag full of drugs in the woods, and I'm pretty sure Luke got exposed to fentanyl. Fortunately, Wayne also had enough of the antidote for it in the bag, or Luke would probably be dead right now."

"Dear Lord! What is fentanyl?"

"It's a synthetic narcotic that's cheaper and easier to make than heroin. And it's a lot more powerful. The amount Luke got exposed to would be like you taking a bottle of your morphine pills all at once—or maybe even more than one."

Jenna's eyes widened in shock, and she put her hand to her chest. "Good heavens!"

"Drug cartels have figured out that they'll make a lot more money by mixing fentanyl with other drugs like heroine and oxycodone. But a lot more people are dying as a result. They often don't even know it's mixed in with the other drugs—or they underestimate how powerful it is." Erin slowly shook her head. "I still can't believe I didn't think of it and warn Luke. But I guess my brain wasn't working right after everything else that happened—which included facing an angry bear, by the way."

Jenna's eyes widened even more. "A bear?"

Erin smiled wryly. "Yep. And your dad is still helping me, even after all these years. A bear and her cub came through the woods near us, but I remembered what he'd said about bears when we were kids, and I was able to fend the mother off—although she probably just lost interest. But I'll tell you the whole story in a bit. I need to quick change before we leave."

"You go, Erin," Jenna told her. "I don't think I can handle any more excitement today, and I'm sure it will be busy there. Just text me with an update on Luke when you can, okay?"

"Okay, Jen," Erin said, giving her friend's arm a quick squeeze before she headed over to the stairs.

"Did they at least catch Wayne and Jesse?" Jenna asked.

Erin turned back to her. "Yes, although I had the dubious honor of catching Wayne—before the bear could catch him." She laughed shortly. "It's part of the long story." Then she ran upstairs as fast as her plastic sandals would take her.

Jenna stood in the foyer with a look of astonishment on her face as she watched Erin go up. Wesley trotted over to her a moment later, rubbing himself against her leg, and she reached down to pet the cat. "See, Wesley? I told you there were bears in those woods. It's a good thing you're a housecat."

"Mrroww," he answered back.

CHAPTER

19

Erin hurried down the hallway to the ER room Luke was in just as Chase McKellar came out.

He closed the sliding glass door behind him and turned around, smiling wryly when he saw her. "Hey, Erin."

She returned the greeting, glancing past him to Luke's room. But the curtain inside had also been closed, and she couldn't see a thing. "How is Luke?"

"He was feeling lightheaded when they brought him in, and we ended up giving him four more milligrams of Narcan. He hasn't had any more symptoms since then, but we'll watch him for a few more hours to make sure."

"Is Jesse still doing okay?"

"Yeah, better than I would've expected. His x-rays looked good, so he won't need another chest tube, and he's been stable otherwise. We got him started on some IV antibiotics, and Colin O'Reilly was just here to admit him. He's going to clean out the bullet wound upstairs. And Wayne Raabe is doing fine, by the way." Chase's lips quirked up into another slight smile. "I heard you were the one who took him out. His head and neck CTs were negative, but you gave him a pretty good concussion, so he'll have to stay overnight for observation."

Erin nodded, though she had a hard time mustering up much sympathy for Wayne Raabe after what he'd done. "Thanks for your help, Chase."

"Thanks for all the patients," he said with a dry laugh before heading to the central workstation.

Erin eased the door to Luke's room open and peeked around the curtain. He was in a hospital gown now, lying semi-reclined on the bed, and his parents were standing on the far side of it. "Do you mind if I join the party?" she asked.

"Erin!" Joanne exclaimed, and immediately rushed over to give her a hug. "Thank you, thank you, thank you. I can't tell you how grateful I am for what you did."

"I'll second that," Greg said, greeting her with a heartfelt embrace as well.

"Hey, this isn't fair," Luke teased. "I'm the patient here, and she's my girlfriend."

Erin smiled and sat down next to him. "Hey, you," she whispered, tenderly brushing a hand over his cheek.

"I need more than that, honey." Luke grinned devilishly and drew her mouth down to his for a brief, but very enthusiastic kiss.

Greg chuckled, turning to Joanne. "Why don't we go get some coffee and come back in a little while?" And on the way out he glanced back at Luke. "I'm glad to see you're feeling better, son."

"I'm feeling a lot better now for some reason," Luke said, grinning up at Erin again. And when his parents were gone he pulled her back down to him, murmuring into her ear, "Have you ever made out with a patient in a hospital bed?"

"I think you can guess the answer to that," Erin responded with a light laugh, trying to ignore the way her body was reacting to his seductive words. They were in an emergency room after all—and he was full of naloxone.

Luke brushed his lips sensuously over her ear. "Mmm, good, because I definitely want to be the first—and only—patient who gets to examine you like this." He gave her earlobe an affectionate bite, and then blazed a path of hot kisses over her neck, sliding one hand down to caress her bottom. "And I promise to be a very cooperative patient if you feel the need to rip this gown off and take me for a ride, Dr. Sally."

"Luke, I think you're still high," Erin protested. But when his seeking mouth captured hers, she couldn't help but kiss him back. As usual, he melted all her defenses.

"I knew it! You OD'd in the woods just so you could make out with your girlfriend!"

They abruptly broke the kiss to see Melinda Mann standing there with a puckish grin on her face. Bandit sat at attention next to her, his tongue hanging out as he watched them.

Luke lay back and smiled at her. "You look too small to know much of anything, Officer Mann."

Melinda rolled her eyes in response, telling Erin, "They're always making fun of me because I'm five foot two and my dog weighs almost as much as I do. And they think it's real funny that my last name in Mann." She gave Luke another wicked grin. "But you're never going to live this one down, Mathis. First you go and make out with your girlfriend in front of the station, and now she has to catch the criminals while you get high with 'em." She chuckled. "It is good to see the straight-laced detective loosening up a little, though."

"Shouldn't you be at the post office, Mel Mann?" Luke teased.

Melinda folded her arms across her chest and glowered at him facetiously. "Shouldn't they give Dr. Pryce your badge, Mathis?"

Erin smothered a laugh. "Be careful, Luke. One word and I'm sure she can have that dog rip your arm off."

"Oh, she knows it's all in good fun. And Bandit would never do that. He loves me. Don't you, boy?" Luke patted his chest. "Come here, Bandit."

Erin watched in surprise as the big dog jumped up onto the bed and lay down with his head resting his head on Luke's chest, looking up at him with puppy dog eyes.

"That-a-boy." Luke playfully scratched Bandit under the chin, and the dog's tail beat furiously against the sheets.

"You should pet him too, Dr. Pryce," Melinda said. "He really is a big baby when there's no work to do."

Erin made no move to touch Bandit, though—not with the memory of him racing around the rock toward her still so fresh in her mind.

Luke laughed softly. "Erin is afraid of you, Bandit. Give her some kisses."

The dog leapt up with amazing agility and started licking Erin's face before she had a chance to move. And she couldn't help but laugh as he continued to assault her with his tongue. "Okay, tell him to stop. I'm convinced he won't eat me alive—although he kind of is right now."

"Hier!" Melinda commanded, and the dog promptly jumped off the bed and sat at attention next to her again.

Erin wiped her face, smiling in amusement as she regarded the pair. Melinda was cute as a button with her short blond hair and lightly freckled face. Yet under the surface she was clearly as tough as nails. And Bandit looked every bit the part of a ferocious dog who would rip someone apart at the slightest provocation. But underneath it all he was, in fact, a big sweet puppy who simply loved the girl he let master him.

"Can we come in?"

Luke looked over toward the now partially open curtain, and all humor faded from his expression. It was time to get back to business. "Of course, Sheriff."

Erin stood up as a woman decked out in full uniform walked in. She was slightly taller than her and probably around sixty, with medium length white hair and brown eyes that matched the color of her shirt. Despite her formal appearance, though, she smiled warmly when their gazes met.

"You must be Dr. Pryce," she said, holding out a hand. "Ellen Gaines."

Erin returned the handshake, impressed by the strength she felt in the other woman's grip. She had a feeling the sheriff could hold her own with anyone—no matter how warm her smile was. "Please, call me Erin."

A dark-haired, ruggedly handsome man in a shirt and tie followed the sheriff in and shook Erin's hand as well, his deep-set blue eyes dancing with humor. "Special Agent Joe Halliday. I've heard a lot about you."

Erin could only imagine. "Are you from the FBI?"

"No, DCI—Division of Criminal Investigation. We're part of the Wisconsin Department of Justice. But I've been working with a regional drug task force for a while now, so Sheriff Gaines called me in."

Luke gave the agent a half-smile. "Although right now it looks like you're more interested in gawking at my girlfriend, Halliday."

Joe chuckled. "If you haven't noticed, your girlfriend is a hell of a lot prettier than you, Mathis. And a woman who can fight off a criminal with one hand and a bear with the other has got my attention, that's for sure."

"What happened with a bear?" Luke asked, looking up at Erin in surprise.

She shrugged, feeling a little embarrassed as all four of them gave her their undivided attention. This was clearly their kind of thing. "Nothing happened, really. A bear and her cub showed up, and I just pointed a stick at the mother bear until she left with her cub. That's it." She was definitely a lot better at telling ER stories.

Joe came over to the bed and shook Luke's hand, clapping him on the shoulder. "I heard you had some excitement yourself, old man. I'm glad to see you're doing well."

"Shit, who are you calling an old man, old man?" Luke quipped. "What do you have, like ten years on me?"

"Not quite," Joe said with a laugh. "I've still got a few years left before I hit the big four-oh." Then he sat on the edge of the bed and his expression sobered. "Sheriff Gaines filled me in about the drugs. We've already been in to see Wayne and Jesse. But Wayne's still pretty confused thanks to your girlfriend—although he had a few more colorful things to say about the bear and seems to think she killed it with her bare hands, no pun intended. And Jesse Torres isn't talking at all. Any idea where they got them from?"

"Yeah, I know who the supplier is." Luke turned to Erin. "Tell them what Jesse said."

Once again, all eyes were on her. Erin wished she at least had a white coat on. "He said Wayne got involved with heroin sometime after Christmas and figured out it was the mayor who was distributing drugs to the dealers. He stole the bag from his house the night he helped Jesse escape."

"You have got to be shitting me," the sheriff said, crossing her arms. "The task force has been working this case hard for over a year and a half, getting nowhere, yet some punk-ass kid could figure it out all by himself? And then he still had enough time on his hands to assault an officer, help Torres escape, and probably kill the mayor's wife?"

Joe's lips twisted into an acerbic smile. "No matter how good our undercover agents are, there's still no substitute for the real thing."

"Frank Murdock had help from the inside, Joe. That's why you weren't getting anywhere," Luke said. "Torres told Erin there's a dirty cop involved, but he didn't know who it was."

Joe turned to Erin. "Did he give you any other names at all?"

"No," she responded, feeling guiltier than ever. She knew there were probably a lot of names on that flash drive.

"Think about it," Luke told him. "The only way they could've stayed a step ahead of us all the time was if they had information about exactly what the task force was doing. So I'll bet the cop we're dealing with is on it. And he's probably the one with the closest ties to the mayor."

Joe whistled softly. "The narcotics investigator for New Dublin."

"Who happens to be our assistant chief of police," Luke said with a grimace. "And he wouldn't give up doing narcotics after he got promoted or add more staff like we needed. No wonder."

The sheriff slowly shook her head. "Ed Finks. The man always was way too cocky for his own good."

"He drives down to Mexico every three or four months, supposedly to visit friends," Luke told them. "My guess is that he brings the drugs across the border himself, cutting out the middle man to improve their profit margin. I'll bet he even uses his badge to help get him past border patrol. And he just so happens to be returning from another one of those trips tomorrow. Erin said Wayne was supposed to meet the mayor at Maguire Park on Monday to exchange the drugs for money. I'm sure Frank was waiting until Ed got back so he could help him take Wayne out. There's no way in hell they would've let that kid go free. He knows too much."

"Wayne told Jesse he thought they might try to ambush him," Erin said. "So they went up to Eagle River and stole a gun and a car from Wayne's brother. Then they came back and hid in the woods."

Luke let out a bitter laugh. "That figures. We spent a day and a half searching the woods up in Eagle River, and it turns out they were down in these woods the whole time."

"Erin, would you mind stepping out for a bit?" Sheriff Gaines asked. "You've been a tremendous help, but we've got some confidential police matters to discuss. And please keep what you have heard to yourself."

Luke took her hand. "Maybe give us an hour or so? I'm sure my parents would love to have you join them for coffee."

Concern immediately filled Erin's eyes. "Just make sure if you start having symptoms again you get someone in here right away."

"I will," he said with a reassuring smile, giving her hand one last squeeze before she left.

He turned back to the others afterward, and his smile vanished. "Until those boys start talking, all we've really got is a bag full of drugs. Everything is circumstantial. But

I don't think we can wait and set up a sting at the park tomorrow. This town is too small, and the mayor is bound to find out about Wayne before then— especially if it turns out Ed is nothing more than a cocky son of a bitch after all, and our dirty cop is someone else."

"Do you think Jeff Kilbride could be involved?" the sheriff asked.

"A week ago I wouldn't have thought he was capable of it," Luke told her. "But nothing would surprise me anymore. Jeff is good friends with the mayor, and he does tend to let other people influence him more than he should."

"Which is a polite way of saying he's more wishy-washy than a laundromat," Melinda commented dryly.

"In any case, Jeff went to visit his son in Minneapolis for the weekend," Luke said. "And it might turn out to be a good thing. It'll keep him out of the loop for now."

Sheriff Gaines stared at him in disbelief. "Your department is knee-deep in a murder investigation and the vicious assault of an officer, and had two fugitives on the loose at the time, and your chief decided to go visit his son in Minneapolis for the weekend? When this is all over Jeff Kilbride will be out of a job, I can promise you that."

"First things first: We need to bring the mayor in," Joe said, turning to Luke. "How much longer do they want to keep you here?"

Luke winced. "Another couple of hours."

Joe nodded thoughtfully. "I think you're right about the mayor; we don't have much time before he catches wind of all this and runs." He shifted his gaze to the sheriff. "Why don't you and I bring him in now for questioning, and Luke can meet us at your office when he's cleared. We've got enough probable cause to hold him for twenty-four hours.

In the meantime we can discreetly track Ed down, or at least have a nice little surprise party waiting for him when he gets home tomorrow." He smiled wryly at Bandit. "And I'm sure you'll have lots of fun looking for any souvenirs Ed brings back, won't you, boy?"

The big dog let out a bark in response, enthusiastically wagging his tail.

APPARENTLY LAWYERS DIDN'T WORK MUCH ON SATurdays—well, except for personal injury lawyers. They seemed to be available twenty-four hours a day.

Erin sat in the hospital lobby and tucked her phone back into her purse with a sigh after she got yet another voicemail. She probably wouldn't be able to find Jesse a lawyer until Monday, and she had no idea what they were going to do in the meantime. The longer they withheld the flash drive, the more Luke's investigation might be compromised. But on the other hand, it was Jesse's best chance to get his life back.

In any case, she needed to speak to the Torres family about where things stood, and the prospect filled her with dread. Police were all over the place, and it would be impossible to keep her identity hidden.

She stood up, eyeing the elevator, and thought about getting on it. But she ended up taking the stairs instead—now wasn't exactly a good time to work on self-improvement.

When she reached the medical floor the unit clerk directed her to Jesse's room, and she nervously headed in the same direction as two sheriff's deputies.

There was a family lounge on the right side of the hallway, and as she was about to pass it she heard a woman inside say, "I can't take Wayne's case, not without a three-thousand-dollar retainer fee this time."

Erin abruptly came to a halt. She paused indecisively a moment, but then went over and glanced into the room.

"I told you, I don't have three dollars, much less three thousand," a man was angrily saying. Another woman stood next to him, and the lawyer—who Erin presumed was the infamous Meredith Armstrong—had her back to the door as the man spoke. "It's not fuckin' right. You can't just leave Wayne high and dry like this."

Erin hastily moved away from the doorway before she was noticed, and continued to listen.

"As I told you and your wife, Mr. Raabe, Wayne has gotten himself into serious trouble, and it's going to take a lot of work to minimize the damage. There's also some serious risk here, given every cop in this town wants to see him hang. And I won't take that risk for free—not for your son or anyone. But I'll refer you to someone who might be willing to defend him." Erin heard her briefly shuffle through a bag. "Here's his name and number. He's young, but he's a good lawyer."

"Hah, a good lawyer! I'll tell you where I can find a good lawyer," Mr. Raabe venomously returned. "In the same place I can find goddamned fairies and unicorns, that's where. C'mon Candy, let's get the hell out of here!"

Erin stepped farther away from the door and quickly pulled out her phone, pretending to be busy looking something up as the couple left the room.

"You know what you call a lawyer on the bottom of the ocean?" Mr. Raabe yelled back in. "A fuckin' good start!"

And with that he roughly grabbed his wife by the arm and jerked her down the hallway.

Erin caught the strong odor of alcohol as they walked by. Both were disheveled appearing and had clearly invested more money in alcohol than in clothes or personal hygiene products. Wayne's dad had greasy, dark hair that clearly hadn't been washed or combed in days, maybe even weeks, and wore a T-shirt and sweat pants that were just as filthy, while the woman was in pajamas.

Their son hadn't stood a chance in life, Erin thought as she watched them. And in that moment she forgave Wayne Raabe for all the terror he'd put her through in the woods.

A few seconds later she heard the lawyer start talking on her cell phone in the room, and she frantically thought about what to do next. If Meredith Armstrong really was in there, then it was her son who'd shot Jesse. There was no way she would take his case…Or maybe there was.

Oh God, I hope Luke forgives me for this, Erin silently prayed. And after taking a deep breath, she walked into the room.

The woman was just putting her phone away and looked up.

Erin met her cold, dark eyes and couldn't get a word out.

Silence hung in the air a moment, and then the lawyer impatiently asked, "Can I help you?" But her tone clearly indicated that she would rather not.

Erin mentally shook herself. "Are you—are you Meredith Armstrong?"

"Yes. Who are you?"

"I—I'd rather not say. But Jesse Torres needs a lawyer, and I think you're the only one who can help him right now."

Meredith laughed derisively. "Are you out of your mind? He shot my son."

Erin eased the lounge door shut and turned back to face her, taking a few steps closer. "Do you know why that gunfight really happened?"

Meredith stared at her through narrowed eyes. "Let me guess, you're going to tell me."

"Jesse Torres is gay. He told your son earlier this year, and Connor has been bullying him about it ever since. Jesse finally had enough, and that's why he challenged him to a gunfight. The thing is, if—or when—all of that comes out, it's going to be really bad for Connor, especially since he almost killed Jesse because he's gay. Don't they have special laws about that sort of thing?"

Meredith didn't bother to answer, but instead said, "So your plan is to blackmail me into defending Torres, is it?"

"No, I'm just telling you why it would be in your best interest to help him. And there's more to the story," Erin added. "Did you know your ex-husband had been running a drug ring, and both Connor and Jesse know he's dealing drugs? Jesse was going to blow the whistle on him if Connor didn't agree to the gunfight."

Meredith said nothing in response, her expression clearly shocked, and Erin wondered if a lawyer had ever been speechless before.

"Wayne Raabe stole a bag of drugs from the mayor's house after he got Jesse out of the hospital," she continued. "But he stole something else—a flash drive the police don't know about. Jesse said it contains files about the mayor's involvement in drugs, and other things as well. Only he and Wayne know where it is, and I told Jesse not to say anything until he has a lawyer who can get him a plea bargain. I'm sure in exchange for your help he won't say anything about what Connor did, and would probably even put in a good word for him—though I do hope your son gets some help for his own problems."

"Fine. I'll take the kid's case and get him a deal." Meredith brushed past her and opened the door. "I'll go talk to him now."

"Another thing," Erin said, stopping the other woman in her tracks. "I doubt Jesse has the money to pay for this. If you do it for free, maybe you can convince his parents not to file a lawsuit against you."

Meredith gave her a long, icy stare. Then she nodded curtly and left the room.

Erin collapsed into a nearby chair afterward, letting out a weary sigh. She really needed to get back to practicing medicine.

"YOU LOOK EXHAUSTED, HONEY," LUKE SAID AS THEY sat in his ER room waiting for the nurse to bring in his discharge paperwork. "Why don't you head home now? I have to go straight to the Sheriff's Office anyway. I'll come over as soon as I can."

Erin shook her head. "No, I'll stay until—"

Scott Ripley suddenly burst into the room, interrupting her. "You're not going to believe this, Luke, but Meredith Armstrong dumped Wayne Raabe as a client. Now she's representing Jesse Torres."

Luke stood up. "You've got to be kidding. Why?"

"Because of a flash drive Raabe stole from Frank the night he broke into his house. Apparently there's a shitload of evidence on it about the drug ring, along with Frank's other activities. Meredith went up to see Raabe right after he got admitted, and even though he's mostly been talking like an idiot, he must've said something about it. But my guess is that he didn't tell her where it was, so she went to Torres. And sure enough, she got him to tell her everything."

"Did they turn over the flash drive?" Luke asked.

"No. Torres says it's in the trunk of the car Raabe stole from his brother. They hid it near a hunting shack in the woods, and half the Sheriff's Department just went out looking for it."

Luke smiled grimly, shaking his head. "So Meredith is defending Torres, who shot her son, all out of revenge against Frank. It makes me wonder if she didn't have something to do with Tina's murder after all."

"Oh, revenge is just the icing on the cake," Scott said. "The DA is up in Torres' room right now, and they agreed on a plea bargain that puts him on probation until he's eighteen, with a clean record after that, in exchange for full cooperation with us, disclosing the whereabouts of the flash drive, and testimony against Wayne. And Meredith convinced the DA to give Connor the same deal since Torres instigated the shooting."

"Son of a bitch!" Luke cursed. "Those boys shot each other. And it could easily have been Torres who cut Ben up, not Raabe. Shit, maybe he even killed Tina Murdock—he was there too. Or Connor could've done it. And now both of them are basically getting off scot-free? It's bullshit!" He turned to Erin, who looked up at him like a deer in the headlights. "Can you grab my discharge paperwork? I need to go find out what the hell is going on." Then he stormed out of the room before she could respond.

With a sick feeling in the pit of her stomach, Erin slowly stood up. She needed to go home and talk to Jenna about all this. *Oh God. What have I done?*

LUKE AND SCOTT WERE HEADING ACROSS THE HOSpital lobby to the stairs when the elevator doors opened and the DA walked out, with Meredith Armstrong alongside him.

"George!" Luke yelled, charging over to them. "You can't seriously be letting those boys off on probation after they shot each other?! And Torres should be held just as accountable as Wayne Raabe for what happened to Ben Watkins. He could've died too, for God's sake!"

The DA nodded, adjusting his glasses. "I understand your frustration, Luke. But both the boys had clean records prior to this, and we've got bigger fish to fry here. Jesse Torres is going to help us with that, and I'd rather negotiate with him than Wayne Raabe, wouldn't you?" He clapped Luke on the arm. "We'll talk more about this at the Sheriff's Office. I just got word from Joe Halliday that they have the mayor in custody. I'll meet you over there."

The DA left, but Meredith hung back. "I think you and your girlfriend need to get on the same page, Detective," she said dryly.

"What are you talking about?" Luke asked, not bothering to hide his antipathy for the woman. "How do you even know Erin?"

"She's the one who told Jesse Torres not to say anything about the flash drive until he got a deal. Didn't she tell you about all that? No, I suppose she wouldn't have. She didn't want to give me her name either when she asked me to represent Torres. Nor would he tell me. But I'm too good at figuring these things out—not that it was difficult." Meredith's lips curved up into a mocking smile. "Tell her I said thanks." And with that she sauntered away.

Luke stood there in shock as he watched her leave. There was no way Erin would do something like that…But then he remembered how she'd treated Jesse in the woods, how she'd protected him, defended him…

He shook his head, reminding himself it was Meredith Armstrong he'd just spoken to. The woman was probably creating trouble where there wasn't any, just for the sheer pleasure of it. No, he wasn't going to believe Erin would have done that to him until he heard the words come directly from her mouth. And if he did, he had no idea what he would do about it.

Next to him Scott said, "What did I tell you? Run. Run like hell."

"You know Meredith. Chances are, it's all one big lie," Luke responded irritably. "Let's get to the Sheriff's Office."

But as they walked to Scott's vehicle Luke started piecing everything together in his mind. Erin had never met up with his parents for coffee after she'd left his room, telling him later that she'd wanted to look around the hospital a little…And he realized then that Meredith might not have been the one who'd lied to him after all.

CHAPTER

20

Joe Halliday was the first one to greet Luke at the Sheriff's Office. "There's the man of the hour," the agent said. "Frank's in the interrogation room with his lawyer, but he's denying everything. And now he says he'll only talk to you."

"Have you brought up the flash drive?" Luke asked as they headed down the main hallway.

"No, we only found out about it after he refused to talk to anyone but you. So I guess you'll get the honors, old man."

Luke grimaced, coming to a stop in front of the closed door to the interrogation room. "I'm not finding the 'old man' thing too amusing anymore—probably because I feel way too old right now."

Joe's lips twisted sardonically. "This job can make you grow old fast, that's for sure." Then he raised two fingers to his temple in a mock salute before leaving. "Good luck in there."

Luke paused a moment to put everything else—particularly a certain woman with green eyes—out of his mind. He needed all his wits about him right now. And with a deep breath he opened the door and walked into the room.

Frank was sitting at the interrogation table with his lawyer, and exclaimed in a huff, "These accusations are absurd, Luke. They have no evidence against me whatsoever!"

Luke took a seat across from them and didn't comment on the evidence. Instead he looked Frank dead in the eye and softly asked, "Do you remember Emily Wheeler?"

The mayor blustered a bit over the unexpected question, adjusting his tie, and finally said, "That was an unfortunate situation. Truly unfortunate. It's a shame she didn't have more self-control."

"The question isn't pertinent, Detective Mathis," the lawyer said.

Luke briefly glanced at the lawyer, and then turned his attention back to Frank. "Really? Emily Wheeler lived in New Dublin all her life—she probably voted for you, Frank. She came from a good family, married her high school sweetheart, and was a great mother to three beautiful kids. Until she got addicted to oxycodone. She could have overcome the addiction, though. She probably would have eventually. Except she started buying it off the street and didn't know what she was really getting. She died of an overdose and left her husband without the love of his love and those kids without a mother. And you think that's not pertinent?"

"Frank had nothing to do with her death," the lawyer smoothly responded.

Luke ignored him this time and continued to stare at Frank in silence for a while. But the mayor kept his own gaze averted, schooling his features into a mask of indifference. It was clear that he had no intention of participating in the conversation any further.

"I'd imagine you weren't too happy when Wayne Raabe stole your flash drive," Luke finally said, adding a little more edge to his tone. "Now there's something pertinent."

The mayor did look at him then, and the mask was gone. Fear—cold and deep and very real—filled his eyes.

"What flash drive?" the lawyer asked.

Frank shifted his gaze back and forth between him and Luke, and desperation quickly supplanted fear. "Leave us alone," he suddenly told the lawyer. "I want to talk to Luke alone."

"I strongly advise against that, Frank. You—"

"Leave us. Now."

The lawyer threw his hands up with a sigh, then gathered his things and headed to the door. "You're making a huge mistake," he said on the way out.

"I want you to turn the camera off," Frank demanded after the lawyer was gone. "I'd like to talk off the record."

"No, I'm not going to turn the camera off, Frank."

"But you could delete part of it later. If I gave you a good reason to, a very good reason, would you do it?"

Luke was pretty sure the mayor had just gone off the deep end. "I might," he slowly answered, as if considering the possibility. Everyone watching on the monitors in the room next door must be enjoying the hell out of this, he thought.

Frank nervously licked his lips, then leaned forward and whispered, "You saw the files, Luke. I have millions in offshore accounts. More money than you can possibly imagine. And I have a place all set up in the Cayman Islands. I was planning to move there when Connor started school up again this fall. As much as I loved Tina, I couldn't deal with her problems anymore. But it's paradise in the Caymans, Luke. And if you let me go I'll share it all with you. I'll give you whatever you want. Just tell them the flash drive belonged to Tina—that she was selling drugs to finance her gambling habit, and you don't have enough evidence to keep me here. We can leave tonight. You won't have to work another day in your life. I promise."

Luke stared at Frank incredulously. Desperation really had sent him off the deep end. And now he could kiss any chance of getting bail goodbye after admitting all that. "No, thanks, Frank. I actually like my job."

"Then I want to make a deal," the mayor frantically said. "Ed Finks is behind the drugs. He's been doing it for years. He brings them in from Mexico, and he forced me to get involved. Really. He threatened me. I was afraid for my life. And he said if he got caught he would take me down with him. But I'll testify against him. I'll tell you everything if I can get a deal."

Luke stood up, shaking his head. "Sorry, Frank. All the deals got used up today."

The mayor jumped from his chair and pounded the table in fury. "You son of a bitch! You'll amount to nothing in this piddly little town. You're nobody. Nobody! Is that what you want? You could have it all! But you're a fool, a goddamned goody two shoes, just like your dad!"

Luke briefly smiled. "I couldn't ask for a better compliment." And with that he headed for the door.

The mayor completely lost his tenuous grip on sanity then. "Ahhh!" he yelled. And in a blind rage he flew around the table toward Luke. But two deputies burst into the room before he could make it more than a few steps. One tackled him to the floor and the other quickly put him in handcuffs.

Joe Halliday came in as well. "We've got the flash drive," he said with a grin. "And it looks like Christmas is coming early this year."

Luke nodded somberly and walked out of the room. Christmas seemed like a long, long way off to him.

"MY GOD, THERE REALLY IS A CHILD BURIED IN THE woods!" Jenna exclaimed in horror as they sat on the living room couch and Erin told her about the grave she'd discovered.

"Anne Marie was my mother's name, and they both have exactly the same birthday. It all fits, Jen. I think my grandparents—well, Helen and Walter—really did kidnap my mother when the real Anne Marie died. And another thing: I remember seeing two small headstones in the cemetery next to Helen's grave. I never looked at them, but those must be the other two children that Bella was talking about."

"We should go there and check it out," Jenna said.

Erin adamantly shook her head. "I'm already convinced, and there's no way I'm ever going back into that cemetery. I've had enough ghost experiences to last a lifetime already, and with my luck the next one would be Walter. I have absolutely no desire to find out what lessons he's supposed to be learning."

Jenna looked at her in concern. "Erin, did Walter or Helen ever physically abuse you in any way?"

"No. Helen would sometimes grab my arm pretty hard when we got into a fight, but she never laid a hand on me otherwise. And neither did Walter. In fact, it was a total shock to me when Bella said he pushed Helen down the stairs."

"Three babies dying can't be a coincidence, though," Jenna said. "If it wasn't abuse, do you think they died from SIDS?"

Erin shrugged uncertainly. "They could have. But babies are at a much higher risk of that between two and four months old. If the other children died within the first few weeks like Anne Marie, it's more likely that they all had some sort of genetic disorder."

"And I know how devastating that can be to a family, especially to a mother," Jenna quietly said. Then after a pause she added, "Maybe that's why Helen used to lock you up when you didn't do what she wanted. It gave her a sense of control, which she hadn't had with the other children. That doesn't make it right, but at least it gives you an explanation. Losing three babies like that would be too much for almost anyone to bear, and it probably sent Helen over the edge."

"I suppose it's possible." Erin remembered how devastated she'd felt over not being able to get pregnant. She couldn't even imagine the heartbreak of losing a child, much less three. But she could imagine how it might drive a person to do crazy things—like kidnap someone else's baby. "You know, I never thought in a million years that I would say this, but I actually feel sorry for Helen Harris."

"It takes a new perspective to change an old perception," Jenna said. "But no matter how ill your grandmother was, it doesn't change the fact that she and Walter committed a serious crime. And you might have real grandparents out there somewhere who still agonize over what happened to their baby." She looked thoughtful a moment. "They would have kidnapped your mother a little over fifty years ago. I've never heard any stories about a kidnapping around here, but we should see what comes up on the internet. And of course, you need to talk to Luke about it. He'll know how to investigate this."

Erin bit her lip worriedly at the mention of Luke's name. "Jenna, some things happened today that I haven't told you about…I think I might have really screwed things up with Luke this time."

Jenna only chuckled, patting Erin's leg reassuringly. "Whatever it is, I'm sure you're making a mountain out of a molehill again. There's an old Chinese proverb you need to keep in mind: 'That the birds of worry and care fly over your head, this you cannot change, but that they build nests in your hair, this you can prevent.'"

"The problem is, I might have created a dragon that's flying over my head right now," Erin responded grimly. "And it will probably burn all my hair off." Then she told Jenna about the encounter with Wayne and Jesse in the woods, and everything that had transpired afterward, finishing with how Luke had stormed out of the ER.

"Oh dear," Jenna whispered for about the hundredth time.

Erin heard how bad it all sounded now that she'd said it out loud. "I'll tell Luke what I did as soon as I see him. I just hope he'll understand and forgive me for it."

Jenna didn't offer any of her usual words of encouragement—in fact, she didn't comment at all—and that more than anything filled Erin with dread. "There's nothing I'll be able to say to make this better, is there?"

"Well, being honest will help," Jenna finally said. "But Luke is so passionate about what he does, Erin. He lives by the rules. He always has. And he doesn't have much sympathy for those who don't. This will be a tough pill for him to swallow, that's for sure...But he is still a man after all. So I suppose if worst comes to worst, you could throw conversation out the window and just seduce him."

"Jenna!"

"Once again, blame it on the morphine," her friend said. "But as the saying goes, 'Desperate times call for desperate measures.' It's a phrase that was actually derived from the writings of Hippocrates, the ancient Greek physician, who stated, 'Extreme remedies are very appropriate for extreme diseases.'"

Erin's lips twisted wryly. "I know who he is, Jen. He also wrote the original version of the Hippocratic Oath, which I took the day I graduated from medical school. It's basically an oath to practice medicine ethically. And I highly doubt the Father of Medicine would appreciate you using his words to...to promote sexual misadventures." Despite herself, she let out a laugh as soon as she said it.

A rueful smile crossed Jenna's face. "No, I suppose he wouldn't appreciate that, would he? And now I really need to go to confession. Things are starting to add up."

Erin grimaced. "For me too. I guess I'll have to go with you."

LUKE ALREADY KNEW. ERIN SAW IT IN HIS EYES AS soon as she opened the front door later that night.

"Did you help Jesse Torres get a plea bargain?" he immediately asked her.

Jenna walked into the foyer and stood next to Erin. "She was going to tell you everything tonight, Luke. Please, come in."

He stepped inside, but continued to pierce Erin with his intense blue gaze. "You knew about the flash drive the whole time, didn't you?"

Erin eased the door closed, then hesitantly turned to face him again. "Yes, but—"

"But nothing," Luke interrupted furiously. "You had plenty of opportunities to tell me, but you decided to help a criminal instead, a kid who instigated a shooting, who was involved in seriously injuring a police officer, who could easily have murdered Tina Murdock, and who knew all about the drug ring—maybe was even part of it." He shook his head in disbelief, pointing toward the back of the house. "Just a few days ago we sat on the swing out there and vowed to always be honest with each other, and then you turn around and do this? Is that how little a vow means to you, Erin? I feel like maybe I don't really know you at all."

Erin was shocked speechless by his harsh words and couldn't come up with a single thing to say in her own defense.

"I'll leave the two of you to work this all out. It's past my bedtime anyway," Jenna told them. Then she gave Erin a quick hug, whispering under her breath, "I think now is the time for desperate measures."

Erin paused to collect herself as Jenna retreated to her room. And when she looked up at Luke there was an intensity in her eyes that rivaled his. "You're wrong, Luke. You know me better than anyone except Jenna. And I've never taken a vow lightly—not ever. But we can talk about this more upstairs."

With that she raced up to her bedroom, giving him no choice but to follow, and went straight to her dresser. She pulled out the white silk nightgown she'd been wearing the night he'd shown up at her window, and turned around just as he reached the doorway.

Luke stopped short, glancing down at the nightgown in her hand. Then he shifted his stormy blue gaze back to her. And for a moment they both stood there, staring into each other's eyes, neither sure about their next move.

Erin finally set the nightgown on the bed and nervously started unbuttoning her blouse. "I—I'd like to change into something more comfortable before we talk," she said, and inwardly cringed at the awkwardness in her tone. She would probably sound a lot sexier trying to sell manure.

And Luke wasn't buying it. "You've got to be kidding me. Do you really think this will all go away with sex?"

Erin watched the anger vanish from his expression, leaving only a hurt look behind. And she didn't like that any better. Hastily buttoning her blouse back up, she walked over to him. "Do you know why Jesse instigated that gunfight, Luke? Because he's gay. And Connor has been bullying him about it ever since he told him. Jesse is upset and confused about who he is and how everyone's reacting to it, and Wayne Raabe has only made things worse. Jesse doesn't need to go to jail. He needs help. And more than anything, he needs to know that people care about him."

Luke sighed. "He's not your responsibility, Erin."

"A lot of people could have said the same thing about me when I was growing up in the house next door. And if they had, God only knows what would have happened to me. But they cared, even though it wasn't their responsibility—people like Jenna's parents and Nolan O'Reilly. There was also a social worker who came to the house every month for over a year, and I doubt she really had to keep…coming…"

Erin's voice trailed off as the image of that social worker flashed through her mind: the woman's friendly face and reddish-brown hair, those eyes the color of a summer sky—Luke's eyes. "Jo," she whispered, finally making the connection.

"Who is that?" Luke asked.

Erin blinked out of her reverie and looked up at him in astonishment. "I keep getting this feeling that I've met your mom before. I thought maybe I'd just seen her at some point when we were in school. But now I'm pretty sure she was the social worker who used to come and check on me. It had to be her."

"Why would she have needed to check on you?"

Erin smiled grimly. "I guess you don't know all my secrets after all. My grandmother—Helen—was a very angry woman, and I became an equally rebellious child. A lot of times we'd get into fights that ended in me being locked in my bedroom."

A different kind of anger sparked in Luke's eyes. "Jesus Christ! She locked you up?"

"It really wasn't that bad after a while. But then I got a little too brave, and she caught me trying to escape down a tree. She locked me in the basement that time, and it was the most terrifying experience of my life—or at least it had been until you got exposed to fentanyl today and stopped breathing. But anyway, I escaped through a window and hid in the Godfrey's shed. They called the police when Walter came looking for me, and then Jenna's mom found me and took me back to the house. But the police really hadn't been too concerned about it all. I'm sure to them I was just another name to add to their long list of badly behaved children. Jenna's mom stood up for me, though, and refused to leave until they got child protective services involved, and I met your mom that night."

"God, Erin," Luke said painfully. "I had no idea you went through all that."

"It's in the past, and I want to leave it there. But I don't know what would have happened if Jenna and her parents—and your mom—hadn't been there for me. Who knows? I might have become just as hateful and twisted as Helen. Or imagine if my father hadn't been found guilty, and I'd been left to his mercy. After years and years of exposure to drugs and alcohol, and God only knows what else, I could easily have become another Wayne Raabe."

"That's ridiculous, Erin. You could never be like him."

"I don't know, Luke. In that environment, and without anyone who really cared, I might have eventually turned out just like him. The thing is, under the right circumstances any of us can become the person we most despise."

Erin reached out and touched his arm. "I also got to see a different side of Jesse in those woods. At one point Wayne threatened to rape me and chop me up into pieces afterward, and Jesse defended me. Later he even explained how to use the gun."

Luke ran a hand through his hair in agitation. "Raabe threatened to rape and kill you?"

"Yes. And when Jesse told him to leave me alone, Wayne said, 'You're a good fuck, kid, but right now she'll be better.' Those were his exact words."

Pure rage contorted Luke's features. "If he'd touched you…If that bastard had touched you…"

Erin grimaced. "You would've killed him. Which is my point exactly about what we can become."

Luke abruptly pulled her against him, burying his face in her hair. "God, it kills me to imagine what you went through in those woods. I'm so sorry I didn't get to you sooner."

Erin held him tightly, grateful to be back in his arms again. And then after a while she looked up at him with a playful grin. "Will you forgive me on the grounds of temporary insanity?"

Luke's mouth gradually lifted into a crooked smile. "Okay, we can go with temporary insanity. But you also have to promise me that you'll never act like a lawyer again—or a cop, for that matter. As it is, no one's ever going to let me forget that you're the one who caught Wayne Raabe."

"Don't worry," Erin responded in a rueful tone. "I already made that promise to myself this afternoon. Practicing law is definitely not for me. And your job makes medicine seem like a vacation in paradise."

Luke chuckled. "Good, I'm glad you feel that way." He gazed at her for a moment, and a slow, devilish grin crossed his face. "But there's one more thing you need to do before I can completely forgive you."

Erin tenderly smiled back. "I'm at your mercy, Detective."

Luke eased away from her and sat down on the bed. "You need to continue that little striptease you started before. And I think you should dance this time. I'll even provide the music." He pulled his cell phone out and searched his music library. "Let's see what I can come up with…Oh, here we go. This will be perfect."

He hit play and Marvin Gaye seductively crooned, "Let's Get It On."

Erin half-groaned, half-laughed in response. "Are you serious, Luke?"

"Oh yes, honey, I'm dead serious." And in tune with Marvin, he softly sang the words to the song.

At first Erin just stood there watching him in amusement. And then she reluctantly started her performance. But she didn't have to dance for long, because as soon as she got warmed up and really put some enthusiasm into the show, it was too much for him to bear.

And by the next song she was learning all about the wonders of make-up sex.

CHAPTER

21

The next morning Erin told Jenna about the Marvin Gaye incident that had resulted from her "desperate times, desperate measures" advice, and they couldn't look at each other without laughing after that. And a few hours later they still hadn't gotten it together, so church was torture of the sort that Erin had never experienced before. Then the final hymn of the service was "Lord of the Dance," and neither of them could manage to sing more than a few verses. Fortunately, one of the most enthusiastic singers in the congregation had been right behind them, and her high soprano voice covered up most of their laughter.

Luke hadn't come because of work—crime, unfortunately, was another disease that didn't take a break on Sundays. But Nolan O'Reilly had been there, and he'd watched them in bemusement the whole time. Usually he attended the service with Colin and his family, but they'd gone to visit friends out of town for the day, so he'd decided to join them instead. Erin figured he probably wouldn't make that mistake again.

"I'm sorry, Nolan. I hope we didn't embarrass you too much," she said as they walked into the church lobby after the service. "I think Jenna and I probably had too much coffee this morning."

"Perhaps a little too much Irish coffee?" he asked, turning to her with a chuckle. "But no need to apologize, lass. Me thinks God has a sense of humor Himself. And I'm sure He smiles down on those who live with a merry heart."

"Mark Twain would say, 'Humor is mankind's greatest blessing,'" Jenna added.

"Indeed it is," Nolan agreed. "Or I'd have been sent to the funny farm long ago."

"And a lot of us would be there with you," Jenna said.

Erin grinned at her. "Although if there were cows on the farm, that might have really tipped you over the edge."

Jenna laughed softly. "I'm actually fond of cows, believe it or not. They're adorable creatures in their own way. And I do sometimes wonder if it isn't actually a blessing itself not to have too many brains in one's head."

"Oh, I know you way too well, Jen," Erin said. "You would like being a cow for all of two seconds."

"Or maybe just one," she responded. "The second I stepped in my own manure I'd be begging to get my brains back."

Nolan let out a hoot of laughter. "Ye'll never appreciate the sweet smell of a rose so much as when ye inhale the fresh scent of manure." And with laughter still in his voice, he said, "But in any case, I would love to continue this conversation over lunch—though perhaps we ought to flush any further talk of manure down the jacks. Would ye care to join me at the Corner Café again? I'd say it would be my treat, but I do believe the treat would be all mine."

Jenna's expression sobered, and she looked at Erin uncertainly.

"I would love to go." Erin glanced around at the few remaining parishioners in the church lobby. "Are Greg and Joanne here? Maybe they would want to join us."

"Colin and Sophia had dinner with them last night, and they all went to the service afterward," Nolan told her. "So if ye ladies don't mind, it'll just be the three of us this time."

"Of course we don't mind," Jenna said. "And never discount the power of three. Good things often come in threes. In fact, there's an Ecclesiastes verse in the Bible that says, 'A cord of three strands is not quickly broken.' And the Declaration of Independence specifically names three rights in one of the most well-known sentences of all time: 'We hold these truths to be self-evident, that all men are created equal, that they are endowed by their Creator with certain unalienable Rights, that among these are Life, Liberty and the pursuit of Happiness.' There were also three wise men from the East who came to see Jesus, bearing gifts of gold, frankincense, and myrrh. And you'll find plenty of trios in children's literature: the three bears who found Goldilocks in their house, the three little pigs, the three little kittens who lost their mittens—"

"The three blind mice," Erin interrupted with a grin. "And don't forget about other famous trios like the Three Musketeers, the Three Stooges, and the Three Amigos."

"Some of us Irishmen are especially fond of being three sheets to the wind," Nolan quipped.

"Which might result in a three-ring circus," Erin said.

Jenna looked around in amusement. "I think we're also the last three left standing here in the church lobby—along with the Father, Son, and Holy Ghost, of course."

Nolan chuckled. "And me stomach is beggin' for a good three-course meal, so I think I'll be off now. I'll see ye ladies at the café shortly."

When Nolan was gone Jenna turned to Erin. "There's a women's bathroom here that has several stalls—in fact three of them, now that I think about it—and a window. Do you want to stop there before we leave?"

"No, I'll be fine," Erin reassured her. "We won't have to run out of the café like our pants are on fire this time—mine in particular."

She had a little surprise in store for Jenna, though. Once they were all settled in at the café and had placed their orders, she said, "I need to use the bathroom after all. I'll be right back." She smiled when Jenna looked at her as if she was certifiably insane, and added, "I guess it was all that coffee." Then she eased out of her chair and headed to the bathroom—or more like the small closet with a toilet in it—and was just a little nervous about the endeavor. But ever since she'd used the bathroom that night at the Shamrock with Luke and found out how well the image of him stealing batteries from the smoke alarm had worked to chase away anxiety, she'd been doing the same thing at home. She could already lock herself in the bathroom there. And now she had the melody of "Lord of the Dance" to distract her here—and it worked like a charm.

She returned to the table, feeling like another weight had just been lifted from her soul. "I'm all good to go," she said, giving Jenna a grin as she sat down. "And yes, that pun was intended."

She joined the conversation they'd been having about the sunroom project that James was working on for them, and found out that Nolan had a keen interest in architecture and construction—of course, there wasn't much that didn't pique his interest, other than rocking chairs. But he offered a few suggestions of his own about the design, and also mentioned that he had a "lady friend" who could get Jenna an adjustable bed with side rails at a reasonable price.

"So what exactly is your definition of 'lady friend'?" Erin teasingly asked him.

Nolan's blue eyes danced with humor. "I'm way too old for it mean what yer young mind is thinkin', that's for sure."

"Well, I believe a lot of your fellow seniors would disagree with you there." Erin's lips curved up into a devilish smile. "In fact, many of them would *really* disagree with you. STDs among the elderly are spreading like wildfire. Just last month I treated an eighty-five-year old man from a local nursing home for chlamydia. Apparently he was the playboy of the West Wing."

Nolan started laughing, and a moment later the waitress brought their food.

"Oh great, now I have to eat," Jenna said wryly. "Right after Erin brings up chlamydia. That figures."

"Hey, at least I didn't talk about the woman I saw right after him who'd left a tampon in for two months. Now that would ruin anyone's appetite."

Jenna and Nolan half-laughed, half-groaned, and the waitress's face twisted into a grimace as she handed them their plates.

When she left Erin smiled ruefully at her back. "I guess I'd better leave a really good tip."

She avoided any further discussion of blood or body fluids after that, and the conversation eventually turned to what had happened to her the day before. She told Nolan about her conversation with Bella, and then about discovering Anne Marie's grave, and his response unearthed yet another unexpected piece of history.

"I've not heard any stories of a kidnappin' meself," he said thoughtfully. "But it would have happened years before I arrived. I was in Dublin attendin' the university back then, and medical school afterward. It wasn't until 1976 that me cousin Deaglan and I moved here with our wives."

"That's odd," Jenna said. "My grandfather's name was Deaglan—Deaglan O'Callaghan—and I think he moved here around the same time."

For a moment Nolan stared at her in shock. "Well, I'll be gobsmacked!" he finally said. "I can't believe I never made the connection before. Deaglan and his wife Aileen had two daughters, Nora and Shannon. Ye must be Shannon's daughter."

"I am," Jenna said in bewilderment. "But how is it possible we could be related? I did a lot of research into my family history. There's no record of your name. And I was just in Ireland visiting distant relatives, and no one mentioned you either."

A pained expression crossed Nolan's face. "That's because it's not a subject devout Irish Catholics would wish to discuss, nor a record they would have wanted to keep. Deaglan and I shared the same grandfather, Tadhgan O'Callaghan. He had an affair with me grandma, but kindly forgot to mention that he was already married. He finally admitted it after she found out she was pregnant with me mam, and she cut off all ties with him. It was only years later that I did some research of me own and found out about all this. I tracked Deaglan down and we became fast friends, and eventually moved here together. Deaglan convinced us to come, tellin' us we'd all find a better life here."

"But Deaglan was really trying to escape from the curse," Erin softly said. "Jenna told me about it."

"You're right indeed. That cursed curse." Nolan shook his head with a grimace. "Deaglan eventually got sick with the cancer, and someone back home told him it was me grandma who'd put the curse on all the O'Callaghan men. Deaglan believed it, and he was riled somethin' fierce. He cursed me back, and we never spoke again. Me wife Màire and I offered to help Aileen and the girls after he died, but she would have nothin' to do with us either. And then Màire died a few years later. Part of me always wondered if there wasn't somethin' to those damned curses after all."

"The O'Callaghans had Li-Fraumeni syndrome," Erin told him. "It's autosomal dominant, and that's why so many of them developed the disorder. It had nothing to do with a curse—or with men. Jenna has it too."

Understanding soon dawned on Nolan's face, and his blue eyes filled with sorrow. "Ah, Jenna, I'm so sorry. Màire and I still tried to do what we could for yer grandma, but when Màire and the twins died I was too caught up in me own troubles to worry about anyone else's. And I'll admit I was a bitter man, and often cursed Deaglan's soul meself. It ate me up inside for a very long time, wonderin' how different our lives might have been if we hadn't come with him, or if I'd never met him at all." He reached over and squeezed Jenna's hand. "But we were family. That's what it all should have boiled down to. And I'm so very sorry we let all those ridiculous notions destroy the most important thing we had."

"It's okay, Nolan. I understand," Jenna assured him. "And we're Irish, so we're prone to ridiculous notions. As they like to say in psychology: 'This is one race of people for whom psychoanalysis is of no use whatsoever.'"

Nolan threw his head back and laughed. "Indeed so. Ye can always tell an Irishman, but ye can't tell him much."

They went back to eating after that, and there was a momentary pause in the conversation. But Jenna only picked at her food. "I never thought about the possibility that there could be other family members not in the records," she finally said, looking worriedly at Nolan. "I wanted to make sure anyone who might have Li-Fraumeni Syndrome knew about it. Do you think there could be others?"

"Ye can rest assured, cousin," he told her. "I did the research meself. Colin, Sean, and I are the only remainin' proof of Tadhgan O'Callaghan's transgressions. All the others appear to have been good Catholics in that respect."

"You called me cousin," Jenna said, her eyes brightening with pleasure. "I like the sound of that."

Nolan chuckled. "Well, me dear cousin, I hope ye like the look of me face too, since ye'll be seein' a lot of it after this."

Erin gave Jenna a grin. "Oh boy. It looks like you're stuck with two doctors now."

AFTER LUNCH ERIN AND JENNA DECIDED TO VISIT Jesse at the hospital. They weren't getting rid of Nolan, though. He gathered up a handful of his retired cronies, along with some of that Irish coffee, and headed over to Jenna's house to help James with the sunroom. "Those dry shites ain't doin' much more than tryin' to kick the bucket anyway," he'd said of his friends. "This'll give 'em somethin' worthwhile to do. And another reason to drink."

Erin smiled at the thought of them as she and Jenna walked through the hospital lobby. She had a feeling Nolan and his friends were going to make James regret offering to work on a Sunday—and he might leave with even less hair than he'd had before.

Then they neared the elevators, and she came to a halt.

Jenna stopped alongside her, following the direction of her gaze. "Do you want to get on?"

Erin turned to her, and it was on the tip of her tongue to say no. But then she glanced down at the cane in Jenna's hand, and an idea occurred to her. "You would really like to see me finally take the elevator, wouldn't you?"

"If you're ready, then yes, I would love for us to get on it together."

"I think I need some motivation, though," Erin told her with a slight smile. "I'll take the elevator if you'll do one thing for me."

Jenna chuckled. "I have a feeling I'm not going to like this. What is it?"

"I want you to get radiation therapy on your hip, and on a few of the other places that are causing you pain."

Jenna's expression immediately sobered. "Erin, we've already been through this. I don't—"

"I'm not talking about trying to cure you, Jen. This is about reducing the pain you're in. And you'll be able to walk longer. I'm sure you'd rather not have me pushing you around in a wheelchair if you can help it."

Jenna softly sighed. "Going back and forth to Madison all the time would be such a hassle, Erin. And it probably wouldn't help that much anyway."

"You're wrong, Jen. There's a good chance the pain will get significantly better within weeks. And you'll only have to go once. A single dose of radiation can be just as effective as a series of treatments in a case like yours, with few side effects. Didn't your oncologist talk to you about all that?"

"I suppose...maybe," Jenna hesitantly responded.

Erin grinned. "It sounds like maybe someone wasn't listening very well." She squeezed Jenna's arm. "Do one treatment for me, and I'll get on the elevator."

"Oh fine," Jenna said in resignation. Then she limped over to the elevator and pressed the up button, adding, "I'll bet you just want to see me get nuked as payback for last Friday when I told you to go screw yourself."

A bubble of laughter started to escape Erin—but it was quickly popped.

"Ladies, this is a hospital!" a nurse said, frowning at them as she walked by.

Fortunately for Erin and Jenna, the elevator doors opened right away, and with guilty looks on their faces they hurried inside.

"I suppose she wouldn't find it amusing if I told her to blame it on the morphine," Jenna muttered under her breath.

Erin did break into laughter then. "We just got yelled at...because you told me to go screw myself."

Jenna hit the button for the third floor. "I did not actually tell you to go screw yourself." Then her lips quirked up into an impish grin. "I just kind of told you that a week ago."

Erin leaned against the elevator wall, and it barely registered that the doors had closed as she continued to laugh helplessly, grabbing her stomach. "I still can't believe...a nurse actually yelled at us..."

But in a matter of seconds the doors started to open again, and she abruptly stopped laughing. "What happened?" she asked, her eyes widening in fear. "Didn't we go anywhere?"

It was Jenna's turn to laugh. "We're on the third floor," she said, stepping out. "Congratulations, my friend. You just took a ride in the elevator."

Erin hesitantly followed her out, glancing back as the doors closed behind her. "Wow, that's all there was to it." She slowly grinned and walked with Jenna down the hallway. "Now I know exactly how I'm going to distract myself every time I get on an elevator. I'll think of that nurse yelling at us because you told me to—"

"Shush, Erin, this is a hospital!" Jenna said, prompting them both to dissolve into a fit of giggles.

In Jesse's room they found a full-blown fiesta going on, with very little room to move. The boy looked a thousand times better, Erin noted. And he had a lighthearted smile on his face.

Then he saw her, and his smile widened. "Papá, Mamá, this is Doctora Pryce," he said to the couple standing next to him.

As soon as he made the announcement the room erupted with happy exclamations, mostly in Spanish, and a path immediately opened for Erin and Jenna to walk through.

"Muchas gracias, Doctora Pryce," Jesse's father said, enthusiastically shaking her hand. "It's a miracle, un milagro increíble, what you have done for mi familia. Jesús told us how you saved him yesterday, and also when he got shot. ¡Es simplemente un milagro!"

"I didn't say anything about you until today. I tried to keep you out of all this," Jesse said. "But Detective Mathis was here this morning, and he knew everything."

Erin grimaced slightly. "Did he treat you okay?"

"Yes, and I think he believes me about not hurting the other cop or the mayor's wife. And we talked a lot about what happened between me and Wayne. He said Wayne is going to have to pay for—for certain things."

A lump of emotion formed in Erin's throat, and she felt her love for Luke deepen even more. "Yes, he will have to pay."

Mrs. Torres took hold of her hand. "I want to give you my thanks too, for everything. Jesús said he promised you he would go to church, and he asked the pastor to come and pray with him this morning. And you are right about making judgements—we should not use the Bible to judge others."

"Sí," Jesse's dad agreed. "We will all pray for strength and guidance, and leave some things in God's hands."

Erin glanced at Jenna, who was staring at her in utter shock. "You know, Jen," she said. "I'm getting really good at making you speechless."

Her friend chuckled in response, and for a while they joined the fiesta.

CHAPTER 22

Ed Finks was completely off the grid, and it made Luke nervous. The man probably always kept himself invisible when he went on his Mexican "vacations," but it was still possible someone had tipped him off about the drug ring being broken up. And if that was the case, he'd have gone right back to Mexico, and they'd never see him again. Frank had been very thorough in his recordkeeping, not to mention his implication of Ed on tape. As things stood, the assistant chief of police was going to be a very old man before he knew what freedom felt like again—if he ever did. But they had to catch him first.

Ed had a live-in girlfriend—one young enough to be his daughter—and they'd brought her in for questioning after locking Frank up. Her face had lost all color when she'd been read her Miranda rights, and they'd had her full cooperation after that. She'd denied any knowledge of Ed dealing drugs, or even using them, but thought he might be cheating on her. And based on her panicked responses during the interview, Luke was pretty sure she'd been telling the truth—either that or she'd gotten some really good acting lessons from Frank. But she expected Ed back early that afternoon, though she had no way to reach him either. He always left his phone at home when he went to Mexico because he wanted complete solitude—to get away from the pressures of being a cop, he'd said.

Luke was sure Ed had a disposable phone, but so far they hadn't found a contact number in any of the files. Frank probably knew how to reach him, but after his breakdown at the Sheriff's Office he'd completely stopped talking—although when agents from the FBI and DEA arrived, he did ask for his lawyer back.

So now it was a waiting game. Sheriff's deputies and detectives throughout the county were on alert for Ed's black, heavy-duty pickup, while federal and state agents, along with members of the regional SWAT team, were discreetly positioned near Ed's house. An ABP hadn't been put out, though, given the delicacy of the situation. Instead, they'd wait for Ed to drive into their net and haul him in when he got home. It gave them a more controlled environment for the takedown. And it would be a fitting ending anyway.

Luke wanted to be the first one to greet Ed when he pulled into his driveway, so he and Scott had staked themselves out inside the assistant chief's million-dollar house down the street from the mayor's, with their tactical gear at the ready.

"This is a pretty nice spread. Maybe it'll go into foreclosure," Scott said, admiring the lavishly decorated living room as they stood on alert by the front windows. "Not that I could afford it even then."

"You wouldn't want this house anyway," Luke told him. "I'm sure there's a lot of bad karma here."

Scott laughed shortly. "I didn't know you believed in shit like that. You think there are ghosts here too?" He wiggled his fingers in front of him and made a spooky noise.

Luke shook his head with a wry smile. "After some of the things Erin's told me, there just might be."

"Christ, she's really got you by the balls, doesn't she?" Scott said. "But then, who am I to talk? I've already had mine pretty much cut off—and that was before I got the vasectomy I probably didn't need." The smoldering anger that had been in his eyes most of the time lately burned especially bright. "But with my luck it would turn out that we never even needed IVF when number five came along."

Before Luke could respond, his cell phone started to buzz. Pulling it out, he saw the call was from an unknown number in Minneapolis. *Shit*, he thought. *Someone probably told the chief what was going on.* "Hello?"

"Is this Detective Mathis?" an unfamiliar male voice asked.

"Yeah. Who is this?"

"It's John Kilbride, Jeff's son. I got your number from his phone. I'm really worried about my dad, and I thought you might know something."

"What has you concerned?" Luke asked, glancing furtively out the window.

"He was acting really strange all weekend, almost like I would never see him again, and it's scaring the hell out of me. But he won't tell me what's going on. Do you know if he's sick or something?"

"He doesn't have any health issues I know of," Luke said. "We are in the middle of a murder investigation. Has he mentioned that?"

"Yeah. And maybe he's just stressed out about it. He and Frank have been good friends for as long as I can remember.

In fact, he was talking about that yesterday. But then he muttered something about how they'd both made a lot of mistakes, and that it was all a big mess."

"What mistakes?"

"I don't know," John answered with frustration in his tone. "He wouldn't say."

"Where is he now?"

"He should be on his way back to New Dublin. He just left a few minutes ago."

"I'll talk to him when he gets home. In the meantime, if you think of anything else he said that might be important, I want you to call me right away."

"Alright, I will. Thanks for your help, Detective Mathis."

"No problem, John." Luke ended the call and put his phone away, shaking his head.

"What was that about?" Scott asked.

"It was the chief's son. He's worried because Jeff hasn't been acting like himself."

"Hah! He's probably feeling guilty since he should be working on a Sunday too."

Luke glanced out the window again. "Jeff's heading back now, so I hope Ed shows his face in the next few hours, or things might get a lot more complicated."

But almost as soon as he said it the voice of one of the sheriff's deputies came across their portable radios. "395 to 28. We have eyes on the prize, heading north on I-94, about eighteen miles from your location. We're shadowing now."

Luke picked up his radio and responded on the encrypted channel they were using, "Copy that 395. Keep us updated."

"10-4," the deputy returned.

"It looks like the party's about to get started," Scott said with a slight smile. Then they quickly put on their tactical gear and readied their guns.

Multiple units called in with updates as Ed got closer, and when he finally pulled into the driveway a swarm of police vehicles closed in behind him.

Luke and Scott rushed out the front door at the same time with guns drawn. "Step out of the vehicle now, Ed!" Luke shouted, running toward him.

Ed Finks looked out the open window in shock. But as realization quickly dawned he didn't get out of the truck. Instead, he hit the gas hard and drove straight into the garage, splintering the overhead door he'd started to open when he pulled in. Then he rammed through the back wall, sending all his neatly arranged tools flying in every direction, and continued to speed down the long backyard.

There were thick woods farther back, and he jumped out of the truck right before it slammed into a tree. But he was surprisingly agile for a man in his mid-fifties. He rolled on the ground to break his fall and immediately got to his feet, dashing toward the cover of the trees.

He might have chosen a different course of action, though, if he'd known the MVP of the police force was there, the one who could intimidate, overpower, sprint, and sniff far better than any of them—and the one who also happened to be the most beloved by children. While Luke and Scott ran as fast as they could in their gear, with a slew of officers behind them, Bandit easily sprinted past them all and caught up to Ed before he'd made it more than a handful of steps.

The dog leapt up, clamping his powerful jaws on Ed's right arm, and tackled him to the ground. Then he continued to pull on the arm, vigorously yanking it back and forth, while the man screamed, "Call him off! My arm! Goddamn it, call him off!"

Melinda, the second fastest member of the force, outran Luke and Scott as well. "Aus!" she commanded, prompting the dog to back off as she jumped on Ed herself and quickly put him in handcuffs.

Luke reached them a moment later, and Melinda grinned up at him. "It looks like a woman had to catch the criminal again, Mathis. You're having a bad weekend."

"You have an unfair advantage, Mann, and you know it," he gasped, pulling his helmet off.

"What, that I don't run like a grandma?" she teased. Then she patted Ed down, removing a knife from his belt and a gun from a leg holster before she hauled him to his feet. "Our dirty cop is going to need some stitches."

Luke glanced at Scott. "You can have the pleasure of reading him his rights since he can't read them to himself. Melinda and I will take Bandit over to the truck—or what's left of it anyway—and see what Ed's brought home for us."

A handful of the other officers had already gathered to inspect the truck when they approached. "Check it out, Luke," one of the Sheriff's deputies said excitedly. "There's white powder all over the ground in front—"

"Get back!" Luke immediately yelled. "Everyone get back! You could inhale fentanyl!"

He pulled his radio out as they all retreated, switching the channel to one used for general communication, and called in, "New Dublin 28 to Comm Center."

"Go ahead 28," the dispatcher responded.

"Have the fire department send the hazmat team to 1419 Woodland Trail immediately. And we need an ambulance for another possible fentanyl exposure."

"28, please confirm you need the hazmat team and an ambulance dispatched to 1419 Woodland Trail for a possible fentanyl exposure," the dispatcher said, not quite able to hide the surprise in her voice.

"10-4," Luke answered.

"Shit," Melinda said as they came to a halt in the front yard. "If I have to go through the decon trailer again, I'm going to shoot Ed in the other arm."

"No, we were far enough away. I think we should be fine," Luke told her. "And leave Ed with one good arm. He'll need it to protect his ass in prison."

"No doubt," Melinda agreed. "I'm just glad you learned your lesson from yesterday. Your girlfriend isn't here to give you CPR this time."

Luke smiled ruefully. "No, she's not. But that's one lesson I'll never forget. And I learned a few more today, like how I should wait for the suspect to turn his vehicle off before trying to apprehend him—not to mention it would be a good idea to unplug the garage door opener." He looked at the mess Ed had made of his house and could only shake his head.

"Was there another lesson?"

"Yeah, that I need to run more sprints."

Melinda laughed. "You'll still never catch me, Mathis. Not in a million years."

LATER THAT EVENING LUKE SHUT HIS COMPUTER down at the police station, ready to call it a day and forget about all the madness for a while. Both Frank and Ed were safely tucked in at the county jail, each blaming the other for everything. But they were only hurting themselves with their lies.

They'd arrested Stella Givens as well, who'd continued to act as sweet as pie the whole time and hadn't quite understood why she was going to jail, even after being confronted with the evidence from the flash drive.

It turned out she and Frank had created a secret bank account in the name of the city called a City Reserve Development Account, with Stella listed as the second account holder, giving her full access to the funds. Over the years millions of dollars from a real city money market account with an almost identical name were transferred into the fraudulent account. Then they'd created fake invoices from the state so the city auditors would believe the funds in the legitimate account were being used appropriately. They'd also made payments to what appeared to be real companies, but were actually just shell companies Frank had created. Too much power had clearly been put into one person's hands—a mistake at any level of government. But Stella had been there so long, and was so highly regarded by everyone, that no one would have thought her capable of such duplicity.

Wayne Raabe should have joined the nefarious little group in jail, but he never made it. He'd started withdrawing from heroin in the hospital, and the symptoms eventually became so severe that he tried to bash his head in on one of the bed rails he'd been handcuffed to. Fortunately, he wasn't as good at head-bashing as Erin was, and the doctor medically cleared him for transfer to a detox facility in Madison, where he would remain under continuous guard by sheriff's deputies until he was released to take up residence with the others at the county jail.

Jeff Kilbride was another loose end they still needed to tie up. As far as anyone knew he hadn't returned to town yet, and he wasn't answering his phone. Sheriff Gaines had stopped by his house earlier in the evening, and his wife hadn't been able to reach him either. Luke suspected he'd caught wind of everything and had gone into hiding. But it was something he would worry about tomorrow. Right now he just wanted to see Erin, and the thought immediately brought a smile to his face.

Just as he started to get up, though, his cell phone went off for about the fiftieth time in the last several hours, and he sat back down with a frustrated groan. News of the drug bust had quickly spread, and he'd been bombarded with one call after another since then. But when he checked his phone he saw the call was from Mike O'Hara, the city council president—and now the interim mayor as designated by the city charter. Luke had informed him of his new title last night after they'd formally arrested Frank.

He hit the talk button. "Hey, Mike."

"Good evening, Luke. I don't want to take up too much of your time. I know you've had a long day. But I just got off the phone with Sheriff Gaines, and I've got an urgent matter to discuss with you. Congratulations, by the way. I understand you played an important role in tracing the drugs back to a lab in Mexico. She said the DEA even offered you the opportunity to join them. That's impressive."

"Thanks, Mike," Luke said, smiling wryly to himself. All he'd really done was find Ed's burner phone. After the hazmat team had cleared the truck—emptying out enough drugs in various secret compartments that even the DEA agents were shocked—he'd inspected the interior himself, figuring if Ed hadn't gotten rid of the phone yet it would be hidden somewhere he could easily reach it while driving. And it had taken him all of five minutes to find it.

Another secret compartment had been built behind the truck's in-dash LCD touch screen, and was wired into the electrical system so that a sequence of buttons or switches already in the vehicle had to be pushed to lift the screen up and access the compartment, such as the power door lock button, the power window button, and so forth. The hard-core drug dealers were all using those kinds of compartments nowadays. But there was no way Luke could have guessed what the right sequence was. He just knew that particular spot was where they often put one of their secret compartments, so he'd smashed the whole thing in. The truck had become government property anyway. And sure enough, he'd found the phone, along with another gun, and a bunch of cash.

Unlocking the phone had been just as easy. He'd figured Ed probably used the same password as his regular cell phone, and that if his girlfriend suspected he'd been cheating on her, there was a good chance she knew it. And he'd been right on both accounts. The FBI and DEA had taken over from there, tracing a number on the phone back to a location in Mexico. They'd contacted the Mexican Federal Police, who'd quickly organized a raid, discovering millions of dollars' worth of fentanyl, heroin, and other drugs. They figured it might be the biggest fentanyl bust they'd ever had in Mexico.

"Do you think you'll take the DEA up on their offer?" Mike asked.

"I don't think so," Luke responded. "Those guys are on the road all the time, and I kind of like being home to cut my own lawn, watch football on Sunday, and kiss my girlfriend goodnight." *Not necessarily in that order,* he thought with a grin.

"I'm glad to hear you say that," Mike said. "I called an emergency meeting of the City Council earlier tonight. And based on the recommendation of Sheriff Gaines, I'd like to offer you the job as Chief of Police. The council members unanimously agreed. This mess is going to be national news tomorrow, and we want someone in that position who will represent us well. It will also make you the youngest police chief in New Dublin history, by the way."

Luke sat there in shock. "That's quite an honor, Mike," he said after a moment. "I appreciate the confidence you have in me."

"I hope there's not a 'but' coming next. We need your leadership, Luke. I tried to contact Jeff once Sheriff Gaines gave me the go ahead. He didn't answer, and I left messages requesting he be at the meeting, but he never showed up. Have you heard from him?"

"No, not a word. Something is going on with him, but I don't know what. I'm not even sure it has anything to do with the drug ring. Frank or Ed probably would've put the blame on him by now if he was involved. They've certainly spread enough of it around. But they haven't mentioned him once, and his name isn't on any of the files we recovered from Frank's flash drive. But whatever's going on with him, he's not in the right frame of mind to lead the police force, that's for sure."

"So you'll take the job?"

Luke paused in thought. It was his dream job, he realized...But he knew without a doubt he'd still choose Erin when the time came. It wouldn't even be a hard decision. No title was worth more than love. Nothing was worth more than love. But he would have one hell of a thing to put on his resumé in Boston.

"I'll act as the interim police chief," he finally said. "And we'll see what happens after the dust settles. Once an election is held the new mayor will probably want to pick someone else anyway."

"We've got a lot of policies and procedures to revamp after this," Mike told him. "And one of them is how the police chief is selected. We've already decided that the final decision will be made by the city council from now on, so I can guarantee the job will be yours for as long as you want it. And I do hope that's a long time. Congratulations, Luke. We'll make the announcement tomorrow."

SHORTLY AFTER LUKE LEFT THE POLICE STATION, Jeff Kilbride walked in. He aimlessly wandered the halls for a while, then finally ended up in his office—though he knew it wouldn't be his office for long.

He glanced at all the pictures on the walls, pictures he'd pretty much ignored for years now—his family, colleagues and friends, himself at various stages of his career...One picture in particular caught his eye. It was the one his parents had taken of him in his Army fatigues right before boot camp. He'd been so excited to start a new chapter in his life then. He was finally going to be somebody.

But the Army had never turned him into the man he'd hoped to become, and he'd spent the next forty years of his life wallowing in anonymity. Not even being named Police Chief had been enough to satisfy him. He'd only gotten the job because of Frank anyway.

Tina had always made him feel important, though. She'd made him feel like a man. And he'd loved her for that. But she'd also brought out the dark side of him, the deep, dark, ugly side he'd always tried to keep hidden, and he'd eventually given in to lust, casting aside his friendship with Frank to have her. But he hadn't meant to continue the affair for long. He'd certainly never intended for things to get so out of hand.

He was sure Frank didn't know about his involvement with Tina. But like a pesky sliver stuck deep in the skin, the truth would work its way out eventually. It usually did. Mistakes were inevitable when it came to deception, and he and Tina had made too many of them. They hadn't been careful enough—and not just with respect to the pregnancy she'd planned to abort. They'd spent way too much time together when they shouldn't have. Tina had even stayed with him at the hotel for the police conference he'd just attended in Madison, telling Frank she was driving down to visit her sister in Illinois. Someone was bound to put two and two together eventually—if they hadn't already. And with his DNA all over the crime scene, the evidence would be overwhelming and the outcome inevitable: He was going to end up in prison for Tina's murder. It was only a matter of time. And his wife would never forgive him. His sons would hate him. He would die in anonymity. Alone. Poetic justice would be served.

He figured Frank had probably found out that Tina was cheating on him with someone—more than likely because of the pregnancy—and then put a hit out on her. His friend would never have gotten his own hands that dirty. And he wondered if the killer had been lurking somewhere in the shadows while he'd still been there with Tina himself that night—and Frank had conveniently been at City Hall.

But Jeff bore him no ill will. Frank had always been good to him. It was his own fault that all this had happened. He was the one who'd betrayed their friendship. He was ultimately responsible for Tina's death. And he could think of only one way out of the mess he'd made.

He sat down in the brown leather chair behind his desk and slid his pant leg up, pulling his Glock from the leg holster he was wearing. Then he leaned back and ran his fingers slowly over the smooth, hard surface of the barrel. And while he stared at it he thought about God for the first time in a very long time, and wished that He really did exist, that there was a greater force he could turn to at a time like this. He might have hope then—hope that he could get through this mess somehow, that he could get through everything life dealt him. There would be a deeper meaning, a higher purpose to his life if God existed, and maybe then he wouldn't feel so dissatisfied, so empty all the time—an emptiness that nothing else had ever been able to fill.

But he'd seen too much in his thirty-six years as a cop. He knew God couldn't possibly exist.

With that thought in mind he quickly scribbled a note. And without hesitation, he lifted the gun to his head and pulled the trigger.

The world went dark for an instant. And then he woke up. He felt himself separate from his flesh and float upward, weightless. He gazed down at the motionless body slumped over in the chair below him and knew it was his body… But somehow *he* was still there. He could still see, and hear, and think.

As the wonder of it dawned on him he saw a light—the light he'd joked about so many times in his life. It grew and was like nothing he'd ever seen before—an incredibly bright, shimmering light. It was almost as if the light itself was alive…

He headed toward it, irresistibly drawn in by some unknown, magnetic force, though he wasn't afraid.

And a moment later he learned how much more there really was.

CHAPTER 23

"You have powdered sugar on your face," Erin told Jenna.

"Where?" she asked, wiping her mouth.

"Right here." With a grin Erin dipped her finger into the bowl of powdered sugar on the kitchen counter and dotted her friend's nose with it.

Jenna laughed, then reached into the bowl and flicked some back at Erin. "You have more."

Erin returned the favor. "No, you have more."

It was open season after that. In a fit of giggles they soon had powdered sugar everywhere.

"What in God's name are the two of you doing?"

They both abruptly stopped laughing and turned to see Luke leaning against the kitchen doorway, shaking his head in bemusement.

Erin brushed some of the powder off her face with a sheepish smile. "We decided to try our hand at making donuts. But we found out it's a lot easier to buy them."

"Don't move," Luke said when she reached for a kitchen

towel. "I want to take a picture of this." And with a chuckle he pulled his phone out.

"No, Luke," Erin protested. "Please don't take a picture."

"Come on, just one." He aimed the phone at them. "Now put a smile on your pretty, powdered sugar-coated faces for the camera."

"Luke, I take horrible pictures, really," Erin said. "Don't you remember what happened in seventh grade? I had that awful grimace on my face for the school pictures, and they never retook them. I was the laughing stock of our class all year."

"I forgot about that," Jenna said with a grimace of her own. "I felt so bad for you. And then you refused to have any school pictures taken again after that."

Erin hastily brushed off the powered sugar, glancing at Luke. "See. Me and the camera do not get along."

Luke grinned. "Too late. I already got a picture."

Erin winced. "And I probably look like I'm sucking on a lemon."

"No, it looks like a bag of powdered sugar blew up in your face." He came over and planted a quick kiss on her lips. "But you taste even sweeter." Then he grabbed a donut off the plate on the counter and took a healthy bite, giving her a devilish grin afterward. "These are really good. But I hope it doesn't mean handcuffs are off the table."

Erin laughed at the remark, though a helpless blush still crept over her cheeks.

"Ah, I think I'll go grab the broom," Jenna said.

"Oh, don't play innocent with me, Miss Godfrey," Luke teased. "Erin confessed it was you who gave her the advice about how desperate times call for desperate measures."

A guilty smile crossed Jenna's face. "Okay, I confess that may not have been the best advice I've ever given."

"Well, who would have guessed that communication actually works?" Luke said dryly, and polished off the rest of the donut.

"Let's change the subject, please," Erin told him. "I'll go get the broom. And then you need to tell us how you caught Ed Finks."

Luke chuckled. "Bandit is actually the one who caught him. He tore up Ed's arm pretty good in the process, and we had to take him to the ER. Your old boyfriend Chase stitched him up."

Erin rolled her eyes. "Chase is not my old boyfriend. And if you say that again, you'll be the next one in handcuffs."

Luke gave her another devilish grin. "Your old boyfriend asked if you were the one who bit Ed."

Jenna choked back a laugh, and Erin shook her head at them both and went to get the broom. When she returned, Luke told them about Ed's capture from the beginning—while he stood by the counter pigging out on another donut.

"My God, Luke," Erin said in dismay after he finished the story. "If Ed had gotten into the woods, he probably would have started shooting at you."

"Probably. But I had my safety gear on. I knew it might get ugly. I just hadn't expected it would get that ugly." He grinned at Jenna, who'd gone to sit at the kitchen table. "I guess he learned the whole desperate times, desperate measures thing too."

She laughed ruefully in response. "You're never going to let me forget about that, are you?"

"I'm never going to let either one of you forget about it,"

he said, pulling the milk container out of the refrigerator and pouring himself a glass. Then he grabbed a third donut and sat down across from her.

Erin leaned the broom against the wall and joined them. "So if Ed was in Mexico, do you think the mayor is the one who killed Tina?"

"Frank is the ex-mayor now," Luke told her. "Mike O'Hara, the president of the city council, took over. But it's possible he hired someone to do it. Frank has been feeding us so many lies I doubt even he knows what the truth is anymore."

"Truth is lighter than air and best friends with the wind," Jenna remarked. "One of the many reasons I don't envy you your job."

"I don't think many people do," Luke said. "But in any case, Tina was pregnant, and it wasn't Frank's. The father's DNA was all over the crime scene, including under her fingernails, so chances are he was the one who murdered her. But right now we have no idea who he is."

Jenna's eyes widened in disbelief. "Good Lord! This whole thing just keeps getting uglier, doesn't it?"

Luke smiled grimly. "Yeah, and I haven't even told you everything. We arrested Stella Givens today, too."

"Stella!?" Jenna exclaimed in shock. "You must have made a mistake, Luke."

"I wish I had," he said. Then he recounted the laundry list of crimes she and Frank had committed.

"I just can't believe it," Jenna whispered. "Stella…"

Luke nodded, taking a big bite of his donut. "Yep. Sweet-as-pie Stella Givens."

"Why on earth would she do those things?" Jenna asked, flabbergasted. "My God, she's been on the parish council at church for as long as I can remember."

"At least she wasn't on the finance council," Luke said, tongue-in-cheek. "But the answer to your question is greed, Jenna. Pure and simple greed. And Jeff Kilbride, the police chief, might be involved in some way as well. Mike O'Hara was going to ask him to step down today, but we think he may have gone on the run. Mike asked me to fill in as chief until all this gets sorted out."

Erin felt uneasiness stir inside her with the news. "Do they want you to take the position permanently?"

"It's just temporary," Luke assured her, seeing the worry she couldn't quite keep out of her eyes. "They'll eventually bring someone else in." He would tell her the rest of the story later—he knew he had to after the whole Jesse Torres affair, though it would probably bother her even more. But for the moment he deflected any further conversation on the subject by telling them about yet another interesting development.

"The FBI is going to be busy up in Eagle River too, thanks to Wayne Raabe. The Sheriff's detectives figured out why Wayne's brother Zeke never reported his car stolen. It wasn't to protect his brother—it was to protect himself. It turns out good old Zeke had stolen the car first, from a parking garage in Fort Wayne, Indiana a couple of months ago. He was doing something called VIN cloning. Basically, he would steal a car and replace the VIN number—the unique ID number every vehicle has—with one from a similar car that'd he'd find parked somewhere else. The number is usually on a plate in the dash, so all he had to do was take a picture of it, or write it down. Then he'd create fake documents and a new plate using that VIN number to sell the stolen car."

"So it's like identity theft, but of a car," Jenna said. "Boy, people sure do think of everything to keep you busy."

"You've got that right," Luke agreed. "But Wayne uncovered a huge scam by stealing the stolen car, and now his brother is in a whole hell of a lot of trouble, too."

Erin's lips twisted into a wry smile. "I hope he can pay for his own lawyer."

Just then Luke's cell phone went off, and with a mental sigh he pulled it out. But it was only his dad this time—who wasn't really looking to talk to him anyway. They spoke briefly, and with a teasing grin he handed the phone to Erin. "My dad's been trying to call you, but you're not answering. Is your phone in the car again?"

Erin shook her head regretfully. "No, I think I might have lost it for good this time—and I checked the car twice." Then into the phone she said, "Sorry about that, Greg. I've developed a very bad habit of misplacing my phone."

"No apologies necessary," he told her. "I'm the one who's sorry for bothering you. But I've got a staffing emergency in the ER, and I'm hoping you can help. The locum tenens doctor who's supposed to work the day shift tomorrow can't make it because of a death in the family, and I can't find anyone else to cover. Chase McKellar is already doing a twenty-four-hour shift—on top of already working the twelve-hour day shift on Saturday—so I absolutely have to find someone to relieve him by morning. And if it comes down to me filling in, it won't be pretty."

"I'd be happy to help. But can I start working there already?" Erin asked in surprise. "I just turned in the paperwork last Thursday, and from what I understand, getting a license to practice in another state usually takes weeks."

"Rome wasn't built in a day either, but it probably

could have been done in two if enough people had been determined to do it. And I had two days to get enough people." Greg chuckled. "I also had a little luck and the right connections."

Erin smiled, glancing out the sliding glass doors in the kitchen. "It's funny you should say that because we have our own little Rome project going on here. James Burnett started building a sunroom for Jenna this morning, and Nolan brought a bunch of his friends over to help after lunch. Then the neighbors called in half of New Dublin this afternoon, and now it's almost done."

Meghan Carey had stopped by with her husband and kids and a pan of brownies—most of which had been eaten by the half-drunk Irishmen, who'd brought a lot more than Irish coffee themselves. It turned out Meghan's husband was an electrician, and when he found out about the sunroom he called in everyone he could think of—including the building inspector—to come help. They'd all asked Erin about her adventure in the woods, of course, and after repeating the story twenty times she'd figured out how to make it sound more interesting. Then she and Jenna had taken Meghan and the kids down to the pond to listen to the swans while the men worked—mostly to keep the children away from the Irishmen after Bella asked her mom what "tits on a bull" were.

"I heard about all that," Greg said in amusement. "Colin mentioned he talked to you when he called to check up on Nolan. He thought his dad had been drunker than a monkey's uncle when he told him Jenna was their long-lost cousin."

"I'm pretty sure he thought I was the monkey's hammered aunt when I said Jenna really was his long-lost cousin." Erin laughed softly, remembering her conversation with Colin. He had his father's sense of humor and a slight Irish lilt he'd picked up from him as well. "I told him I would make sure Nolan and his friends were sober before they drove home, but he warned me that it wouldn't be an easy task to get five drunk old Irishmen to cooperate. And he was right. I ended up driving them all home." And in the process she'd learned plenty more interesting ways the Irish used the English language.

"I know firsthand how hard it can be to get one Irishman to cooperate," Greg said dryly. "Come to think of it, maybe I should call Colin back and make him work the ER shift tomorrow. That ought to rile him up a bit."

Erin smiled as she imagined how that conversation would go, having just found out how good Irishmen were at quarreling. "No, I'll do it if all the paperwork is in order."

"Yes. I was able to get you approved for a locum tenens license, which will be good for ninety days at a time. We've given you temporary privileges at the hospital, and our malpractice carrier approved you for coverage as well. Those were the biggest hurdles. I can have one of our IT people meet you in the ER tomorrow morning to get you set up on the computer, and I think you should be good to go after that."

"Perfect. What time should I be there?"

"It's a 7:00 a.m. to 7:00 p.m. shift," Greg said, and apologetically added, "I hate to ask you to do this on such short notice, Erin, but I'm desperate at this point. As you know, it can be a real challenge to staff an ER twenty-four hours a day, especially when there aren't enough ER physicians to go around."

"I understand, Greg. And I'm glad I can help."

"Thank you, Erin. I'll stop by in the morning to see how things are going. And I'll make this up to you somehow, along with everything else."

"Don't worry about it. And I owe Joanne a lot anyway, so I think we can call it even. She helped me out when I was a kid, though she might not remember. I only just made the connection myself."

"No, she's never forgotten about you," Greg told her. "She just hasn't said anything because she wasn't sure you would want her to."

Erin smiled painfully. "Until recently I wouldn't have, I suppose. But please give her my thanks. And I'll be sure to tell her myself next time I see her."

"I will. But as they say, 'What goes around comes around.'" Greg chuckled. "And right now it's come around to me being in dire need of an ER doctor, so I'm glad we're all on this merry-go-round of life together. I'll see you tomorrow, Erin."

"Okay. Goodnight, Greg."

Erin ended the call and handed the phone back to Luke, who raised a brow questioningly. "What's going on?"

"It looks like I'll be working in the ER tomorrow. The doctor who was supposed to cover the shift can't make it, and Greg couldn't find anyone else to fill in."

"What about Chase McKellar?" Jenna asked.

"He's there now on a twenty-four-hour shift."

"A twenty-four-hour shift?" Jenna blinked in astonishment. "How is that even allowed?"

"No one ever worked shifts that long at Boston General. It's too busy there. But I've heard twenty-four-hour shifts are pretty common in smaller ERs."

Jenna shook her head. "I wouldn't want to be a patient

in the twenty-fourth hour, that's for sure—or even the sixteenth. It should be illegal." As soon as she said it she gave Luke a chagrined look. "No offense against your dad."

"No offense taken," he said. "I'd like to ask him about that myself. New Dublin ER is busy enough that I would imagine a doctor isn't guaranteed to get even an hour of sleep between patients—not that it can be guaranteed in any ER. And it's a fact that going without sleep for twenty-four hours is like being legally drunk."

Erin grimaced. "It's a good example of what I've told Jenna about before. Doctors are generally held to a different set of standards than the rest of the human race, and hold themselves to those unattainable standards most of all. It gets ingrained very early on in training—we should work harder and longer than everyone else; we shouldn't need to sleep as much or even take time to eat until everything else in done; and we should pretty much have all the answers to everything. We're just not supposed to have the imperfections of the rest of humanity. I'm sure that kind of mentality is one of the reasons why doctors are more likely than most other professionals to abuse alcohol and drugs, among other things."

Jenna's brows furrowed. "What other things?"

Erin hesitated, then said, "The divorce rate is higher, and so is the incidence of depression. On average at least one doctor commits suicide in the U.S. every day. But it's something no one wants to talk about." It was a subject she herself would never have considered bringing up before now. "We're expected to be superhuman. We want to be superhuman. And when we realize we're not, we don't know what to do." She smiled tenderly at Jenna. "I'm just glad you turned me back into a human again, my fairy friend."

The concerned look on Jenna's face only deepened. "It

seems to me that in your profession there needs to be as much compassion for the doctor as there is for the patient, and yet you rarely get very much at all. It's no wonder so many doctors buckle under the pressure. Can't Greg find someone else to work, Erin? You deserve a much longer break than you've had. And Nolan was looking forward to teaching you how to use a real drill tomorrow—not the kind you use on people's bones."

A slight smile pulled at the corner of Erin's mouth. "The truth is, I actually own a real drill and know how to use it. I just didn't say anything to Nolan since he was having so much fun showing me how to do things. I think it reminded him of the old days at the hospital. But everything will be fine tomorrow." She squeezed Jenna's arm reassuringly. "I have your understanding and compassion, that's all I need. In fact, I'm looking forward to going back to the ER. I really do need it as much as it needs me. And I'm sure Luke will be happy that I'm staying out of trouble. Isn't that right, Detective?"

"Yes, that's right," he said over a mouthful of donut.

Erin brushed some powdered sugar off his face with a grin, and turned back to Jenna. "I am going to call Nolan, though, and ask him to stay with you until I get back tomorrow. I'm sure he would be more than happy to. And his car is still here anyway, so I can pick him up before my shift and bring him over."

"I don't need a babysitter," Jenna protested.

"Just humor me, okay? Then I won't worry about you while I'm gone. And you can nurse Nolan's hangover this time."

"If I say no, will you tell Greg you can't work?"

Erin chuckled. "I've already dealt with five stubborn

Irishmen today, so you're out of luck there. I won't change my mind now." She got up and put a donut on a plate for Jenna. "You better take one of these before Luke eats them all. I'm going to run upstairs and look for my phone again. It's got to be somewhere."

And she eventually did figure out where. Just when she was about to throw in the towel again it finally dawned on her that the last time she had the phone was when Luke called right before dinner to let her know he couldn't make it. And while she was talking to him she'd gone to get washcloths for the Irishmen. So she looked in the hallway linen closet, and there it was.

Laughing at herself for being so absent-minded, she called Nolan and made arrangements to pick him up in the morning, then headed back downstairs, smiling over the conversation. Poor Nolan. Jenna really was going to be his nurse tomorrow.

But she forgot all about Nolan's hangover when she saw Luke in the foyer putting all his gear back on, with Jenna standing alongside him. "What's going on?" she asked, hurrying over to them.

Luke turned to her, and there was a haunted look in his eyes. "Patrol officers responded to a report of gunfire at the PD and found Jeff Kilbride dead in his office."

"Oh my God, that's awful," Erin whispered. "Was he murdered?"

"No, it looks like suicide." Luke slid his gun into its holster on his belt. "He left a note for his family, and one of the officers read it to me on the phone. It said he was sorry to end things like that, and he hoped his wife and sons would forgive him someday. And he also took full responsibility for Tina's murder. He wrote that things got out of hand, and he wished he could take everything back."

Erin's eyes widened in shock. "*He* was the one who killed her? But why?"

Luke grimaced. "My guess is because of the baby. Women are a lot more likely to get murdered by a male partner when they're pregnant. We'll get a warrant for his DNA, but I'm pretty sure it'll be a match. The thing is, some of his fingerprints were at the crime scene too, but we excluded them because he said he forgot to put his gloves on right away. They were only on the door, and he had been one of the first officers to arrive at the scene. But that's probably why he hadn't wanted DCI to get involved either. Unlike us, they would've requested he provide a DNA sample. We never even thought to consider him a suspect."

Luke didn't mention that Jeff grew up on a farm, and had a military background, so he was also more likely than most to have worked with barbed wire before. It all added up to him being the killer…And yet it didn't, his gut told him. But he shook that feeling off for the moment. He'd probably just eaten too many donuts. "Anyway, I've got to go. This'll take a while to investigate, so I'll head home afterward."

"No, I don't want you to be alone tonight," Erin said, grabbing hold of his arm before he could turn away. "Come back after you're done—please. I don't care how late it is."

Luke opened his mouth to give her all the reasons why he shouldn't, but then stopped himself and nodded instead. Knowing the night was going to end with her in his arms would make everything else a whole lot easier.

Jenna went over to the foyer table. "Here, we had some spare keys made for the front door. I thought you should have one too." She pressed a key into his palm and briefly squeezed his hand.

"Thanks, Jen. I'm sure Erin doesn't want me throwing rocks at her window again." Luke gave them both a ghost of a smile, then headed out the door.

Erin softly sighed after he was gone. "What a bad ending to a good day."

"We don't have to let it end badly," Jenna said. "Come, let's go outside and watch the fireflies. We can put that nice new deck to good use."

Erin nodded and followed her out. The Irishmen had decided to extend the deck beyond the sunroom so that she and Jenna would have an unobstructed view of the whole backyard. And now, looking out at it as they sat down, she realized what a great idea that had been. Those Irishmen were smarter than they wanted people to think.

It was another clear night with a sky full of stars. Hundreds of fireflies once again danced to the tune of the crickets, while a slight breeze softly rustled through the trees in the distance. Moonlight shimmered over the pond, where the frogs and birds had a concert of their own going on. And for a few minutes they just sat there enjoying the sights and sounds of the night.

"It's hard to believe you were ever worried about me being bored here," Erin eventually said. "I'm still waiting for that to happen, by the way."

"I'm kind of hoping it does happen now," Jenna remarked. But then her lips quirked up into a playful smile. "Although maybe not quite yet. I'm looking forward to doing more research into your mom's past. Who knows? You could be related to Einstein or Thoreau—or even the President." She made a face. "Okay, let's just go with Einstein or Thoreau. But anyway, it's all very intriguing. And now we won't be able to go to the library tomorrow like we'd planned. Is there any chance you could call Greg and tell him you can't work after all?"

Erin chuckled. "For the last time, Jen, I'm not backing out."

"Are you really sure you're ready to deal with all that again, Erin?"

"Yes. In fact, I've never been more ready. When I go back to work tomorrow I'll be better prepared to take care of patients than I ever was before, because now I know how to take care of myself. And it's all thanks to you. I owe you for so much, Jen. You have no idea."

"Oh, please. I owe you a lot more."

Erin smiled at her affectionately. "Then I guess we'll owe each other forever."

Jenna smiled back. "I guess so."

Erin gazed out at the pond, and after a moment her expression sobered. "I don't know if it's such a good idea to dig any further into my mom's past, though. I mean, look what happened between Nolan and Deaglan. Maybe it's better to just let it go, like everything else in the past." And after half a century it would probably all remain a mystery anyway. Last night she'd told Luke about Anne Marie, and he'd looked some things up for her on the computer. She'd been sickened by the number of missing children across the country, but they hadn't found any record of an infant who'd disappeared around the time of Anne Marie's death.

"Okay, we'll let it go," Jenna said. "If that's what you want."

Erin nodded. "I think so. And the same goes for my father. Luke is pretty sure he left town, which is probably for the best. But even if he comes back it doesn't really matter. That's another part of my past I'd like to leave there."

"There's a difference between ignoring your past and

coming to terms with it. Do you think you've done that?"

Erin thought about everything that had happened since she found out Jenna had cancer. "I think I've at least made a good start," she finally said. "Though I'll probably never completely come to terms with the fact that my father killed my mother, or that I had to grow up without parents. I don't know if it's possible to ever really get over things like that." But it occurred to her that she didn't feel the old bitterness and anger anymore, the dark heaviness in her soul that talk of the past usually left her with. And she knew then that she really had come to terms with a lot of things.

But it wasn't just acceptance she felt for her mother now. It was so much more. Somehow, someway, despite death, a whole lot of misconceptions, and twenty-six years spent trying to forget her, she realized the love they'd once shared had still managed to find its way back to her.

Smiling softly, she sat there enveloped in the warmth of that love as she watched the fireflies flicker around her, almost as if they were winking their approval, sharing the moment with her in joyful celebration, reminding her that there was indeed an amazing and powerful force in the universe from which all love was born.

Erin turned back to Jenna, feeling a shift take place inside her, the dawning of a new, deeper understanding of life and how it needed to be lived, an understanding that her friend had really been trying to teach her all along. "I think you're right that the meaning of life lies in self-discovery—in finding the truth within us. And I know now that part of the journey has to include understanding how the past influences our thinking and behavior, otherwise we'll end up like those cows on the hill in your poem. But beyond that, there's no use in obsessing over the past, or the future either. We need to embrace every moment right now, to be grateful for what we have instead of always looking for something different, something more. And above all else, we need to love ourselves and others no matter what. It's all so simple and yet so complicated. But it's the only path to inner peace—the key to unlocking all the wonders of eternity." She grinned. "There I go, rhyming again. And I'm sounding more like you every day."

"Actually, you sound like Thoreau," Jenna said. "One of my favorite quotes is—"

"I know exactly which quote you're thinking of," Erin interrupted. "It was the first one you told me when I got here: 'You must live in the present, launch yourself on every wave, find your eternity in each moment.' I think that quote has been stuck in my head ever since."

"And now you won't need CPR on the beach."

"No. I can actually swim." Erin shook her head with a laugh. "I wouldn't have guessed in a million years that I would ever learn how to swim. In fact, if you'd told me ahead of time about half the things that would end up happening here, I would've said that you really did need a brain scan because none of it was even possible."

Jenna smiled, lifting her gaze up to the stars. "I have a feeling there are more possibilities than you or I could ever imagine…And I think your journey here has only just begun."

AFTERWORD
(THE REAL STORY)

One of the first people who read this book wondered how much of it was actually fiction.

My response was that many real-life events inspired it, though I changed the details somewhat to fit within the framework of a single story or to protect privacy. And unfortunately—or fortunately, depending on how you look at it—Erin's story is in a lot of ways my own story. My father was a less benign version of Helen Harris who used to take out all his unresolved anger on my mother, and to a lesser extent on my five siblings and me, continuing a cycle of abuse that had started in his own childhood. But my parents divorced when I was ten, and afterward my dad became a "born-again Christian." He then used religion as an outlet for his hatred. And he soon became quite adept at terrorizing others with words from the Bible.

After they divorced, my siblings and I lived with my mother most of the time. But she'd always struggled with mental illness and was too lost in her own world to have any real concept of being a mother. There were no hugs or words of affection growing up. No rules, or curfews, or making sure homework got done. I'm still amazed that six kids managed to survive in an environment like that, though three didn't graduate from high school. And I learned that if there's anything worse than not having a mother, it's having a mother who's there but not really there at all.

Like Erin, I've been claustrophobic since childhood, though not as severely. I avoided elevators whenever I could and used to keep the bathroom door slightly open if possible—which usually resulted in some combination of animals and/or kids coming in. So I eventually learned to at least close it more often! Most people are somewhat afraid of being trapped in an enclosed space—unless your name is Houdini—and millions of people around the world have full-blown claustrophobia. It's actually a complex disorder (as most disorders are), and a number of factors usually contribute to the development of it. But I think for me the most significant causative factor was an event that happened when I was around five. An older girl lived across the street from us, and I liked to hang out with her. But one day, for reasons I'll probably never know in this lifetime, she locked me in her shed and beat me with a stick. I can only recall a few bits and pieces of the incident, and I have no idea how I got out, but I remember going home and curling up on the couch. I was wearing a dress and looked down at the welts on my legs, and it was like I was looking at someone else's legs—which is something the mind often does to help a person cope with trauma. But interestingly, I never talked about the incident with anyone and never associated it with my claustrophobia until I was writing this book. Like Erin, I've always preferred helping other people with their problems rather than dealing with my own. I think a lot of physicians are like that, and it's one of many things that needs to change in medicine.

Other real-life events were a source of inspiration for this book as well. For example, there really was a well-liked city treasurer in Illinois named Rita Crundwell who embezzled millions of dollars from the city she worked for and "invested" the money in her horse ranch. In fact, it's not uncommon for horses to be used in money laundering schemes. And it's a sad thing that such beautiful creatures are used as a screen to cover up the ugliness of human greed.

I've also done my best to write the medical cases accurately. Variations of these scenarios have all happened to an ER doctor out there somewhere. And the child abuse case was one that I dealt with myself, and took extremely personally, having grown up with an abusive father.

I treated the child the first time, and the case was even more dramatic in real life than I related in the book. Afterward, I truly had felt like saving that child's life validated all the hard work and sacrifice that had been required to become a physician, and made up for all the times—the many, many times—when I'd felt like I wasn't really making a difference. Sometimes patients have even outright said so, usually the ones who didn't get narcotics. But I wasn't working when the child was brought in the second time. The ER physician on duty that day later told me what the neurosurgeon had said after the child died, the words Erin quotes in the book. And when I heard them myself I felt like a piece of my heart had been ripped right out of my chest, a piece that I don't think I'll ever get back.

Parts of the book have also been inspired by my experience helping a friend—who I'll call by her middle name, Lee, for privacy reasons—through stage 4 breast cancer. I first met her in the ER as a patient and gave her the initial diagnosis. She'd come in alone that day, and I quickly learned that she was an incredibly strong, independent woman, though also very reserved. But I told her she was going to need help dealing with her diagnosis, that someone should come and be a part of the discussion regarding treatment because this wasn't something she could or should cope with on her own. But she said there was no one, and I'll admit that I had to hide a few tears when she told me that and left alone. (Unlike Erin, I've always been a crier. I haven't once been able to watch the movie *Scrooged* and not cry when the little boy finally speaks.)

In any case, I made arrangements for Lee to see a breast surgeon a few days later, and I called her during my shift the next day to see how she was and to remind her about the appointment. I don't call patients back every day, but I will always call if the circumstances warrant it. And I'd felt an immediate connection with Lee, probably because we were a lot alike. But when I talked to her she sounded very uncertain about seeing the surgeon, mostly because she was intimidated by the prospect of driving to a hospital she wasn't familiar with in a bigger city. I knew there was a good chance she wouldn't follow through, so I told her I would take her. I'll never forget that moment. I remember thinking it was probably a bad idea—I really didn't know her after all. And I wondered if I'd be crossing some medicolegal line that would get me in trouble, which is a truly sad commentary on medicine these days. But I didn't feel like there was a choice. I was off the next day and she needed help. That's what it all boiled down to. And I heard the gratitude and relief in her voice afterward (she also said so, but her tone expressed a lot more than her words), and I knew then that I'd made the right decision.

I thought it would be just a one-time thing, though. I'd bring her in to see the breast surgeon, get the ball rolling, and they would take over from there. But life rarely works out exactly like we plan. The surgeon, who I'd never spoken to before, was very matter-of-fact. She basically told

Lee there was little she could do, that the prognosis was extremely grim, and she should get her affairs in order (and then after saying all that she did a breast biopsy).

    I was horrified, and it's another moment I'll never forget. I'd given bad news to many, many patients over the years—and to Lee herself—and I couldn't imagine being so callous about it. This was a human being after all. But I think the surgeon misinterpreted Lee as being aloof and uncaring because of her stoic personality. I knew differently because I'd taken the time to really talk to her. And I think this critical interaction between a doctor and patient is often not taking place anymore because of the dehumanization of medicine—it's become more about numbers than people. Doctors are numbers. Patients are numbers. And in a profession that is supposed to be about treating human beings, and requires as much skill in psychology as biology, a model like that will never work.

    But after witnessing the interaction between Lee and the surgeon I vowed that I would do whatever I could to help Lee. And so began my journey of seeing medicine from the patient's perspective, which I'd never really had to do before. She was referred to an oncologist, who was just as matter-of-fact as the surgeon had been. She told Lee that she probably only had weeks to live and didn't think palliative chemotherapy (chemotherapy intended to prolong life or improve symptoms, but isn't a cure) would do much. In the book Jenna chooses not to get chemotherapy, partly because I wanted to emphasize other important aspects of treatment, not the least of which is maintaining a sense of humor and remembering to laugh every day. But there is no right or wrong answer when it comes to palliative chemotherapy. It should always be the patient's choice and supported either way.

Lee did want to go ahead and get chemotherapy, and I was with her for every session. We became friends, and the weeks turned into months. Despite being told she only had weeks to live, Lee survived for fifteen months after her diagnosis. Much of that time was actually spent without palliative chemotherapy either, due to complications. But Lee had the most potent drug available, one neither the breast surgeon nor the oncologist ever offered: a positive attitude. She lived despite cancer. She never let it define her. She chose to live while she was dying rather than die while she was still living.

One of the most important lessons I learned from this experience is that no patient should ever be given a timeline for his or her death. Yes, patients need to be appropriately informed about their diagnosis, and they need to be adequately prepared for their death—just as we all do—but they should never be bundled into an "average." The range of possibilities should be discussed, with an emphasis placed on what is possible—that is, the numbers on the right side of the bell curve. More power needs to be put into patients' hands in determining their fate, that with good treatment and a positive attitude there is no reason they can't be counted among those who live as long as anyone else has with their condition—or even longer.

When patients hear that they have a certain number of weeks or months to live based on an average, they're much more likely to follow that timeline. It's not necessarily because of statistical probability, but because of the power of the human mind. If we believe something will happen, it's much more likely that it will happen, good or bad. There is nothing more potent on this earth than the power of the human mind. And it's a weapon that's vastly underutilized in medicine.

I could go on and on about that, but I'll move on to another topic I could go on and on about: the paranormal. I actually did go on and on about it, and I had to rewrite this section because I ended up with far too much material to put into an afterword. So I think at some point I need to write a book specifically about my experiences with the paranormal, which have been many, along with a discussion of near-death experiences and some of the rather illogical and unscientific arguments that have been used to dispute them. And of course, the paranormal will play a part in the sequel to *An Eternity in a Moment*.

But as far as the paranormal goes, the first time I saw a ghost was when I was around age six, and it happened just like I wrote in the book when Erin wakes up to see the ghost next to her bed. I know the skeptics will say that I was simply in a state between dreams and consciousness and imagined the whole thing. But I've woken up over 16,800 times since then and have never seen anything like that again. I later found out that a man had hung himself in the house, and that my mother had been terrified living there. My father worked the night shift, and she would often hear footsteps, or would feel like someone was touching her, and even felt the bed shake at times. Ironically, because of my mother's mental health issues, I would never have believed her if I hadn't had such a vivid experience myself.

A lot of paranormal things have happened since then, both inside and outside of the hospital setting. But the one I really want to discuss is my most recent experience, the one that I think is also the most extraordinary and meaningful.

By November of 2016, I'd been helping Lee for a year. She'd overcome one complication after another: sepsis due to a port infection (the permanent IV line in her chest), a deep pressure ulcer on her tailbone from lying in the hospital bed for so long when she was sick, almost monthly lung taps to drain cancer fluid out, and a punctured lung when she had a new port put in. But everything eventually began to take a toll on her. She was getting sicker.

That, and other things, were taking a toll on me as well, unfortunately. In addition to helping Lee, I had to have a hysterectomy (which I'll discuss later) and was working full-time in the ER. I also had the most important job of all: being a parent to two teenage daughters. Their dad and I had divorced several years previously, and he wasn't in their lives much, so they were depending on me too. One night I was especially overwhelmed, sitting alone in my family room, and thought that the burden on my shoulders had become too much to bear. But as that thought crossed my mind I suddenly saw an incredibly bright flash of bluish light to my left, encompassing the whole left side of my peripheral vision. It only lasted a second and was gone, and for a moment I sat there wondering what had just happened. There hadn't been any light coming in through the windows, or any other source I could identify. And nothing seemed especially different afterward—other than I was too shocked to feel sorry for myself anymore.

The rest of the night was uneventful, but not long after that I started seeing a bluish colored ball of light—and sometimes more than one—in my left peripheral visual field. It's continued ever since, and I'll see it pretty much every day, usually multiple times a day, and it will only be to my left. I can be anywhere when I see it: at home, at work, driving, at friends' houses. It seems to happen randomly most of the time, though more often if I'm feeling down, and is gone within a second—or at least, it seems to be. (You'll understand what I mean by that in a moment.)

As a physician I know all about the flashers and floaters and various visual anomalies that can happen to people, but this didn't fit anything I'd ever read about in a medical textbook, or anything I'd ever read or heard about otherwise. Still, if someone else had said it was happening to them, and I'd never experienced it firsthand, I would've told them that there had to be a medical explanation and they should get their eyes checked. But I'd had a normal eye exam within months before all this started and knew my eyes were fine.

There was simply too close of a connection between what I'd seen in my family room that November night and the blue ball of light that I kept seeing afterward for it all to be a coincidence. As crazy as it seemed, part of me was pretty sure it was a spiritual presence of some sort, perhaps one of the angels I'd never quite believed really existed.

For months I didn't tell anyone about it except Lee. I'm a physician after all, and I couldn't have anyone thinking I was crazy. I'm also well-versed in the sciences. I'd aced every biology, chemistry, and physics class I took in school, and what I was seeing wasn't in any of those textbooks either. Part of me was also worried that this ball of light might not necessarily be a good thing. Even though I'd never felt anything negative about it, I couldn't be entirely sure that it wasn't a less than benign spiritual attachment, or didn't portend something bad. So I decided to go to a medium.

I scheduled the appointment in February of 2017 and had a couple of weeks to wait before the appointment day. In the meantime, my maternal grandfather became ill. He was one of the few positive role models I had growing up (along with my grandmother and several teachers), but he'd been suffering from advanced Alzheimer's disease for years and had long since forgotten who anyone was, though he'd otherwise been well at the time I made the appointment. But a week later he developed pneumonia and ended up dying early in the morning on the day I was scheduled to see the medium. Of course, I know what the skeptics will say—it was just another coincidence (such an easy, meaningless word to use).

I doubted it was a coincidence, though, and went to see the medium that day. She told me the blue orb was a guardian angel and thought it was a female. But she didn't have anything more to add at first, and we started talking about other things. Then out of the blue—no pun intended; they just come naturally—she said the angel's name was Janelle. It immediately struck me how close that name was to Jenna, the most spiritual figure in my book. I'd started writing the book a little over a year before I'd met Lee, but had stopped about six month later, when I was a little less than halfway done.

There were a number of reasons I'd stopped writing. Around that time I found out about the death of the abused child whose life I'd previously saved. I also witnessed the firing of a female colleague that was done in such a reprehensible manner it led me to turn in my resignation at the hospital we worked at. And amidst all that, I went through a bad breakup. All in all, I lost several pieces of my heart in a very short time, and I'd pretty much forgotten about my book. But I began writing again a few months after Lee passed away and finished the book about a year later.

I would be doing a disservice to a lot of people if I didn't mention another issue that was going on during this period of my life. In 2012 I had an Essure procedure done. The Essure device is a metal and fiber coil that is placed into each fallopian tube as a permanent form of birth control and is marketed as a non-surgical alternative to having a tubal ligation. But several months after the procedure I began experiencing noticeable pelvic pain. I figured it was related to scar tissue that normally forms in the fallopian tubes after the procedure, and that it was something I would just have to live with. However, the pain continued to worsen over time, and by 2016 I opted to have the implants removed (about two and a half months after I met Lee), which required a hysterectomy. The gynecologist told me after the surgery that the Essure device had perforated my left fallopian tube at some point—likely months ago—and had basically gotten stuck to my colon because of extensive scar tissue formation. She gave me pictures, and I now have proof that my pain tolerance is very high!

But this really isn't a laughing matter. The device could have killed me—and has killed other women. It's also caused significant complications for thousands and thousands of others. I did some research after my experience and was horrified to discover how inadequate the studies had been regarding the device. I'd trusted the system, in particular the FDA (the federal agency that regulates devices like these), and found out that my trust had been misplaced. I won't go into all the details—that's a book in itself. But the story behind the device is a perfect example of how money often trumps morality in our society. And when that happens in both the government and in medicine, the results can be catastrophic for patients. I would suggest watching the Netflix documentary *The Bleeding Edge* if you want to learn some of the shocking details regarding the multibillion-dollar medical device industry and the FDA.

Anyway, getting back to my appointment with the medium, it was eventful in another way: My grandfather came through. The medium said he was quite weak. But he planned to stick around for his funeral and was then going to prepare a place in Heaven for himself and my grandmother, who was still alive and well. I'd already told the medium that my grandfather had passed away that morning, so I wasn't sure I could really make much of the conversation. I'd given her plenty of material to work with after all. And it could have been a lucky guess that she mentioned my grandmother was still alive. But she also said that I would experience the death of a friend soon, and I hadn't told her anything about Lee, who was seriously ill at that point, and would end up passing away two weeks later.

Ironically, the thing that really convinced me about the legitimacy of the experience was something that happened right after I left the medium. When I started my car the SiriusXM station was no longer on channel 8—the '80s station—as it should have been. Instead, it was now on channel 130—the EWTN Global Catholic Radio Network. I knew for a fact that the radio had been on channel 8 when I turned the car off before going in, and I hadn't even known there was a Global Catholic Radio Network, much less ever listened to it.

My grandfather had been a very devout Roman Catholic. He was strict, but he never terrorized people with religion as my father had been prone to do. He'd worked hard and experienced plenty of hardship in his life, but he still always had a twinkle in his eye. And I could relate almost every positive experience I'd had with religion to him and my grandmother. So I knew it was absolutely no coincidence that my radio had gone from channel 8 to channel 130. My grandfather was letting me know that he really was there.

Even so, I still wasn't entirely convinced that I had a guardian angel—or maybe even more than one—following me around. I was no longer afraid to talk about it, though, and I'm pretty sure a few people now think I'm certifiably insane. I also told some of my coworkers and was surprised to learn how many of them have had paranormal experiences.

But my doubts would persist for another year—until the day I had a random encounter with a five-year-old boy in the ER.

The only person up to that point who thought they'd seen the blue orb was a nurse I worked with. But I'd already told her what I'd been experiencing, so it was hard to know if the power of suggestion had something to do with it. And another medium I went to (to get a second opinion) also said the orb was an angel, though again, I'd told her why I was there right away and didn't think to withhold that information to avoid influencing her in any way.

But a couple of months later I was working in the ER and walked into a male patient's room. His wife and two children—one of whom was the five-year-old boy—were sitting to my left, and I briefly saw the blue orb near them in my peripheral vision. I've often seen it during patient interactions, so I didn't think anything of it and began talking to the patient. Then all of a sudden the little boy got up and started swatting at the air right where I'd previously seen the orb, clearly focused on something that wasn't visible to the rest of us. His parents immediately reprimanded him, and he hid behind his mother's arm and peeked up at me. I looked back at him and knew right away that he'd seen the orb. A child I'd never met before, whose name I didn't even know, had seen what I'd been seeing for over a year. I was shocked, awed, and relieved. I wasn't losing my mind after all.

The patient and his family didn't know I wasn't crazy, though. And the last thing they needed right then was to think they were dealing with a doctor who should order a psychiatric consult on herself. So I didn't say anything about the orb and was going to leave it at that. But two days after the event, on Good Friday, I woke up early in the morning and couldn't stop thinking about the boy. I remembered how scared he'd looked when his parents yelled at him—he certainly hadn't looked scared when he was swatting at the orb—and I thought I should talk to them about why he'd probably been acting that way.

I went to the hospital later that morning and called his dad, who was doing well. But he hadn't remembered how his son had behaved, even though he'd reprimanded him for it at the time, because he'd received several doses of a potent narcotic in the ER that day. I spoke to his wife afterward, and she recalled the incident vividly. She apologized, thinking he'd tried to swat at me, and said he'd been acting perfectly fine up until then and had never done anything like that before.

I was a little nervous about how she would react to my explanation for his behavior and eased into the conversation by asking if she'd be offended by spiritual or religious topics. (And if I heard the slightest reservation in her voice I was ending the conversation right then and there!) But it turned out she was a very spiritual person, so I told her about my experiences with the blue orb and how her son had swatted at the same spot I'd seen it in their ER room. Then I gave her my conclusion (or my diagnosis, if you will): Her son had the ability to see spirits.

Right away, with tears in her voice, she said that he'd previously recognized a picture of her dad in their house and spoke about him as if he knew him, though his grandpa had died before he was born, and no one had ever pointed him out in the picture or talked about him. (I think mom still had a lot of unresolved grief over his death.) But when she'd asked her son how he knew who that was, he told her his grandpa had said so when he played with him in his dreams. She hadn't known what to make of it then, but now she did (and hence, the happy tears): Her son really did know his grandpa.

She told me she was going to ask him more about what he'd seen in the ER after we got off the phone and offered to let me know what he said. I reminded her that he's seemed scared when they reprimanded him for his behavior, and she should reassure him that what had happened wasn't anything bad. I also suggested she not give him any prompts that might influence his responses (as I'd learned from previous experience). So she only asked open-ended questions like, "Tell me what you remember seeing," and didn't mention specific things like angels or ghosts.

I'd expected that if he said anything at all it would be what I already knew: He'd been swatting at a blue ball of light flying around. It never once occurred to me that he'd seen more than that. So when his mom called back later and told me what he said, I was utterly shocked.

He hadn't seen the blue orb at all. What he'd seen was a figure standing next to me, facing the bed. He couldn't identify it as a man or woman, it never spoke, and he'd only seen it from the back. And he said it was big, like the size of a refrigerator. His mom also asked him to draw a picture, and he drew two of them, which she sent to me. Keep in

An Eternity in a Moment 449

mind that this is the work of a five-year-old several days after the event.

FIGURE ONE

FIGURE TWO

It's evident that he drew a head and body in both pictures (with only a head and torso apparent in the second one). But the part that I find especially interesting is the area he told his mom was silver, the area on the figure's back. In the first picture it's a solid square shape, but in the second picture the silver areas are separated, even though the overall picture is less detailed. At first I had no idea what he might be drawing. But then it occurred to me—wings. He depicted them as closed in the first picture, and as two distinct structures in the second one. An angel with wings. And that was the final piece—literally—that absolutely convinced me of the existence of angels.

These pictures are noteworthy in another way too—it appears that he drew on angel with dark skin. If you think about all the images of angels that have been depicted in our culture: in paintings, books, murals, stained glass windows in church, on the internet, etc., how often do you see angels with dark skin? Almost never. The boy who drew these pictures is Caucasian, and we live in a predominantly white community. If his mom had inadvertently given him a prompt to draw an angel, and he'd drawn it from his imagination, I highly doubt the angel would have dark skin. I think this is a message I'm supposed to pass along: Not all angels are white.

I know there are a lot of people out there who will think all of this is ludicrous or made up, but I've related everything that happened as accurately as I can. And as Mark Twain would say, "Truth is stranger than fiction, but it is because fiction is obliged to stick to possibilities; Truth isn't." Many have credited him with this quote as well: "If you tell the truth you don't have to remember anything." The truth is—it's a lot easier to tell the truth.

I also believe in integrity. Without integrity we are left with no moral ground to stand on. And with no moral ground to stand on, we are bound to fall—as individuals, as a society, as a civilization.

A few years ago I wrote this in my "book of thoughts" as well: Rich is the penniless man who lives with honor. Pitiful is the rich man who lives without it. And the one with neither is surely not a favorite of God or the Devil.

In any case, it's up to you to decide what the truth is. (As Jenna will say in the next book, "I'm just trying to save you from a few surprises later.") But never forget that our actions in this life really do matter, more than we can possibly know. And love matters most of all. So if there's one quote worth remembering more than any other, it's this one:

> Your Heavenly worth is weighed
> In the love you leave on Earth.

I hope you enjoyed reading *An Eternity in a Moment*. Please pass along the message of love to others.

And if you have a minute to post a quick review online at Amazon.com or barnesandnoble.com, I would greatly appreciate it!

More information is also available at: www.kcarothers-books.com

Made in the USA
Columbia, SC
24 November 2018